ANIMAL ATTRACTION

A WOLF HOLLOW SHIFTERS NOVEL

NIKKI JEFFORD

ANIMAL ATTRACTION
Wolf Hollow Shifters, Book 5

First Print Edition
ISBN-13: 979-8507927500

Professionally edited by Roxanne Willis and Per Se Editing.

Cover design by Najla Qamber.
Interior design by Nada Qamber.

www.NikkiJefford.com

For my wild and wonderful readers.

 chapter one

ANY TIME THE strong and mighty Kamari howled, every wolf in Glenn Meadows joined his chorus. That afternoon, he strolled by Hailey, who lay on her belly in the open field, surrounded by her female friends. She was soaking the end-of-summer warmth into her fur like it was water and she was preparing for the dry season. Kamari's acute yellow eyes took her in with a clear sense of ownership that always had Hailey warring between submission and giving the older wolf a healthy reminder that she had the strength to tear open his throat.

After passing her, Kamari raised his proud head of gray fur and howled. Hailey lifted her snout off the ground and howled along with her group. In the near distance, the rest of the pack could be heard echoing the call. Soon, males were running on four legs into the field and assembling around Kamari.

The rally turned riotous as the males snarled and bit one another, some jumping onto their hind legs to spar with their opponents.

Hailey adjusted her seating for a better view, and

Hailey's friend mimicked her movements to take in the show of friendly male rivalry. Mid-ranking members pinned weaker wolves to the ground and nipped at them until hearing a cry of surrender. Kamari chased after Byron, a strong male Hailey had grown up with and shared a fleeting relationship with the summer past. She considered Byron her last fling, an affair they had carried out mostly in human form. Dalliances no longer held appeal for her, though. Hailey was ready to settle down with a mate.

The two males tore through the meadow. Byron zigzagged through the tall grass, his lips pulled back in a smile as he leapt ahead before Kamari could nip his tail.

Eventually, Kamari caught the younger male by the hind leg. Byron cried, then flipped over on his back in surrender. Snapping and snarling, Kamari straddled the other male until Byron licked his muzzle, signaling the game was over.

Kamari had won. His role as the pack's alpha male had been undisputed ever since Hailey's parents willingly relinquished the role two moon phases ago. Her brother Hector had never wanted to be alpha, and her father still held on to the hope that he would find a pureblooded female, join her pack, and have a litter of pups.

What the Glenn Meadows pack needed was an alpha female—a position Hailey felt ready to claim as soon as their soothsayer, Flora, stopped interfering. It was not the way of wolves to consult the alignment of planets and other such nonsense the old woman deemed vital for decisions and matchmaking.

To Hailey, it was an easy choice. With no pureblooded

males around for the claiming, she would choose the next best option—an alpha male.

She would choose Kamari as her mate.

The males divided into smaller groups and took off in different directions, some for the forest, others the community center. Hailey yipped at her group to get going and give her privacy with Kamari. The females sprang into action, going after the males.

That left Hailey and Kamari alone in the field together. The older wolf prowled over and brushed against her side. She stood still while he circled her, sniffing at her rear and rubbing along her lean, powerful body before nuzzling her snout and resting his nose above hers.

Mine, his actions said.

Yours, Hailey agreed by allowing his attention.

She crouched down and slid under his chin, pressing against his chest rough enough to push him back a step. Kamari jumped at her and extended his front paws, holding her down, but not pinning her as he had done with the males.

Hailey freed herself from his grasp and licked his muzzle. He pushed his head against hers. She pushed back and they kept at their amorous play until Kamari yipped that they should return to the community center.

Wanting more time with the alpha, Hailey backed against his rear, trying to engage him in further cuddling and play. Her heat was coming, and it was a testament to his self-control that he did not mount her on the spot.

Kamari barked and started toward their village. He stopped and turned his head to see if she followed. When he saw Hailey still standing in place, he barked louder. She returned his bark and started after him. The alpha male's commanding disposition was one of his many appealing traits.

Once Hailey joined him, they ran side by side through a patch of forest into the next meadow. The land sloped upward slightly, with a narrow stream trickling past large stones. An additional area of woods divided the bowl-shaped meadow from another open field. There were many open spaces in Glenn Meadows, the place their pack had settled while Hailey was still a pup, nipping at Hector to get him to play, exploring under her mother's watchful eye, and marking the territory that was to become her permanent home.

She had been born a wolf.

Four legs and fur. A predator. A pureblood. A survivor. Wild.

Typical wolf shifters, on the other hand, were born in human form—unable to make the transformation into their animal skin until sometime around their twelfth year.

The urban wolf shifters who had formed a pack with her parents after the pandemic shed their animal forms as though casting off a coat until they were ready to put it back on. Their offspring behaved in a similar manner. They all seemed to identify with their human side first and foremost.

Not Hailey. Hailey's wolf was always with her, twitching in her limbs and watching the world through her eyes.

"More wolf than woman," her father was always boasting.

She recognized that same wildness in Kamari, despite

his heritage as a shifter from the old human world. His animal instincts were sharp. He spent more time in his wolf form than human. Too bad she would have babies rather than pups with him. Only a pureblooded male, born in his fur form, could give her pups at birth. It was a phenomenon that no one, not even Flora, could explain.

Whatever the reason, it was time for Hailey to let go of that dream. Babies eventually grew into children, then teenagers. Once they came of age, she would nurture their animal side and teach them everything she knew about surviving in the wild as a wolf.

The sun slanted through the next grove of woods, late afternoon light pushing through the trees. Kamari and Hailey stopped at the forest's edge before a blanket of green wild grass spread into the meadow where their pack's village was built.

Two sets of deerskin clothing had been left on the ground. Standing beside the skins, the wolves shifted into their human forms simultaneously, grabbing their handmade garments as they straightened out onto two legs. Kamari shook out his pants and fringed leather shirt before putting them on over his thick, muscular legs and broad shoulders.

Hailey did not mind that he was her father's age. Kamari was a striking wolf who commanded obedience and respect from the pack. In human form, he was robust with a deep, pleasing voice.

While the handsome older male secured his pants, Hailey pulled on a fringed skirt that reached her knees before covering her breasts with a tanned skin halter that left her toned midriff exposed. Blonde hair framed Hailey's cheeks. She never tucked it behind her ears as many females did, especially when flirting with the males. Hailey liked the feel of her hair on her face when she wasn't in her fur, but she did keep it short–less washing and combing. She had the lightest hair in the pack, which turned almost white during the summer months and fell into supple waves that had all her friends sighing with envy.

"I think it is time to organize another hunting trip," Hailey announced.

Kamari rubbed his fingers along the short bristly growth on his chin. "We'll take Paxon, Ellis, Skeet, and Byron."

"Good choices," she said, pleased. Hailey lifted her chest, but Kamari's brown gaze burrowed into her eyes.

"After the hunt, I wish to claim you as my mate," Kamari stated.

Heat flushed over Hailey's skin and tingled along the back of her bare neck. Her heart felt lighter inside her chest, like the sun rising at dawn. She blinked several times while her mind rejoiced at the thought of being bonded to this worthy male.

Kamari stepped in front of her. "Do you want this, Hailey? I know I am older."

Hailey's eyes widened. "I want this. I don't care about age." The words gushed out of her mouth like breaths she had been holding. "I don't want anyone else."

Smiling, Kamari brushed back the hair falling over her left cheek. Her white-blonde strands slid through Kamari's callused fingers, landing right back where they had started.

"You have such a pretty face," he said huskily.

Her heart skittered. They had never been intimate—never even kissed, though their wolves had nuzzled. Hailey wondered if Kamari might kiss her now that they had exchanged promises. He touched her cheek, then took a step back.

"I will speak to your father."

"My parents will support us," Hailey said.

"I will speak to him nonetheless."

Hailey pursed her lips and glanced across the field.

"Come," Kamari said, "the afternoon grows late."

They walked side by side barefoot through the grass to their pack's village, which was surrounded by a wall of thorny branches. Nails protruded from a wooden gate that was guarded at all times. Seeing their approach, Seamus, a shifter in his third decade with shaggy brown hair, pulled open the gate to allow them passage.

Kamari nodded at him and Seamus nodded back.

The ground inside was packed dirt, all plant life worn down over the years of their tribe living together in an enclosed space made of crude huts and tents. Within the walls, no shifting was allowed. It was how they kept out rabid wolves and other dangerous beasts. Everyone walked in on two legs, including the chickens that pecked at the earth in every direction. The birds had been introduced over a decade ago when a shifter named Horton stole some from a human's homestead. A couple of the chickens had escaped several years ago. Hailey still salivated at the taste of those squawking birds when she discovered and devoured them outside the walls of the village. They were supposed to be rounded up and brought back, but she had succumbed to temptation when it came to an opportunity for a fresh kill with new flavor. Hailey believed in rewarding her wolf whenever possible.

They passed a group of elder women seated on blankets, gossiping while working on garlic braids. Multiple sets of eyes took Hailey and Kamari in. The alpha nodded at the women. They smiled, then turned their attention back to the garlic and conversation. Only one remained silent in their party–Sydney, the girl they had taken in from the Wolf Hollow pack. She weaved the pieces of garlic in her lap while continuing to stare at Hailey. There were members of their village who said the girl gave them the willies, but Hailey merely stared back until Sydney dropped her gaze.

Hailey and Kamari were nearly at her parents' hut when a howl raced across the meadows and through the gates, bringing a hush over their village.

The howl came again. No one answered. It was not one of their own. Hailey cocked her head to the side and listened intently.

Her parents emerged from their hut. As soon as they saw her, they came over and stared at Hailey expectantly. She blinked once and said, "Werewolf."

chapter two

WITH HER BONE necklace, fringed top, and skirt adorned in fur and feathers, Hailey's mother, Geraldine, was the image of feminine strength. Unbound, dark blonde hair ended in thick layers that swept over her shoulders. She nodded. "It must be Aden from Wolf Hollow."

Hailey's father, Jefferson, growled. "Nothing good ever comes from Wolf Hollow."

Hailey folded her arms. She had to agree with her parents. The visit her brother and cousin had made to their closest neighboring pack had been interrupted when a rabid wolf attacked the territory in broad daylight. According to Alexa, she and Hector had been treated abominably. They had subjected themselves to Wolf Hollow's odd masked mating dance only to be mocked the following morning for their concerns about safety.

Hailey pursed her lips, recalling Alexa's account of the dance. Why would the shifters put a wolf mask over their human faces rather than transform into their true animal forms? It did not make a lick of sense to her.

Beside her, Kamari had turned to oak. Deep gouges

wrinkled his forehead when he frowned.

Flora had been the next to visit Wolf Hollow after word reached them that the pack's prize pureblooded male had returned after a three-year absence. Hailey had thought perhaps fate was intervening to provide her with a pureblooded mate who could give her pups and continue her family's line.

But even Wolfrik had not passed Flora's cosmic approval.

It sounded to Hailey as though the fates did not favor Wolf Hollow.

"What do you want to bet he brings bad news?" her father asked.

Bad news or good, the pack's single females raced from their huts, finger-combing their hair in urgent strokes. Two of the females jogged up to Hailey. Layla tugged her skirt up, showing off lean tanned legs, while Violet pulled her leather halter down to reveal more of her bust.

"How many males are coming?" Violet asked, breathless from her sprint over.

Hailey's frown stretched into a smirk. "Only one. Sorry to disappoint."

Violet slapped the heels of her palms over her eyes and groaned.

"Single? Mated?" Layla bounced on her feet.

"It's the werewolf," Kamari said gruffly.

Layla stopped springing in place. Her shoulders sagged. "Oh. Why do you think he's come?"

"Maybe to take the girl back to her family," Hailey's mom suggested.

Hailey shook her head. "No. She's with us for good.

He's here with news."

Violet stared at Hailey and blinked several times. "How do you do that? You should apprentice with Flora to become a seer."

"Not happening," Hailey said with a vehement shake of her head. "One fortune teller is plenty."

Kamari pressed in closer to her while Hailey's parents nodded their agreement.

"But who will guide us after Flora joins the spirit pack?" Layla asked.

Hailey looked at Kamari and grinned. It was on the tip of her tongue to reply, "Your alphas will guide you," when Aden's howl came louder and closer.

Sighing, Hailey started for the gates. "Someone must answer him."

"I'll do it." Hailey's mom unfastened her top from her neck mid-stride, then pulled off her skirt, followed by her bone necklace. As she strode past the families and friends emerging from their homes, she let them know who approached.

After Geraldine cleared the gate, she crouched over the earth and shifted. Her proud, unmistakable call filled the blue sky overhead.

Hailey looked over to see that her brother Hector had joined their group. Her father caught him up on their imminent visitor.

"Let us meet him at the gate," Hailey said.

Her family and friends fell into step with her. The pack members who had begun crowding at the entrance made room when they saw their approach. Hailey's mother led

Aden in. They were both naked and Hailey was struck by Aden's hulking form. He seemed bigger than the last time he had come to their village. Such a shame he was a werewolf and not a wolf shifter. Coupling in animal form was not impossible, but the act would prove painful to a wolf. The elders said it was the equivalent of a stallion mounting a pony. Hailey did not appreciate being compared to ponies, but the warning had certainly deterred the single females from offering Aden anything other than friendly conversation during his occasional trips to Glenn Meadows.

Aden was difficult to read, with his relaxed stride and neutral expression. Beside him, a massive grin had blossomed over her mother's face. She looked through the crowd and, finding Hailey, met her gaze with a jump of her eyebrows.

Hailey's heart skipped a beat, not in the pleasant kind of way but with a feeling of foreboding.

"You can return to your homes," Hailey's mom addressed the pack. "Aden has a proposal to discuss with my family, nothing critical."

That only piqued their curiosity further. Packmates continued to linger and stare as Hailey's mom led Aden over. "Layla. Violet. Go fetch Flora at once."

Hailey's friends took off in the direction of the seer's hut while Aden was escorted to her parents' site. Along the way, her mother scooped up her clothing and necklace and put them back on. Four eager faces awaited them. Hailey's younger siblings arranged furs around a fire that had just been lit outside the hut and laid out a loincloth for Aden to wrap around his waist. Noah jostled the logs around, coaxing the flames to take hold of the dry wood. Luna invited Aden to take a seat on a cushion made of deer hide. After he'd secured the loincloth around his thick waist and settled into the cushion, Luna handed him a mug of water. While the werewolf drank, the family of purebloods settled in around him.

"Cameron, we'll need another cushion for Flora," their mother said.

Hailey settled into a spot across from Aden. Her parents flanked her, leaving Kamari to sit beside Hector. As their pack's unchallenged alpha, Kamari had every right to sit in with her family and hear Aden's news.

Hailey's four younger siblings—Luna, Jaxon, Noah, and Cameron—took their places on either side of Aden. They were litter mates, all in their eleventh year. Hailey's parents had been moon blessed with the birth and continued survival of their second, and final, litter.

Watching her younger siblings sitting tall, attentive, and respectful tugged at Hailey's womb. She could feel Kamari's attention on her and for once, she avoided meeting his gaze. Instead, she focused on Aden.

"Is all well in Wolf Hollow?" her father asked.

"Yes, thank you," Aden answered.

"No recent attacks?" Jefferson prodded.

Aden clenched his jaw and gave him a hard stare—one the older, pureblooded male returned.

"Humans from the city attempted an attack. We took care of them."

Kamari snarled.

"Humans?" Geraldine frowned. "This is the first time I have heard of them leaving their cradle." It was her way of referring to the decrepit structures the last surviving humans clung to.

"They were after one of their own," Aden supplied. He continued with an account of the events, his lips loosening to share pertinent information for their pack's awareness.

When Aden finished, their circle went silent until Geraldine spoke. "I don't expect the remaining humans will venture back over the mountain. They can only deduce that their leader and his men are all dead, and they will not wish to follow in their footsteps, especially with no good reason to take such a grave risk wandering into the wild."

Aden nodded. "Our conclusion as well."

"What became of the woman they were after?" Hailey asked. The werewolf had failed to mention the fate of the human who had run from her tribe.

Aden folded his thick arms over his muscled chest and sat up taller. "She suffered a blow to the head and has remained unresponsive, though she continues to breathe. The wizards at Balmar Heights are keeping her alive."

"For what purpose?" Kamari demanded.

"Once she awakens, she will help us infiltrate her brother's compound and free the wolves imprisoned there."

On either side of Aden, the mouths of Luna, Jaxon, Noah, and Cameron all hung open. They stared up at the werewolf with rapt attention and awe.

"I want to help free the wolves," Jaxon said.

Luna nodded beside him. "Me too."

"And us," Noah and Cameron said simultaneously.

Their father looked them over before returning his gaze to Aden. "Are there any purebloods in captivity?"

"Wolfrik claimed to be the only one."

Kamari huffed. "How fares your pack's pureblooded male? We were told he was too unstable for our Hailey. The poor beast will likely never claim a mate."

"Kamari." Hailey spoke his name firmly. There was no reason to be rude to Aden.

The werewolf flashed his teeth in a rare smile. "Wolfrik is happily mated with a child on the way."

"What's this?" Jefferson growled and shot to his feet. Glowering across the fire at Aden, he shook his fist. "Our Hailey wasn't good enough—is that what you're saying?"

"Sit down, Jefferson," came the croak of Flora's voice as the old woman hobbled over to their group. Layla and Violet helped the seer onto a cushion beside Hector. "Thank you, girls, now shoo."

Violet rolled her eyes before taking Layla's hand and striding away, head held high as though taking her leave by choice.

Flora leaned to one side and then the other, tucking her legs in with a groan. Father sat slowly and folded his arms.

"Stop your glowering," Flora snapped. "I told you Wolfrik and Hailey were not meant to be."

"She is right, my dear," Geraldine said. She was the only one in their circle smiling brightly. "Aden has come with wonderful news. A pureblooded male has arrived in Wolf Hollow seeking a pureblooded female to claim." She threaded her fingers and looked into the dimming sky, likely thanking the moon for such fortunate tidings.

Hailey felt the familiar stir inside her womb. A longing, deep in her soul, called out for a mate who could give her pups. Her wolf perked up in the subconscious of her mind. She could feel her heat coming on faster and stronger. It became nearly impossible to sit still. Looking over when she repositioned herself, she saw Kamari frown.

"Who is this male?" Jefferson asked Aden, but it was Flora who answered.

"A wanderer," she mused, adding, "from southern territories."

Aden shrugged. "He and his brother have distinct accents and speak to one another in tongues."

"Brother?" Hailey's mother perked up. "There are two?" Her eyes gleamed in the dimming light.

"Yes," Aden said. "Both unmated, though only one expressed interest in a claiming."

"And you told me he specifically seeks a pureblooded female," Geraldine rushed in.

Aden nodded. "That is what he said."

"Hailey, you must leave for Wolf Hollow first thing in the morning and meet this male," her mother said. Kamari growled, showing teeth. Ignoring him, Geraldine looked to their seer. "What say you, Flora?"

The old woman pursed her weathered lips and stared into the flames. Everyone kept silent, even Kamari, as the seer's eyes glazed over. Her head looked too heavy for her neck as it listed forward, chin practically touching her chest. If her eyes weren't open, Hailey would have expected the elder had dozed off. The seconds inched along like the tiny legs on millipedes. Flames crackled steadily from the logs Noah had arranged.

Finally, Flora spoke. "What does this wolf call himself?" she asked, her eyes still fixed on the fire.

"Diego," Aden answered.

Wood popped and crackled gently.

"And his brother?"

"Rafael."

Sparks shot out of the burning logs and the flames rose higher. Flora leaned forward and pressed her wrinkled fingers over her lips.

Geraldine stared from the fire to Flora. "What does it mean?" she asked somewhat shrilly.

Rather than answer her question, Flora leaned back and yawned. "Hector, help me up."

He did as asked, picking the old woman up and setting her on her feet as though she weighed no more than the deerskin dress covering her ailing frame.

"I am tired," she announced to the circle. Her eyes landed on Hailey. "You should rest, as well. Tomorrow you will go with Aden to meet these males." With those final words, Flora left their circle at a measured pace.

Mother clapped her hands together and lifted her head to the sky, blinking back tears that glistened briefly over her irises.

"We must send an escort," Jefferson said.

Hector huffed. "Don't look at me. They don't want me back."

"I will go," young Jaxon said, standing.

"Why not me?" Luna challenged. "Perhaps the second brother is younger and will want a mate in time."

"Neither of you are going," their mother said. "You are too young."

The siblings shut their mouths and remained seated, waiting to be dismissed. Watching them respect their mother filled Hailey with pride and hope. It was a warmth that spread from her heart to her belly and down to her core.

"I will go," Kamari announced coolly.

The warmth pulled away from Hailey at the tone of his voice. Kamari would have made a wonderful mate, but even he had to understand this opportunity could not be turned down without exploration.

"Is that wise?" Geraldine asked, looking Kamari over. When she stepped in front of the alpha, it was as an equal. Scrutinizing his face, she frowned. "Can you remain impartial, Kamari?"

"I want what is best for Hailey, same as you, even if it means stepping aside."

A pained stabbing sensation twisted inside Hailey's chest as some of her excitement turned to sorrow.

Her father walked over and placed his hand on Kamari's shoulder. "You are a good alpha, Kamari, and the male I trust most to stay with my daughter until the claim is made."

The alpha nodded and left abruptly. Watching his retreating form, Hailey chewed on her lower lip. Meanwhile, her youngest siblings dispersed, leaving only Hector behind. He joined her side, staring in the direction that Kamari had disappeared.

"A word of advice, sister. Steer clear of the elder Jager's moonshine. It could make you do things you later regret."

She nodded. "Anything else?"

"Good luck."

She grinned.

After Hector's departure, Hailey ducked down to follow her mother inside her parents' hut. The thatched ceiling was low, creating a cozy den of blankets. Geraldine sat down and stretched her legs in front of her, pointing her toes.

Hailey sat beside her, shoulder to shoulder, leaning against her mother. Her throat quivered the tiniest bit and a sudden sadness seeped into her soul. What a strange day. She had awoken thinking Glenn Meadows would be her home for life, and now this could very well be her final night with her pack.

Geraldine put her arm around her daughter, speaking while looking forward, as though it was too painful to stare into her face.

"You will need to form your own pack with your mate."

Hailey nodded. Glenn Meadows already had an alpha, and it had grown overcrowded.

"Once the claim is made, you can invite some of our pack to join yours," she continued.

The weight pressing down her shoulders and chest lightened somewhat. Hailey would not be entirely on her own. Some of her friends were itching for a change of scenery and males. Poor Layla and Violet were related to just about every family in Glenn Meadows with the exception of Hailey's family.

"Find territory not too far away so that we may visit once in a while."

Hailey's heart clenched into a fist. Tears rarely appeared on her face, but tonight was an exception. An unfamiliar sensation filled her eyes and spilled down her cheeks. When warm lips kissed her cheek gently, a fresh flow of tears streaked down the sides of her face.

"I am so proud of you, my girl. And so happy. Mother Moon has answered my call to deliver a pureblooded male to give you many pups and protect you and your family with his life." Geraldine sniffled. When Hailey risked a glance, she saw her mother's eyes glistening, but she was smiling through the tears. "Tonight, you will sleep in here with me one last time. Your father will spend the night with Hector. In the morning, we will have one last family meal before you head out with Kamari and Aden."

Hailey stiffened. It was a five-day journey on four legs to Wolf Hollow. The trek would be made entirely in animal form—just her and two unmated males.

There was one rather awkward problem with that.

"My heat has come early."

chapter three

DENSE WOODS SLOWED Hailey's pace halfway to Wolf Hollow. Ferns tickled her furry legs as she trotted through the thick foliage, sniffing out the route Aden had taken from his pack to hers. Following the werewolf would have been easier, but Geraldine had spoken with the males before their departure, instructing them to give Hailey a couple hours of lead time.

In animal form, it would be near impossible for the males to keep off her.

Her mother took it as another sign that Hailey would soon be mated and expecting her first litter.

Hailey found it inconvenient. Once reaching Wolf Hollow, she would have to remain in human form until her heat passed. She didn't plan on inciting a riot among all the single males in an unfamiliar pack. At least the journey would eat up five of the days, leaving her a couple more before it was safe to shift into her wolf.

Her heat was another trait that set her apart from regular wolf shifters. Not all pureblooded females experienced it, but the chances were more likely. The females in Hailey's family line were blessedly fertile, according to her mother.

When the sun dropped from the sky and the moon reigned the darkness, Hailey sniffed around until she found some nice overhanging brush, then dug through fallen leaves and dirt until she had made herself a nice shallow hole to curl into.

Kamari and Aden would be turning in about then, as well. It had been decided before their departure that the males would shift into human form each evening to prevent their wolves from racing through the night to catch up to Hailey.

"Safer for you to remain in wolf form while sleeping," her mother had said.

So long as there were no lone wolves around to get a whiff of her, Hailey thought. If any rogues tried to hump her, she'd make them bleed. It was an annoyance she hoped not to encounter en route to meet her future mate. He, Diego, was the only male she wanted on her back.

Diego, she repeated in her head.

He had been searching for her, Aden said. Well, not her specifically, but a pureblooded female. They had both been holding out for one another. That was all that mattered.

Diego's journey from afar spoke to his superior survival skills.

Hailey looked forward to meeting him very much.

STOMACH FULL OF rabbit, Hailey raced through the woods on the fifth and final day of her journey. She had gotten used to dodging trees and the numerous roots forming ridges above ground. Sensing her destination in the distance, Hailey slowed her speed. It was time to let the males catch up.

Her steps had slowed, but her heart had not. Tail twitching, she prowled through the underbrush, sniffing the ground one moment, then lifting her head the next.

The sound of an animal crashing through the forest made her pause and hold as still as the mountains. A gorgeous male wolf with gray-and-white fur came to a stop and howled. He appeared distracted and had yet to catch sight or scent of her. That lasted the span of a blink. The moment the wolf lowered his muzzle, his golden eyes landed on Hailey. He jerked in place, then stilled and stared at her openly.

Instead of baring her fangs, Hailey remained poised. Arousal blazed beneath her tail. Her heat permeated the air between them, growing stronger, beckoning the male to answer the call of nature.

The male sniffed the air. He took his first step toward her. Captivated by the stranger, Hailey remained in place as he circled her.

The male moved with a confident ease and strength. He was young, like her, and powerful. He gave off an air of virility and might.

Instinct and attraction brought her wolf to heel, and pleasure swept through her when the male stuck his snout by her rear and remained in place for a good, long sniff, as though drawing her heat out by his lungs.

A warm, wet tongue slid between her hind legs. He lapped at her, testing her sex hormones.

Hailey glanced back at him. When his tongue flicked in and out again, she closed her eyes, her body relaxing as it yielded in a way that was wholly unfamiliar yet felt instinctively natural.

The male moved to her hind flank and rubbed his face against her. She flicked her tail but remained in place. Wasting no more time, the male mounted her. Hailey held his weight on all four legs and paws. She could have easily thrown him off. Instead, she swept her tail to the side and allowed him entry. Nails digging into the earth, she kept upright while the male humped her. Furry front legs grasped her backside and pressed into her lower belly while the male's hind legs shook with vigor.

The male had latched onto her fully, his soft chest hunched over her rump, muzzle breathing in deep above her back. As his penis swelled, Hailey's vaginal wall constricted. He could not impregnate her without a full moon, but they could end up stuck if they did not stop soon.

Hailey felt incapable of pulling away. Her wolf wanted this male, wanted his pups, his affection, protection, and loyalty.

Howls in the distance jolted Hailey out of a fervid fog. She lurched forward, freeing herself from the male. He slid from her back, landing seamlessly on his front paws.

The call of Kamari and Aden rose again.

What had she been thinking? She had come to

meet a pureblood, not mate with the first new male she encountered in the forest.

More howls arose, these ones unfamiliar and numerous, originating from the nearby pack that made up Wolf Hollow.

Hailey sprang past the blinking male and took off running. She followed the chorusing wolves and her nose, racing westward. The male who had humped her gave chase. She ran faster and faster, not slowing until she streaked into an opening in the woods filled with shifters mostly in human form.

The smell of roasted wild game filled her nostrils.

Several males in wolf form stared at her and began to sniff the air. Hailey growled. She needed to shift before she started a brawl. For several heartbeats, her wolf held on—wanting to fend off the males stalking toward her. A young woman spoke to them in a commanding voice. Hailey was too distracted to pay attention to her words, but the males did, despite her heat. They shifted into their human forms and grabbed clothing from the ground. While the males dressed, Hailey drew away from her animal, taking on the shape of her human half. She stayed low to the ground as her paws morphed into fingers and toes. Fur receded into fair skin. Her ears and snout shrank. Blonde hair fell over her cheeks and the back of her neck.

Hailey stood up and looked around, taking in all the strangers staring at her. Everyone was clothed. She lifted her head and chest in defiance. The cool night air teased her nipples into stiff peaks. She was not about to cover them. All she had were her hands, and such a gesture would communicate weakness.

A phantom ache settled between her thighs where the male wolf had swelled inside her. She wasn't used to the transfer of physical sensation from her wolf to her human form, and it perplexed her now.

While the shifters gawked at her, Kamari and Aden raced in, coming to an abrupt halt before taking on their human forms. Kamari looked her over quickly, his brows furrowed. She nodded at him to convey her well-being. The trip over had been without incident or harm . . . well, not entirely uneventful, but no one else needed to know of her deviation—other than the other party, whomever he may be. Had the male followed her to the glade? She had a feeling he had. Hopefully, he would keep his mouth shut and leave her alone.

And hopefully her wolf wouldn't stray again. Meeting new males was exciting and all, but she was here with a clear purpose. Unlike Sasha and Wolfrik, Hailey would not settle for anything less than a pureblooded mate.

"I am Hailey of Glenn Meadows," she said to the group who had gathered around them. "I was told there was a pureblooded male interested in meeting me."

The silence that followed felt like a great void. All eyes turned to a tall, tanned, muscular male with dark brown hair down to his shoulders. Beside him was a delicate-looking female wearing a floral cotton dress, her blonde hair secured in a ponytail, watching Hailey with a frown. A forced smile appeared on the male's lips.

"I am Diego, a pureblood from the south. I am very sorry you traveled all this way, but my interests have landed elsewhere." He placed his arm around the female by his

30

side. She immediately blushed, setting off whispers and wide eyes among the pack.

Apparently, Hailey wasn't the only one hearing this news for the first time.

Unsure what to do next, she stared at the pair. This hadn't been what she was expecting, and she did not appreciate being made to look like a fool.

Kamari grumbled beneath his breath. "I ought to rip out that cur's throat. He sends for you, then goes after another female. No one in this pack deserves you—especially not their faithless guest."

Hailey's heart constricted. How could this be? Why hadn't Flora warned her? What good was a seer who did nothing to spare her this indignation?

Keeping her head held high, Hailey looked over the males, as though she, too, would sooner pick one among them. All she wanted was to run back home with Kamari, make their claim, and put this nonsense behind her.

The woman with long brown hair who had commanded the wolves to shift walked over with a warm smile. "Thank you for coming. I am Sasha."

Kamari huffed, but Hailey welcomed the greeting from another pureblooded female—even one who had not taken to her brother. The female had a friendly and diplomatic air about her. She wore a short cotton dress with stripes.

"You are very welcome to stay as long as you like," Sasha continued. "Diego is not the only pureblooded male visiting our pack. His brother, Rafael, is here as well."

Hailey followed Sasha's gaze to a gorgeous naked

man with short brown hair. His skin was the color of acorn tops, showcasing muscles as defined as mountains and the valleys that ran between them. He held an air of exotic mystique, sensuality, and defiance.

Sparks went off inside Hailey's chest the way they had in the fire during her last night in Glenn Meadows when Rafael's name was spoken before her pack's seer. The male was staring at her like he had never seen a female before, which was lunacy. In his eyes, she saw lust and anger. His hand covered his genitals, drawing Hailey's eyes to his fingers. It was as though his palm was gripping her gaze and forcing her focus on his sex organ.

In that moment, she knew with certainty that his wolf had been the one to mount her. Perhaps she had found her pureblooded mate after all. Her wolf approved, and she always trusted her animal instincts above her human ones.

Hailey relaxed her attention, flicking her eyes back up to meet Rafael's. He narrowed his eyes as though she were his enemy—a peculiar reaction. Was this male at odds with his animal side?

Perhaps he desired a moment of privacy to introduce himself.

Hailey took a step toward the male, only to see his nose wrinkle and lip curl as though he had gotten whiff of a skunk. Spinning on his heel, he stormed off into the cover of the woods.

 chapter four

THE GROUND CUFFED the bottoms of Rafael's feet with brutal opposition as he stamped down the nearest trail. Dark shadows pressed upon him as night swallowed the sun and dimmed his surroundings in cave-like obscurity.

His wolf and his brother were determined to ruin his life. He should have never jumped on that female's back. There was only one type of female he refused to screw, and that was purebloods. He should have had no problem resisting a mate-obsessed huntress, but tonight his wolf had failed him.

Damn Diego to the moon and back. Just because his brother had willingly allowed a sly female to domesticate him, it didn't mean Rafael had to accept the same fate. Thankfully, the next full moon was another three weeks out. Females had a frightening tendency to turn fiercely hormonal during that special time of the month when their ovaries howled for procreation.

No way was he sticking around to risk fathering a litter. He would rather roam the earth alone for the remainder of his days.

"*Hermano*, wait up," Diego yelled at his back.

Rafael's hands fisted. He had never wanted to hit his brother before this moment. This is what came of pursing a mate.

Rafael continued his heavy stride away from the glade. Away from the Wolf Hollow pack. Away from *her*.

Diego fell into step beside him, tucking strands of his long hair behind each ear.

"I should have waited to send word to the neighboring pack." He shrugged. "I did not expect to find my forever mate so quickly."

Find her? More like become ensnared.

Rafael huffed in disgust. "I never dreamed that I would see the day that my brother would become a whipped wolf."

Diego snarled, drawing a grin up Rafael's cheeks. It was about time the fool got a taste of his rotten mood.

"Lacy is the love of my life."

Rafael burst into laughter. He stopped to clutch his stomach, pitching forward. Diego narrowed his eyes. Rubbing phantom tears away from his eyes, Rafael straightened up.

"Lacy is a liar. What kind of female that age is still a virgin? She is clever. I'll give her that. She dangled the bait and you snatched it up like a bloodthirsty hound."

Diego lifted a fist.

Raising his brows, Rafael watched to see if his brother, his most loyal and constant companion, would fight him over a woman he had met mere days ago.

Just as suddenly, Diego lowered his fist and spread open his palms in a placating gesture. "I don't expect you to understand, but I am sorry, Raphy. This changes our plans, I know."

"This changes *your* plans." Rafael folded his arms. "I'm leaving—with or without you."

Diego blinked several times before nodding. "Will you at least stay for my claiming ceremony with Lacy?"

Claiming ceremony, Rafael sneered in his head. It was Wolf Hollow lunacy. If a male wanted a female, and she wanted him back, the male took. He mated. He claimed. What he did not do was ask permission from elders and schedule a ceremony for his pack to witness. Rafael would sooner sleep naked atop a bed of fire ants than be a spectator at Diego's claiming ceremony.

His brother, who knew him better than anyone ever would, took one look at his face and slumped in defeat. Watching the humor and spark fade clawed at Rafael's heart.

"Maybe." When Diego looked up hopefully, Rafael huffed. "No promises. Thanks to you, I now have a pureblood problem on my paws."

Diego's brows furrowed. "The female from Glenn Meadows? She cannot expect you to fill in for me."

Rafael laughed darkly. "She might after allowing my wolf to mate with hers right before her arrival."

Diego's eyes bugged out. "She what? You did what?" With a grin and shake of his head, Diego proclaimed, "You are *loco*. How did this happen?"

"After our little chat, I ventured out to cool off and bumped into her on her way in."

"Well, that's one way to let off steam," Diego said smugly. If his lips did not release the bemused smile fixed across his cheeks, Rafael really might have to smack him. "She is pretty," Diego added.

La mujer esta hermosa. Hailey looked like a moon goddess.

"She was eyeing me like meat at the gathering," Rafael grumbled.

Diego laughed. "You know what I think? I think fate brought us here."

With a frown that could have felled a tree, Rafael's chest contracted on a breath filled with displeasure. "Four legs brought us here. Fate had nothing to do with it."

"Brother, will you truly never take a mate?" Diego asked gently, his tone turning grave.

"You know why." Rafael's mouth clamped shut and his jaw tightened around the trauma of memories long past.

Fortunately, Diego let it go. "Fate or four legs, I appreciate you sticking around for my ceremony. You are my only family. *Mi mejor amigo.* I don't expect you to settle down with the pack, but I am happy you will see me claim Lacy." Diego tilted his head. "Should we head back?"

And give that she-wolf another opportunity to sink her claws into him?

Harsh laughter rumbled down Rafael's throat, rattling around like stones inside his ribcage.

He dropped to the ground on his knees and glared up at his brother, still warring with feelings of family loyalty and betrayal.

"I'm going to see if there's any good game left in these woods. Don't expect me at dinner . . . or breakfast. In fact, don't plan on seeing me anywhere near the glade until you give up your freedom to that *puta*." Diego's snarl made Rafael laugh. "Don't expect me to like her just because you do. Howl if you need me."

Rafael took on his wolf form before his brother could admonish him. *Freedom*, his last human thought bellowed like a battle cry.

His wolf responded with disobedience, racing straight back to the glade to get to the female.

 chapter five

MOST OF THE Wolf Hollow packmates resumed their conversations and idle tasks around the community cauldron, showing little interest in the new arrivals. Hailey was glad to be left mostly alone.

A curvy female with long brown hair sauntered over, eyeing Kamari up and down, paying particular attention to his genitals. Her bright smile conveyed pleasure in what she saw.

Back in Glenn Meadows, the females assumed that Kamari would eventually claim Hailey and didn't bother flirting with him. It did not bother her to see this young brunette feasting her eyes on the alpha. Kamari was a male deserving admiration. He was not hers, not like the wolf in the woods.

"I am Camilla," the female announced. She wore a short, constricting dress that looked more like a hindrance than anything else. Flipping her long hair over her shoulder, she lifted her head to stare into Kamari's eyes. "My little sister joined your pack. How is Sydney?"

"The girl is keeping out of trouble, earning her place,"

Kamari said gruffly.

Camilla bobbed her head. "Good. I am relieved to hear it. Thank you for taking her in." When Kamari made no answer, Camilla twirled a section of her hair around her finger. "Your pack was charitable in preventing a young female from being sent to her death. Sydney did a terrible thing. But banishing one so young into the wild would have been horrible too. Thank you." Camilla lowered her head.

It lightened Hailey's mood to see a member of Wolf Hollow express appreciation. "Rest assured, your sister is safe and will remain so with our pack."

Hailey was pleased to see Camilla flash her the same bright smile she had expected was only for Kamari. "You're nice and so pretty." The female moved closer and leaned in with a conspiratorial gleam in her eyes. "We had no idea Lacy snatched Diego up." Camilla clucked her tongue as her gaze moved to the petite blonde now surrounded by several females. Diego, like his brother, had fled the glade—something she was trying not to take personally. "I underestimated her." Camilla's words were seasoned with admiration. Returning her attention to Hailey, she sighed dramatically. "Males can be so difficult. Is it the same in Glenn Meadows? It must be. Well, you came all this way. No reason not to have a bit of fun. Come with me and I'll introduce you around."

Sasha cleared her throat. Wolf Hollow's pureblooded female had remained in place, a few steps away, waiting patiently while Camilla spoke.

"First, I will take our guests to find clothing to borrow for their stay."

NIKKI JEFFORD

"Oh, right." Camilla looked directly between Kamari's legs and giggled before turning once more to Hailey. "Come find me later." With another flip of her hair, Camilla walked off, swaying her hips.

"Follow me," Sasha said cheerfully.

Hailey and Kamari fell into step behind the pureblood and her green-eyed mate, Tabor, over a path made wide enough for them to walk two by two.

"Your timing is fortunate." Sasha looked over her shoulder repeatedly to address them as they made their way through the woods. "We recently returned from a successful supply run. The garments we gathered are still being sorted in our communal cabin."

"Watch out for the roots." Tabor took his mate's hand, keeping hold of her even after she stepped over an insignificant tuber.

Sasha threaded her fingers through Tabor's. With her head turned to regard him, a warm smile filled her cheeks.

Hailey rested her attention on them as she would a pair of animals behaving oddly. Surely Sasha knew every inch, rock, and tree of her territory. She was a pureblood, the strongest of all females, yet she allowed her mate to escort her along the trail as though she were fragile.

Hailey's cousin had made Sasha out to be a bitch from hell. From what she observed, Alexa's account had been unfair. Then again, Alexa was a bit of a hellion.

The path rounded an enormous uprooted tree that had taken a layer of earth with it on its horizontal plunge. The dry loam remained caked to the bottom trunk. Heavy woods caged the hollow. Although favorable as coverage,

40

it could also keep enemies hidden.

"It's just ahead," Sasha announced.

They reached a small clearing that had been made to accommodate a small cabin with wood walls. Even in the dark, Hailey could see where repairs had been made with nailed boards in some places and logs in others.

Tabor went ahead of the group to prop the door open with a rock and enter the dark structure. Moments later, a faint light filled the frame, illuminating the entrance in a welcoming glow.

Sasha went inside.

Hailey paused at the doorway and swung around, not surprised to find Kamari's eyes on her. He went in ahead of her, ducking his head, though it appeared the structure had been built to accommodate height and bulk. After listening for any type of warning and hearing none, Hailey entered the cabin.

A glass oil lamp rested on a table, filling the space with enough light to inventory the contents of the cabin. Axes, shovels, and tools from the old world adorned one wall—kept in place with nails that jutted at various angles from the wooden barrier. Furry wolf-shaped masks stared vacantly from another wall, nails sticking out from cutout eye holes.

The furnishings were sparse. A bed was covered in a mound of strewn clothing.

Sasha gestured to the messy pile. "Go ahead and look through the stash. Choose whatever outfit you want."

Tabor and Sasha held back while Kamari and Hailey approached the bed. Once they began picking through the garments, the mated pair began a private conversation. Hailey ran her hands across worn cotton with faded patterns. Numerous dresses, some skirts, pants, and soft shirts covered the bed.

"Scavengers," Kamari said in a low voice only for her ears.

She nodded twice, inclined to agree.

Kamari kept his hands by his side while she rifled through the pile, selecting a pair of tan-colored pants. "Try these."

Taking the pants from her, Kamari stepped into each leg while Hailey watched to see if they fit. The waistband appeared as though it would work until the zipper settled in place and Kamari attempted to secure the final fastening. The button stubbornly resisted overlapping the thin notch meant to secure the pants around the male's hips.

"I'll leave it open," Kamari said.

Hailey turned back to the mass and selected a large gray shirt with short sleeves. When she turned again, she caught the brief flicker of longing the alpha directed at her.

"Thank you," Kamari said, grabbing the shirt and hastily pulled it over his face.

She turned before she had a chance of seeing that unsettling gaze again. Digging through the garments, Hailey found a short white skirt dotted with tiny pink flowers. The fabric had ruffles along the edges and a matching strapless top that stretched over her head before compressing over her chest.

Sasha joined them, gesturing at the clothes mound with a smile. "It's nice to have extra for a change. We're planning another trip into the suburbs to search for baby clothes." Her hand slid down her torso, resting on her belly. With that motion, Hailey understood her mate's overprotective behavior.

"Congratulations," Hailey said.

Sasha beamed. "Thank you. We are hoping our wee one is born with powers like my mate."

It seemed an odd thing to wish for, but then the Wolf Hollow shifters were a peculiar bunch.

Sasha and Tabor exchanged a tender smile.

"We have three packmates expecting, and an infant in the den," Sasha said with glowing cheeks. "Shall we have dinner?" she asked, sliding her hand over her belly once more.

Hailey was ready to leave the confines of the cabin and get back outside. She led the way out, halting outside the door when a pair of glowing eyes stared up at her. It did not matter that she was in her upright form; even her human sight would have recognized him anywhere.

"Oh," Sasha said, coming up behind her. "It's either Rafael or Diego—probably Rafael."

The light that had been glowing at their backs dimmed and went dark. A moment later, Tabor joined them. "I wonder what he wants." Tabor got in front of Sasha, focused on the wolf. His shoulders were relaxed, but clearly he wasn't taking any chances with his pregnant mate.

The wolf trotted up to Hailey and nudged her leg. She opened her palm and held it below his muzzle, feeling a moist nose touch her fingers when the wolf brushed his face against her fingers.

"Look at that, he likes you." Sasha stepped around her

mate and flashed Hailey an encouraging smile. "I know you just put on clothes, but perhaps you would like to shift and introduce your wolf."

Hailey chewed on her bottom lip. No one else knew that she and Rafael had skipped introductions and jumped straight to mating. No one needed to know.

Hailey crouched in front of Rafael and rubbed the backs of his ears.

Hello again.

He leaned his head into her hands and briefly closed his eyes. An urge to rub her face into his soft fur was hampered by their present company. Hailey needed time alone with the pureblood, but she couldn't shift. Not yet.

With a final stroke of the wolf's head, Hailey straightened and faced Sasha. "I must remain in human form another two days at least. My wolf is in heat." Sasha's brows furrowed. "Do you not experience these from time to time?" Hailey asked.

Sasha's mate cleared his throat softly and muttered, "I'll, uh, be just over there." He shuffled away, remaining close by, though he turned his attention to something on the ground.

"No, I never have," Sasha said. "That's remarkable."

"Hailey comes from a long line of pureblooded wolves." Kamari's chest puffed out as though speaking of his own ancestors.

Rafael's wolf nudged Hailey again. When she didn't pet him, he moved in front of her and sat on her feet. A laugh burst through her lips. A pleased smile reached Sasha's eyes.

"Perhaps we ought to leave the two of you alone. Maybe this friendly fellow here should be the one to shift."

Without waiting for a response, Sasha took off, first collecting her mate where he stood nudging at a stone with his toe. They sped down the trail, making themselves scarce.

Kamari looked down at the wolf on Hailey's feet with a frown. "This is one of the purebloods?"

"Rafael," Hailey said.

The wolf looked up at her and grinned. If there had been any doubt left in Hailey's mind as to who he was, the pair of golden eyes gleaming up at her would have settled the matter.

"Do you want me to leave?" Kamari asked.

The alpha's eyes contained familiarity and warmth. His presence brought her comfort. His scent kept her grounded. If Kamari left, she would be surrounded by strangers for the first time in her life.

Invisible vines twisted around Hailey's heart and squeezed. She could avoid meeting Kamari's inquisitive gaze, but she could not block him out. His stare marked her as sure as the sun in an open field.

"I would like a moment alone with him, but will you stay in Wolf Hollow a little longer?"

"Of course." The words burst out of Kamari's lips. He started toward her, then abruptly stopped, gripping his own arm as though he had to hold himself back. "I only meant for now. I'll wait for you in the communal glade."

"Thank you," Hailey whispered, still dodging his gaze.

Kamari left without another word. She listened to his footfalls until all trace of the alpha faded. Night sounds filled the space left behind by Kamari. Crickets chirped all around them. A frog croaked from a nearby tree. Somewhere in the hollow, a wolf howled.

Hailey got to her knees in front of Rafael and met his golden gaze. "It would be nice if you shifted so we could get to know one another." The wolf nudged her shoulder, bringing a laugh to Hailey's lips. "I wish I could join you in fur form, but we don't want a repeat of earlier . . . or maybe you do."

With smiling lips, the wolf nodded his head.

chapter six

THE FEMALE'S SOOTHING voice put Rafael at ease. He enjoyed her fingers in his fur, stroking his head and scratching behind his ears. It was as though she knew exactly where he wanted petting. He'd never allowed another being to touch him this way before. Rafael despised humans and would sooner trust a rabid wolf than a person of any age, gender, or disposition. Despite the female's current form, he knew what the female—Hailey—really was. A shifter like him. She was his, even though he felt the grip of his humanoid half fighting a mate claim with this healthy, attractive, and fertile female.

Everything would go much smoother if Hailey shifted back into her beautiful wolf form. Animal instinct was far superior to a battle of defense and ego. He'd mount her, mate her, bite her, and claim her. His two-legged half would simply have to accept that.

Reluctantly pulling his head away from Hailey's attentive fingers, Rafael licked her hand. His tongue ran over smooth, slightly salty, skin.

Gentle laughter shook the female's chest. He liked

seeing her happy. Crickets chorused around them, undisturbed by the flirtation taking place between a wolf and a woman.

Rafael nudged the female's leg. When she ran her hand from his neck down the ridge of his back, a silent sigh of contentment rustled along his spine. As good as the pets felt, this wasn't what Rafael had wanted to communicate. If Hailey shifted, she would understand. They would finish what they had started, then make their claim beneath the stars. By morning, all the single males would know that she was his and to keep off. Not that they would stick around for long. Despite what the Wolf Hollow elders said about rebuilding their community, the pack was already too crowded for Rafael's taste.

What they said was human-speak.

Strength in numbers.

Rafael and Diego had been a pack of two from the moment they had lost their parents.

Having a female by his side would be a welcome change. They would run free. If they found a safe spot, perhaps he would breed with her. He padded around Hailey.

"Where are you going?" Soft laughter filled her voice.

He nudged her back with his nose. When she tried to turn to face him, he put his full weight into pushing her from behind.

She gave a startled gasp as she fell forward, catching herself on her wrists, now on all fours. It was the correct position; wrong form.

"Hey!" Hailey said in a chiding tone. "What was that about?"

Rafael barked as she settled on the ground, seating herself with her legs tucked in as she studied him with furrowed brows. He barked again.

Hailey spread open her palms. "Sorry, buddy. I have to stay this way for the next two days or so. How about you shift? I would really like to meet you face to face."

This set him off barking at full volume. His humanoid half would ruin everything. He could practically hear the commands shouting in the dark. Lifting his muzzle, he barked his would-be master away. Hailey winced, her gaze darting in the direction of the glade. Then she returned her attention to Rafael and his insistent yipping.

"Shh. No bark, okay?" Her voice was so gentle and sweet even as she tried to shush him.

He didn't listen, not even when Hailey leaned forward and tried to placate him with soft pets. Rafael wanted to see her wolf. The smell of her lingered in his mind. He breathed in and out craving her heady scent in his nostrils. His tail swished with impatience. He barked harder.

Hailey stood up and grabbed her head, groaning in exasperation. Throwing her arms to her sides, she stared at Rafael with fierce olive-brown eyes. "I can't shift. I'm in heat. Do you understand? Are you in there somewhere, Rafael? You know what that means, so tell your wolf to simmer down."

Heat.

Rafael's next bark cut off. His body stilled as thoughts, and the chorus of crickets, swarmed him like a dark cloud of incessant mosquitoes.

Hailey's wolf was in heat.

The realization made it through, giving Rafael a

window in which to take control and propel himself into a rapid shift. It was like falling out of a tree. His claws had barely retracted when his body jerked and he found himself sprawled naked and twitchy on his side in front of an unwelcome audience.

"¡Mierda!"

Hailey's lips parted. The moon gave her hair a silvery shine and turned her skin to porcelain. Even though she was now clothed, there was still plenty of smooth, supple skin on display beneath a short skirt and tube top. There wasn't a scratch or scar on the woman. Did they pamper the pureblood like some kind of show wolf in Glenn Meadows? Her kind was not meant to be sheltered. Now here she was, probably expecting him to claim her and become her loyal protector.

Not happening.

He sprang to his feet.

With graceful poise, Hailey held her ground and watched him with a curiosity that made Rafael feel lightheaded.

Danger, he warned himself. He couldn't let her beauty mask the threat staring him head on as surely as the rare predator issuing a challenge.

"That word you spoke, what language is it?" she asked.

"Spanish," he grumbled, as though the question offended him. What really provoked him was her interest. Her perfection annoyed him. He took issue with the way her white-blonde hair formed soft waves that framed her proud square jaw and elegant nose.

She didn't look like she belonged in the wild.

"Aden said you came from the south," she noted.

"We did," he answered gruffly. "We've also been to the west and the north. Next, I'll head east. I'm always on the move."

Rafael folded his arms over his chest. He had covered himself in front of her the first time, but he would not do so again. This hormonal female needed to be set straight. Within his wolf's consciousness, he had registered the revelation that her wolf was in heat. No wonder the animal in him had mounted her. Any male wolf would have done the same. It was nature, nothing more. Relief fueled his resolve.

"Once my brother claims his female, I am leaving."

Wrinkles disrupted the smooth plane of Hailey's forehead. "You plan to leave?"

"That's what I just said."

"Alone?"

"Exactly." He lifted his chin, daring her, a stranger, to advise him to stay and claim her. *Just how brazen was this she-wolf?*

At the moment, she looked more confused than demanding. Hailey rubbed her earlobe between her thumb and finger, frowning. "But wolves are pack animals."

Rafael laughed humorlessly. He prowled up to her, dropping his arms as the flawless features of her face filled his vision. "Why don't we cut to the chase. You're here because my dumbass brother sent for you and, let's be honest, you came running because you're desperate to breed with another pureblood. There's nothing you want more than to birth litters of cuddly little pups to frolic through fields and give your life purpose."

A low growl rumbled from Hailey's throat. Her inquisitive expression was no longer filled with warmth. Good, he was getting through to her.

"My brother could have given you what you wanted, but unfortunately, another female got to him first. Sorry you wasted a trip coming here, though I imagine you don't leave your pack very often, if ever, so it was probably good you got a chance to see a little more of the world."

Hailey's jaw tightened. He saw a vein pulse in her smooth neck.

"You're wretched," she cried.

"I'm a lone wolf, sweetheart. Not interested. That's all you need to know."

Hailey's olive-brown eyes hardened. "Tell that to your wolf," she snarled.

"You said it yourself, you're in heat. My wolf's actions can hardly be blamed. Why didn't you wait until your heat passed to come here? What did you expect?"

Fingers curled, Hailey backed away from him with a vicious snarl curling her upper lip. Her ferocity had the unfortunate effect of turning him painfully on. It had been easier to insult her when she appeared docile. With her hackles raised, his groin responded with the same rapid speed as dry wood catching fire. If he wasn't careful, the flame might spread into a blistering desire that consumed all rational thought. He had to get hold of himself before he tackled her to the ground, ripped off her clothing, and buried himself between those smooth, milky legs.

Hailey's pale face filled with color. Bone-white teeth gnashed together, and rage flashed in her eyes.

She appeared too angry to notice his hard-on. When she spun around and took off running, Rafael felt his heart catch for a moment and tug in her direction.

He needed a new focus pronto. He grabbed himself in a punishing grip and pumped hard and fast, casting himself into the throes of self-pleasure.

The crickets ignored the furious strokes and smack of his fist. He did not hold back. Did not go gentle. Pleasure and pain became one until he came on the soil where the she-wolf had stood condemning him with her thunderous glare.

Oh, yes, he was a scoundrel. Arrogant. Beastly. A wild thing. Wretched, indeed.

Better to be alone than to end up like his parents.

chapter seven

AS PROMISED, RAFAEL made himself scarce. Until Hailey left, he didn't trust his wolf to stay away from her, so he borrowed a bow and arrows from Tabor and hunted down his meals by hand and cooked them over a fire in front of a cave near a river. The spot had a small piece of grill that fit over a rocky fire pit and a few other handy tools for a cookout.

Two days after his encounter with Hailey, he stood roasting a raccoon over a fire pit at midday. The Wolf Hollow shifters ate twice a day—in the morning and in the evening. They even had a gong to call them to supper like dogs. Rafael ate whenever he wanted.

He turned the meat over the grill, then stepped away from the heat and smoke, swiping the back of his hand over his forehead. The sound of the crackling fire filled his head and temporarily replaced his troubled thoughts. All of this time in his human form had given him a chance to ponder where he would go after Diego's claiming ceremony. There would be no more company and conversation. No teaming up to hunt big game. Silent nights without laughter.

Dammit. He was back to thinking again.

Frowning at the flames, Rafael felt his heart char along with the meat.

This was bullshit. How could his brother do this to him? Diego should tell his piece of tail that her place was by his side, wherever that might be.

Unfortunately, there was the whole baby thing. Lacy wasn't a pureblood, which meant screaming infants in need of community protection. Such a hindrance.

If his brother had held out just a bit longer, he could have had himself the kind of female who didn't need a tribe to protect her young.

A growl vibrated inside Rafael's chest. He wanted to claw away all thought of his brother with Hailey. Seeing them together would have been torture. Just the idea of it made his teeth elongate and fur rise over his arms.

"No!" he shouted.

He closed his eyes and pulled in deep breaths filled with smoke.

Meat. Lunch. Eat. He repeated the three words in his head until his thundering heart simmered down.

Once the outside of the meat was charred, Rafael put the fire out and waited for his meal to cool. He looked around at the still woods beyond the cave, then walked with hurried steps to the river to have a drink and splash water over his face. The cool liquid invigorated him inside and out. He was ready to feast and think about something other than pesky females—like which direction he would head. Fall was on the horizon. Perhaps he would travel east for a bit, check out the Midwest, then drop back down to warmer winter climates. Or maybe he would spend a winter in the snow. The decision was his and his alone. He was freer than he had ever been.

Rafael lifted his chest, only to have his shoulders droop the very next moment.

The concept of freedom felt rife with loneliness.

Dragging his feet back to the campsite, his clouded thoughts had him trudging to the grill with his eyes out of focus. The sight of a naked male seated on a boulder made his head jerk and claws punch through his nails.

Wolfrik, Wolf Hollow's only pureblooded male, held a leg of cooked meat to his teeth. He ripped off the flesh and chewed loudly, looking at Rafael with eyes that smirked.

"Help yourself," Rafael grumbled, retracting his claws. It wasn't the sharing he minded so much as the surprise intrusion.

Wolfrik should have howled or called out before entering his space. Although this was the wild wolf's territory, there was such a thing as animal etiquette. The smart thing would have been for him to announce himself.

Oblivious to his barbarism, Wolfrik opened his jaw wide and ripped into the meat. At least he hadn't taken the entire raccoon. Rafael would have been forced to fight him if he'd overstepped and, judging by his body mapped in scars, an altercation with Wolfrik could only end up bloody.

Rafael shoved his fingers into his pants pocket and dug out a switchblade he had borrowed from the pack's communal shed. Crouching beside the cooked meat, he sliced off a strip and stuffed it into his mouth. Rafael chewed and chewed. The raccoon meat was tough as tree bark.

"Good stuff," Wolfrik said between chews. He lifted the leg he'd ripped clean off the raccoon above his head like a club he meant to bring down over a foe. With a wolfish grin, the male returned the leg to his mouth and bit off a chunk of flesh.

As soon as he felt certain the meat wouldn't choke him, Rafael swallowed. "Did the female from Glenn Meadows leave?"

"Hailey?" Wolfrik picked a small bone from his mouth and flicked it to the ground. "Saw her and her escort in the glade earlier."

"Why is she still here?"

"Maybe it has something to do with you still being here." Wolfrik lifted his brows and smirked, then fished out another bone.

Ignoring the remaining meat, Rafael paced alongside the fire. "I told her I wasn't interested." Wolfrik's laughter and smug grin rankled his nerves. "Something funny?" Rafael demanded.

Wolfrik sucked his fingers clean and wiped his hands on his muscular thighs. Lacerations, welts, and lines of angry red raised skin marred his tan skin. The male had as much reason to hate humans as Rafael. The other pureblood had been held captive for several years, so Rafael didn't blame him for sounding unhinged.

Wolfrik rested his palms flat against his thighs and looked him up and down. "By hiding out here, you established your role as prey with Hailey as the huntress.

You think she's going to give up because you tucked tail and ran? Think again."

Rafael stopped pacing and gritted his teeth. "I'm not hiding; I'm sending a message. You would think she would have more self-respect and go home."

"Nah," Wolfrik said. "A strong female doesn't give up that easily. Look how my Kallie wore me down. Big difference, though. I made sure I established myself as the hunter during our courtship."

Rafael had no doubt there. Wolfrik didn't seem like the type to settle down with a mate, yet he had claimed a female and had a baby on the way.

"Couldn't ask for a better mate. Brave. Independent. Attentive. Gives me my space. Never nags. Sexy on two legs and four," Wolfrik boasted. "She will be the best mother. And she saved me from Hailey."

Rafael's head jerked. "What do you mean, she saved you from Hailey?"

Smug smile on his lips, Wolfrik stood and stretched, flexing his muscles in the process. He wore his scars with pride.

"I'm a pureblood. Hailey's a pureblood. Some of the elders got the idea we should mate."

Rafael had to fight back a snarl.

Wolfrik shrugged. "At least she's not chasing you down. Maybe it has something to do with your brother keeping her company."

"Diego's doing what?" Rafael may have yelled his question. Whatever his volume, it was drowned out by a rumbling bear-sized growl. "Is that a—" Rafael didn't bother finishing his sentence. Wolfrik was already on the ground shifting, head first, snarling before his tail had even formed.

Rafael unfastened his pants, yanked them off, and dropped to all fours. He shifted and caught up to Wolfrik at the river. Across the water, a burly brown bear stood on its hind legs and bellowed. Rafael snarled alongside Wolfrik. The hair along the ridges of their backs stood and ears flattened.

The bear crashed down and paced along the river's edge. Rafael and Wolfrik kept pace across from him. There was snapping and snarling on one side, answered by a grumble on the opposite. The bear lumbered along, not crossing over, but not leaving the water's edge, either.

Water flowed between them. At least the animal was respecting Wolf Hollow territory. Rafael would have left it at that, but Wolfrik's teeth were bared and his growl indicated he wanted to engage. Rafael wasn't keen to fight a bear, though he would in a heartbeat if his pureblooded friend led the charge. At the moment, he was a guest of his tribe. There were packmates to protect . . . and Hailey.

The bear turned to face them, setting Wolfrik off. The male's roar likely had the earthworms quaking beneath the ground. Saliva dripped from Wolfrik's fangs. The bear huffed again and again. He started back up the way he had come, stubbornly following the water's edge.

Wolfrik jumped into the water and growled. The bear huffed louder. Water splashed as Wolfrik raced across. The bear ran several feet back then stopped, jerked around, and roared.

Any swears Rafael might have flung became snarls with every spring of his legs across the river. No sooner had he cleared the river than a second bear crashed through the trees to join the other. One full-grown brown bear was alarming enough. Two had Rafael's survival instincts kicking into full gear.

The growls that followed were deafening. Excitement, fear, and rage filled his bones. He fed off the adrenaline and manic snarls coming from his friend.

The second bear charged Rafael. His nails slashed at the air in front of him. Wolfrik jumped between them and the bear stopped short. The beast stood, bellowing through gigantic teeth.

The first bear was still huffing. The sound grew louder and more insistent. The bear who had started to charge Rafael dropped down. With an agitated snort, he and his friend took off running into the woods, away from Wolf Hollow.

Good. You better run.

Rafael turned and started for the river. He needed to run back to the glade and make sure Hailey was okay.

His ears twitched at the sound of Wolfrik running, not back across the river, but away. His footfalls receded in pursuit of the bears.

Rafael growled in frustration. He couldn't leave his wolf pal to fight alone. Running after Wolfrik, he barked, trying to make the male see reason. But Wolfrik was like a hawk swooping down after prey. Single-minded, stubborn *pendejo*. Did he want his child to grow up without a father?

Ferns whipped past Rafael's face. It all became a

blur of green as he sprang through the brush. He heard a crashing sound ahead, followed by a curse. Racing forward, Rafael came into a small opening and jerked to a stop.

Wolfrik had shifted to human form and was staring at a pile of bones. The pull to communicate distracted Rafael's wolf enough to transform to his two-legged self. Standing up, Rafael took in the crude mound of human skeletons stacked chest high. A single skull sat at the top, jaw wide in terror.

Rafael found himself making the sign of the cross. He had observed urban shifters making the gesture in the past and the motions came to him unbidden. Something about the bones, some of which still had skin attached, filled him with dread. He wanted to get far away from the monstrous display, and yet he couldn't stop staring at the horror before him.

Wolfrik circled the pile, kicking at the bones. "Those bears weren't just bears. They were shifters."

"How do you know?"

"Because they took a shit back here—human shit. Didn't bother digging a hole and covering it up, either. Filthy fucks." Wolfrik hocked, then spat beside the heaping pile of death. Rafael felt the urge to cross himself again.

Wolfrik stared into the woods. "A bear pair; I don't like it."

"Are they responsible for all this?" Rafael had never seen such a mass of human remains.

"Nah, we took care of killing these human scum," Wolfrik said. "Too many bodies to deal with. Left them for scavengers and maggots to do their work."

Rafael gave the pile a hard stare. "This is a lot of bones."

"Impressive, I know." Wolfrik smiled, showing all his teeth.

Needle point chills pricked at Rafael's skin. "What were this many humans doing out here?"

Wolfrik selected a femur from the pile and smiled maniacally. A gleam entered his eyes as though, in looking at the bone, he recognized a vanquished foe.

"Their leader's sister ran away—led them straight to the slaughter."

"Will more come looking for their fallen comrades?" Rafael demanded. If humans had found their way to Wolf Hollow once, they could do it again. Leaving Diego susceptible to attack was not an option.

"We executed the leader and his underlings," Wolfrik said, still looking at the bone with tissue decomposing on the surface.

Well, if there was an argument to be made for large wolf packs, the macabre mountain of remains certainly spoke volumes about strength in numbers.

Wolfrik tossed the femur and leaned forward as it sailed past trees, watching it like he was considering shifting and fetching the revolting piece of bone. The pureblood's fingers twitched over his thigh.

"Once Sparrow wakes, we'll return the favor when we attack what's left of the cockroaches on their turf," Wolfrik announced. Rafael gave a start as he continued. "I knew all the handlers and wardens operating the cages and pit fights, but Sparrow has knowledge of the entire compound and operations."

Rafael folded his arms. He didn't like the sound of this

one bit. "Where are you keeping this Sparrow, and why go back?" There was no one who understood the need for vengeance better than Rafael, but he also knew how easily revenge could turn into a suicide mission. There was no glory in providing humans with an easy target. No justice in handing them another trophy.

Wolfrik's jaw tightened. "There are still wolf shifters trapped in that hellhole. The wizards are keeping Sparrow alive. Hopefully she's not so brain-damaged when she wakes as to be useless to us." He shrugged. "I'll give her until after the birth of my child. If she hasn't come to by then, the wizards need to let nature take its course."

Rafael scrubbed his jaw. "Humans, wizards, bears—anything else my brother needs to know about his new home?"

"Pretty sure he can handle it," Wolfrik said.

Diego was travel-seasoned and tough, but that didn't ease the frown on Rafael's face. "Was that the bear shifter who came after your packmate?"

Wolfrik jabbed his toes into one of the large paw prints that had pressed deep into a patch of loam. "I don't know. He was operating alone before. Maybe he has a friend."

"Or family," Rafael said.

Wolfrik shrugged like it made no difference. "Well, I'd better tell my council and order extra patrol in this area in case those lugs make the mistake of crossing the river. They can play with human bones all they want, so long as they respect my territory. You sticking around?"

Grimacing at the skull, Rafael shook his head. "I should check on my brother."

"Right," Wolfrik said with a laugh. He went up to the nearest tree and peed on the trunk. Dick still in hand, Wolfrik turned to the next tree and did the same before shaking himself off. He squatted, grunted, then straightened and shook his head. "Don't got a shit in me at the moment."

Rafael expelled a breath of disbelief.

"Your mate is one lucky female," Rafael said, ribbing the other pureblood. It helped take the edge off the grim spectacle.

Wolfrik smirked. "Maybe one day you'll join the club."

And like that, the dark cloud returned to muddy up Rafael's mood. With a chuckle, Wolfrik snatched the skull off the bone pile. "Don't look so glum. It could be worse. You could be this guy." With that, Wolfrik tossed the skull over his shoulder. It hit the remains with a ghastly clack.

They dropped to the ground, shifting on all fours into fur, then took off running for the hollow's glade. Wolfrik was in his element, and he was fast, but Rafael's wolf wanted to get to Hailey. They raced each other through the thicket until reaching the dirt trail, where they picked up speed. Wolfrik growled when Rafael started to pass him. Ignoring his friend, he pushed on, not flagging for an instant.

They passed a couple of shifters standing on two feet as they ran headlong down the path. As they neared the glade, Wolfrik veered off down a narrow trail. Rafael continued on the direct route—following the scent of his intended mate.

The glade was mostly clear, except for Lacy and her partner on meal duty. Beneath the shade of a tree, Diego sat beside Hailey. The sight made Rafael want to tear his brother apart.

His vicious snarls jerked Diego's attention away from Hailey. They were sharing a log, sitting way too close.

Diego's brows drew together as he aimed a stern gaze at him. "No, Raphy!"

Rafael's mouth practically foamed at the indignation. He snapped his jaw.

Hailey stood and folded her arms, glaring down at him. His brother's displeasure was one thing; hers shoved the growl right back down his throat. He lifted his head to look at her and wagged his tail.

With a heavy sigh, Hailey flung her arms out. "Your human half wouldn't like you to behave this way. Understand? Are you in there, Rafael? Get your animal under control. Better yet, pay more attention to your wolf. I like him a whole lot better." She spun on her heel and stormed into the woods.

Rafael trotted after her.

Spotting him, Hailey groaned. "You have got to be kidding me."

She started running down a path. Rafael gave chase, springing with each step. His lips drew into a smile as he kept pace with his favorite female. He liked this game.

Looking over her shoulder, Hailey yelled, "Just go away."

She looked from side to side, searching her surroundings. When the path reached a fork, she launched herself down a new trail and kept looking over her shoulder. Rafael wagged his tail in greeting. Hailey huffed and jogged forward. Woods closed in around them. The thick green canopy teemed with insects, wildlife, and arachnids going about their business while the wolf chased his woman. A bird halted its song to watch them pass beneath its branch, then flitted to a neighboring tree.

Hailey looked back again, but it was the wrong moment to take her gaze off the earth in front of her. She yelped and went airborne, arms thrown in front of her body as she fell onto the ground.

Rafael sprang forward, his heart racing.

Was his female hurt?

She had already flipped around when he reached her and was rubbing her foot. "Didn't see that dang root. I blame you," she said, wagging her finger at Rafael.

Her light tone held no pain in it, but she kept rubbing her toes. Rafael walked over and licked her foot.

A startled laugh puffed through Hailey's lips. "Oh, you think that will make it all better, do you?" She reached out a hand and scratched behind his ears.

If her change in mood was anything to go by, he really was improving her condition, so Rafael licked her foot again, then her ankle, and then her lower calf.

Laughter burbled from Hailey. "Hey, nothing wrong with my thigh," she said as he made his way up her leg. "Don't need a saliva bath. Don't need–"

Her stream of words ended when he nosed his way beneath her short skirt. The heat of her wolf was not present, but a poignant scent emerged, one his human half recognized as arousal.

Shift, female, he urged, but he was the one who shifted.

 chapter eight

HAILEY MOMENTARILY FROZE as Rafael's wolf stuck his head straight up her skirt. The cotton held in the heat of his breath against her thighs and sex. She gripped his fur to yank him away before he could stick his tongue where it had no business being. Her hands grasped onto hair. With a blink and a gasp, Hailey saw that Rafael had shifted into human form and was kneeling with his face pillowed between her legs.

She shoved him away and scrambled backward. As soon as she stopped, she squeezed her legs shut.

What she really wanted to do was go back over to Rafael, the man, and strangle him. The sight of him made her seethe. His face brought back his barbaric words. No one had ever spoken to her with such vulgarity and censure.

Her wolf had trusted his. Hailey would have given him her heart. No drama. No games.

Every male should be so lucky.

She would have been the dream mate. But oh, no. How had he reacted? Like a manic beast caught in a steel trap. He made her out to be a desperate female, salivating after a mate. Even now, he glared at her and demanded, "Why are you still here?"

He crouched on his arms and knees, his arm muscles flexed as he held himself above the ground.

Hailey's jaw clenched. She had never felt such raging hatred toward another shifter. They picked themselves off the ground and stood apart, glowering at one another.

"I am making sure my heat has passed before I leave," she said defensively.

If she'd been trite, she could have pointed out that he was the one with a boner. It was big and bulging, like the rest of him.

"Why were you talking to my brother?"

"He was the one talking to me."

"About?"

"Why? What's it to you?" Hailey folded her arms.

"My brother already has a mate."

"Not yet."

Rafael's snarl prompted a bird to squawk before flapping away.

Rolling her eyes, Hailey explained, "I don't mean that in an 'I intend to interfere' kind of way—despite your poor conclusion as to my character. It was friendly conversation, nothing more." Her anger turned inward. Why was she attempting to justify herself to him? "I plan to leave tomorrow. Fear not, Rafael. By the time the next moon rises, we won't have to see each other ever again."

With those words, she took off in the direction she'd been fleeing, watching carefully for roots. She wasn't about to look back and risk tripping again. She had no desire to look upon the beast. And by beast, she meant man. Too bad such an agreeable wolf form was wasted on him.

He acted like she was after him, yet he was the one who kept chasing her down. Faithless brute!

His brother had turned out to be nice. He'd apologized again for sending a shifter to fetch her and explained that his intention had been to visit Glenn Meadows himself, until Jager insisted he stick around a little longer and sent Aden instead. After Hailey forgave him for any wrongdoing, he had regaled her with tales of the brothers' adventure across the continent. With each new story, Hailey had found herself developing a case of wanderlust.

Suddenly, she wasn't so sure about returning to Glenn Meadows. When Rafael had first rejected her, her initial reaction was to run to Kamari and tell him she could not wait to leave.

"I will speak to your father when we return home," he had said.

But she was no longer certain about claiming the alpha, either. There was a whole wide world out there. As much as she hated to admit it, Rafael was right. She had barely left the thorned walls of her home or surrounding fields.

Maybe it was time to stretch her legs beyond these mountains and woods.

ONCE MORE, RAFAEL found himself angry, aroused, and feeling very much like his uncovered pelvis and genitals—like an asshole and a dick.

If Hailey had descended from urban wolf shifters, it would have been a different story. He would have flirted and teased his way between her legs. The female was gorgeous, proud, and sexy without seeming to be aware of her flawless beauty. In the past, he had met purebloods who put on airs. It had been a pleasant surprise to meet Sasha and Wolfrik, who did not behave as though the moon revolved around them. Hailey was a revelation as well. When she said she was leaving, he believed her, and it left him with a peculiar feeling of displeasure.

Rafael glanced down at his hard-on. Masturbate or apologize? Decisions. Decisions.

If this was to be Hailey's last night in Wolf Hollow, it was now or never.

Rafael sprinted after her. Clouds of dirt lifted off the trail with the pounding of his feet. Grit rubbed between his toes.

A head of wavy white-blonde hair moved at a hasty clip through the greenery. Even when Rafael was close enough for her to hear him, she kept going, not looking back.

"Hey, hold up." Hailey ignored him. He jogged to her side and matched her steps. "It's nothing personal. I'm not interested in a mate. End of story."

Eyes on the trail ahead of her, Hailey huffed. "You should tell that to your wolf."

"Yeah, he has a mind of his own." Rafael scrubbed his jaw.

"Why is that?" Hailey asked, sounding more curious than vexed.

"I don't know. This has never happened before." The

whole thing was weird. Rafael supposed it had been Hailey's heat that got his wolf all riled up and confused.

Hailey pursed her lips, obviously unimpressed with his unenlightened answer. If she were to shift now, Rafael wondered if her wolf would have as little control as his. It was a theory he did not want to test.

"So, you're returning to your pack?" he asked instead.

"For now."

"If you want to know more about the world beyond your meadows and this hollow, feel free to ask me . . . before you leave, I mean."

"Your brother already shared stories with me, and I'm leaving soon."

Hailey's arms swung as she walked with long, lean limbs that looked ready to whack him if he got too close. The smell of her pussy lingered in his nose. He had to ball up his fingers to keep from ripping down her skirt and tasting her. He knew better than to fuck a pureblood. It was akin to a claiming. He might as well bite her, because something primal happened when two purebloods bumped bones. It was probably nature's way of ensuring the survival of the species.

The sound of Wolf Hollow's gong rang out through the forest. The wrinkle of Hailey's nose made Rafael chuckle.

"No dinner bell in Glenn Meadows?"

"No," she answered.

He should stop walking alongside her like a dog on a leash. He ought to leave her alone and make himself scarce until she was really good and gone.

But the danger had passed. Hadn't it? She had no

more interest in him. Unable to decide, he continued with her to the glade.

Shadows fell as night descended. His stomach rumbled. He had not gotten to eat much of his raccoon before being disturbed. There was plenty of food in the hollow's communal cauldron. He might as well get something to eat.

Smoke and the smell of stew filtered in through the trees. Wolf Hollow packmates joined them on the main path, heading in the same direction of fire and food. A familiar giggle caught his attention. The busty brunette he had tangled with after first arriving flipped her hair back and grinned at him. He could not recall her name. She winked but didn't approach. Maybe it had something to do with the blonde he couldn't seem to part ways with.

If he wanted to, he could drag the brunette and her friend into the woods for another threesome after dinner. The two females had been eager participants up for anything. Rafael should eat his meal with them. He cringed, recalling their incessant chatter and flirting. It was overkill and exhausting. He'd gone so far as to cover one of their mouths with his hand while pumping into her.

Taking a sidelong glance at Hailey, he wondered how the blonde behaved when bedded. There was a seriousness in the way she held herself and spoke, a soulfulness in her gaze that called to him. What did she look like when she smiled?

As though hearing his silent question, her face lit up. It was as though the sun had reversed direction to rise up from the horizon and chase the night away.

Rafael's heart lifted until he saw what had brought

about this joy.

Hailey's escort, the older male who had traveled with her, stood in the glade, arms folded, watching their approach. The male was ripped and had aged well. Although cropped short, his hair was not receding or thinning. There were silver threads running through the light brown strands, but they had yet to take over. He had the air of a puffed-up elder who knew his place at the top of the command chain.

Rafael felt his gums aching from clenching his teeth. Releasing the tight hold his jaw had taken, he ran his tongue over his teeth and relaxed his shoulders, strolling up to the male alongside Hailey.

"I see your dad's still here."

Not taking the bait, the male lifted his cleft chin and flashed Rafael a languid grin.

Hailey gave a slight jerk at his comment, turned, and stared with surprise, as though not expecting to see him still at her side. Her smile was gone.

"Kamari's not my father; he's my alpha."

Those words were like maggots inside his gut. The adoring look she'd shot the male made Rafael's stomach crawl and itch to punch *esa estupida boca presumido que tiene* in his smug mouth. The alpha oldster looked amused rather than insulted by Rafael's dad comment.

"Let's grab a bite," he said to Hailey.

She nodded and hurried to his side. They walked away, leaving Rafael behind like a pesky insect.

It looked like the pureblood had a protector after all. They might already be fucking or, if not, would be very soon—and more. A growl vibrated deep within Rafael's throat.

Mine.

His wolf was going to be seriously pissed off with him.

A bubbly giggle preceded fingers that brushed his arm. "It's nice to see a man without pants—or a shirt—for longer than fifteen seconds." The female who had joined him in a romp several nights ago slipped her hand over his ass cheek and squeezed, then let go with a grin. "Want to have a bite with me and Camilla? We've missed you these past couple days."

Rafael found himself leaning away from the brazen she-wolf. "You go ahead. I need to have a word with my brother."

Still smiling, the female swept her long dark brown hair over her shoulders and lifted her tits. "Of course. Diego's over there talking to Tabor. You know where to find me." Hips swinging, she sashayed in his direct line of sight.

Rafael sighed. He didn't know what direction "over there" was supposed to be, nor did he have any interest in finding the frisky female later.

He tramped into the glade and searched the faces gathered. Lacy sat on a log near the fire with a friend, but Diego was not hovering near them as Rafael would have expected. Ever since meeting the skinny blonde, Diego had put himself on a short leash, so he couldn't be far. Rafael was right; he spotted his brother leaning against a tree trunk, conversing with Tabor. He'd heard rumors that the shifter was part wizard, but he had yet to witness a display of power.

As soon as Diego saw him, he nodded, said something to Tabor, and headed over. "Everything all right, *hermano*?"

Rafael sniffed dismissively. "It will be once that

pureblood returns home." Even as he spoke the words, they didn't ring true in his heart. "Why were you talking to her?"

Diego released a windy breath and ran both hands through his hair. "I was just being nice. I felt bad. Now you're mad at me, and so is Lacy."

Rafael's eyebrows lifted. "Lacy's upset?"

"She won't come out and say it, but I can tell she's displeased." Diego looked to where the blonde sat, finishing up her supper.

"Sounds like a good time for us both to hit the road," Rafael remarked.

He wanted nothing more than to get the hell out of Wolf Hollow before Hailey. Every time he watched her walk away, he felt his wolf snapping just below the surface.

But Diego's gaze was fixed on Lacy. As though sensing his attention, she set her bowl down, reached up, and pulled her hair free from its elastic tie. Diego was practically on his toes watching as she shook her long, light, slightly messy hair over her shoulders. When she began finger-combing the strands, Rafael huffed and walked away—leaving his brother gaping.

He was about to dish up when howls rose in the distance. The shifters in the glade cocked their heads and looked at one another.

"Wolves from Glenn Meadows." He heard Hailey's voice before locating her. She stood with her bowl cupped in her hands, Kamari behind her as she stepped forward at the sound of the howls. "I wonder why they've come."

 chapter nine

ELATION AND CONFUSION overcame Hailey as four familiar wolves entered the glade. Sasha arrived on foot, along with several members of her council, apparently to greet the newcomers.

The wolves ran up to Hailey and Kamari. Their wagging tails receded as they began the shift. The figures who crouched naked on the ground were all young, single shifters: Byron, Skeet, and Hailey's dear friends, Layla and Violet.

Happiness at seeing their faces turned to fear. "Is everything all right back in Glenn Meadows?" Hailey demanded before her packmates had a chance to stand.

They lifted from the ground, smiling.

"Everything is fine," Layla said.

Hailey tilted her head. "Then why are you here?"

Violet laughed. "Good to see you too." She eyed the crowd with a mischievous grin. "So, who is the lucky male you're going to mate?"

Groaning inwardly, Hailey was spared having to answer when Sasha entered their circle.

"Welcome to Wolf Hollow. I'm Sasha."

Smiles turned to pursed lips as the new arrivals looked Sasha up and down, assessing her. The poor pureblood had no idea of her infamy back in Glenn Meadows. Hailey suspected Sasha wouldn't care even if she knew everything Alexa had said about her.

"You're welcome to dish up now or after we find you clothes," Sasha continued in her gracious manner. "Hailey knows where the communal cabin is and can show you clothing to borrow whenever you like." With a final grin, Sasha left the circle, heading to the line at the cauldron.

They were quiet for several heartbeats before Byron said, "She seems nice—nothing like the bitch Alexa painted her as."

"She is nice," Hailey said.

Her packmates looked at Kamari, who nodded. "They have been good hosts, though I cannot say the same of their guests."

"What do you mean?" Layla asked the question, but all four faces looked to Hailey for an explanation.

"I'll tell you on the way to the shed, unless you want to give the single shifters a longer look." Some of the good humor returned to Hailey's tone. Ever alert, she took note of the hungry gazes checking out the newcomers.

The way Byron and Skeet puffed out their chests, they had noticed, as well.

Layla teased out her hair with her fingers until it fell into voluminous, if messy, strands over her shoulders. Violet's thick, gently curling hair was always bouncy. She puckered her full lips and took a look around.

Two males rushed forward. They weren't as big and muscular as the rest, but they were certainly eager.

"I'm Wiley and this is Justin," one said, gasping as though he'd used up the last of his oxygen.

"Can we dish you up stew?" the other male asked.

Layla chuckled. "My, aren't you two chivalrous."

"And adorable," Violet added.

The young males shared a wide-eyed look.

"I'm taking them to the shed first," Hailey said.

"We'll come with you." Two females had appeared on either side of Byron and Skeet. "Unless you want to join us for dinner now. Clothing optional." A curvy brunette winked at the males.

Hailey held back a sigh. Seeing the way the shifters fawned over her friends made the sting of Rafael's rejection all the harsher. This was the sort of attention she had been hoping for upon her arrival. Rafael had said it wasn't personal, but it was impossible not to take it as such. He had taken one look at her after she shifted and discarded her in the most brash manner.

The light chatter stopped. Hailey blinked and found her friends studying her.

"We will be right back. I promise," Byron said. "First, we need a moment with our alpha."

Hailey gave a start when she realized Byron was referring to her, not Kamari. Feeling a rush of pride turn to concern, she looked at the older male, but he was turned slightly away from their group, speaking with Jager.

"Come." Hailey cleared her throat. "We will return shortly."

Kamari looked over and nodded at her, then resumed his conversation with Jager.

Once they were on the path to the shed, and Hailey had confirmed no one trailed them, she let her friends know the situation with Diego and Rafael.

"What assholes!" Layla cried.

Byron smacked his fist into his palm.

Before her friends' uproar threatened to shake the trees, Hailey lifted her hands for them to stop. "Discussing this won't change anything. One has his heart set elsewhere. As for the other, I wouldn't want to mate with the beast anyway. He's a complete and utter wretch."

Skeet hocked and spat on the ground. "No good mongrel," he grumbled.

Hailey turned to Layla and Violet, whose fingers curled, ready to give Rafael a piece of their mind. Hailey didn't want that. Better to ignore the brute and be on their way.

"Now tell me why you're here."

"Your mother sent us," Violet answered.

"My mother? Why?"

"She told us to join you and your mate," Layla rolled her eyes on the last part, "and start a new pack."

Hailey stopped walking. "Right now?"

Byron nodded. "No reason to wait."

"You agreed to leave home?" Hailey looked into the four faces of her friends, letting it sink in. Her mother had spoken of this, but she hadn't expected it to happen this soon.

"We're ready for adventure," Layla said, bouncing on the balls of her feet.

"And mates," Violet added. "We're all pretty much

related at this point—time to branch out."

"Yeah, I'm not interested in claiming one of my cousins," Skeet said, wrinkling his nose.

"Feeling's mutual, cuz," Layla said. When Violet laughed, Layla shook her finger. "Hey, he's your cousin too."

"Second cousin."

"Still . . ."

Violet nodded and groaned.

While they teased, Byron sidled up beside Hailey. He had a smile that could warm a winter day.

"We were hoping we might find a few single shifters in Wolf Hollow to join our new pack."

"Two females and two males, to be exact," Skeet said.

"Or more. It's nice to have options," Layla said.

"Ahem." Violet jerked her head at Hailey. "We'll need three males now."

Hailey's lips parted, but no words came. She did not want a male from Wolf Hollow. But her spirits lifted at the possibility of exploring the world. Her smile dropped.

"I told Kamari he could claim me."

She had already planned it before Aden came calling. After Rafael's refusal, it had seemed natural to accept the alpha as her mate.

"Ugh." Violet yanked on her hair and squeezed her eyes shut.

"What do you mean, ugh?" Hailey asked defensively. When Violet pouted, Hailey put her hands on her hips.

Skeet cleared his throat. "I think what my cousin is trying to say is that we don't want to go back to Glenn Meadows."

"Kamari can come with us and Hector can step in as

alpha back home."

"We don't want Kamari to come with us," Violet said. "We want you to be our alpha, not him. This is our chance to explore and do things our own way without an old-timer telling us how it's done."

Hailey's hands moved from her hips to cross over her chest.

"What if we come across more purebloods?" Violet asked.

Hailey chewed on her lower lip. Her friend brought up a good point. Maybe she didn't have to give up on her dream of pups. All along, she had waited patiently in Glenn Meadows, hoping for a mate to stroll in. This could be Hailey's chance to venture into the wide world and search for her heart's desire.

Waiting hadn't gotten her anywhere.

But what about Kamari? He would be disappointed if she didn't return home with him.

Hailey clasped her hands together and squeezed. "What if Kamari wants to come with us?"

Violet shook her head hard enough to send her curls flying. "We can't let that happen."

"I'll speak to him." Hailey lifted her chest.

"What will you say?" Layla asked.

"I don't know yet."

Hailey led her friends the remainder of the way to the shed and stood back while they dug through the clothing. Their conversation faded into the background of her mind, where her churning thoughts circled like leaves caught in whirlpools.

Kamari would want her to come home. If she did not, he would insist on coming with them to lead their pack. They would inevitably claim one another and mate. Having a baby would mean establishing shelter. Hailey did not want to settle down. She wanted a chance to run free. She wanted pups. She wanted both. Only a pureblood could give her what she wanted. It always came back to that.

chapter ten

Usually, Diego helped Lacy clean up after dinner, but tonight she turned her back to him anytime he approached. She busied herself collecting bowls from her packmates as they finished, offering up warm smiles that made her cheeks dimple.

The female was so damn cute and innocent. Giving Lacy her first kiss had been more erotic than making out with a woman of experience. The feel of her soft, inquisitive lips parting for him filled Diego with wild energy.

His brother had it all wrong. Lacy hadn't tamed or leashed him; she brought out instincts that he had never experienced before–the need to protect and mate. This was a new stage of life, one that felt both exciting and natural, an ancient calling that brought man and beast to the center of the circle of life.

His eyes tracked Lacy's movements. Desire throbbed in his cock when he watched her bend to collect bowls from several females. The faded material of her cotton dress dragged up her long slender legs.

Lacy straightened and carried the bowls to a basket

full of dirty dishes. The scrawny male who was her work partner added more—the basket now nearly overflowing.

Lifting his chest, Diego strode toward them. The young male eyed him warily before reaching for the basket. "I'll take these to the river to rinse off."

"No. I'll do it," Lacy said.

"Allow me," Diego threw in.

She didn't spare him a glance, speaking into the basket rather than to him. "I said I will take care of it." With that, she lifted the basket, hugged it against her, and took off down the path to the river.

Frowning heavily, Diego watched her hurry away.

This was all his brother's fault.

No. That wasn't true.

Lacy had chosen to punish him for being friendly to Hailey. Unlike Rafael, he had a winsome personality that extended to both sexes. And he had felt guilty—guilt that faded once he apologized to Hailey.

One of the traits he admired about Lacy was her kindness toward her fellow shifters. Apparently, that did not extend outside her pack.

A flare of abnormal anger raced up his spine. It faded just as fast. This was ridiculous. Lacy was his. They had made promises, exchanged hearts.

The female had never had a man before. It was time to remind her that nothing had changed and that he wasn't going anywhere.

Walking along the trail, Diego tried to think of what he could say to bring back Lacy's smile. He had only meant to speak briefly with Hailey. But then she had shown such interest in his travels that time had swept by, caught up in a gust he never saw coming. He would have spoken the same way to anyone who asked about his adventures. But maybe it had looked to Lacy like he was showing interest back by talking and laughing for so long with the single, pureblooded female.

He was almost to the river when he heard Lacy scream.

Thought left his brain as he lunged ahead, practically flying with each sprint over the path. His feet were in the air when he leaped off the slight lip where the trail went down to the river.

Heart thundering like a buffalo herd, Diego raced the remainder of the way to where Lacy stood at the river's edge, a broken bowl at her feet in the rocks. Her face was ashen, but she appeared unharmed. With a shaky hand, she pointed across the river.

At first, he only saw two naked female shifters from the Wolf Hollow pack, bathing in the middle of the stream a ways up. They looked in the direction that Lacy pointed. That was when Diego noticed the large, naked male on the opposite side of the Sakhir, dick in hand, whacking off.

One of the females shrieked and ran for shore while the other glowered in the male's direction.

It had to be another shifter. Humans weren't dumb enough to walk into the woods alone—especially not naked. The guy was a big, hairy, bearded, muscled mass with a tight grip on his dick. He had acted lewdly in front of Diego's woman. What else had the miscreant planned? Diego bellowed in rage.

It had to be the bear shifter who had kidnapped Elsie

and attacked the hollow after she escaped. The pack had chased him in this direction. He was one dumb beast to return. Soon he would be a *dead* beast for bothering the females.

Diego ripped off his shirt.

"No!" Lacy cried, her eyes widening as he unfastened his pants.

The bastard didn't retreat or so much as flinch. He just kept pumping away, his focus on the naked female who stood frozen in the river.

This was Diego's pack to protect. He needed to give this pervert a reason to never return to their borders.

He yanked his pants down, only to be stopped by frantic hands grasping his arm.

"Please, don't go," Lacy begged him. "Wait for help. Diego, don't leave me."

During his pause, the female who had run to shore shifted and howled. No sooner had she stopped than she howled again.

Seemingly unconcerned, the male across the river gripped his cock like it would fall off if he didn't hold it in place.

Answering howls rose from the glade.

Diego pulled away from Lacy. He wasn't going to just stand there and let the pervert get away with jacking off in front of the females. The bear shifter needed to be chased off and given a reason to think twice about returning. Obviously, he hadn't learned his lesson the first time.

Tears splashed down Lacy's cheeks as she murmured, "No, no, no," but Diego was already on the ground, shifting—his wolf's instincts taking over. His female's distress fueled him with purpose.

On four legs, Diego jumped into the river, running and then swimming. His ears twitched at the sound of barking behind him, wolves arriving to back him up.

In the meantime, the bear shifter had sense enough to retreat. Once Diego reached land, he raced to the spot where he had last seen the brute and quickly picked up his scent. Nose hovering an inch above the ground, he sniffed, rushing from spot to spot.

Another wolf, still dripping water from the river crossing, joined him. Wolfrik. The hollow's pureblood streaked ahead. Diego followed, catching up quick. A third wolf joined them. Rafael. Together, they barreled past trees and leaped through brush.

The intruder's scent changed from human to animal, pungent and strong. They heard his roar before catching the sight of his big, brown, furry butt retreating through the forest. Sensing them, the bear spun around and roared. Birds that had probably been sleeping peacefully seconds before squawked and flapped from the trees. The three wolves slowed their steps, prowling closer with caution, teeth bared, growling.

Howls seemed to light up the sky. More wolves were coming. The bear didn't stand a chance.

Standing on two legs, the bear bellowed his outrage.

The three wolves spread apart to surround him. Diego prowled head on, while Rafael and Wolfrik flanked the bear from either side. The bear turned, facing them each in turn with a mighty roar that did nothing to stop them from closing in.

When the bear roared at Wolfrik, the male lunged. Out of nowhere, a boulder-sized mass charged through the brush, knocking Wolfrik onto his back. A second bear had appeared. Rafael yipped in surprise when a third one charged him. Fury and fear set Diego off snarling and snapping at the bear who had stood at the river while his brother and Wolfrik battled the other two.

The bear swiped his paw at Diego's head, missing him by a hair when Diego crouched on the ground before popping back up. His teeth snapped, saliva dripping from his lips. He streaked forward and bit the bear's leg, unable to tear flesh in his haste to get away before the bear took another swipe at him. His foe dropped to all fours and roared.

Nearby, his brother raced around the second bear.

Wolfrik jumped onto his hind legs, attacking the third bear. Deafening snarls and bellows were cut off by a cry of pain. The scent of blood filled the night air.

Piercing howls arose. More of Wolf Hollow's packmates were approaching at rapid speed.

The bears took off running.

Before he could give chase, Diego noticed Wolfrik lying on his side, bleeding on the ground. When he came in for a closer look, the other pureblood growled in warning as though expecting Diego to attack him while he lay wounded and vulnerable. Diego backed off.

A group of about a dozen wolves ran into view and stopped. The female pureblood, Sasha, walked up to Wolfrik, sniffed, and whimpered in distress.

chapter eleven

HAILEY AND HER friends were breathless when they reached the glade. She had wrestled with indecision—whether to shift and join the Wolf Hollow pack in their call to chase off intruders.

"It is not our territory to defend," Byron had reasoned.

Violet had nodded her agreement. "If they need our help, we'll aid them. Otherwise, we should keep out of their affairs."

So her friends hastily dressed before their group raced to the communal space where everyone seemed to be yelling to be heard above the rest.

Wolfrik sat on a stump with his arms folded, staring down at the dirt while a young woman with a gently swelling belly and thick brown hair waved exasperated arms in front of him. "If I have to raise this baby alone, I will hunt you down in the afterlife. Do you hear me, Wolfrik?"

"I'm fine," he grumbled.

"You're fine. What about your wolf?" his mate asked shrilly. "Raider said you were bleeding out from the side."

"Raider should mind his own damn business," Wolfrik

growled.

A group of males flung strings of curses as they spoke with shaking fists. Diego's intended mate sobbed while her friend hugged her. A petite young woman with silky long straight brown hair stood crying while a male three times her size rubbed her back in a slow circular motion.

"I am so sorry," the female choked out. "I never dreamed Brutus would come back."

"See what trouble your sister has brought to our pack?" one of the hollow's rare elders bellowed at Tabor.

The male rubbing the female's back stopped and snarled at the elder.

Hailey's mind spun. It was all a bit much at once. She looked around and, spotting Kamari, rushed over. His eyes lit upon her. He met her halfway, reaching out to touch her arm.

"Are you okay?" he asked.

"Yeah. What's going on?"

Hailey's friends joined them, closing their group into a tight circle.

Kamari huffed. "Bear sighting. I don't understand what the big fuss is all about. The bears respected their boundary."

"It sounds like Wolfrik was hurt," Hailey said, glancing over her shoulder.

"The pureblood is a fool who goes out of his way to fight. Be grateful you didn't end up becoming his mate," Kamari said.

Hailey was glad of it, but her heart still went out to Wolfrik and his mate—his mate especially.

"Wow, Alexa was right about this place. It really is a mess," Layla mused.

"We leave in the morning," Kamari announced.

Their circle went quiet and the conversations around them became muffled. Hailey could feel her friends looking at her.

She opened her mouth to tell Kamari there had been a change of plans, but the words lodged inside her throat. Their alpha had given them a command. That was the problem. As long as Kamari was around, he was the one in charge. If Hailey told him her desire to start a new pack, he would either coax her into returning home or insist on leading them.

It was time for her to make her own way in the world.

Seeming to pick up on the discontent, Kamari folded his arms and struck an imposing figure.

"Let's see if there's any stew left," Hailey said quickly.

"I need to talk to Hailey. Layla, dish up an extra bowl," Kamari said.

Layla pursed her lips and looked at Hailey, who nodded for her to go on ahead. While her friends walked away, Hailey found herself tucking her short hair behind her ears. Trying to come up with the right words to convince Kamari they should part ways made her stomach queasy and her nerves raw.

Kamari looked around and lowered his voice. "Jager was considerate enough to alert me to a bear shifter sighting that took place along their southern border earlier in the day. I'm guessing the sighting that just happened at their northern boundary were the same bears. There is a witch wolf shifter here one of the bears was after. He attacked the hollow about a week ago and was chased off.

The group that just came back said there are now three bears. We shouldn't run into any trouble when we head out the eastern crossing for home."

Kamari stopped talking and looked to her for a response.

It was her opportunity to tell him what she really wanted, but once more Hailey found herself unable to communicate her desires. This was her moment to take a different path. Now that an opening appeared before her, she found her palms sweating and heart racing.

"Hailey?" Kamari's eyebrows drew together.

"That's good," she said, nodding vigorously, avoiding eye contact.

Kamari's shoulders relaxed. "I'll shift and check it out tonight just to be sure the bears haven't wandered east. Stay with our group and don't shift until I'm back."

Hailey rejoined her friends on a log away from the ruckus still going on as the hollow's elders issued orders. Layla handed her a bowl of stew.

"You didn't tell him, did you?"

Sighing, Hailey sniffed above the bowl. "Deer," she said, more to herself than her friends.

"It's a bit cold, but good," Violet said, taking a bite.

Hailey ate with deliberate bites, chewing slowly as she surveyed the gathering in the glade. Her friends did the same. The single shifters who had shown such interest when her friends first arrived were now part of the drama unfolding beneath the stars.

She looked from face to face until spotting Rafael and Diego on the outskirts, expressions tight. Diego's mouth moved while Rafael listened, arms folded. Rafael said something and the brothers clasped hands briefly before Rafael turned and circled the glade before choosing a southward path.

Hailey jumped to her feet. "Take this," she said, shoving her bowl at Layla. "I'll be back."

She didn't wait for a response. Heart thumping in her chest, Hailey hurried after Rafael.

The moon and stars were smothered above the forest canopy. A dark figure moved briskly ahead.

"Rafael," she called out.

The figure stopped. Hailey freed her hair from behind her ears and jogged up to him.

He regarded her with an expression she could not read.

"Bears were spotted earlier in this direction," she said.

Rafael stared at her for several heartbeats before responding. "I know. I was the one who spotted them."

"Oh." Hailey lifted her hand toward her ear, then brought it back down to her side, fingers clasping the skirt and bunching it up in her grasp.

Rafael took a step closer. "Is that why you ran after me? To warn me?"

"No." Hailey looked him square in the eyes.

His gaze held before drifting down her neck to her breasts, then snapping back up as though remembering himself.

"I want you to teach me how to be an alpha."

Rafael's brows rose. A second later, he huffed. "I thought you already had an alpha."

"My friends and I want to start our own pack." Rafael's laughter fueled Hailey's resolve. She folded her arms over her chest and glared at him. "What's so funny?"

Swiping at phantom tears, Rafael shook his head. "By today's standards, you and your friends are too domesticated. You wouldn't last a week in the wild."

Hailey's nostrils flared and her breath came out hot. "Are you calling my wolf weak?" she demanded.

"I'm calling you too tame," Rafael answered, leaning forward.

His smug, cocky smile made her want to rip his throat out. The insult tunneled all the way to her animal side, bringing out the beast. Hailey jerked forward into Rafael's startled arms as her legs caved in.

"No," she cried out, as her bones thinned and her body shrank.

The skirt fell down her waist, which was now sprouting fur. Her hands turned into paws against Rafael's chest. She pushed off him, landing on the ground on all fours. The skirt fell loose, but the tube top remained stuck around her middle. When she was fully transformed, the fur rose along the ridge of her back. A low growl thrummed between her clenched teeth. Rafael stared down at her wide-eyed. Unlike his wolf, hers knew not to cozy up to his human. He was disrespectful and untrustworthy.

She snarled one more time before taking off.

The glade had too many shifters in human skin, so she ran south. She knew better than to go where bears had passed, which meant finding another trail off the main southern path. East might lead her to Kamari, and she did not want to see him. He had told her not to shift while he was away—another male trying to command her.

I am a wild thing, her wolf reminded her.

The trail reached a clearing in which stood a grassy knoll surrounded by boulders. Hailey ran up the gentle slope. Up top, her lungs longed to howl, but she didn't want Kamari to hear her, so she kept her lips shut.

The stars speckled the sky overhead. Fresh air filled her lungs. Her heat had passed. She was free to roam, and run, and go wherever she damn well pleased. Free of the infuriating shifter who refused to help her.

Hailey shook her body, trying to free herself from the piece of clothing circling her back and belly, but the article remained stubbornly attached. She rolled on her back to no avail. Once she was back on her paws, the sight of a gray-and-white wolf brought a snarl to her lips.

Rafael stalked up the knoll, golden eyes on her.

She snapped. He stopped briefly, then continued placing one paw in front of the other, ignoring her snarls.

When he reached her, she didn't hesitate. Hailey lunged and bit his furry hide. Rafael snarled and bit her above her furry leg. That set her off, and suddenly they were a tangle of growling, snapping, ferocious beasts jumping at one another and biting. Rafael pinned Hailey down. She rolled away, scrambled back to four legs, and grabbed him by the neck. He jerked out of her hold, jumped onto his hind legs, and tried to wrap his arms around her face. Snarling, Hailey backed up, then raced forward and head-butted him.

They took off racing around the knoll, nipping and growling, taking swipes and bites at one another. Hailey stopped abruptly and Rafael tripped over her, fell, and rolled before coming back to his feet. He growled his frustration.

Hailey's lips pulled back into a grin that said, *I'm not the same wolf you humped on my way in.*

Rafael's golden eyes flashed. He darted forward and jumped onto her back. Hailey bucked him off.

Triumph lifted her snout to the sky. This wolf's human had called her tame. Now he knew she wasn't some docile wolf he could mount and mate at will.

He tried again, and again she threw him off, taking pleasure in his increasingly manic snarls.

She could have run off, but she liked this game—enjoyed taunting and teasing him . . . until the wolf gave a forlorn cry. He wasn't to blame. She could tell he wanted her despite himself. Her heat was no longer a factor, so it must be something else. Why was his wolf's behavior so at odds with his human's?

Hailey gave Rafael a gentle nudge of sympathy. The wolf's human should really listen to the wise animal within.

This time, when Rafael hopped onto her back, she held steady, pushing her human side out entirely. This moment was between wolves, two purebloods humping in the night.

Thoughts dissipated. The wolf on her back belonged there. His underbelly arched over her and his furry arms clutched her sides. It didn't take long. After he finished, he twisted around, positioning them end to end. They were stuck. The tie-up made it awkward to get around. Rafael wanted to go one way, and Hailey the other. She growled several times as Rafael pulled her along, the tug like a rope. They padded their way in this stumbling manner down the knoll and around a boulder. When, at last, they were able to break apart, Rafael remained with Hailey as though still attached.

The two wolves nestled in between the boulders, snuggling against one another. Hailey's wolf would have been content to remain this way all night, but her human half was as strong as her animal. While the wolf slumbered, the human steadily clawed her way back up to consciousness.

chapter twelve

HAILEY LAY ON her side with her legs tucked in and a wolf beside her. His fur felt soft against her naked skin. A lingering sense of satisfaction pulsed below the surface, only to be replaced by an ache of longing to share in their wolves' joining by intertwining man with woman.

But Rafael was not currently a man, nor did he want her. He had even refused to help her. She despised him.

Her body betrayed her. Her clitoris swelled as her blood vessels dilated and passage slicked.

The steady breath at her back meant she still had time to get away before Rafael's wolf scented her arousal. It would trigger him to shift.

She scrambled away on hands and knees, not looking back for fear of seeing golden eyes watching her, or worse, stubborn brown ones. Once clear of the boulder, Hailey stood and tugged the top loose around her waist back up over her breasts.

She looked at the dark sky. How much time had passed? If she was lucky, less than an hour. She hadn't run far and didn't think she had snoozed for too long.

What had happened? Her mind felt foggy, like her wolf was holding back details. One thing was certain—their animals had mated, and this time there had been no one to interrupt them.

It didn't matter. No full moon meant no pups.

Hailey placed a hand on her flat belly. Uninvited tears welled in her eyes. She had waited all her life for a pureblooded male to come along. One finally had, and mounted her wolf twice, but wouldn't claim her. It felt worse than if he had ignored her entirely.

They were compatible. Her wolf trusted his.

The man was a mongrel for putting her through this torment. If his wolf wanted on her back, he could damn well do the right thing and claim her, mate her at the full moon, and give her pups.

Huffing, Hailey dropped her hand from her belly. Like that would happen. He wouldn't even help her get her new pack started.

Well, he'd unwittingly done her one favor. She was riled up enough to hunt Kamari down and tell him she and her friends were heading off without him. They could still be neighbors once she found a suitable location. Maybe she wasn't ready for a journey across the continent, but it was a start. She'd do it without Rafael's help and free from Kamari's commands.

She hurried in the direction of the glade, relieved to find the borrowed skirt on the path. Rafael's clothes had been tossed into a nearby heap, revealing that he had shifted shortly after her. It was surprising he hadn't run in the opposite direction as fast as his two legs could carry him. His wolf had obviously not given him that option.

Picking up the skirt, she shook off the dirt, then stepped into the garment and tugged it up to her hips. Hailey finger-combed her short locks, smoothing out the soft waves, and proceeded to stride forward with her head held high.

It surprised her to see her friends where she had left them. Maybe not that much time had passed.

Her group had been joined by young single shifters who sat on the ground in front of the log, talking to the visiting shifters. They were holding mugs and taking sips between laughs.

Violet twisted a curl around her finger while listening to a tall, toned male who leaned his head toward hers when he spoke. Layla tipped her mug back. When she brought her head forward, she saw Hailey and waved energetically.

Hailey walked over, trying to force a smile to her lips.

Layla stood up on wobbly legs. "Hailey, meet our new pack!"

"New pack?" she looked from her friend to the small group that had joined theirs.

Layla nodded. "This is Hudson, Chase, Wiley, Justin, Emerson, Gina, Zadie, Nudara, Rosalie, and Camilla."

Looking at the barely familiar faces, Hailey could no longer fake a smile. This was not what she had in mind. Maybe an extra four from Wolf Hollow—not ten.

"I am so ready for a change of scenery," a busty brunette said. Beside her sat the female who had introduced herself to Hailey as Camilla when she first arrived. She was the next to speak. "Where exactly are we going?"

A tall, curvaceous blonde flipped her long hair over

her shoulder and lifted her chin. "We should go west. Nothing terrible has ever come from that direction."

Several heads nodded.

Layla tried to hand Hailey her mug. Hailey wrinkled her nose. "What is that?"

"Moonshine." Layla hiccupped, then giggled.

Hailey shook her head before looking down at the blonde. "We're going east." She made the decision in the moment. Hailey wasn't going to let a stranger take over her pack.

The blonde's amused smile felt like claws extending along her skin.

"Glenn Meadows is to the east."

"We'll be passing Glenn Meadows and continuing east," Hailey informed her.

The other female met her eyes, unblinking. Hailey held her stare. A redheaded female took the bossy blonde's hand and squeezed, but the woman wouldn't look away from Hailey.

Camilla huffed. "Why do you want to come anyway, Em? I thought you liked being on the council."

The blonde flicked her gaze to Camilla, smile dropping. "What's the point of being on the council when they continue to roadblock my simple request? If Jager can't handle a same-sex claim, then maybe it's time to leave."

"You said council majority was in our favor," the redhead beside her said.

Em huffed. "One step forward, two steps back. You heard the elders tonight. They want to drag us back to the dark ages. A bunch of cavemen is all they are. Think they need to guard the women while the 'fairer sex' cooks and has babies."

"Did I miss something?" Hailey pursed her lips.

Layla took a gulp from the mug before nodding. "Yup. After the incident with the bears, the Wolf Hollow elders forbade the females from bathing in the river. They're supposed to stick to the pond within the territory, where it's safer."

Hailey raised her brows. Em met her eyes. "See what we're dealing with here?"

Hailey rubbed the back of her neck with both hands. "I think there's been a lot of excitement and you should all get a good night's sleep before you make a decision to abandon your pack."

"Abandon?" Em barked. She got to her feet and placed her hands on her hips.

The group went silent.

"Yes, abandon," Hailey said, not backing down. She wasn't trying to be rude, simply pointing out the obvious. "Glenn Meadows has reached its capacity and figured out how to keep the tribe protected. Wolf Hollow is rebuilding its population and has been dealing with attacks and more losses. Is this not so?"

Em's eyes narrowed. The redhead, who appeared to be her lover, got to her feet and placed her hand on the blonde's shoulder. "She has a point. You're needed here, Em. Jager might not appreciate that fact, but the rest of us do. Think of your baby sister. Don't you want to be around for her? And what of Jordan? What about when she and Raider have young? You'll want to be around to be an aunt, won't you?"

Camilla scoffed and rolled her eyes. "All the more reason to leave," she muttered.

The curvy female with dark brown hair seated beside her patted her leg and flashed her a sympathetic grin.

Em turned to the redhead, her features softening as they stared at one another. She lowered one arm and touched the other female's cheek. "We'll sleep on it, but first I want to speak to Jordan and Raider—maybe my dad. And check on little Franny. Come with me?"

"Of course."

Hailey was relieved to see the two females walk away hand in hand. Hopefully, everyone Em came into contact with would help talk her out of leaving. It wasn't that she did not like the aggressive blonde; it's that she saw them butting heads daily, and that's not what Hailey wanted for her new pack.

She glanced at the shifters who lingered. With any luck, they would have second thoughts, as well. It was one thing to make plans in the heat of the moment, with the help of moonshine, and another to go through with leaving the only home and pack they had known. Maybe, by morning, they would see reason.

One way or another, she was eager to put distance between herself and Rafael.

RAFAEL SAT UP slowly, taking in his current surroundings with human eyes. The boulders surrounding him made up a rocky nest with a narrow passage leading back to the grassy knoll.

He waited, breathing steadily, biding his time. Without seeing her transform, he was aware of Hailey shifting. He remembered mounting and mating her in crisp detail as though his human brain had been shoved inside his wolf's skull for an up-close experience.

When she pulled away from his wolf to make her exit, he shifted and kept his eyes stubbornly closed, feigning sleep. Sightless, he listened to her leaving and waited. Rafael feared that if he saw Hailey in all her naked glory, he would succumb as his wolf had and give in to his lust.

He waited longer, not wanting to catch up to her on the trail. This was getting out of hand. Twice now their wolves had intertwined. Thank the Goddess with her mysterious moon magic for regulating a female wolf shifter's fertility to its fleeting window of opportunity during full moons.

He would never willingly condemn offspring to the harsh reality he was forced to live in. If two purebloods could not protect their pups, as his parents had failed to do, then what hope was there? It was easier to have no children to worry over. No mate to break his soul if she were killed.

Death was like desperation in this cursed world of theirs. Plenty to go around.

And so Rafael stayed behind longer than necessary before leaving the knoll and collecting his clothing. After getting dressed, he trekked eastward, arcing away from the den. He'd find a rocky ledge to sleep under.

Tomorrow Hailey would be gone. She'd leave and he could relax until it was time for his own departure. For the first time in his life, he would be a lone wolf—no more

Diego to howl and pal around with. No family. No friend. No mate. Alone.

Rafael tried not to think too much about the first time he had seen Hailey's wolf. Heading in the direction where they had first met made it difficult to think of anything else. Her appearance had been so unexpected. The beauty of her white fur and moonbeam eyes filled his head. The memory of her intoxicating scent tickled his nostrils. She'd had the regal air of an alpha female—calm, collected, and fearless.

Unlike tonight, she had yielded to him quickly, stood patiently as he sniffed and licked and then mounted.

Fur sprouted over his arms as he remembered her beneath him.

Not again!

Rafael had two choices: keep his clothing on and try to contain his wolf or undress before his wolf took over and ripped at the garments to get free of the fabric.

He took in a deep breath and slapped himself in the face.

"Think of fire and rivers and caves, mountains and valleys, forests and . . . legs—long, sexy, moonlit legs wrapped around my waist. Shit! No!"

Now Rafael had an erection. Well, maybe it would help keep him human. Looking at his arms, he saw the fur had thickened. *Mierda*. Hard and hairy. Just great. What was next? A furry dick?

Cursing, Rafael unfastened his jeans with fingers that were turning to paws. He clawed them the rest of the way past his knees and ankles. Sharp nails raked his chest as he freed himself from the shirt and got onto all fours.

"You already had her," he tried to reason with his wolf, but the beast would not listen.

The ground flew beneath his paws as he charged down the trail. Stopping abruptly, he sniffed the air and picked up her scent headed east rather than back to the communal glade. Charging through underbrush, he leaped over fallen trees obstructing his path until locating a narrow trail. Her clothing had been discarded, tossed over a fallen log. Picking up the change of odor made Rafael's tail wag.

Once her scent became stronger, he slowed to a trot, then a walk, going still when he picked up voices—one male and one female. He recognized the feminine voice at once. Without a second thought, Rafael shifted and crept closer, taking stealthy steps over the soil. Keeping out of sight was much easier in the dark.

He approached near enough to make out the words and crouched over the ground, not bothering to leave the trail. Hiding in the brush would do no good if it rustled with his movements. So he hid in plain sight, naked, tanned skin melding in with the dirt path.

"I want to see more of the world," Hailey's voice drifted to where Rafael eavesdropped. Anger and frustration laced her words.

"It is not safe out there for you or your friends." Rafael was not surprised to hear Kamari's voice lecturing her.

"Nowhere is safe," Hailey countered.

"Glenn Meadows is. We have the right population, location, and fortification. We made it a safe haven to protect families and females like you."

Rafael half stood, nostrils flared, one fist ready to

shove in Kamari's imperious face. A surge of shame filled him at having said much the same thing to Hailey earlier, when the irony was he felt wolves were meant to explore. The truth was hard to admit. He didn't want anything to happen to her. Despite his best efforts not to, he cared about what became of her and had feared that her inexperience would get her and her friends killed.

But what was the alternative? It was playing out before him in dialogue.

"What do you mean by that? I'm a pureblood," Hailey snapped.

"I only wish to protect you, Hailey. You know what happened to the rest of your litter mates before the fortification. You were too young to remember, but I will never forget the grief your parents went through. I would never want you to experience that kind of heartbreak, especially when there is no good reason to. Any children of ours would have the protection of our tribe, our pack. No harm would come to them. They would grow up safe and loved with their parents, grandparents, aunt, uncles, and cousins."

Rafael barely dared breathe, awaiting Hailey's answer. Would Kamari's coercion work on her? He clamped his mouth shut to contain a snarl. Violence swirled inside his chest, blasting into his head. Hailey had submitted to him, not to the older alpha from Glenn Meadows. She had come to Rafael asking him to teach her, essentially requesting he become her new alpha in the interim.

If Kamari coaxed her back to his pack, it would be too late. The alpha would claim her and end any future for the female beyond the only life she had ever known.

Hailey was a proud and beautiful shifter who deserved a chance to run free.

"You know I will be a good mate to you," Kamari continued.

"Yes, I know that, and I love my family and our pack. I just want a chance to do something different. Give me a year to explore, then I'll return and claim you."

"No." That one word was spoken with grave finality and a hint of anger. "I'm done waiting, Hailey. I waited when your mother hoped to make arrangements between you and Wolfrik, and then with one of these interlopers. None of these males were interested. I am. I have been since you came of age. You are too. You said so on more than one occasion. This is what comes from leaving Glenn Meadows. You are confused and agitated. Once we are back home and mated, you will settle back down and find your contentment restored."

Rafael nearly spit on the ground.

"I am beginning to question that very much," Hailey growled.

"More confusion." Kamari sighed heavily.

"My mother wants me to explore. That's why she sent my friends."

"She thought you would be claimed. Your mother would not want you to go into the wild without an alpha looking over you and your friends. I will do no such thing. We return home after breakfast."

Before he could think it over, Rafael jumped up and swaggered into view of the arguing pair. "You won't, but

I will," he announced.

Hailey sucked in a breath of dismay. Kamari jerked his head and turned, glowering as he faced Rafael. They were all naked. Rafael's eyes tripped over a long, dark shadow. Kamari was erect, a sight that turned Rafael's smug smile into a ferocious snarl.

This alpha elder couldn't wait to get Hailey back home to claim and control. Would Hailey's wolf yield to the alpha's as she had for Rafael, or would Kamari fuck her into submission? And what of her human side? Just seeing Kamari hard for her made Rafael want to shift and bite the other male's dick off.

"What are *you* doing here?" Kamari asked in disgust.

"Offering my aid to a female capable of making her own decisions." Rafael lifted his brows in challenge.

Kamari grunted. "You've changed your mind? You wish to claim her now?"

"Hailey doesn't have to be claimed. What she needs is an alpha."

"What do you know about being an alpha?"

"More than you."

Kamari narrowed his eyes to slits. "You're a fool who would only get Hailey and her friends killed."

"We're not a bunch of helpless pups," Hailey cried out. "You've seen us hunt. You know what we're capable of."

"You've only left our territory on extended hunting trips a handful of times, and all with the supervision of me or your parents." When Hailey pursed her lips, Kamari growled and jabbed a finger in Rafael's direction. "You would put your trust in him—a male who *rejected* you."

109

The bastard couldn't seem to say the word enough times. It was cruel and unnecessary and licked fire across Rafael's chest every time he caught Hailey wince with dejection.

His decision not to mate had nothing to do with Hailey's desirability. Unlike Kamari, Rafael wasn't selfish. He knew he couldn't fulfill the pureblooded female's needs. Better to set her free.

He turned and faced her, expression softening as he shut Kamari out. "I will teach you to be your own alpha, and once you are ready, your life will be yours to lead in whatever direction you wish."

Hailey's lips parted. Eyes locked on his, she gave a slight nod. "Thank you."

Kamari puffed out exasperated breaths of disbelief, then seemed to suck them all back in. Chest inflated, he ground his teeth together and shot Hailey a narrow-eyed glower. "I cannot promise to wait for you, Hailey."

"I don't expect you to," she answered solemnly.

"An alpha should have a mate and offspring."

"I understand."

One moment Kamari was as stiff as a log; the next, he seemed to cave in on himself. Tears filled his eyes as his head and shoulders sagged. "You have no idea how much I care about you, Hailey," he said in a watery voice. "My heart is yours. There is no one else."

Rafael rolled his eyes in private. It was as though he had disappeared from sight when tears tracked down Hailey's cheeks.

"I'm so sorry," she said in a voice that broke. "But this

is something I need to do. You know I'll come back. I want to see my family again, and you—even if you're mated when I return."

When she took a step toward him, Kamari jerked away, turned, and stormed off.

"Kamari, where are you going?" Alarm filled Hailey's voice.

"Home," he grumbled without turning around.

"But—"

"There is no reason for me to wait until morning." The words sounded like an accusation.

Rafael sprinted forward, catching up to Hailey and jumping in front of her. "Let him go," he said gruffly, irritated to see her running after the other male.

Hailey tried to peer over Rafael's shoulders. She leaned forward on her toes, not noticing her nipples brush his chest. He noticed. So did his cock.

"He should wait until morning and make sure no one wants to go back with him," Hailey said stubbornly. "He should at least say goodbye to the members of our pack staying behind and to our hosts in Wolf Hollow."

Rafael's throat quaked with possession. "Let. Him. Go. You're mine now." He was pleased to see Hailey turn her full attention where it belonged, meeting his stare—even though her upper lip curled back in anger.

"I'm not yours," she snapped.

"As of this moment, I'm your new alpha."

"You said you would teach me to become my own alpha," she said accusingly.

"And I will, but until then, you will obey me."

With a growl, Hailey lifted her hand, but before she could slap him, Rafael spun her around and captured her wrists behind her back. Gasping in outrage, Hailey thrashed and tried to buck him off, reminding Rafael of her wolf's eventual submission. His cock seeped at the tip in anticipation of a joining that would never come.

"I have a duty to keep you alive and make you strong," Rafael barked at her. He had to channel his rage before his lust took over and he ended up mounting her. Once he crossed that line, there was no retreating. He would pump her full of seed, then guard her for the rest of their days. Neither of them would ever be free again.

"You're a wretch!" Hailey shoved her back against him, but all it did was bring her firm cheeks flush against his cock.

He snarled at her, as though she were the one holding him down. "And the world is a wretched place. Better to learn that from someone who cares whether you live or die. It might be hard for you to believe this, but I want you to succeed. Purebloods need to have each other's backs. We don't have to be mates to be loyal. I will teach you everything you need to know to survive in the wild, but first I need you to submit. Without a claim, there can only be one alpha. Are you able to submit to me?" A mate was an equal, and he could not risk putting her in that position. He turned his question into a command. "Submit."

Hailey struggled for several more heartbeats before going still. "Fine," she said begrudgingly. "Since I'm such a threat to your highly prized independence, I submit."

Body slackening, Hailey got onto all fours, her rear

in the air, to demonstrate with her body what her words had stated.

This wasn't what he had asked of her. It felt more like a taunt than surrender and it took all of Rafael's self-restraint to stop himself from mounting her on the spot.

 chapter thirteen

DIEGO TOOK SEVERAL steps toward Lacy, then slowed as though wading through rushing waters. She still clung to her friend's side. His female, if he could call her that anymore, was obviously angry with him. Diego had ignored her pleas not to run after the bear shifter. But he'd done it for her.

This bear had barged in twice now. There was no turning off Diego's instincts to take on a threat head-on.

Maybe Rafael was right about the danger of claiming a mate. Like their father, Diego would not hesitate to run straight toward certain death, all for a female.

What Rafael did not understand was that it was already too late. Diego was in love. Lacy could change her mind and still he would stay until he was certain the bears weren't returning.

Casting a last forlorn look at Lacy, he lowered his head and trudged westward into the woods. There was less foot traffic in the direction of the hollow's Forest of the Ancestors. Sasha had a cave she had kindly offered up after Diego announced his intentions to claim Lacy.

The pureblooded female had figured Diego was used to a lot more privacy in his travels.

"I'm staying with my mate in his cabin, so the cave's all yours if you want," she had said.

Sasha had figured right.

Diego trekked that way now. He had hoped to share the cozy enclosure with Lacy after their claiming. Now he wasn't sure of anything. The cute blonde was an anomaly as mysterious as the cosmos. Sides of her he had never expected emerged daily. She was sweet, but also spunky. Bashful one moment, passionate the next. Shy, then forward.

When Hailey first arrived and practically announced herself as having come to claim a pureblood, Lacy had revealed another layer. She had grabbed Diego's arm and narrowed her eyes at the Glenn Meadow's female in a manner that could only be described as possessive. It had pleased him.

But the thrill of Lacy's attachment was short-lived.

Gone was their playful banter. The teasing and flirting ceased. Lacy had appeared upset and directed her ire at him.

Diego did not know what to do or say. Lacy was a virgin, and he had never engaged in a relationship outside of sex.

So he trudged over the forest path, the darkness filling his mind and movements with gloomy weight. He left behind the camaraderie of the group to mope in silence.

A pair of glowing eyes watched him approach from a tree branch above. As he passed, the owl's head swiveled, keeping Diego in its sight. He looked back and saw it still staring at him.

A fallen leaf got stuck beneath his foot. Diego stopped and pulled it off, then continued. The canopy of trees made the path look like a dark tunnel leading to the cave. Sasha's quarters were a fair distance from the glade. Diego wasn't sure he wanted that much privacy. Maybe he should turn back. There was a nice fire burning in the glade, and old Jager had brought over a batch of his moonshine to help calm nerves.

The hoot of the owl made Diego's heart take off at a gallop.

"*Mierda*." Diego wasn't usually one to feel spooked.

He turned and glared in the direction of the owl. To go back to the glade felt craven. Diego lifted his chest and chin like a true master of the wilderness. He was not afraid to be alone. He just didn't like it, and he couldn't understand how his brother would get by on his own.

A memory of their mother came back to him like a spirit descending from the stars. A beautiful gray-and-white wolf watching her pups play.

Rafael knocked Diego over on his back. Diego kicked at the air, batting at his brother while they nipped at one another. Their mother dashed over, joining their play, nudging Diego and taking gentle nips at him without biting. Diego squeaked and kicked, egging them on. He grabbed hold of his mother's neck when she dipped down, letting go as she batted him with her paw. Diego jumped to his legs and raced around in a circle as his mother and brother pursued him.

He rolled onto his back and barked, loving the attention. His mother bounded over, springing over the meadow grass. With gentle nips, she grabbed at Diego's short, flailing legs, then moved to his side as he rolled over.

Rafael mimicked their mother, except that he actually did bite with his sharp little teeth. Diego barked at him. Mother pushed Rafael away. Once they'd settled down, she slathered their faces with her tongue, her eyes beaming with pride and all the love in the world.

The stars blurred through Diego's watery eyes as he looked up at the sky.

"Te quiero, mama."

The endless sprinkle of light overhead seemed to pulse as though the galaxy containing them was quaking. Head tilted back, Diego watched, transfixed. A shimmering sensation filled his soul. It had been too long since he had revisited his mother. Unlike his brother, he chose to hold on to the happy memories. Rafael held his fist around her final fate.

Diego wished he could have known what his mother looked like in human form—wished he could lay eyes on the woman she'd been just once. But he and his brother had been too young to shift, and their mother had kept to the same form always.

He had seen his father transform into his human skin—a man crazed by grief. The cruelty Diego witnessed still shook him to his core. Their father had taught them one final chilling lesson before deserting them in favor of death.

He had taught them to fear mankind.

DESPITE THE SMALL fire he had built up near the cave's entrance, Diego shivered. He still couldn't get over the fact that his brother would be spending evenings like this after he took off. The bastard had better come back and visit him. Maybe he would make a friend along the way.

Diego sighed. If only Rafael wasn't committed to his unhappiness. Pureblooded females were scarce. Finding one who was the right age, single, beautiful, and good-tempered was rarer still. Rafael was a fool—a damn stubborn fool.

With a shake of his head, Diego turned his back on the forest outside and edged his way toward the belly of the cave. A nice sandy spot had blankets arranged for a peaceful sleep away from all the night sounds and packmates yipping and whimpering as they dreamed at night curled up in wolf form.

The arrangement would be comfortable in either shape. Diego took a seat in the center of the comfy nest and sprawled out on his back. He was just deciding whether to remain this way or shift for the night when the sound of a small rock hitting a larger one jolted him upright.

In the opening of the cave, he made out Lacy's silhouette. He could see her clearer as she paused beside the fire, hair pulled back into a ponytail.

"Diego?"

Chest warming, he stood and stared at her, filled with elation and a wariness that she had changed her mind about their claiming and come to deliver the news away from prying ears.

"What's going on, Lacy?" She twisted her fingers in her hand, avoiding his gaze. "Are you having second thoughts?" Diego demanded, having reached the end of his patience—done with the guessing games.

Her arms dropped to her sides and blue eyes locked onto his. "No! Are you?" There was fire in her voice and a tremble in her chin.

"You're the one who has been avoiding me." He took a step forward, but hesitated, unsure whether to stand his ground or go to her. It was so hard to tell what she did or did not want from him.

Lacy provided no help when she cast her eyes downward, pulling her blonde rope of hair over her shoulder and studying the ends. "I thought maybe you wanted me to back off."

"Why the hell would I want that?" Diego hadn't meant to yell, but Lacy was so far off the mark, it was as though they were speaking in different languages.

Lacy stopped fiddling with her hair and flung her arms out to her sides. "So you could woo the pureblooded female."

Diego blinked rapidly. It felt like smoke had gotten into his eyes. "I have no romantic interest in Hailey."

"You were smiling and laughing together," Lacy accused.

Diego reared back. "So you're saying you don't trust me?"

"That's not what I'm saying. It just looked like you were interested."

"I just told you I wasn't . . . I'm not."

Lacy yanked on her hair, loosening the tie holding it

together. She clutched her head, fingers digging into the blonde locks covering her scalp.

Taking a calming breath, Diego evened his voice into a soothing timber. "What's really going on, *mi cielito*?"

"What does that mean?" Lacy asked in a soft voice.

Diego stepped closer. "It means my little sky . . . my heaven."

Glossy blue eyes stared back at him. He almost imagined he felt the waft of her breath emanating from the rapid rise and fall of her chest.

"You're so worldly and I—" Lacy shrugged. "I've never stepped outside Wolf Hollow, not even to go on a supply run." She pulled her hair loose. Diego watched the silky, light strands of her hair thread between her fingers as she pulled it back up and secured it in a lopsided ponytail. "As you know, I have no experience, have never seen the world. You're the first male I ever kissed. I am so afraid to disappoint you . . . scared I won't be enough. That once you have me, you'll realize it was a mistake."

"*Mi amor*," Diego cried out. "Do not say such things. Do not even think them. "*Te amo*. I love you now and forever."

"I love you, Diego," Lacy proclaimed with an iron will that left nothing open to interpretation.

Diego stormed over and picked her up. Lacy squeezed her arms around his neck.

"You could have died today," she practically yelled at him. "I've never felt so scared."

With his female in his arms, gripping him tight, Diego's breath came out in heavy exhalations. "You never have to worry about me," he said, though it pleased him that she did. "I know how to survive, *mi amor*. Nothing can keep us apart. I will always protect you." She moaned. "*Mi vida. Mi reina. Cariño.*"

Their lips fused. Lacy rubbed against him and dug her fingers into his back as though his endearments had turned her feral. Her little gasps for air as Diego invaded her mouth made him as hard as the cave walls enclosing them. Waiting to claim his feisty little *loba* in body and soul was turning into a torturous interlude, but Lacy was worth every second of celibacy. He would respect her wishes. Treat her like a moon goddess. Be the best mate he could possibly be.

Diego carried Lacy to the blankets, lowering them until they were seated in front of one another. Lips swollen and cheeks a devastating shade of pink, Lacy reached up to fix her ponytail.

Diego ran his hands over her arms as he lowered them gently into her lap before slipping his fingers into her hair and releasing it from its binding. He set the stretchy tie onto a nearby rock, never taking his eyes off the beauty in front of him. With gentle strokes, he smoothed her silky hair over her shoulders.

"*Chica bella*," he murmured.

They leaned forward at the same time, lips meeting halfway. He pressed his palms against her hips, sliding his fingers over her curves and up her sides until they reached her breasts. He cupped the small mounds, circling his thumbs around her nipples until they budded.

Lacy gasped in a breath. Diego released her from their kiss to lower his mouth to her breast, wet the thin fabric of her dress with his tongue, and nip gently at the hard peaks. Moans filled his ears as he attended to her opposite breast with the same deliberate attention.

A hand slipped beneath her skirt. Her pussy was already seeping, and it made Diego groan in satisfaction, for it was his duty not only to protect his female, but to bring her pleasure.

There were years of neglect to make up for—not that Diego was complaining. To find a woman untouched in this savage world of theirs was like stumbling upon a blossoming utopia that had somehow escaped the apocalypse.

"I wish to see you naked, *mi cariño*. Is that okay?"

Face flushed, Lacy nodded. As he tugged up her dress, she lifted her arms, helping him free her from the garment. Diego fisted the fabric, his gaze soaking in every inch of smooth, light skin. She could use a little more meat on her bones, but she was perfect in his eyes, from her toes and long slender legs to the thatch of blonde hair between her thighs and perky breasts that taunted him beneath a sweet face that blushed profusely.

"*Bella. Eres una mujer muy hermosa.*" He lifted her dress to his nose and inhaled deeply. Closing his eyes, he breathed again, her scent permeating the cotton.

His dick swelled inside his pants, weeping at the end. Diego tossed the dress onto his shoulder and unfastened his pants, giving his erection more room to expand, hoping the action would not startle Lacy—that she would trust him.

She said nothing and made no movement, fixated on his actions.

Taking a last breath of her dress, Diego folded the garment and set it on a rock near her hair tie.

He didn't need to mate her to satisfy his urges. There were other ways.

"I wish to taste you, *mi amor.*" His voice came out raspy. He didn't ask for permission. She could tell him to stop if she wanted.

Using one hand, Diego pushed her back gently onto the blankets. Soft pops from the fire sent sparks of light out into the dark entrance that he now faced, on his knees above Lacy. He spread her legs and there was no resistance. He dipped down and inhaled, eyes rolling back at the heady scent of her arousal.

Lacy trembled but remained pliant in his grasp.

A growl vibrated from deep within Diego's chest and with it, the intoxicating scent intensified. He could wait no longer. Lips parted, he took his first lick. Full-bodied feminine arousal coated his tongue.

Dios mío.

It was his last coherent thought before spreading her apart and burying his head between her thighs to feast.

Lacy's moans filled the cave. Her fingers tore at his hair and yanked as though she was the one holding him prisoner to her pleasure. The more he licked, the more she seeped. He bathed his face in her arousal and sucked the juices from her clit. Lifting her hips, Lacy shoved at his tongue.

It was a good thing he had taken her dress off, or he would be ripping it away now.

Diego grabbed her by her ass and dug in like a dog

after a juicy bone. Lacy cried out at the same time a fresh spurt of potent glaze slicked his greedy tongue.

"Fuck me!"

Diego blinked and lifted his head to make sure the vulgar command had really originated from his sweet female's lips. A sheen of sweat glistened between her breasts, which rose and fell with panting breaths.

"*Mi amor*, there will be plenty of time for coupling once we are mated."

"Now," Lacy said, her eyes blazing.

Diego chuckled. It was impossible not to let his head swell with knowledge of her satisfaction. The female was quickly coming undone.

"That's enough for tonight. We can play again tomorrow."

Hot from his exertions, Diego pulled his shirt over his head and tossed it aside. He intended to pull Lacy against his chest and try to calm his raging desire enough to get some sleep.

Lacy had other ideas.

"Now," she repeated with a growl that threatened transformation. The sound echoed against the walls. Her eyes began glowing. On hands and knees, she prowled the short distance to him.

Diego's head jerked in surprise when her teeth elongated. With a look of possession, Lacy's pupils dilated, blotting the blues of her irises. She lifted onto her knees and gripped his shoulders.

"Diego, you are mine and I am yours. I claim you as my mate." Sharp teeth pierced his neck. Her canines sunk in deeper.

Closing his eyes briefly, Diego groaned. His heart sped and sweat dampened his hairline as though he'd gone into a fever. Lacy held on as though she had caught dinner and was waiting for the life to drain from her prey.

Diego gripped her hips and spoke gently. "Enough, *mi amor*. I am yours. You can let go now." When she ignored him, he stroked the back of her head. "I must claim you back, *mi amor*. This is your desire, *verdad*? You want me to claim and mate you."

The piercing clamp on his neck loosened. Lacy released him and drew back.

"I'm sorry," she said sheepishly.

"Oh, *mi cariño*. You never have to apologize for being rough with me. I would have waited, but now I must complete our bond."

Diego's teeth scraped over Lacy's delicate neck. Her moan brought out his canines. With her head tilted back and eyes closed, Diego held his female in his arms and claimed her.

chapter fourteen

JAGGED ROCKS EMBEDDED in the trail slowed Hailey and Rafael's progress back to the glade. The trail that meandered east was more rugged than the rest, not to mention they were unfamiliar with Wolf Hollow's territory. The outer areas were less traveled, especially this one that headed toward Glenn Meadows. The two packs rarely met up.

Rafael led the way, exerting his position as alpha.

Mangy wretch, Hailey thought to herself. Except that he wasn't at all mangy.

Muscles corded in smooth, bronzed arms that pulled at low-hanging twigs, snapping them from trees and tossing them aside to clear the way. She could hardly avoid the sight of his toned ass, just as tan as the rest of his magnificent body. Hailey liked that he kept his hair shorter, with long strands at the top that sometimes fell over his forehead and feathered the space above his eyes in seductive wisps.

Diego's hair was the same length as hers. He was the shaggy one. As friendly as he had been, Hailey was relieved he was spoken for. She felt no attraction to him. Rafael, on the other hand, riled her up and sent the wrong signals to her body—certainly to her wolf.

He had decided they would return on foot so as not to tempt their wayward wolves into another round of mindless humping.

"Which direction will we head in after leaving Wolf Hollow?" Hailey asked. Since he was facing forward, she went ahead and addressed his ass. It was as fine a backside as she had ever seen, and it wasn't like he had eyes in the back of his head to catch her staring. She could appreciate his body and disdain him at the same time.

"We'll start out eastward. Watch out for the big rocks." Rafael's head dipped forward as he stepped over rough terrain.

Removing her gaze from his rear end, Hailey looked for the solid clumps impeding the path. "Why east?" she asked.

Rafael stopped and turned, his focus on her feet as she navigated over a pile of particularly large, coarse rocks embedded in the trail. The uneven edges looked sharp enough to lacerate skin.

After Hailey cleared the rocks, Rafael continued forward. Maybe he wasn't a complete wretch. Or maybe this was her first lesson in becoming an alpha leader—keep an eye out for danger and obstacles, alert her packmates, and make sure they made it through.

"The coast is to the west—too many cities crawling with human vermin. I've been informed of the wizards living to the north and would sooner avoid making their acquaintance. My brother and I came in from the south through a town I don't wish to revisit. The place gave us the willies."

"So, we head east." It's what Hailey had wanted. She wondered what Rafael would think about leading a large pack. "In addition to my four friends, there are about ten members of Wolf Hollow who want to join us."

"Too many," Rafael said without stopping or taking time to consider.

Hailey's lips lifted into a big grin. If only he knew how much their instincts were aligned. Perhaps it was a pureblood thing.

"We can take two at most, though I'm inclined to keep our group down to six."

She nodded even though he wasn't facing her. "Your brother and his future mate are intent on staying in the hollow?" she asked. Rafael snorted derisively. "Do you plan on seeing him again?" Hailey pressed.

"He's my brother. I will visit when I can."

After Rafael's moody tone, Hailey figured he was finished making conversation. When he swung around without warning, she gave a squeak of surprise. Dark eyes sized her up. Rafael pressed his lips together in a firm line and folded his arms. Hailey mirrored his stance, covering her breasts with her arms.

"You do know you'll have no more clothes, right? No blankets, cushions, or trinkets. No bowls, mugs, or hairbrushes," Rafael fired off. "No tools of any kind. We'll hunt and eat as wolves. There will be no more cozy campfires or social circles. Are you prepared to let your animal take charge?"

Hailey met his gaze and lifted her chin. "Like you, I spent my adolescent years as a wolf and nothing else."

"And what is the longest stretch of time you've given your wolf since then?" Rafael asked.

Frown tugging down her lips, Hailey thought hard to remember. She was constantly shifting back and forth. Every day she was one or the other at some point. How long had she held one form for an extended period?

"That's what I thought," Rafael said with a huff.

Hailey's spine stiffened. "It won't be a problem, though I'm sure to miss your pleasant conversation so very much," she said sarcastically.

When Rafael looked over his shoulder, she gave him an eye roll. He chuckled and swept loose strands of hair off his forehead.

"What about our wolves and their"—Hailey's cheeks heated—"attachment?"

"They'll just have to work it out of their systems." Rafael shrugged.

How could he be so nonchalant about their attachment? She would never understand the male denying himself a mate by choice. It was unnatural and exasperating.

"You and I will shift into human form during the full moon to ensure our wolves don't breed," Rafael added. "Anyone who comes with us must agree to the same. The wild is no place for pregnant women or babies."

"Understood," Hailey said with a nod. For now. Her plan was to scope out a spot to start a new tribe that would build a perimeter and slowly expand.

She had no need to share that information with the

male who would be leaving them. Once Hailey learned everything she could from him, they could part ways—or sooner if the partnership turned problematic.

They continued at a slow but steady pace toward the hollow's communal glade.

"When do we leave?" Hailey asked.

"After my brother's claiming ceremony the day before the next full moon."

"So, we'll stay in Wolf Hollow until then?"

"Yes."

"Okay."

Rafael stopped, looked back at her a moment, and gave the barest nod before continuing. They reached the spot where Hailey had undressed. She saw that Rafael had chosen that spot to do the same, which brought back the familiar confusion. He had said he wanted nothing to do with her, yet he kept chasing her down. Was he interested, but unwilling to admit it yet? When he spoke of the full moon and not mating, was he in fact considering the possibility?

She studied him in the dark—a healthy, strong, virile male. It made her insides molten and her ovaries purr.

Rafael's head was bent, looking at the clothing, but making no move to touch them. As his eyes moved her way, Hailey quickly turned her attention to an overhanging branch so that he wouldn't catch her perusing every inch of his body like a she-wolf in heat.

"Get onto all fours."

His command snapped her out of her fog and gave her a jolt. Eyebrows drawn together, she scanned his face for signs of desire, but grim determination gripped his jaw.

"Why?"

"We'll shift and sleep there in that soft soil." He nodded at a small opening in the forest with moss and rich earth unhindered by rocks, roots, and logs.

"But our wolves—"

"Need training," Rafael said gruffly.

"You don't train wolves." Hailey scowled.

"Wrong word choice," Rafael acknowledged. "Resistance is obviously futile, so we need to allow them to become acquainted. The more time they spend together, the more they'll simmer down and get into a routine."

Hailey eyed the shadowed patch of earth Rafael had indicated but made no move toward it. Her skin felt hot despite the cool night air.

Rafael walked past their clothes to the loamy space. "Better to have at it out here than in front of an audience."

Glaring at him, Hailey stormed over until they stood face to face. She spun around and dropped to the ground in front of the mongrel.

"Is this what you want?" she demanded, lifting her ass in the air.

The memory of his wolf swelling inside hers, locking them in the throes of bestial pleasure, made her slick with unintended desire.

Growling, Rafael fell to his knees behind her, grabbed her by her hips and pulled her against his erection. Hailey moaned.

"Shift," Rafael snarled, fingers digging into her sides, rough enough to bruise.

Her pussy throbbed between damp folds. Hailey had to bite her tongue to stop herself from begging for him to fill her throbbing passage, thump against her hips, and break down the trembling dam building inside of her.

Rafael's grip tightened and pulled a whimper from her lips. Pain was irrelevant. Need overwhelmed reason. His hard tip poked at her slick opening.

Yes. Please. Mount me. The words she did not dare utter aloud screamed inside her head.

The head of his thick manhood drew back. Hailey's next whimper sounded pitiful. She might as well have begged.

His hardness pressed against her again without penetrating. So close. He had only to thrust to join their bodies.

Mate me. Please.

Hailey stretched her arms in front of her and braced herself for penetration.

Pressed against her, Rafael's body shook. "Shift," he pleaded in desperation, each of them begging for different outcomes.

Gritting her teeth, Hailey snarled. *Pride over pleasure,* she thought, enraged, right before she did as her alpha demanded and shifted.

AFTER RUTTING AND being released from their tie, the two wolves curled up beside each other on the soft earth. Fur pressed against fur. Rafael laid his head on the ground. He smacked his lips several times, content. Beside him, his female fell into a quick slumber. He remained awake, ears twitching, listening for any threat lurking in the woods. The croaking of frogs, chirp of crickets, and distant hoots communicated that all was well.

Lifting his head, he stared with glowing eyes into the darkness, teeth bared in warning at an invisible foe.

His serenity faded. He stood and looked down at the radiant pureblood. Their coupling was incomplete. He had yet to impregnate her. They would have to try again.

She gave a big sigh, indicating her desire to sleep. Rafael's unrest wasn't helping. He licked her muzzle a couple of times, then lowered himself onto his belly beside her and made another survey of the towering trees surrounding them.

It was safe. They could sleep.

The female's breaths evened out. Her body twitched from time to time. Rafael pressed against her and closed his eyes, memorizing her scent as he drifted off.

It was daylight and he watched his mate lead their litter of six pups out of her den. The rambunctious fur balls yipped and bit at one another, grabbing legs with needle-sharp teeth, pulling at floppy ears, and chomping down on tails that wagged too close to their mouths.

Hailey barked at them to settle down. When the little hellions ignored her, she grabbed the most rebellious of them by the scruff of his tiny neck. He cried out in dismay and kicked his legs as she walked up to Rafael and deposited the whelp in front of his paws.

Keep your son in line, her eyes said.

Rafael smiled. The pup just needed exercise.

Barking for the rest of his brood to join them, Rafael sprinted for a nearby field. Excited yips followed at his tail. When he reached the grassy expanse, he stopped and allowed his pups to jump at him. Rafael sprinted away and led the unruly group in circles. Small paws sprang over the earth, barking in delight at the chase. Hailey joined them, brushing up against Rafael. One of their pups tripped and rolled over the emerald grass.

Running in circles, they became one mass of gray-and-white fur blurring together, fading into the landscape.

Rafael found his size reduced to that of a pup. Hot sun blazed in a too-bright sky over dusty, parched earth. The grass below his paws turned brittle. Dirt coated his pads. He yipped at Diego, who snoozed in the shade. His brother opened his eyes briefly, then closed them.

Their mother stood in the open, head lifted, sniffing.

Rafael wondered if his father was on his way back. He was hungry and restless. Bounding up to his mother, he yipped. She lowered her head and touched her nose to his.

Stay with your brother.

Rafael watched her stalk off, scenting the air. The twitch of her ears and brief wag of her tail spoke of a treat soon to come. She stalked through the woods on a mission.

Rafael glanced back at his brother, who appeared deep in sleep. Then he looked in the direction his mother had gone and padded after her. As he trailed her through the forest, he picked up the scent of a fresh kill. Saliva rolled off his tongue, splattering in small drops over the cracked earth.

It was hard not to charge past the trees after his

mother, but he did not want her to grab him by his neck and carry him back to the den.

There were hidden wonders in the woods that Rafael was ready to discover. His grumbling stomach egged him onward.

The shade did little to block out the heat, and soon Rafael was panting, craving water as much as meat. He could not hear his mother. There seemed to be no sound at all, as though the drought had sucked it all away along with the water.

The hairs along his back began to prickle. The heat felt thick and ominous. He wanted to cry out for his mother, but his throat was as parched and silent as his surroundings. Rafael dragged his feet forward. Where was she? He stopped and looked around, unsure whether to continue or return to his brother.

The confusion in his young head and the quiet of the forest was interrupted by a horrible clanking snap, the likes of which no animal had ever made. His mother cried out in pain. Her terrorized cries filled the forest and became louder. No. It wasn't that the yelps were louder, it was that Rafael had gotten closer—running to save her. Racing across a hostile landscape to witness her end.

Heart speeding with his breath, Rafael woke up in his human skin soaked in sweat. He sat up blinking and panting, looking around. This wasn't right. Where was he? The woods were lush and dark. The wolf at his side wasn't his mother or brother.

He gasped in breaths and clutched his chest. The white wolf beside him lifted her head and placed it in his lap, staring up at him with eyes that seemed to stare straight into his soul. Keeping perfectly still, she kept him in her comforting gaze.

Rafael lowered his hand to pet her head but stopped himself before his fingers touched fur.

Those eyes. Those fierce, loving eyes held so much compassion, as though she knew everything that had ever happened to him. There was no judgment or expectation in that gaze. What a beautiful being.

Tears spilled down Rafael's cheeks.

Hailey pressed her head deeper into his lap. Her soft fur brushed against his thigh and tickled the tiniest bit.

Rafael laughed. "Only you could love a wretch like me."

He stroked the velvety fur on her head, which helped to steady the rise and fall of his chest. The tears cooled and dried on his face.

"I'm sorry I can't be your mate, but I will do everything I can to teach you how to survive in this world. You will be stronger for it, and I hope that one day you will find a worthy mate."

Except that was a lie. He never wanted another male to claim Hailey. She was his, even if he could not have her.

Rafael stopped petting her and gently eased the delicate head from his lap to lie on his side by her. He closed his lids, resting his eyes, though not expecting to sleep. He'd sooner stay away from the nightmares hiding in the shadows of slumber. Instead, his mind returned to their unruly, adorable pups. They'd seemed so real. Something hopeful and warm spread across his chest. He shifted his attention back to his mother, blotting out more favorable dreams before they had a chance to hold their shapes and cause him to do something that could not be undone.

Rafael concentrated on being a wretch instead of a dummy.

When first light came, he got up and dressed. He stood for what felt like hours, waiting for Hailey to rouse.

"Shift," he commanded. As soon as she obeyed, he threw her clothes at her. "Now get dressed."

chapter fifteen

BLISSFUL REST AND a beautiful morning were ruined by Rafael's grouchy voice and rude actions. He flung Hailey's clothes at her like they were on fire and chucking them against her was the only way to put them out.

"Good morning to you too," she grumbled.

Hailey knew what this was about. Rafael was still pissed at her for trying to tempt him into coupling. Most males would be thrilled to have a woman bend over for them, but oh no, not Rafael. Their wolves were getting all the action while Hailey couldn't seem to stop setting herself up for rejection. She blamed the wretch standing over her, glowering like a beast whose prey had gotten away. His imposing presence and bold commands got her hot and bothered.

There were small purple bruises on her hips where he had grabbed her. She wished the impressions his fingers had made didn't excite her. He'd left his mark, but stubbornly refused to leave the one she craved most.

Hailey stood and put on the top and skirt. She spun around, facing Rafael, and put her hands on her hips. "I'm dressed. Happy now?"

Rafael scoffed and rolled his eyes.

Hailey did the exact same, bringing a smirk to Rafael's lips.

"What now?" she asked with a smile.

"Breakfast at the glade. It's time I met your friends and assessed their value to my pack."

His pack? Hailey puffed out a vexed breath.

Rafael's smirk stretched over his cheeks. "Got something to say?"

"Nope. Lead the way."

"You first. Think you can manage not to trip and fall?"

Fluffing her hair out, Hailey took striding steps to the path in front of him. "Think you can keep your eyes off my ass?" she challenged, right before she swayed her hips and started for the glade.

A growl issued behind her. Smiling to herself, Hailey swung her arms as she took purposeful steps back to the communal gathering.

At least she wouldn't have to be the bad guy, telling the Wolf Hollow shifters they weren't invited to join them. Rafael was good at barking orders and being a general ass—not to mention his talent for denying shifters their deepest desires. She hoped Hailey's friends would accept him as their temporary alpha.

When they reached the glade, Hailey was dismayed to find her friends sprawled out on the ground where she had left them—passed out and snoring, from the look of it. Empty mugs were tipped over, littering the area around the dozing shifters. Skeet had drool in one corner of his mouth. Violet's arm was draped over her eyes while Layla lay on her stomach beside her, head on her arms. Byron was on his side, a gentle smile on his lips. The shifters they'd kept company with earlier were noticeably absent. They had probably built up a tolerance to moonshine, unlike Hailey's packmates.

"Oh no," Hailey said.

Rafael folded his arms and sniffed the air. "Why is breakfast not ready?"

Hailey looked around and noticed other shifters circling the cauldron while scratching their heads. A young male paced in front of it. "Lacy never showed up for breakfast duty."

"My brother," Rafael said in alarm. He had his clothes off in seconds, then dropped to the ground.

Springing to action, Hailey did the same and was soon dashing after him through the forest.

Had the bears returned and harmed Rafael's brother and Lacy? She matched Rafael's speed, prepared to join him in battle if that was what it came to. Hailey had no idea where they were going, but Rafael must have picked up his brother's scent. He ran without pause, leaping over fallen logs and flying through the forest in a blur of gray-and-white fur.

Rafael didn't stop until he reached a cave. His ears twitched, then morphed. As soon as Hailey noticed him shifting, she did the same and jogged after him as he entered the cave. She reached his side, coming to a stop where he stood rigid, staring in.

The shadows within were not enough to hide Diego

and Lacy, naked and tangled in each other's embrace. Sunlight angled inside the cavernous space, creeping up the edge of their blanket and reaching for their toes.

"So you decided not to wait, after all." Rafael's dark laughter filled the cave.

Diego jolted upright, blinking rapidly. He shielded Lacy with his body. She gave a squeak of surprise and yanked at the blanket, but their bodies effectively weighed it down.

The couple had fresh bite marks on their necks. A stab of jealously pierced through Hailey's abdomen. If only Rafael had done the same to her.

An unhappy growl vibrated from Rafael's throat. "I stand corrected. You decided to skip the claiming ceremony."

Diego shrugged lazily. "Lacy and I didn't want to wait any longer. Raphy, you are looking at a mated male." Happiness shone in his brown eyes and toothy grin.

Face flushed, Lacy remained pressed against Diego's back as though he were a shirt she was trying to squeeze into. Her blonde hair was messy with thin strands standing on end. Swollen lips were moistened with the tip of her tongue.

Rafael clamped his jaw shut and glowered into the cave.

"Congratulations," Hailey offered.

"Thank you, Hailey." Diego took her in and raised one brow, his lips forming a secretive smile. "And what are the pair of you up to?"

"Making sure the two of you hadn't become a bear's breakfast," Rafael snapped. He took a menacing step forward. "Speaking of which, your new pack mates are standing hungry in the glade, fretting over the disappearance of your *mate*."

He spit the last word out like it was a fly that had sailed inside his mouth. Hailey winced. Lacy gasped, her eyes widening behind Diego.

"Oh my gosh! I didn't mean to sleep in." She grabbed her dress. In her hurry to get it over her head, she ended up struggling and tipping over.

"Relax, *mi amor*. I'll help you make breakfast. It's not as though they'll starve." Diego took her dress, shook it out, and carefully lowered it over her head.

She knew she should give them privacy, but Hailey couldn't seem to pry her eyes away from the endearing scene of two newly mated shifters lovingly tending to one another.

Rafael looked over at her and snarled. "Come along."

She followed him, stepping away from the mouth of the cave and into the bright morning sun that shone through the wide opening in the canopy.

Rafael hocked and spit on the ground. "Whipped dog," he muttered.

"You don't want your brother to be happy?"

His lips drew back into a wretched grimace. "That smile you saw on his face is because he just got laid. Wait a few months and see how thrilled he is answering to his mate when she starts ordering his sorry hide around all the time. She was angry he spoke to you, but she couldn't say anything about it—not back then, before they were mated. Now she has him right where she wants him."

Hailey studied the rough grooves in Rafael's forehead

and cheeks. "Were your parents unhappy?" It was the only explanation she could think of for Rafael's deeply rooted hostility toward a mate claim.

His eyes narrowed and she thought she must have hit the mark, until his words said otherwise. "There was never a pair as loyal and in love as my parents."

Feeling utterly confused, Hailey bit down on her lower lip. "I don't understand what you have against life mates."

"*¡Dios mio!* You are so naive."

"Then enlighten me!" Hailey flung her arms out at her sides.

Rafael sniffed dismissively and stormed away from the cave. Once Hailey caught up to him, he stopped and jerked his head at the forest. "I'm not waiting for Diego's mate to make breakfast. We'll shift and hunt. You know how to hunt, *si*?"

"I'm an excellent hunter." Hailey lifted her head and chest. It was a fact that came out as a boast. She didn't mean to flash him her tits, but unless she turned her back to him, it was impossible not to have them jiggling under his nose as they moved about naked.

Rafael's chin dipped and his gaze fastened over her breasts. The lust dilating his pupils made her nipples prickle and stiffen. Casting a look over the muscular male, she noted the erection twitching like a tail between his legs.

She would have been pleased if she weren't so frustrated.

"I would never boss my mate around," she said. "I think mates should be partners and friends."

Tendons stretched in Rafael's muscled arms when he

folded them over his chest. He met her gaze and lifted a brow. "What happens when your partner dies?"

"We all die eventually," Hailey said.

"What if your partner dies young? What if you're left to raise your pups alone?" Rafael's voice grew loud and bitter. "Would you seek revenge if you could—if you knew who killed your mate?"

"I—" Hailey's jaw hung open at this dark turn.

"Wild wolves don't know any better," Rafael said with a shake of his head. "Purebloods—shifters, we understand pain and sacrifice. We can make a choice not to tempt fate into turning love into a goddamned nightmare. Now shift, so we can go kill an unsuspecting bunny that probably has a mate nursing their kits back in their hidey-hole."

Not taking the bait, Hailey shrugged. "If he has kits, they'll leave the nest soon enough and make more rabbits for us to hunt down. It's not as though they have to wait for a full moon or a picky mate to claim them."

She braced herself for Rafael's outrage, but he surprised her by throwing his head back to bark out a laugh. His arms relaxed and the earlier scowl unfastened from his mouth. With the briefest of smiles, he lowered his magnificent body to the ground. "Well then, let's go ensure rabbits don't take over the world."

Hailey joined him on the ground. Face to face, on all fours, their eyes met and they shared a heated look. The wanting felt like torturous bliss. Her ovaries seemed to think they might see some action yet, and her genitals responded in kind. Gravity tugged at her heavy breasts, pulling Rafael's gaze down with it.

She heard voices emerge from the cave, Diego speaking to Lacy as they hurried out.

"Time to shift," Rafael said.

After the transformation, they shot through the forest, intent on the kill. It kept them from going at it . . . like rabbits. Hailey sniffed the underbrush, determined to root a rabbit out of hiding and show off her skills.

They quieted their steps, stalking through the forest in full predator mode. Padding over the earth, Hailey watched the underbrush carefully, searching for the barest quiver in the low-hanging leaves.

Birds twittered overhead, their chirps sounding like taunts.

Rafael stuck his nose into thick underbrush, sniffing loudly. Hailey stalked past him, ever watchful. She became singularly focused. Patience came naturally to her. Once she set her mind to something, she could wait for hours—days even—to achieve her goal.

As morning took a stroll toward afternoon, Rafael ran around poking at bushes. Hailey distanced herself from the male and the noise he was making. She hid near a tree and watched a sunny spot on the trail. Time passed, and she was rewarded for her perseverance when a rabbit hopped out to sun himself. His tiny nose twitched back and forth as he nibbled on bits of vegetation.

Hailey kept very still, scarcely breathing. Even her heart slowed to the barest pulse. She became a part of the forest, blending in with the trees, air, and earth.

The rabbit hopped closer, then froze and hunched. When no threat presented itself, he resumed twitching, long whiskers brushing over the dry soil as he searched for weeds. He grabbed a fallen leaf that was still green and nibbled on the edges.

He turned around and lifted his ears briefly before going back to his leaf.

Hailey sprang to action. Dropping the leaf, the rabbit dashed away, but not before she grabbed him by the back. The bunny screamed, a sound that made her heart thunder with triumph. She bit down, sinking her fangs through warm blood and flesh, cutting the rabbit's next shriek off with her jaws. Her teeth ripped through fur, tearing out chunks of meat and devouring her kill before it went cold.

When Rafael appeared, she tried offering him what remained, but he shook his head and sat on his haunches, seeming to enjoy watching her feast.

She finished up what she could before dropping the remains on the ground. Hailey licked her lips and swallowed. The fur around her mouth was wet with blood. Rafael walked over and began cleaning it off with his tongue.

Howls arose that Hailey recognized as her friends. She lifted her head and answered them. The call was issued and answered until the small group found her. Hailey was glad to count no more than four wolves.

Skeet growled at Rafael. The pureblooded male was on him in a flash, grabbing Skeet's wolf by the neck. Skeet cried out and got on the ground. Rafael put a paw on his back and held him down. Out of the corner of her eye, Hailey saw Byron crouching as a growl rose in his throat. Before she could bark to stop him, Byron attacked.

 chapter sixteen

RAFAEL LAUNCHED HIMSELF at the attacking wolf. As soon as he got a good hold on the other beast, he clamped his jaws tight and drew blood. The other wolf snarled and snapped his fangs.

His foe was male. Rafael had not liked the familiar way in which this one had looked at Hailey. This felt like a challenge for the right to mate her. Rafael would have to hurt the offender, maybe even kill him. He had no place in his pack.

Teeth sinking deeper, he shook his foe violently. The other male's growl pierced Rafael's ears and made his heart thunder with fury.

Hailey's three other friends circled the fighting wolves, barking in confusion and worry while his female stood back and watched.

The other male swiped at Rafael with his claws, trying desperately to free himself.

Hailey barked at him to submit.

Rafael released the male and readied himself for the second attack when the growling started anew.

Another bark issued from Hailey.

The other wolf looked at her, then at Rafael. His lips lifted as he bared his teeth and snarled.

Hailey's friends joined her in barking at the rebellious male. This only served to encourage him.

Snapping teeth came at Rafael's neck. He jumped at the male, raking his claws down his back. There was a piercing cry. The other wolf darted away, hunching with his head lowered as he slunk over to his friends, a slight limp to his gait. They lined up next to their wounded friend and looked to Hailey for instructions.

It was time they met their new alpha. Rafael shifted. One commanding look from him to Hailey had her doing the same.

"The one who attacked me, what's his name?" Rafael demanded while Hailey was still crouched over the ground.

"Byron. His wolf has always been more rowdy than the rest, but you don't have to worry about him. He's a skilled hunter, strong, loyal, and a good friend."

Rafael clenched his teeth as Hailey sang the other male's praises.

"A good friend—is that all he is? Because he seemed to want to fight me for you."

Hailey straightened and pursed her lips. "Byron and I aren't lovers; not anymore."

A snarl burst out of Rafael. That settled it. Byron had no place in his pack.

Once the four friends had shifted, Rafael's glaring eyes shot immediately to the mongrel he had fought. The brown-haired male was muscled, tan, and—sadly—lacking in defects. Unlike Kamari, Byron was the right age for Hailey.

Rafael ran his tongue over his teeth, recalling the taste of Byron's blood in his wolf's mouth. So long as he remained Hailey's alpha, no one else could have her. She was to train under him. That meant no courtships and no rutting, unless it was Rafael's wolf on hers. While their animals answered the call of nature, he would have no interference.

While his thoughts swirled, Hailey updated her friends and made introductions.

"Why should we follow him?" A female with thick, long, loose curls and skin darker than his own demanded.

Rafael couldn't remember her name, even though he had heard it moments before. Only one name burned in his mind. Byron glowered right back at him, having the audacity to size him up like he meant to take a swing at his face.

Bring it on, Rafael thought with a smile.

"He refused to claim you, so what business does he have joining *our* pack?" The curly-haired female asked.

Rafael's chuckle earned him a nasty glare from the dark beauty. "First of all, this is *my* pack. *You* need *me*, not the other way around. Your purebloaded friend understands and accepts this; so should you."

The female gaped at Hailey. "Is this true? You're okay with this mongrel taking over, Hailey?"

With a frown at Rafael, Hailey turned to her friend and softened her gaze. "I know he's a wretch, but he'll only stay with us long enough to show us what he knows about surviving in the wild, which he's been doing his whole life. I asked him to."

The female who had spoken looked at her other

friend, a young woman with messy rich brown hair that tumbled down her shoulders.

Rafael wasn't so wretched as to look at either woman's genitals. There was only one female he yearned for.

"I suppose it's all right if it's temporary," the other female said slowly.

"I don't like him." Byron folded his thick arms over his chest.

"We need him," Hailey said firmly.

Rafael smirked at Byron. The other male narrowed his eyes.

"His feelings don't matter, since he's not coming with us," Rafael announced.

"What?" the friends cried collectively.

Rafael lifted his chin. "Your survival in the wild is dependent on your loyalty and ability to act as a team. Disobedience jeopardizes our safety."

"I am loyal to my pack," Byron bit out.

"You need to be loyal to me," Rafael fired back. "Your wolf's first reaction was to attack me, so you'll understand why this won't work. Maybe you can stay in Wolf Hollow and find yourself a mate."

"I'm not staying in Wolf Hollow."

Hailey walked over to Rafael and put her hand on his shoulder. "Give Byron another chance. I'm sure you don't expect every wolf to roll over the second they meet you."

One of the females scoffed and rolled her eyes.

Rafael scratched his chin. Hailey had a point, and he liked the gentle press of her hand on his shoulder.

"Fine, but if he can't keep himself in line, he's out."

Hailey nodded. "Sounds fair. Byron?"

The other male stared at Rafael for several long heartbeats before dropping his arms. "Agreed," he said.

"Good. And the rest of you," Rafael said, "can you follow my lead?"

"Sure, why not?" the dark-skinned female said. "It's not like you're going to be around long."

Rafael chuckled. "Careful, I might stick around longer than you think."

Abruptly, Hailey pulled her hand off him like his skin had scalded hers. Lines formed over her forehead like ripples in a pond. She was a hard one to read. Rafael would have thought she'd be happy if he stayed longer. He hadn't planned to, but once the words were out, they felt right.

"Tell me your names again," Rafael said to the other three.

"Violet," the dark-skinned one said, with a toss of her dark brown curls. "Think you can remember it this time?"

The others stared him down in challenge; even Hailey raised a pert brow.

Good, they were spirited. Rafael grinned. His pack had spunk.

Not his. The reminder jabbed at the back of his skull like a woodpecker after insects.

His for now.

THE SEVEN SHIFTERS who made up Wolf Hollow's council sat in a semicircle facing Diego at dusk. He had been asked to join them after dinner. When Lacy asked if she should come, too, the elder Palmer had instructed her to stick to her cleaning duties.

Now he sat on a hard stump outside Jager's hut being stared down through the ashy smoke of the elder's fire. Their somber mood was at odds with the happy occasion, in Diego's opinion. Only one friendly face stood out in the crowd. An amused smile puffed out between Emerson's rosy cheeks. Diego wanted to believe that whatever came of this ambush, Sasha would have his back, even though she looked very serious at the moment with her deep brown eyes studying him as though he were a stranger.

Jager's wrinkled fingers formed a steeple. "Did you pressure Lacy into an early mate claim?"

Diego nearly laughed. Emerson winked and began weaving her long blonde hair into a braid over her shoulder.

"No," he answered, unable to mask the humor from his voice. His smirk would be no help in convincing the council, but he didn't care. This was none of their concern and he would never tell them the truth—that Lacy had been the first one to bite. Remembering how his shy mate took charge filled him with passion and pride.

"Do you think it's funny to coerce an innocent?" the elder Palmer asked.

Diego nearly choked on the smoke. He stood up to suck fresh air into his lungs and snarl at the shifter accusing him of such foul activities. "I have never pressured a female, certainly not my beloved."

Sasha nodded and flashed him an apologetic grimace. "Of course not. The two of you made your intentions clear."

"But they were supposed to wait until the full moon celebration for their claiming ceremony," Jager said. "The pack is becoming unruly. Mate claims are taking place in secret." The elder aimed a narrowed gaze at first Sasha and then Wolfrik, but the pureblooded male was preoccupied with pushing back the cuticles on his fingers with his nail.

When Jager turned his attention to Emerson, she dropped her braid and scowled back at him. "Why are you glaring at me? I'm the only one patiently waiting for the council's approval to claim Gina."

"We are not discussing that right now," Jager snapped.

Emerson jumped to her feet, smile going up in smoke. "It doesn't matter anymore. Gina and I are leaving Wolf Hollow to join Hailey's new pack. You all can do whatever you want and find a more malleable shifter to fill my spot on the council."

The blonde's braid loosened, freeing itself from its weave as Emerson jerked her head and arms in agitation.

"Emmy, you can't leave," Palmer said in haste.

"I'm not the only one," Emerson announced triumphantly. "A whole group of us plan to go, even Camilla. It's our decision, Father."

Eyes pleading, Palmer stood. "We need you here, Emmy. Your family needs you. Your pack needs you. Isn't that right, Jager?" He swung a glare at the old shifter. "Give my daughter your blessings to claim the female she loves at the next full moon ceremony, you old bastard.

Emerson's put her life at risk for this pack again and again—more than most of the rest. She deserves her pick of mate."

Diego sat back down slowly, not that anyone noticed. The heat was no longer on him. Indeed, the angry voices across from him appeared to attract the flames and smoke. It billowed into their faces. Brows furrowed and nose twitching, Raider waved it away with one large hand. Smirking, Diego slouched on the log and let the council duke it out.

The wrinkles in Jager's face seemed to multiply. "I won't stop them, but don't expect me to offer up my moonshine or toast the union."

Palmer growled.

Emerson laughed humorlessly. "I don't need your foul liquor, old man, nor your blessing." She jerked away from him and walked the three short steps to Palmer. "Yours is the only blessing that matters to me, Papa."

Palmer beamed and kissed Emerson's cheek. "Gina is a beautiful woman. You have excellent taste, my dear."

Heidi, another mated shifter from the den, snorted at Palmer's boast.

"Can we please get back to the business at hand?" Jager asked, waving his arms for attention. "Everyone, I implore you to take your seats."

With a flip of her hair, Emerson returned to her stump, plopped down, and crossed one leg over the other.

Jager redirected his attention to Diego. "I will take your word for it that your early claim on Lacy was executed by a mutual understanding."

"Don't just take my word for it, ask her yourself."

Heidi pursed her lips and nodded.

Sasha scooted to the edge of her stump and raised her voice. "When I saw Lacy at dinner, she looked like a happily mated female."

"Yes, I observed the same," Raider said.

"Be that as it may, it is time to restore order," Jager announced. "What is this you say about packmates leaving the hollow?"

Emerson looked at Diego and held his gaze. They were both aware of the plans the visiting shifters had made with some of the single shifters in Wolf Hollow . . . and with Rafael. It had come as a relief more than anything else when his brother shared his change of plans.

Rafael would not go into the wild alone—not at first. It eased Diego's troubled heart considerably. Now that he had claimed his true love, he wished the same for Rafael. He hoped that spending more time with Hailey would lead to a mate claim. Wolves were not meant to be alone. Rafael deserved happiness and the love of a good female.

When the soft pops of the fire filled the silence rather than answers, Palmer cleared his throat. "Emmy?"

Sighing, Emerson scratched at her neck and recited names of shifters who had expressed interest in leaving. By the end, Jager's eyes were bulging so far out of his sockets, they looked ready to fall into the fire and burn up like coals.

The rest of the council did not appear any happier.

"And what of patrols?" Sasha demanded, a hand going to her belly.

"They cannot desert their pack like this," Jager said. "We won't allow it."

Raider shook his head and sighed. "Let me speak to them."

"I'll talk to them with you," Palmer said.

"Damn Glenn Meadows wolves stirring things up," Jager grumbled. "Nothing good ever comes of their visits."

 chapter seventeen

THIS WAS IT. This was goodbye.

It felt like the earth was crumbling out from beneath Rafael, and not just the bits of rock tumbling over the edge of the bluff where he sat with Diego, staring out at a valley transformed into a dust bowl by the climate's breakdown. Brown sand piled up into wave-like drifts below their dangling toes, all traces of green long since buried and turned to dust.

Rafael grabbed a rock and chucked it into the void. The stone sailed far before dropping and disappearing into the grains of that desert landscape. It was clear to see why Wolf Hollow's border stopped here.

The sight of it made Rafael's stomach feel as hollowed out as a rotting tree. "So, this is your new home," he said somberly.

"Not this." Diego jutted his chin forward, making Rafael's heart lurch.

It wasn't as though his brother was in danger of tumbling forward, but just the idea of him plummeting that back-breaking distance made every muscle in his body tense.

"Wolf Hollow is actually quite beautiful," Diego continued. "Miles of lush green forest, rivers, fields, glades, a waterfall, and a pond." He smiled contentedly. "It wouldn't matter if the pack lived in a desert. My home is with my mate."

Rafael eyed the purpling bruise on his brother's neck. "I knew the wench had teeth."

"Careful," Diego growled.

Rafael scoffed and rolled his eyes. "As long as she makes you happy."

"Raphy, I've never felt this content. Love is a blessing."

Love was a curse, but he kept his mouth shut on that topic. There was no convincing Diego otherwise.

Rafael scooped up another rock and chucked it over the edge. A light breeze blew over his bare chest. The whisper of fall teased the sheen of sweat over his brows and seemed to sway through his bones like branches in the wind.

The two Wolf Hollow shifters patrolling this area walked by on four legs, glancing briefly at Rafael and Diego before trotting near the bluff's edge to resume their sweep of the southwestern corner of their territory.

"I can't believe this is really goodbye," Diego said, his voice thick with emotion. "I never thought we would part ways."

The wind ruffled his brother's shoulder-length hair. Rafael had to look away to ease the stab of pain cutting through his soul. His fingers dug into the parched earth, grains of sand spilling through his calloused fingers no matter how tightly he tried to hold on.

"Life is full of endings," Rafael said darkly.

Diego turned his head. "This is a new beginning, brother, not an end. It is the start of a new journey for you, as well."

Rafael flattened his palm and brushed the sand particles off his skin. It did feel as though he had a purpose now, and at least his female understood that he was the one calling the shots.

While Lacy's lips had pouted when the brothers announced they would spend one final day together—just the two of them—Hailey had nodded and flashed Rafael a sympathetic smile. The pureblood from Glenn Meadows knew what it was like to leave behind family. Unlike Lacy, she had chosen to step away from her sheltered life and embrace the unknown. Her courage satisfied Rafael. Pretty much everything about her was pleasing to the point of frustration.

The only tension between them was sexual, and even that was something any hot-blooded male with a pulse had to appreciate. It stroked Rafael's ego to have an alluring beauty want him. But it also put him in danger of losing control. If his human half joined his wolf in rutting with the pureblooded female, a mate claim was inevitable, and he wouldn't do that to himself or to her.

A crescent moon illuminated the wispy clouds converging over the sky for an early end to the day. Rafael sent up his silent thanks to the celestial body for keeping his species' procreation in check. At least by spending more time together, Rafael could ensure Hailey knew how to handle herself in the wild. He wanted her to be safe, especially once he was no longer around to protect her.

Hailey and her friends were eager to leave. Rafael could hardly blame them when there was more drama unfolding in the glade. He could care less about Wolf Hollow's council interfering with their packmates wanting to bail. Rafael wouldn't have allowed even half of them to join their group. It was the outcry and woeful tears he had no desire to witness. Some members of the pack were taking it personally that others desired to depart. A couple of them were siblings, potentially facing the same gut-wrenching separation Rafael and Diego faced.

"Hailey would be a good mate for you," his brother said now.

Rafael waited for his anger to flare, but all he felt was the breeze. "Yes," he acknowledged, "but I don't want a child, let alone a litter."

"You can't let the past decide your future, Raphy."

Rafael grunted, eyes on the wasteland below. It reminded him of similar dust heaps surrounding the first home he ever knew. The air had left his throat constantly dry.

"You've been a great brother, and you would make an even better dad," Diego insisted.

Rafael scooted back and got to his feet. "Fatherhood is in your future, not mine, *hermano*. But I have no doubt the role will fit you well."

Nodding, Diego grabbed a rock and threw it over the edge before standing and dusting off his hands. Somber eyes stared into Rafael's.

"Mother, may she run forever free, would have wanted you to find a mate and have pups. Father too."

Rafael wanted to laugh. The only thing their father had

ever truly cared about was their mother. He had gone mad with grief. The once-mighty wolf turned reckless and mean until he found his beloved's scent. It was a cruel trap set out by the hunters who had killed his mate. He knew it, but he went anyway. Rafael could still remember his father's pitiful cry in the distance, filled with pain and defeat.

These memories were better left buried in the ground with the bones of creatures long gone.

Why did Diego have to go spoiling their last day together?

His brother switched topics to the changing season and how different it would be to weather the cold in one place, but it was too late for Rafael. His mind had already wandered where it had no business stepping foot. That damn dream had brought back the worst day of his life.

Upon hearing his mother's cries, Rafael had dashed through the brittle timber, dry from extended drought.

He came upon her, circling in terror, dragged down by a massive steel trap that had caught her delicate front leg in its metal jaws. The head of a dead cow lay on its side over the dusty ground. The scent of beef was all over the trap—deadly bait for luring in a wolf.

Rafael's whimper made his mother go still. When her eyes landed on him, he felt pinned in place and his cries shushed.

She barked at him to leave her, but Rafael was as rooted in place as the slowly dying trees. She struggled with each step, blood seeping where the trap's angry jaws refused to let go. Rafael urged her along past brambles and beetle-ridden bark. When she fell, he cried for her to get up.

She cried back, pleading for him to leave, but Rafael would not. He would never leave her behind and vulnerable.

There came a distant thundering that made Rafael glance briefly at the sky, but the rumble was a tremor in the ground.

He looked to his mother for direction, and that was when he saw something strange taking place. Her fur disappeared before his eyes, leaving behind something that was not his mom, nor any animal he had ever seen before.

Thick dark hair flowed from her head like a horse's mane, but that was where the equestrian resemblance ended. Large brown eyes bored into his, making him shrink away. The creature's mouth moved and a foreign sound emerged. Urgency lashed from her tongue, but none of it made any sense to Rafael.

«¡Vete! Prisa, Rafael. Debes irte ahora. Rafael."

It was that one word he kept hearing over and over, directed at him. *Rafael.*

The rumbling in the earth grew louder.

"Por favor, Rafael. Por dios. Déjame y vete.» Her arms lifted, clasped together by the horrid steel trap. "Rafael. ¡Vete!"

She had named him before she died. Rafael had seen her human face once, heard her voice—beautiful in spite of her terror for his safety—words spoken before her tongue was silenced forever.

An elbow jabbed him out of the hellacious cavity of his memories. Rubbing his shoulder, Rafael glared at Diego.

"I've been asking you a question. Where has your mind gone?"

It was better if he didn't know. Rafael had never told Diego that he had seen their mother in her human form, and though she had begged him to leave, he had stayed. He had stayed and it had done nothing to help save her.

He pulled Diego in suddenly and gave him a tight hug, chest to chest. His beloved brother, whom Rafael had helped name once they were old enough to shift into their human forms.

Chuckling, Diego slapped his back. "I'm going to miss you too, Raphy. You'd better get your ass up this way again to see me soon."

Rafael grunted. "I'll come back and make sure that mate of yours is keeping you happy."

"You don't have to worry about that." Diego smirked.

For his brother's sake, Rafael prayed to the moon goddess that Lacy would remain a pleasing mate. His brother deserved no less.

"Watch out for bears," Rafael said.

"Safe travels," Diego replied, throwing in a cheeky, "Beware of the full moon."

Rafael's grumble set his brother off laughing. At least one of them found amusement in the situation.

chapter eighteen

DURING THEIR FIRST week of travel, home stuck to Hailey like a silver thread as unyielding as spider's silk stretching from her heart to her childhood meadows, streams, and mountains.

Every movement eastward took her farther from her familiar territory. The smells and very air filling her nostrils were distinctly changed. The landscape was all new. Woods gave way to great plains stretching on for hours of sunbaked exposure that pulled on her tongue until it hung limp and dripping between her teeth. There were moments where home felt like an oasis and the rest of the world an inhospitable husk slowly withering away. Days where she felt she had made a terrible mistake. Would she ever see her mother, father, and siblings again? Would the passage of time all but erase her from their memories?

Then their small group would reach an awe-inspiring sight, like a vast river cutting through rising mountains and the welcoming shade of trees clustered on both sides of the wide waterway.

In Glenn Meadows, there had been regular meals

thanks to her tribe's communal efforts. Meat and fish were smoked and stored. Chickens were raised. Vegetables and other edible plants were grown. They knew the best places to forage close to home.

Yesterday, Hailey had only caught one mole. The day before that, not one of them had eaten. With all the distance they were covering, they could all use a hearty meal.

The first lesson Rafael had taught them was to never eat anything they hadn't caught themselves. Today they would work together to hunt down big game.

Sunlight sliced through the canopy as the seven wolves stalked out of the woods to the tall grass of an arid plateau, following closely behind Rafael. In the end, only one member of Wolf Hollow had left the pack to join them. Byron had come, too, and, ironically, become fast friends with Rafael. Males—go figure. What mattered to Hailey was that their pack worked together and kept one another safe and fed. So far, she was happy with their dynamic and grateful Rafael had agreed to lead them. While his human half was a wretch, his wolf was a natural leader tuned in to the larger world.

Their alpha led them through the grassy plateau, steering clear of surges in the land that could expose their presence. Hailey's place had been established nearest their leader, always the one to follow directly behind Rafael. She observed the way he scented the air, veering away from certain paths while charging through hidden openings in the forest at breakneck speed, snatching a rabbit before it had entered Hailey's sight.

The landscape wasn't the only thing changing.

Animals previously foreign to Hailey would pop up from beneath the ground or scurry up a rocky butte. She had licked her chops earlier at the sight of rabbit-sized furry creatures with short, rounded ears nibbling on grass before dashing out of reach between rocky crevices.

Skeet had tried unsuccessfully to dig one out, barking in frustration when his efforts produced nothing more than scattered pebbles and soil.

With an amused grin, Rafael led them to the open plains with its grassy coverage where, sure enough, the antlers of a bull elk appeared, moving with caution while the wolf pack crouched low to the ground, as unseen as tiny ants. Another elk joined the first, then a whole herd stepped out of the forest, joined by mothers with calves.

The wolf pack crouched lower, hidden in a sea of grass, soundless and patient. As they moved across the plain, the straw rising from the ground rustled against the animals' long legs.

A feeling of confidence murmured through Hailey listening to the herd approach. There was no doubt in her mind that they would bring one of the animals down and fill their bellies with tasty meat.

It wasn't until Rafael shot forward that her heart lurched, along with her legs. The group moved in tandem toward the herd. Hoofed feet sprang to action, pounding across the earth, grass now whipping their flanks. When the herd split into two, the wolves split off, following both groups to single out the weakest. Hailey led Layla, Skeet, and Hudson after the females and calves.

They ran so close to the fleeing animals that Hailey

could feel the ground tremble below her paws. She sprang up and down, half running, half flying across the plateau. The ground sloped upward. She charged forward and got a quick look at the full expanse. Seeing that Rafael, Byron, and Violet had singled out a weakened elk who had fallen dangerously behind, Hailey made a swift arc, leading her group to rejoin Rafael's.

Her brain sparked with excitement, driving her forward, faster and faster with energy to spare.

Rafael grabbed the elk's leg, releasing it in the next instant when the beast kicked out. His herd abandoned him without a backward glance. The animal tried desperately to catch up as the wolves closed in. Hailey and her group matched the beast's speed, flanking him from the opposite side. Rafael lunged and snapped at the elk's side, sending their prey wheeling over sideways. They came at it with snapping teeth, but the elk managed to right himself and make one last feeble attempt to get away.

Watching her dinner try to flee gave Hailey a surge of adrenaline. She shot forward and sprang at its face. Wide, terror-stricken eyes took her in as she flew at the animal. Hailey opened her jaws and latched on to its neck. Her teeth sank in, effectively turning into a vicious anchor, pulling the elk down into the depths of the grass. Her packmates attacked from all angles. Hoofed legs kicked out sideways, then at the sky when they got the animal onto its back, belly exposed for their dining pleasure. Gradually, the kicks turned into jerks, then twitches, before going limp as the wolves tore its belly open and turned it into a gory feast.

Consumed with hunger, Hailey ripped out chunks of warm, blood-soaked meat. The wet slurp and smack of gorging filled her wolf's ears as their pack chewed through the carcass and filled their bellies. After devouring their first big group catch, they all wore crimson smiles.

THE FOLLOWING MORNING, the sky lightened in increments and with it, the temperature rose gradually.

Satiated from the previous day's feast, Rafael's pack stretched and curled over soft green turf. Contented smiles marked their faces even in slumber. Rafael's muzzle rested on Hailey's back. They were the only two who slept together. No one mentioned the arrangement. They did not speak of anything in the human tongue, for they had not shifted into those cumbersome forms since leaving Wolf Hollow.

With the moon growing rounder every night, Rafael and Hailey would soon need to shift and wait out that period during the full moon's fertile gravitational pull.

A meadowlark landed in the grass near the wolves and tittered. Its head turned side to side above its bright yellow feathers, beady black eyes taking in the furry travelers as it commenced a cheerful serenade. Closing his eyes, Rafael allowed himself and his pack to rest a little longer. He nuzzled his face against his female's coat and reveled in her happy sigh.

It was important to him that Hailey experience the wonders and the awakening of moving through nature, leaving their prints upon the world, and the wild calling rooted deeply in their ancestry. He could not imagine any other life, not comprehend keeping still, settling into one place. The meadowlark sang his agreement.

The fur pillowing his face felt divine, but daylight and new landscapes beckoned.

Rafael stood and yawned, sending the meadowlark into a flutter of yellow wings against blue sky. Hailey's eyes blinked open. Lazily, she lifted her head and stared at him. Rafael walked over and nuzzled her.

More heads lifted. Hudson, the shifter who had joined them from Wolf Hollow, got to his feet and stretched. Byron stood next. Violet shot Rafael a sullen look and tucked her head in as though she meant to go back to sleep. It wasn't until all of her packmates were on their feet that she joined them with a low grumble. Violet's mood lightened as they set out on the next adventure.

He led them on a path beaten into the earth by buffalo herds. The amber rays from above followed their progress along the trodden prairie. Dipping down into valleys, they trotted their way south for a stretch before picking up the pace eastward. When the trail climbed, Rafael slowed his gait. Sun struck the ridge they crested and scattered its light across the distant dazzle of lakes and rivers.

Seen from this vantage, the fate of the world appeared reassuring in her endless abundance and beauty. Nature provided. Nature protected. Nature prevailed.

A howl soared free from Rafael's throat. That joyful call pealed off his tongue and lifted off the ledge like an eagle in flight. One day, the earth would claim his bones, but today, the sky claimed his soul.

Wolves chorused behind him. Rafael lifted his head again, eyes closing against the blinding sun. They made a sound unparalleled by any other species. Their electrifying song echoed across the valley, spreading for miles.

A little after midday, they came upon a pristine lake surrounded by swaths of lush green grass and clusters of tree shade. Stopping beneath the canopy's dense screen, Rafael shifted to his human form. Following his lead, their pack morphed from four-legged wolves into a giddy group of naked humans.

"What a beautiful world we live in!" Layla yelled, as though her friends' ears might not work yet. She bounced on the tips of her toes, seemingly unconcerned by the way it made her breasts shake.

Skeet nodded. "I can't wait to tell the tribe all about our adventures after we return."

"I can't wait to tell my dad about the elk we took down," Violet said, lifting her chest.

"That was awesome," Hudson said.

Byron lifted his hand for Hudson to high-five. The guys smiled proudly.

"What now?" Violet asked Rafael. It was good to see her human half falling into line as swiftly as her wolf had.

"I thought you might enjoy a swim break." Rafael jutted his chin in the direction of the lake.

Violet and Layla took one look at each other and squealed before racing for the water's edge, the guys following on their heels, leaving Rafael alone with Hailey beneath the shade. It felt an age since he had seen that smooth, beautiful face with cheeks that dimpled like imprints in the clay along a riverbank when she smiled even slightly. Bright blonde, springy hair framed eyes filled with tears that remained captive within the olive-brown circles of her irises.

She didn't need to speak for Rafael to understand the emotions cascading over her face. He could read her the way his wolf instinctively knew whenever she felt thirsty, hungry, tired, anxious, promiscuous, content, or irritable—the last of which was a rarity with the good-natured female.

Her watery gaze spoke of wonder and joy—an awakening. The tug of Rafael's soul intertwining with hers stole his breath. He had crossed vast stretches of the continent, and yet the most dangerous boundary stood five inches below him. Their wolves behaved as though they were mates. He thanked every faraway star across the galaxy they had not bitten one another and made a lasting claim. The true test fast approached. The aptly named Hunter's Full Moon might be the greatest foe Rafael had ever faced.

He had to prevent his wolf from breeding with hers. This barrier must not be crossed. It was easier to keep his distance when they were in human form . . . or so he had hoped. But seeing the world in her eyes, he was overcome with the need to hold her and kiss her, then make love to her in nature's embrace during their precious moments alone while the others laughed and splashed in the distance.

Face full of wonder, Hailey breathed out. "I have no words."

"Have you forgotten how to speak?" Rafael laughed.

Looking at him with eyes that glittered like stars, she

answered, "I remembered how to live."

An ever-expanding and deep longing stirred within his chest, burrowing into his heart.

He felt something for her. Something he was terrified to acknowledge.

With love came loss. That pain was no mystery to him. He could not go through it again.

Straightening, he pulled his eyes off her, focusing on the lake. "Time to join the others," he said.

Hailey fell into step beside him. "Is this where we're staying for the full moon?"

"Possibly. We have another two days at our disposal, but this looks like a good place to lie low."

Their group was neck deep in water talking with barely a breath between words, as though making up for the weeks spent entirely in wolf form without human conversation. Rafael made his way to the narrow stretch of pebbled beach where the others had waded in. The sun-warmed stones pressed into the arch of his foot. Stepping into the lake, he gritted his teeth. Its cold stung on contact.

Hailey sucked in a breath behind him.

Laughing, Layla lifted her hand above the surface and waved. "Come on in, you get used to it."

Hailey waded past Rafael. When the water reached just below her hips, she dove in, popping up two seconds later, hair dripping and lips grinning. "Refreshing," she announced.

Layla nodded. "There's nothing like this at home. What about in Wolf Hollow, Hudson? Do you have any lakes in your territory?"

"One," he answered. "It's really pretty with a waterfall, but compared to this, it seems like more of a pond."

Rafael waded through the cool waters up to his chest. When he was deep enough, he dipped his head back, soaking his hair. He ran his wet hands over his face and head, squeezing the water back out.

Byron watched him. "How long are we staying here?"

"Through the full moon."

"I'll start a fire."

Rafael gave him a nod to go ahead.

Layla swam the few strokes to Hudson and stood, water cascading from her hair to her shoulders and running in rivulets between her breasts.

"You miss home?" she asked.

"Not really."

"What about your packmates? Your sister?"

"I miss my best friend. My sister can take care of herself. What about you? Did you leave siblings behind?"

"Yeah, but they're younger, and I didn't have to leave my best friends behind."

Hailey and Violet smiled back at her.

Sighing, Hudson said, "I just needed a break, you know?"

"Yeah, I do," Layla answered. "Something different. Something new."

"Exactly."

"Would you ever return to your pack?"

"I'm not sure."

Rafael swam away from their chatter, cool water sliding over his muscles and limbs. Arms wheeling over his head and legs kicking, he made his way to a fallen tree submerged partway in the crystalline shallows. Gripping the sodden bark with his toes, he lifted himself out of the water, balancing on the log.

Water droplets rolled down his back and chest. He scanned the opposite side of the lake in the distance. The land on the other side led to rising mountains far more beautiful than anything human hands could ever sculpt or carve. Rafael felt humbled in its wake. He was reminded of his insignificance in this grand and mighty world. It was the most freeing feeling he had ever known.

While the others spoke of home, Rafael lifted his head and surveyed the uncharted wilds. He had returned home.

LATER THAT EVENING, after the moon turned the lake silver, Rafael emerged from sleep to the pop and crackle of a steady fire. He lay on his back, staring up at a clear sky full of stars. Looking into that heavenly expanse, a soft hum filled his head and a feeling of being watched back.

The fire sputtered in agitation at being disturbed. Rafael turned his head toward the heat and saw fresh twigs poking out above the flames. A slender arm pulled back. Hailey sat on her knees, leaning over the rocky perimeter Byron had made. Firelight danced over her exquisite, full breasts, and shadows played along the underside of her curves and the crevices of her smooth, beautiful body.

Three wolves slept curled up in the shadows beyond the fire. Two were noticeably absent—Hudson and Layla, no surprise. They knew to enjoy their fun before the full moon.

Hailey sat back and watched the flames, becoming

hypnotized by the movement of light, unaware of Rafael watching her.

This was the first night they had not cuddled up together. Like his wolf, Rafael had wanted her the moment he saw her shift and rise from the ground, as proud as a queen from a bygone era.

Agreeing to lead her pack temporarily had been a risk. As he had feared, they were becoming closer. He wanted her even more. His dick responded to the sight of her, as hard as the towering pines they had passed through on their way to the lake. It jutted straight up—an arrow aimed at the moon.

Hailey looked over, straight at his pulsing organ, as disobedient as his wolf. She made no sound, didn't even blink, as she lowered her hands to the ground and moved toward him on all her hands and knees. Wavy blonde hair curtained her face as olive-brown eyes blazed a path that crossed the few feet to where he lay breathing rapidly. A fresh flow of blood rushed to his groin. A bead of moisture glistened at the tip.

The distance between them was short, but Hailey took her sweet time.

Rafael had held himself back every time he was tempted to lose control and plunge into this gorgeous female. The question was now whether he could hold *her* back, if she was the one to mount him.

chapter nineteen

THE WAXING MOON called to Hailey, keeping her from sleep. Light emanating from that heavenly orb might as well have been rays of sun beaming at her eyelids every time she tried to settle in for the night.

Awareness fluttered through her body like the wings of time. Her chance for mating continued unfulfilled. A mate and motherhood eluded her, despite being in her prime. And finally, when she had found a powerful pureblooded male, he denied her for no good reason. It was the most infuriating thing she had ever experienced with another shifter.

The male had no idea of the torment her body put her through in his presence. It wasn't enough that her heat cycles had started coming more frequently months before, as though her body was tired of waiting on her to get on nature's schedule and mate already.

She felt her own wolf slipping from her control. If Rafael insisted on rejecting her, she didn't want to cuddle with him in any form. She frowned into the flickering flames, steadying the angry racing of her heart. All this time in the wild, her wolf had given over her full affection, trust, and loyalty to their pack's alpha.

Being human again, she felt the first sting of betrayal.

At some point, Rafael would leave them—abandon her wolf.

It didn't matter to her that he had made that clear from the start. He should have tried harder to keep his wolf at bay. Better yet, he should have ceased being a cantankerous wretch and claimed her. Most frustrating of all was the desire she felt—like an incessant itch that needed scratching and scratching and scratching. It was a flaming ache between her thighs. Yet another need Rafael stubbornly turned his back on. If his wolf was going to mount hers, his human half might as well do the same and build something more out of this partnership.

When the fire guttered, Hailey stood to gather more sticks. There was no shortage of tree limbs lost to winds and scattered across the ground. She spared Rafael a passing glance. The insufferable vagabond lay stretched out on his back, chest rising and falling, a faint smile over his lips. Naturally, he would have no trouble slumbering peacefully—comfortable enough to lie face up, genitals on full display.

His penis rested flaccid against one muscled thigh, nesting above dark wiry hairs covering his scrotum. She took a good, long stare, trying to convince herself she did not want his sex organs anywhere near hers.

Returning to her task, Hailey grabbed as many sticks as she could carry, choosing thick pieces that weren't overly long. Byron's wolf looked up and made a brief note of her activities before lowering his head and seeming to doze off once more. Skeet and Violet were near him, curled up. Hailey had kept her eyes closed earlier when she had heard Layla and Hudson make whispered plans. She had waited until long after their footsteps had faded into the forest to open her eyes, sit up, and watch the fire. Hailey was grateful they had left the campsite to enjoy one another out of earshot. It would have added another layer of sexual frustration to the mass building inside her.

Hailey made herself useful by feeding more sticks to the fire. It crackled to life, flames licking the dry twigs. Several small pops followed. Her eyes went out of focus. For a moment she saw only waves of flashing light. Then she felt a gaze with a heat to rival the flames warming her skin.

Hailey looked over, half expecting to find Rafael sitting upright, but he remained flat on his back. His eyes were open and on her, and a massive erection jutted below his belly button.

The ache between her legs built into a throbbing inferno. She knew he would not come to her, so she went to him, crawling over the earth filled with infinite life thriving beneath the surface, a miraculous cycle of birth and death beneath her knees and palms.

She could feel moonlight on her back. The thick head of Rafael's penis glistened above silky foreskin stretched over his expanded length. The size of a male's sex organ did not matter much to Hailey so long as it did its job, though she was pleased by the monolith before her. She was wet enough for a male of his size.

Rafael watched her climb over him. It was as though

the earth was holding him down; as though, like her wolf had for his, Rafael the man was submitting to her.

So she took him. She positioned her sex over his veined shaft and, after her initial guidance, seated herself over his hips, fully penetrated. Hailey gasped, the way she had upon taking that first step into the cool lake. Now she was submerged in wet, needy heat. The aching throb nudged her into action—rocking her hips, riding Rafael with abandon, as though he might get away if she weren't fast enough.

Something untamed and savage woke inside of her. Nails digging into the male's shoulders, Hailey threw head back, her spine arching while her hips bucked.

Rough hands reached up, not to pull her off, but to clasp hold of her breasts. Rafael met her thrusts with his own, ramming up to burrow deep inside her.

She closed her eyes and kept her face toward the moon. Rafael rolled her nipples between his fingers, then slid his hands down her sides, resting them on her hips, urging her with speedy shoves of his hands to continue riding him as her breasts bounced freely.

One of the wolves whined. Hailey was too far gone in the throes of pleasure to concern herself over Byron's startled whimper. Hopefully, he would go back to sleep. When he made more noise, Rafael growled, "Hush up," and the whining stopped.

Roping an arm around Hailey's back, he rolled them around, reversing their positions. Rafael's hungry gaze replaced the cold orb of the moon. His pupils burned like coals as he moved with slow deliberate pumps, pulling one of Hailey's legs over his chest, hooking her ankle behind his neck.

With the ground at her back and her alpha inside of her, on top of her, Hailey entered a state of bliss that was infinite and ethereal. She was no longer human, nor wolf. Thoughts escaped her. She moved with the body joined to hers. He seemed to grow inside her, the way his wolf did right before tying them, bound by nature's call to mate and breed.

Life. It was the only coherent thought Hailey could muster. The point of life was life and more life.

Rafael panted with pleasure, thrusting in and out, burying himself to the hilt, then pulling away to thrust again.

They were blanketed by stars and warmed by their shared heat and the fire radiating over their skin.

Her nerves vibrated. Heart pounding, Hailey felt its pulse most strongly at her core, around the male shoving himself between her thighs. As she tightened, he expanded inside her, filling her so completely she was stretched over his thick length.

Rafael grunted with the extra effort it took to move inside her. He pushed deep and rammed against the spot pulsating as rapidly as her heart.

Hailey half moaned, half howled at the onslaught, losing control of her throat and the continuous stream of ecstasy erupting through her lips as it burst open the dam that had been welling at her center.

It felt like a star exploding under water. Fragments shot off in all directions in a wave of liquid fire, then drained from her thighs. She felt herself washed away in the moment, satiated and spent. Hailey sagged over the earth, head no longer lifted, but lolling over the grass, regaining her breath as she relished her long-overdue climax.

Her release was followed by Rafael's, filling her once more with warm spurts that flooded her womb. The alpha's body jerked above hers, releasing more seed than she could hold. He spilled down her thighs. Without the moon at its fullest, it didn't matter how much got away.

As though sensing her thoughts, Rafael pulled out and away from her. His hooded gaze turned to rounded eyes that stared down in horror and anguish. Something cold washed over his features, dousing Hailey in its wake.

"That," he growled, "can never happen again."

He stormed off toward the moonlit lake, leaving behind words that blistered her heart.

The bliss she had felt turned to outrage. Hailey had thought that if they ever coupled in human form, their relationship would strengthen, but she had been terribly wrong. Rafael would never change his mind. At that moment, she finally understood that he would rather be miserable alone than happy with her.

She scrambled to her feet. Byron's head popped up. He met her eyes and whined.

"Quiet." She didn't mean to snap. "Stay," she added before taking her first step away from the warmth of the fire to follow Rafael to the lake.

She wasn't going to lie there soaked in his scent. She needed to rinse off too. The wretch would just have to deal with her company while they shared the lake. But not for long.

WHAT HAD BEEN a crystalline blue lake during the day now looked like a black hole leading to eternal damnation. Rafael headed straight for it, cussing in both Spanish and English with every step he took.

He had gone and done it—let down his damn guard. If it had been a random female, it would not have mattered, but he had promised himself he wouldn't use Hailey that way. That she had initiated the coupling made no difference. He had eagerly participated and was still awash in the lingering satisfaction of flipping her around and taking her fierce and fast against the earth.

And now she would expect him to claim her.

It wasn't too late to avoid that cursed fate. Thank the moon he didn't have to worry about any of his seed bearing fruit.

But that didn't mean he was free and clear. Already he had become too attached to the pureblooded beauty. He had known it was a terrible idea and now this . . . it was a catastrophe. They would have to part ways. That was always the plan, but Rafael needed to remind himself of that fact as many times as it took to drill through his skull.

He wouldn't leave her and her friends while they were so far from their familiar grounds. What to do then? Turn around after the full moon? Spend the winter together and lead them back in the spring?

While he pondered ankle deep in water cool enough to sting, Hailey stepped into the lake. Rafael kept her in his peripheral vision, not trusting himself to stay away if he saw her naked and glistening with sweat from their exertions.

"You should not have followed me," Rafael grumbled. "I am in no mood for company right now."

"I did not follow you. I came here to rinse you off of me." The bite in her tone made his head jerk.

She strode past him, making a brave show of sinking deeper into the bone-chilling depths without pause until submerged to her neck. The water around Hailey rippled as she rubbed her arms over her skin.

Rafael folded his arms, keeping his distance in case this was some ploy to get him to wade in with her, after which she would launch herself into his arms and ride his cock beneath the water. As alluring as the prospect was, he had to keep his ground before they ended up making babies beneath the full moon.

Hailey didn't stay in the icy reservoir for long. Her arms sluiced angrily with each stride she took back to shore. With the water no longer covering her, she pressed one arm over her breasts and held her other hand over her pussy.

Rafael snorted at the ridiculousness of her covering herself after they had just rutted.

Hailey glared at him.

"I meant what I said. We can't do that again," Rafael said. "Not that I didn't enjoy myself, but—"

"I can't do this anymore," Hailey interrupted. Rafael's brows drew together. Hailey avoided making eye contact, instead looking past him to the campfire. "I thought that I could settle for friendship, but I can't."

The temperature felt as though it had dropped twenty degrees. Anguish shivered in Rafael's spine, but he forced every muscle in his body to turn to stone.

"What do you mean?" he asked in a low voice as cool as the lake.

"I think we should part ways tomorrow." Hailey met his eyes, her gaze piercing. "You can wait out the full moon here while my friends and I put distance between us."

Rafael stiffened. "You don't know where you're going."

Unblinking eyes stared back at him. Hailey folded her arms, covering her breasts in a tight embrace. "I don't know where I'm going, but I can find my way home."

"So, you're going home? Back to Kamari, I suppose." It was impossible to mask the bitterness from his voice.

"No," Hailey said. "I like it out here. There's still so much to explore."

Rafael nodded, but instead of relief, his jaw tightened with worry and something else he did not want to think about. He wanted to continue exploring the world with her, but to do so, he would have to claim her. Hailey was right. It wasn't fair. There were too many feelings between them, growing stronger every day. If he could never claim her, then he had to let her go. Delaying their separation would only make it more painful. Ironic, when the whole point had been to avoid this kind of turmoil.

Rafael nodded. "Tomorrow we go our separate ways."

The look of disappointment in Hailey's eyes was one Rafael feared would haunt him in the lonely days and nights to come. She headed back to the fire, dragging his gaze with her. It would be one of his last opportunities to commit her lean, supple legs, graceful curves, and slender arms to memory. Water droplets rolled down her back into the crevice of her lovely cheeks. He would have loved a chance to grab hold of that bottom and take her from behind, but that was never happening. The coupling should have never occurred in any position or form. She had felt too good on his cock. A perfect fit, if such a thing was possible. Now she was walking out of his life, washed clean of him in every sense, dripping with the last of the lake water that slipped free of her skin.

Rafael's nostrils flared. Claws pricked at the tips of his fingers and his heart surged inside his chest, racing in a feeble attempt to catch up to Hailey while his legs remained stubbornly locked in place.

Every instinct howled to go after the female and claim her as his own. Rafael had to remind himself why he could not do that. He called the horror of that long-ago day to the forefront of his memories. It had been carefully stored and carried with him throughout the years, trapped inside his mind as merciless as that steel trap his mother had stepped into.

Hoofbeats thundered inside his head. Rather than hide from it, he ran toward the memory the same way he had rushed to his mother.

"Por favor, Rafael. Por dios. Déjame y vete. Rafael. ¡Vete!"

He never had a chance to see her with his human eyes. Over the years, he had pieced together an image of a dark-haired goddess who sacrificed herself for love.

When Rafael would not leave, she looked away from him, long, dark hair whipping around her shoulders as she searched the area. She looked up and stilled for a brief moment.

The ground shook harder.

Pound. Pound. Pound.

Stark terror filled his mother's eyes. Dragging the horrid steel trap with her and dripping blood, she scooped Rafael into her arms. He gave a startled yip, but that was all. This figure was foreign, but familiar. He trusted her completely. He wanted to lick away her wounds and burrow into that warm space against her chest.

His mother, however, was running out of time. She could not spare a quick hug or rub of her cheek against his head. Wrist shackled she used her arms to fling Rafael into the air. Shock overtook him. He had trusted the woman, and she had tossed him away. Fear gripped him next as he free fell, his tiny legs kicking to find purchase. Then he landed on something solid above ground—some kind of platform in the trees, surrounded by a low wooden wall covered in twigs and leaves.

Rafael scampered around the edges looking for a way out. There was one opening, but he stopped short, looking at a distance too far to jump. A sad whimper trembled off his lips. Below him, his mother hobbled away in her wolf form. It was as though he had imagined the female figure with her silken hair and strange sounds.

Eager shouts cut off his next cry. These sounds were deep and rough with no trace of compassion.

His mother lifted her head and issued a warning howl to any wolves within hearing distance. Rafael hunched down in fear, peering over the ledge in fright.

Thunder rolled into view in the form of three horses. He had seen their species roaming wild before, but never in this manner with tall, broad figures atop them. Dust billowed in clouds around the horses' hooves. Gleeful smiles stretched over the men's leathery faces. Their dark eyes were full of ill intent.

Rafael's mother erupted. Her snarls were deafening; her bared fangs were the nightmare of foes. In spite of the trap, Mother made lunges at the group—ears flat against her head. The horses shied away and whinnied in terror. Rafael had never seen her so fierce.

The men patted the necks of their mounts, speaking in coaxing tones before communicating with each other. The three brutes reached for coils of rope at their sides. They tossed the rope into the air. The frayed strands spun, whirling above their heads, up high where Rafael stood frozen, watching in confusion. Then they threw the rope, with swinging arms, directly at his mother, who snarled in fury.

Rafael did not know then what was happening. He knew it was something horrible. Later, he pieced it together with more clarity.

Those bastards lassoed his mother's neck, tightened their nooses, then, fists tight around the ends of their ropes, kicked their mounts into a gallop. They took off in opposite directions with his mother in the center of their trap. In this cowardly manner, they killed her in the most horrific way.

Rafael's heart broke the moment his mother's head was torn off her body. He would have cried and kept crying if he had not heard her voice inside his head, calm and loving, this time without worry or urgency, only reassurance and comfort.

«Silencio, mi amor. Debes esperar hasta que se vayan. Mantente en silencio. Estás a salvo.»

He thought he felt hands holding him back and turned, hoping to see that the woman had leaped from the wolf's body to land alongside him on the platform above. There was nothing to see, and yet he was not alone.

The next time he looked below, the men and their horses were gone. His mother had disappeared with them.

It was to be part one of his parents' tragic end. Soon after, those same men would use his mother's body as bait to catch his father.

Once Rafael was older and able to shift, he realized the reason his mother had shifted back to her wolf form to face her attackers. They would have known what she was if they had come upon her naked female form. No begging would have saved her. The men would have raped her, then killed her so she would not return for vengeance.

Rather than go out with whimpering cries, she had chosen to race for death's door in a rage that echoed across the land long after those monsters ripped her apart.

Rafael could not risk going through that kind of loss again. The pain of it had killed his father as surely as the trap laid out beside his dead mate's body. Father had walked into it willingly.

If not for Diego, Rafael would have lost the will to live. But he would not abandon his brother the way their father had. They had left that awful place and kept on the move ever since—until Diego found a home in Wolf Hollow.

Rafael would never stop running.

And he would never claim a mate. Because if anything were to happen to Hailey, it would be the death of him.

chapter twenty

HER SHIVERING BODY woke Hailey from sleep at dawn. The fire had burned out as surely as the hope in her heart that Rafael would change his mind and claim her as his mate. During their brief time together in the wild, he had come to mean so much more to her than merely a pureblooded male of opportune age.

She enjoyed his company, the warm and deep timbre of his voice, the sound of his laughter, the sight of his smile, the way the light reflected off his brown eyes, and the scruff on his face. His muscles were as beautifully sculpted as the towering mountain ranges they had crossed. She appreciated the way he handled the pack. Would she be able to lead them with as much skill?

She would do her very best. Hailey was still part wolf and pureblood. Survival instincts were passed down and born into her, as much a part of her as her fingers and toes—claws and fangs.

She could do this. She wouldn't have to go about it alone . . . unlike Rafael. Maybe she would have felt bad for him if he wasn't choosing solitude for himself.

Another shiver racked her body. She felt too forlorn to put the effort into starting another fire. Everyone else was cuddled up in fur form, including Layla and Hudson, who had returned while Hailey was asleep, and Rafael. The last thing she wanted was to shift and end up snuggled up to the brute who acted as if claiming her would signal the end of not only civilization, but the world.

She scowled at him in his warm fur.

Hailey curled into a tight ball, wrapping her arms around her knees. She shut her eyes, trying to close out the cold, but keeping still did her no favors. The slow, soft pad of paws moved toward her right before a furry figure nestled beside her—Rafael lending his warmth as though to apologize for his human half. Hailey kept her eyelids closed tight, holding in the tears. Eventually, she fell back asleep.

Byron was the first to rise and, thankfully, got the fire going to ward off the morning chill. When Hailey sat up, he nodded a silent greeting at her and she nodded back. She scooted away from Rafael's wolf, getting as close to the fire as she dared. Knees pressed into her chest, she let the heat of the flames warm her skin.

One by one, the others shifted. They went into the woods to relieve themselves, taking turns before returning to the fire.

Hailey kept her attention on anything and anyone who wasn't Rafael, as though they had already parted ways.

"We're going to need to hunt again," Byron said.

"Yes, please." Layla patted her flat stomach.

Violet flashed her a sly smile and raised her eyebrows.

190

Skeet sat cross-legged in front of the fire, ripping pieces of grass out of the ground and throwing them into the flames absently. He looked in Rafael's direction. "How did you and your brother take down game with only two of you?"

"We managed."

The sound of his voice made Hailey's jaw tighten. "Will you be able to manage alone?"

She had not meant to ask the question aloud, but there it was. Despite everything, she was still worried about him. At least she had been able to keep her tone neutral.

"Yes." Rafael's eyes locked on hers.

The breath left her lungs for the length of that shared look. Hailey returned her attention to the fire.

"Alone? That's not for a while, right?" Violet asked. When neither Rafael nor Hailey responded, she raised her voice. "Right?"

Hailey looked at Rafael, then chided herself for her habit of turning to him for decisions. Their partnership was over. It was time for her to lead her pack. Squaring her shoulders, she pushed off the ground to address the group. Standing above them fueled her resolve.

"We always knew Rafael's time with us would be temporary, and I'm grateful for all that he has shown us in our short time together. Rafael is not interested in joining our pack long-term. The full moon presents an opportunity for him to remain behind in human form while we get out of range to keep our wolves apart. First, we'll hunt and make sure Rafael fills up on enough meat to tide him over while he's on two feet."

Toes digging into the cool, moist earth, Hailey braced herself for some kind of protest from the group. When they nodded their understanding, a breath puffed out of her like a cloud sailing through blue sky. Her friends were unfailing. She had their loyalty and support. It meant everything to her. She would not let them down.

"Now's as good a time as any to track down a meal," Byron said, lifting himself off the ground.

Hailey flashed him an appreciative smile.

"I could eat," Layla said, following his lead.

"Me too," Hudson said.

Soon, they were all standing–everyone except for Rafael. He smiled with amusement and something bordering on acceptance. Hailey's lips twitched at the humor of her group standing to go on a hunt when they would need to crouch right back down to the ground to shift. But that wasn't what this moment was about. It was about solidarity. An agreement. A pact made between her and her remaining group members.

Looking each one of them in the eyes, Hailey nodded. "Let's see what kind of game these woods have to offer."

As Hailey LED her pack up the next summit, a blue dusk began to haze across the wilderness.

She had lived in a natural setting her entire life, and yet she felt this journey had allowed her to step outside for the first time in decades. Everything felt new yet familiar. She knew these woods. They had been her home before, and she would make them so again.

Their bellies were full after gorging on another elk they had taken down as a team. It had been late afternoon when Hailey and her pack said their final goodbyes to Rafael. He had wished her luck. She had replied, "May Mother Moon watch over you." And that was that.

No change of heart on Rafael's part. No hugs. And certainly no tears.

Hailey had fought the urge to run from him as fast as her legs would carry her. She had to think about her whole pack and set a steady pace. Luckily, her wolf was able to leave Rafael behind. She wasn't sure how cooperative her animal would have been if Rafael had been in fur when the hour of departure was upon them.

The landscape narrowed, funneling down to an earthen pass that yawned open, revealing a river, forest, lakes and expanding mountain ridges in the distance.

Hailey lifted her head and howled. Her pack mates echoed her howl. They stood still, listening for an answering call. Her ears twitched as she stood on the edge of the world waiting to hear from Rafael, but only the hoot of a concealed owl answered her.

They made their way down the slope and into the gathering shadows. Moonlight glowed over pine needles and lit a beaten path that threaded through the forest. Ever alert, Hailey stopped when they reached pools of reflective water, clear enough to see straight down to the stones layered below the shallows. After everyone had a drink, she led them out of the forest and into a boulder field.

This was where they would spend the night.

Byron selected a smooth, flat rock to lie on, his furry

front leg dangling over the edge. Skeet sniffed around, peeing on select boulders before settling on a spot. Violet plopped down several feet away from her cousin, her head up watching the rest of their movements. When Layla and Hudson nestled together in a patch of moss, Hailey's back and tail sagged. It felt as though she was missing a limb and could not hold herself as tall as she once had.

Not caring where she settled in, so long as it was dry and the terrain was pliant, she curled in with a heavy sigh. Each new sight and discovery felt dull without Rafael there to experience it alongside her.

She rested her muzzle over her front paws, blinking sadly at the imposing, inanimate shapes of the boulders and the shadows they cast underneath the nearly full moon.

After everyone had settled in, Violet got up and padded over. She shifted beside Hailey then nudged her side gently with her hand. Waiting until Hailey had made the transformation, Violet smiled at her with concern. Her shoulders and eyebrows squeezed upward. "Hey, what happened with Rafael?" her friend whispered.

Hailey cast her gaze out over the terrain and saw that the rest of the pack kept their heads down, conserving their energy.

"Nothing," Hailey answered. "He said from the start that we would part ways. I decided it would be wiser to cut ties sooner rather than later."

Violet wrinkled her nose and pursed her lips. She leaned in closer, locking eyes with Hailey. "But Byron and I heard the two of you together last night. I thought maybe he had come around to claiming you."

Hailey blinked several times. She had heard Byron's whimper of concern, but had not been aware, until this moment, that Violet had also heard them.

"That changed nothing—not for him," Hailey said.

A huff of disgust blew past Violet's lips. "I don't understand that male at all. Seriously, what's wrong with him?" Hailey shook her head. Huffing again, Violet said, "Well, screw Rafael. His loss. The biggest. He'll never find a mate as remarkable as you."

"That's the whole point. He doesn't want a mate . . . ever."

"Well, he's a moron."

An unexpected laugh burst out of Hailey. She covered her mouth and glanced at the wolves still sleeping soundly.

"Yes," Haley said. "An obstinate wretch."

"We don't need him."

"No, we don't."

"*You* don't need him." An intense glow filled Violet's eyes.

Hailey stilled, unable to agree.

"Hailey." Violet paused after her name. "You don't need that mongrel. You've got us—your loyal friends and family. Your pack."

Slowly, Hailey nodded. "I know, and I love you all. Now let's switch forms before we freeze our asses off on this mountain pass."

T HEY LEFT EARLY the next morning. Hailey set a steady pace, leaving the mountains behind and entering a vast expanse of woods. Upon picking up the scent of elk, their pack took up the trail in pursuit of their prey. Their steps slowed as they caught up to the herd.

Hailey and her friends were already skilled hunters. They prowled silently from behind, following the herd's progression through the forest step by step as the sun moved across the sky. It wasn't until the elk entered a prairie that their pack made their move.

Hailey led the charge, sprinting through long strands of grass that whipped at her flanks. Warm afternoon air blew over her fur with each spring of her paws. One of the elk was noticeably injured. He limped behind as the wolves closed in. The rest of the herd shot off into the woods without a backward glance. Knowing he would never make it, the elk stopped running, lowered his head, and charged Hudson with his antlers. Hudson jumped away while Byron snapped his jaw near the elk's already wounded hind leg. The animal kicked out with his hooves. Byron dodged the blow and snarled viciously.

While the elk was distracted by the males, Layla lunged at its side, bringing the animal down. They attacked all together, ensuring their prey didn't rise back up. The elk thrashed and kicked dangerously close to their heads, but he never got a chance to turn over.

Fangs that had been snarling now ripped and tore through its tough hide to get to its meat. The animal flopped around briefly, like a fish out of water, before going still.

Hailey chewed hungrily. It was the most meat she had ever eaten in such a short period of time, but they were covering great distances that made hunger an ever-present beast gnawing at their bellies.

After feasting, they took a brief nap.

Hailey led the pack southward. The prairie disappeared into forest. Woods became open plains. In the distance, she saw a butte jutting from the open terrain surrounding it like a dried-up moat. She headed for it with a slow gait, belying the heavy meal.

Nettle grew tall and thick among the ungainly vegetation filling in the space between trees and boulders. They passed wildflowers in purples, pinks, and yellows. Whorls of red tubular flowers boiled with bees at work beneath the last blazes of sunlight.

Hailey scanned the open expanse, sniffed the air, and flicked her tail as she listened. A vast emptiness filled her senses. Resuming their journey across the land, they trotted past the bones of a large bird that had been picked clean. Buzzards circled overhead, then disappeared as though they had been an illusion that vanished with the setting sun, which turned red as it dropped to the line of the horizon, spilling color across the sky like blood diluting in water.

Hailey picked up the pace. They reached the butte at last light, scurrying up to the flattened plateau at twilight. From that vantage, they could see out across the land for miles into the distance.

The females shifted into their human forms while the male wolves kept guard. Hailey stared into the pale sky, watching it turn blue—the shade darkening by degrees. Tonight, the full moon outshone the stars, stealing their luster and washing them away with its far-reaching beams of light.

Hailey felt herself opening beneath those mystical rays, like the pink, red, and white cosmos they had passed bursting into bloom at the touch of the sun.

As the temperature dropped around her, warmth radiated from her thighs, building into an inferno of need.

No. No. No.

Her heat couldn't be returning so quickly. Not now. Taking in steadying breaths, she reminded herself that it wasn't her heat. She was in human form, not wolf. This was the ache of longing, and she felt just as powerless to prevent the breach over her body as she did when experiencing her wolf's heat cycle. She could no more stop her lungs from expanding with breath, or her heart from its steady beat.

As the full moon reached its apex early in the evening, Hailey's mind wandered to Rafael. Was he thinking about her at this same moment under a shared moon? Did he regret not chasing after her as she had hoped?

Probably not. He was too stubborn, too wretched, too much of an obstinate beast to choose love over loneliness.

As she released a heavy sigh, her friends scooted closer, sandwiching Hailey atop a swath of grass that dipped into a shallow bowl protected from the wind. It was to be their bed for the night. For now, the three of them were content to take in the view of the wilderness they had covered as it dimmed and shadowed beneath the moon.

Violet stretched her arms behind her and leaned back, tilting her head. Her body arched, breasts lifted for the moon's gaze.

"Look at that big, beautiful moon." Violet sighed as though it was a male wolf she could never reach.

"Kinda makes you want to howl, doesn't it?" Layla chuckled.

Lowering her head, Violet shot her friend a wry grin. "Speaking of howling, what's the deal with you and Hudson? Have you found your mate?"

Layla glanced at the spot where they had last seen the males before they slunk off to sniff around and mark the area. She shrugged one bare shoulder. "Nah, we're just fooling around." Layla ran her hands through her hair. "Beggars can't be choosers."

Violet stared at her wide-eyed for several beats before bursting into laughter. "You're terrible. Hailey, shove her for me, will you?"

Smiling, Hailey bumped her shoulder against Layla's. Her friend rubbed it in mock indignation.

"He's not that bad," Violet said.

"Oh, he's not bad at all." Layla winked. "I'm just saying there isn't much of a choice."

"At least you get a—" Violet's next words were cut off by a distant howl.

Hailey sat at attention, absorbing that faraway howl as though it was the first splatter of raindrops after months of drought. She jumped to her feet, wanting to holler across the earth.

Here! I'm up here, Rafael.

He had changed his mind and chased after her. They would be together again and this time it would be forever until they left this world for the next.

Hope was a sticky web, wrapping itself around her heart before a spider jumped on and injected it with venom.

The netting inside her head untangled during the second howl that channeled through her ears and echoed inside her aching chest.

Not Rafael. Not any wolf she had met before.

Answering howls burst off the butte from the throats of their male pack mates.

Hailey's shoulders slumped. She sat back down and wrapped her hands around the back of her neck, elbows locked, arms pressed over her breasts.

"That wasn't Rafael, was it?" Violet asked.

"No."

"Then who is out there? Another pack? A lone wolf?"

"That," Hailey said, "is a full-blooded wild wolf."

"Not shifter?" Layla asked.

"He's more pure than I will ever be." Hailey peered into the dark with a wondering gaze. Of course they existed and likely thrived in the wilderness. But Hailey had never seen a true wolf. They didn't have any need for or interest in shifter packs and tribes, other than to avoid them the same way they would steer clear of humans.

Violet nudged her in the side with her elbow. "*He*?" She raised her brows.

Layla snickered. "Someone's feeling desperate."

Violet made a face at Layla, then put her hands on her hips. "You said it yourself, slim pickings."

"He can't shift."

Violet fluffed out her long curls. "So, we do it doggy style. My animal's not opposed."

"Oh, you're bad. What if he wants you as his mate afterwards?"

Violet grimaced. "Yeah, that would be a problem."

"And cruel," Hailey tossed in.

"Fine," Violet grumbled. "I'll stay away from wild wolves."

They settled back into the grass, listening for a call that had gone as silent as the stars.

"Maybe our guys scared him off," Layla said. "Don't take it personally, V."

"Shut up." Violet laughed.

Hailey smiled and it felt good. She tried to wrap the warm feeling of friendship around her and let it chase away some of the gloom seeping into her heart. Byron padded into view, making his way to Hailey and stopping a foot away, sitting on his haunches. Hailey reached over and scratched him behind his ears. His tail thumped once over the ground. Then he stood and walked back out of view.

Layla and Violet watched, not uttering a word until he was out of sight.

"What was that about?" Layla asked.

Hailey looked in the direction Byron had gone and smiled. "Byron just wanted to check on us before we go to sleep."

"You mean check on *you*," Layla enunciated.

Her suggestion breezed over Hailey without the slightest tingle or flush of her cheeks. Violet twisted her lips to the side, studying Hailey's face.

"The two of you made a good couple. Would you ever consider claiming Byron as your mate?"

"What if it was between Kamari and Byron?" Layla asked. She lifted her knees and pressed her elbows into them, her hands cupping her cheeks as she peered at Hailey.

"Kamari's an alpha," Violet said.

"But Byron's younger and hotter . . . and he's here."

"Hmm." Violet rubbed her bottom lip. "Maybe it's a question of where, not who. Does Hailey want to eventually return to Glenn Meadows, or continue on this path with our new pack?"

"I would like to live closer to home—eventually," Layla said.

"I wasn't asking you."

"Doesn't mean I don't have an opinion. Don't you want to see your family again?"

"Eventually," Violet said.

Hailey's friends looked at her and raised their brows.

"I would like to see my family again too," she said. "I don't know about Byron or Kamari. I need time to heal." Heal her broken heart.

"Cheer up. Maybe we'll come across another lone wild wolf." Layla waggled her brows.

Violet smacked her playfully on the shoulder. "Oh my gosh, you're the worst."

Layla returned her friend's smack. "Maybe that's how purebloods were first created."

Climbing into the grassy bowl, Hailey pressed against her friends to share their body heat. With a last glance at the moonlit sky, she wondered the same thing.

Had an urban wolf shifter wandered into the wilderness long ago and mated with a wild wolf? Was it a female or male who crossed that first boundary, creating a new breed of wolf? Then after, had more urban shifters done the same? Had their offspring bred with the offspring of another wild and urban wolf to create the first purebloods?

Maybe it went back even further in time before the rise of civilization to a shifter among the first humans to inhabit lands roamed by wolves.

With her eyes closed, Hailey's mind continued to reach out for answers. Unlike humans, her kind had never recorded written histories. They had always kept their species hidden from those who would misuse or hunt them.

Her mind created its own version of the past as she faded into the night. She saw the land, as wild and vast as the territories they had traversed. Stared back at a time when modern technology and cities did not exist.

The natives, her parents had told them, once lived off the land as they did. They likely had shifters among them, perhaps lived among them harmoniously. Maybe it was one of their ancestors who had left the tribe to mate with a wild wolf.

Pulled into a tumultuous slumber, Hailey dreamed of a pale-skinned woman aboard one of the floating vessels her elders spoke of from the old world.

Waves surged up as high as mountain peaks while thunder crashed overhead. The boat lifted and fell, tipping far enough to dip into the ocean as though drinking from the sea. Screams filled the night. Lightning flashed and Hailey saw herself standing on the deck, gripping the railing, her dress and blonde hair drenched.

The next flash struck the mast and lit it on fire. A rolling wave seemed to throw the boat right out of the ocean. Hailey's knuckles turned white. When the boat landed, a loud crack split sea and sky. It was a terrifying sound, more so because it had not thundered from above. She looked down at her buckled silk-and-leather shoes, half expecting to see the deck broken apart.

Another wave rushed in as she was looking at her feet. Her scream was drowned beneath the icy slap of saltwater, chilling her to the bone. The beastly storm nearly dragged her into its depths.

"We're going down!" a male voice shrieked.

Hailey saw no one. She could hear them yelling, cursing, and screaming, but the world was blurry. Another glance down revealed rising water covering her buckled shoes, inching its way up her stockinged legs.

With one hand holding tight to the railing, she yanked off her shoes, then snagged her nails over the stockings and pulled, freeing herself from her garters next. The dress was too tight. She couldn't reach the fastenings in back.

Terror gripped her tighter than any bodice as she let go of the railing entirely. Amid the shouts and screams, she begged the ungodly creature inside her to come to her aid. Save her. She promised never to shut that part of herself out again.

There was no answer. She reached around her back and grasped with numb fingers that slipped over the buttons. Maybe she had to be fully naked for the beast to heed her. Unable to free herself from the constraints, she bellowed in fear and frustration.

"Please!" she screamed over the rumbling sky.

She ripped at her drenched skirt and petticoats, hands shaking with cold as she tried to tear it apart. With another desperate wail, she fell to her knees and attempted to

ANIMAL ATTRACTION

work the dress over her head.

Where was the furry beast when she needed it? This wasn't only about her survival. Surely some instinct would come out to save them both. The boat lurched, sending her rolling across the deck, luckily inward.

Her next scream turned into a snarl. She clawed her way out of the fabric smothering her. A monstrous surge tossed her yelping into the waves. Disoriented and drowning. In a panic, all four legs kicked to the surface above. Her muzzle lifted above the crashing waves, where wind howled and thunder boomed.

The boat capsized beneath the next punishing crest. Lightning seemed to reflect off the jagged waves.

The wolf swam, instinctively orienting herself toward the closest land mass. She was not a creature of the ocean and wanted to escape this churning nightmare as swiftly as her legs would carry her. But there was no running through water, only menacing swells trying to drive her into the bottomless depths. Merciless waves crested, the sea foaming at the mouth.

HAILEY AWOKE IN a cold sweat, nearly choking on the water she imagined clogging her throat. Blinking rapidly, she calmed her breathing and rubbed at her damp hairline.

She managed to return to sleep, but it was as though the dream was waiting to resume, like an unfinished memory. Like a past life rediscovered.

205

chapter twenty-one

TINY LEGS CREPT over Rafael's body where he lay buried beneath leaves, moss, and twigs. He didn't want to attract any unwanted visitors with a nightly fire. Neither did he wish to expose himself to the elements or predators. He kept his hands clasped around his genitals. Bugs had no business crawling over his junk. The thing creeping down his back made him twitch. He wasn't getting any sleep, but it wasn't as though he could trek naked in the dark.

At least he had made it through the full moon.

To be safe, he would spend the next couple days on foot. Hailey had told him she planned to head southeast, which meant he needed to go northwest . . . except they had come from that direction and Rafael did not feel inclined to backtrack.

Maybe he should go north and spend his winter in the snow. Chill the fuck out.

His muscles tensed as the creepy, crawly thing approached his ass. He reached one hand around and flicked it, rustling the leaves slightly. While it was no bed of roses, he had slept in worse conditions. Creepers and critters were manageable. It was humans and vulhena he had to watch out for.

Rafael didn't expect to see either out here, far from the crumbling cities and suburbs. His encounters with the unnatural hybrid creatures were thankfully rare. In their travels, he and Diego had noticed that vulhena appeared to keep to the outskirts of the cities still inhibited by the last surviving scum of humanity. It was, in his opinion, most likely why the Wolf Hollow pack had problems with the creatures.

The hollow wasn't deep enough in the wilds, but they liked its proximity for gathering supplies from the suburbs. Yet another reason Rafael had never wanted to settle down with a pack that had turned tribal. At least he knew Diego could take care of himself. His brother was no longer the forlorn little pup whimpering when their father threw rocks at them and raised his hand to strike if they got too close.

It was their father who had found Rafael in the hunters' hideout in the trees. He had arrived frantic on four legs, sniffing the ground like he intended to inhale every last speck of sand. When Rafael had cried in relief, his father lifted his muzzle, a flicker of hope in those golden eyes, hope that faded when he saw no sign of his beloved on the platform with his son.

For the second time that forsaken day, Rafael witnessed the strange transformation of beast changing into something different. The sight was not comforting as it had been with his mother. The man crouched over the earth radiated fury and violence. His fingers dug into the bloody earth left behind. Sharp eyes scanned the hoof prints beaten into the ground. The grooves in his face were like deadly crevices, and his frown snuffed out all trace of joy.

Rafael found himself cowering and backing away as this stranger stood and came toward him. He reminded him too much of the hardened men who had come by earlier. Rough hands shot up and grabbed Rafael. He cried out in alarm and the man smiled without warmth, nodding his head.

«*Muy bien niño. Debes temerme. Debes temer a todos   los hombres.*»

Rafael squirmed in his arms. The man, his father, reached a hand toward his head like he might stroke him. His hand hovered and shook above Rafael's small ears.

"*Debes ser fuerte, hijo mío. Tú y tu hermano. Tu madre quería que vivieras. Sobrevive por el bien de ella. Cuídense el uno al otro. Y aléjense de los humanos.*"

He understood that his father was giving him a command. The words did not matter. The warning was there. Any trace of compassion leached from his father's face and fingers as they tightened around Rafael and he stormed past dead trees. He gained speed, making Rafael bunch up in dread. The ground was still a long way down and moving fast as his father's legs pounded over the dusty earth. He didn't stop until he had reached the den. Diego was sniffing around and gave a startled yip when he saw them. Rafael was tossed to the ground; he rolled onto his feet.

"*Quedense! No me sigan.*" He pointed a finger at each of them, then at the ground.

Rafael and Diego stared up in confusion and fear.

Then their father got to the ground and shifted into wolf form. Diego began wagging his tail at once. He gave a bark of excitement and raced over, only to be snarled at. Tail between his legs, Diego whimpered and crouched over the ground.

When their father stalked away from the den, Diego followed, which meant Rafael had no choice but to trail him. He could not let his brother be captured by those brutes on horses who had killed their mother.

Noticing that they followed, Father turned and snarled. *Stay here. Don't follow me.*

When they continued pacing after him, he shifted into his human form, stood, and bellowed his words from before.

"Quedense! No me sigan."

He picked up a rock and threw it at Diego. The stone hit him in the face. An ear-splitting cry made the hairs on Rafael's back rise. He growled, showing his teeth at the man who now smiled.

"Muy bien, Rafael."

With a nod, he stalked off on two legs, heading back in the direction of the clearing where his beloved had been torn apart.

This time, Rafael made sure Diego did not follow.

Such memories were a plague on Rafael's soul, but they did the job of setting his resolve. The tiniest expression of kindness was enough to reel Diego in. Rafael always had to be the one on guard. He had been unable to prevent his brother from falling for Lacy's honey-coated smiles, but at least she didn't intend him any harm.

The only thing left to protect was Rafael's heart.

At first light, he pushed free of his earthen blanket. Leaves fell from his body as though he were a tree shedding his covering in fall.

Rafael brushed off the debris, peed on a tree, then stretched before making his way to the lake. He rinsed off in the icy water, feeling awake and ready to leave this spot.

He headed eastward the way he had seen Hailey and her pack go. Starting on the same route was all he intended. Hailey meant to steadily drop down to the south as her pack progressed eastward. Rafael would keep to the east, then head up north.

They were long gone, anyway. Still, the more distance between them, the better for his wolf when he shifted.

Even without claws or tools, Rafael was a seasoned hunter. At midday, he came across a stream in the forest with foot-sized fish flitting through water as clear as the air he breathed. When Rafael's shadow fell over them, they darted off. He lowered himself beside the gentle stream, dipped his arm in, and held it still.

With all the patience and time in the world, Rafael watched the water—not moving a muscle. Eventually, the fish returned. Unblinking, he followed their gliding movements near his submerged hand that had settled like a clamshell over the sandy bottom.

Several fish came close. Breath steady, Rafael let them pass on. He waited for the right moment when a fish passed directly over his open palm. In a blur of motion, Rafael scooped it out of the water and tossed it onto land. The fish flopped frantically in the dirt as Rafael lifted a stone as large as his catch and brought it down in a killing blow.

Dropping the stone, Rafael gave a loud whoop that echoed across the forest. Grinning, he glanced back at the stream, half expecting to see Diego on his haunches chuckling. But the boulders were his only companions and the steady trickle of spring water the only sound.

Rafael's shoulders drooped. He wished Hailey and her friends were still with him. Wished she had gotten to see this neat trick of his.

"Ah, well," he said aloud. "A fish is a fish." A fine meal, even if no one had been around to see him catch it with his bare hands.

The trouble was, he now had to make a fire. It was that or shift. Rafael wanted to give Hailey another day to be well and truly gone from his life. Making a fire just to cook one fish felt like a colossal waste of time and effort. It wasn't one of his top skills, since he'd never had much need of it, keeping to wolf form while traveling and enjoying the fires of packs he and Diego made friends with along the way.

With a hefty sigh, Rafael searched for a flat piece of wood, then gathered small twigs and dry bits of grass. It took nearly as much time and effort as catching the fish, but the first sparks were like the first passes of the fish nearing his arm. Determination made him rub the stick against his fire board faster. Once he had a shining ember, he deposited it carefully into the nest of tinder he had built and blew gently. It caught in a gratifying leap of flame. Rafael gave another whoop as he added more sticks to the blaze.

He skewered the fish and held it over the fire, inhaling

the mouth-watering aroma as it sizzled. When it was cooked through but not overdone, Rafael scraped it onto the flattest rock he could find and used a piece of flint he had grabbed by the stream to cut into his meal. He removed the meat off the bones with his fingers, licking them clean with each bite he fed into his mouth.

After he had picked the bones clean, he dropped the large stone he'd used to finish off the fish into the fire and kicked dirt inside until his hard-earned flames were no more. Rafael rinsed his fingers in the creek and bent forward to take in large gulps of fresh, crisp water.

The fish made themselves scarce.

He WAS STILL deep in the forest when he came across a shallow cave embedded in a granite outcrop. It was just large enough for two, plenty of space for him to settle in come dark.

Rafael did a sweep of the area, in the process startling a doe with two young bucks. They dashed out of the brush and ran in rapid hops over the terrain before disappearing from sight.

"You're lucky I'm not in my wolf skin," Rafael called after them.

A pinecone landed on his head and bounced off. He looked up, half expecting to see a squirrel sticking out its tongue, but it was gravity, not a tree rat chucking the cone at him. Rafael kicked it away. He picked up a gray-and-white feather, lightly rubbing a thumb over the rough upper vanes. Near the quill, the vanes turned to downy fluff, as soft and weightless as a cloud.

He would have presented it to Hailey if she were still around—handed it over like a damn flower for her to hold on to before they shifted and took off on the next leg of their adventure.

Rafael released the quill and watched the feather float to the ground before returning to his shelter to perch on a rock outside the opening and await dusk, listening to the crickets prelude the owls. A soft breeze murmured in the pines. Rafael folded his arms over his chest. He prized his independence, but this was a bit over the edge. Crickets, owls, and wind for company . . . there was nothing engaging to be exchanged.

Perhaps it would not be Hailey's beauty, friendly nature, or heat to break him. Maybe it would be the damn wind that convinced him to run after her.

He burst into laughter, slapping his knee.

"A wretch, indeed," he said aloud. "Wretchedly alone."

He glanced behind him into the cozy cavern and laughed harder as his head filled with delightful memories of making love to the determined pureblood. Her warm, tight heat had been bliss against his cock. He could be buried inside her, coupling all through the dark night in their little cave for two, instead of talking to himself.

Hands pressed to his head, he sighed. He would have been a fool to stay with her. And yet he was a fool to have let her leave.

Hopeless wretch.

She was gone now, and a good thing too, because no matter what he felt for Hailey, it did not change his resolve to avoid a mate claim and becoming a father. He treated the path of bonding as he would one leading to a city or a bear den. Nothing good could come from following it to the end. He wasn't like his brother—able to forgive, let go, and move on. Or maybe he was just a coward. Imagining Hailey stepping into a trap, being torn apart . . . he knew it wasn't something he would ever recover from. If he wasn't with her, he wouldn't have to worry about any number of horrors befalling her.

Instead, he crawled into the cave alone with no one to torment him other than the ghosts of his memories.

THE CAVE PROVIDED a secure, dark shelter in which to catch up on sleep. When Rafael roused himself, it was to light flooding the forest.

He emerged from the cave to face another day on the move, his thoughts keeping pace. This was the longest stretch Rafael had ever spent in his human form, and it felt as though it was driving him half mad. He wondered if it was harder on purebloods. Being born a wolf made him believe that form was his dominant half.

A clear sky greeted him, sunlight slanting across the pine trees. The morning was dry and dewless. Rafael left his shelter, pushing on and climbing the steeply forested terrain toward the next summit. He chose the path of least resistance, sometimes making tracks for long stretches. More often than not, he zigzagged his way up and up and up, leaving the pines in his wake as they fell back, unable to continue with him to those mighty heights.

ANIMAL ATTRACTION

A smooth peak snaked above the forest like a trail through the sky. He walked past boulder heaps and sparse scrub with little birds that took off in a flurry at his approach. This much closer to the sun, the heat made him drowsy. Sweat dripped from his body. His naturally tan skin was darkening every day he kept to this form.

Rafael walked all morning. A bit after midday, he picked his way down a gradual slope and searched for a stream. His ears picked up the melodic burble and whoosh of a river before he ever saw it. Following the sound, he traipsed through the woods until reaching the beautiful sight of a swift river. Resisting the urge to jump right in, Rafael walked along the water's edge until he found a narrow sandy spit against a shallow area of the water. He waded in and crouched, letting the current wash away the sweat and grime from his night in the cave and subsequent trek. Opening his mouth, he gulped water down, not bothering to scoop it up with his hands. Rafael splashed his face and scrubbed at the thick stubble bristling over his jawline, chin, and upper lip. Being in wolf form slowed the growth of his facial hair and that on his head—both of which he preferred to keep trimmed. That was about the only thing abandoned suburbs had been good for—a trim and a shave here and there. It wasn't as though he and his brother could travel with a blade when their wolves were always on the move.

His last trim had led him and Diego to Sasha's pack. They had been readying themselves for a shave and haircut in a deserted suburb when they heard the frantic howls. Three shifters from Wolf Hollow had been hunting down a rabid wolf that used to be a member of their pack. He had gotten away, at the time, and bit Sasha's mate before he did—luckily while Tabor was in human form. Tabor had been wounded, but not turned.

Rafael never dreamed that the invitation to spend time in Wolf Hollow would lead to his brother's domestication and to the introduction of an irresistible pureblooded female.

Last night, Hailey had haunted his dreams, riding him as she had before he screwed it all up with his stubborn commitment to bachelorhood. The only time he woke up was from the discomfort of finding himself as stiff as a stalactite. If Hailey had been there, he would have damned the consequences and mounted her on the spot.

All this solitude was giving him too much time to think. Rafael drank more water before stepping out of the river and backtracking through the woods the way he had come in. Boulders rested in dips at the bottom of the ridgeway. Small pebbles rolled down to join them every now and then, loosened by the parched earth.

Rafael found a patch of grass beside a slab of smooth granite. He sat and leaned against the stone, soaking in the heat it radiated and letting the sun finish drying him off. The position was comfortable enough to lull Rafael into dozing off.

He woke to the sound of large wings wafting closely overhead. Blinking and shielding his eyes, he took in the turkey vulture circling around for closer inspection as to whether Rafael was carrion to peck at.

Hell, no!

Rafael jumped up and shook his fist in the air. "Off

with you, scavenger!"

He narrowed his eyes on the ugly flying brute, watching it veer off and fly away, only dropping to his knees once it was out of sight. Enough of this tedious walkabout.

Time to let the wolf out.

chapter twenty-two

THE WORLD TURNED into a kaleidoscope of greens, blues, and browns that whirled by as Rafael raced across mountain passes, over hills, through woods, around boulder fields, and past enormous lakes that stretched on for miles. He leaped over streams and tore through fields.

He wasn't heading north. As soon as he picked up Hailey's scent, there was no other course for him other than the one leading to his female. The trail was faint at first. Rafael had to sniff hard in many places. Other times, he would find a clear path that allowed him to run for a long stretch. He picked up on the familiar odors of the other pack members, but there was only one that mattered to him.

The sun pressed down on his fur. It set. The moon and stars dotted the sky. Dawn came. Days passed. Rafael continued to run.

When hunger gnawed at his belly, he ignored it until it began weakening his pace. Only then did Rafael start sniffing harder for more immediate animal scents, putting his nose to work in search of something he could turn into a meal. Without the pack or a partner, he could not go after his preferred meat. Instead, he had to resort to smaller critters, preferably not too far off course.

As though delivered up by the earth, something moved—well, slithered—on the path ahead. The snake was light yellow with splotches of dark brown and orange circles covering its long, thick reptilian skin. This one looked well fed.

Hijo de puta.

On a menu of things to kill, snakes were somewhere near the bottom of his list. But it was right there in front of him, and Rafael was hungry.

¡Mierda!

Rafael slunk toward it warily. Sensing his movement, the snake coiled and made a rumbling sound deep in its throat that emerged like a raspy, roaring rattle when it exhaled. Fortunately, this was no rattlesnake, despite the similar, disconcerting sound. Rafael had stumbled on a nonvenomous bullsnake. Venom aside, the snake would still try to strike, wrap, and squeeze. Rafael's throat bobbed just thinking about his airways being constricted by coils of the slithering, scaled snake.

Hissing, the bullsnake faced him. Rafael kept his distance, weight on his front paws as he performed a fake-out, acting as though he would lunge. As expected, the snake shot forward as Rafael pushed back out of reach. He did this several more times, heart racing like he was running up a mountain the whole time.

They went back and forth, face to face. Its beady black-and-yellow eyes kept Rafael in its sights. A forked tongue protruded from scaly lips, mouth slightly open, head angled down in defense.

On the next lunge, the bullsnake uncoiled like rope unraveling to stretch across the ground. Rafael used that opportunity to streak around the snake and grab him by the tail.

Lightning quick, the snake whipped around like a fucking boomerang returning straight for Rafael. He released its tail and dashed out of the strike zone not a moment too soon.

Panting, Rafael kept a safe distance away while watching the snake and planning his next move.

Veering off the trail to go around the serpent was very tempting. Wasting hours hunting down a meal—or multiple meals, if the prey was small—was not appealing either.

Wolf versus snake, round two.

Bracing himself on his front paws, Rafael closed in, repeating the same lunge and retreat while the bullsnake struck at the air and recoiled.

Apprehension turned into determination. He would beat this serpent.

Rafael moved back and stood watching the damn thing hiss at him. He paced over the dusty earth while the snake tracked his movements.

Why couldn't it have been a chipmunk, vole, or rabbit scurrying over the path? Or a lizard even? He'd take a lizard over a snake.

When Rafael closed in, the snake's mouth opened wide, that horrid, raspy hiss making his fur stand on end. The serpent moved in quick whips, coiling forward in unpredictable lurches. Its head seemed to float above the ground and sway threateningly.

Rafael backed off, still puzzling over how best to attack. The snake shrank down and quieted, but he wasn't fooled that it had let down its guard. He circled it from a distance. Watching every movement, the snake's head twisted around. As Rafael made another turn, he came in slightly closer.

In a daring, or perhaps stupid, assault, Rafael burst forward and grabbed the bullsnake. There was no way he could hold on without being struck, but he did manage to throw the serpent into the air. All roughly five feet of hissing vermin was airborne. As soon as Rafael released his prey, he jumped back. When the snake hit the ground, he was on it in a flash, ripping a gash through its scales, then dashing out of striking distance.

The rattling sound of the snake's throat seethed with fury. The end of its tail curled and lashed over the ground. It began inching away, twisting every half second to watch Rafael. He held still, giving the snake a couple of feet before pouncing on its tail, claws skewering its skin. Again, Rafael jumped away from his prey. The bullsnake was injured and bleeding, dragging itself through the dirt.

It tried again to face off with Rafael. In the end, his wolf's tenacity paid off. He managed to strike faster than the snake, sinking his canines into the cool skin and biting down hard in a killing blow before the serpent had a chance to retaliate.

The snake lay as limp as frayed rope over the dirt and rocks. Rafael dug in.

At least he didn't have to build a fire.

SEVERAL DAYS LATER, Rafael reached a butte. He followed his nose to the top and wagged his tail as he located the spot where Hailey had slept. Her scent wove its way into his soul and bolstered his resolve.

Rafael lifted his head and howled a mighty call that echoed across the valleys and woods. After the sound faded, he listened intently, waiting for her to call back. None came, but she was out there. He just had to get closer. So he raced down the butte.

Onward.

The pack's trail began heading to the south. He became excited again when he found a deer carcass in a field, left over from one of their kills.

From everything he came across, he could see that the pack was doing an exceptional job of hunting and selecting ideal spots for sleeping. They were also making excellent travel time, which meant Rafael had to push himself if he hoped to catch up to them anytime soon. Good thing he was used to being on the move and was always up for a challenge.

So he ran and ran and kept running, some nights forgoing sleep to keep on the scent—opting for naps along the way. Her scent drew him in. It was getting stronger. He became single-minded in his pursuit.

It was late afternoon and he was running along a plateau above the tree line when the hairs stood up along the ridge of his back. A muffled breeze filled the air with his first whiff of rot. Ears flattening, Rafael slowed and took prowling steps closer. The putrid stink thickened the airways inside his nostrils. Through it, he detected no immediate threat, so he crept along.

Buzzards circled up ahead, then dove down. They did not return to the skies. If this area was safe for them, it meant it was safe for Rafael.

He still kept a keen watch on his surroundings while making his way to the source of that stench.

The scene he walked into was one of death. It had been a gruesome one for the dismembered humans whose guts and body parts were left scattered across the slope for the buzzards to pick clean. Among the flesh and bone were packs—some ripped apart, others left undisturbed. A couple of fishing poles were cast aside as though the people had been on their way to catch dinner. The scene made little sense.

Rafael stayed only long enough to identify the source of the attack. Vulhena. Then he was running from the kill site, heart in his throat. Hailey had traveled through this pass. What were humans doing this far out in the wilderness?

Hailey! His mind howled. *Hailey!* He should have never left her side.

Rafael was panting by the time he reached the bottom of the plateau. He needed to calm the fuck down and regain control of his senses. Hailey's scent was older than the vulhena. She had passed through the area *before* the humans, ahead of the threat.

But where had the vulhena gone?

Based on the carnage he'd stumbled across, those humans had had the misfortune of being discovered by a rare vulhena swarm. The creatures were usually solitary, but Sasha had warned him of this anomaly and how it had been a horde of vulhena working together that ended the lives of her parents and nearly the rest of their pack's elders. The damn pests were adapting. Alone, they were vicious but manageable. Teamed up, they were lethal. Like everything else that had gone wrong in the world, they probably had humans to thank for these unnatural mutations.

Rafael stopped and took in his surroundings. He put his pursuit on hold to investigate, racing from one spot to the next, sniffing. After maybe an hour of this, he determined that the vulhena had come and gone in a different direction than the path Hailey was on. His entire body sagged with relief . . . until the sound of sobbing reached his ears.

Warring instincts clashed. Fight or flight. Curiosity. Fear. Anger.

Anything full human deserved to die. He could finish off what the vulhena had missed. It would be a kindness to the survivor left behind.

With silent footsteps, Rafael prowled into the woods. The scent of humans was strong. They had come through here on their way to the plateau. Usually it was the straggler who got picked off first, but in this case, it appeared that lagging behind had spared someone's life.

Not for long.

Rotting flesh once again corrupted the air—that and the stink of feces from both humans and vulhena. His lips drew back, canines clenched in a silent snarl.

What Rafael found were two bloody bodies and a little girl standing over them crying. Her sob cut short when she saw what prowled from the woods. Eyes wide, she whirled around and ran.

Hijo de puta!

Had this child's parents not taught her to never run from a predator?

They wouldn't be teaching her any more lessons, good or bad, from the looks of it. The two corpses in the path were a man and a woman. Rafael could catch faint traces of their terror, or maybe that was coming from the little girl sprinting out of sight. She was lucky he was a shifter. If he had been full-on wolf, she'd be as dead as her mangled mother and father. The two humans weren't dismembered like the rest of the group. Vulhena liked to rip their food apart, but it looked as though they had already gorged themselves on the slope, then killed these two more as an afterthought. There was still flesh left on the bodies.

On closer inspection, it looked like the man and woman had been running toward their doomed group rather than away from the carnage. Rafael studied the footprints in the soil, how they pressed into the earth with more force as they had run toward the plateau. He glanced in the direction the girl had run. Best guess, the parents weren't running to aid their group, but to lead the vulhena away from their child.

His stomach hardened like a boulder. It dragged his lumbering steps.

He should leave her, let the woods finish her off. She wasn't his problem, and she was a human.

She was a child.

The girl looked no older than six.

"¡Mierda!"

Rafael gave a start at his words. He hadn't realized he had shifted. Well, shit. It was like his subconscious had decided what he ought to do.

He took his time following the path, hoping he would not find the girl and could be on his way. Farther down the path, he came across two faded backpacks that looked as though they had been tossed into the brush.

What the fuck were these humans doing trekking through the wilderness?

Rafael stared at the bags, scratching the thick stubble on his chin. He snatched the two bundles and continued.

There was a worn path beaten into the earth by dozens of booted feet and a few bare.

Rafael was a seasoned tracker. He didn't need his wolf to find the narrow, hastily made path through a thicket that scratched across his skin. He shoved the prickly bushes aside and peered over a stretch of woods sloping downwards toward a ravine.

Bedrock rose from the earth alongside mossy trees. Rocky outcrops were stacked in haphazard clumps like large log piles. The girl scampered up a large boulder, her bare toes gripping the steep slope with an efficiency that would have impressed a mountain goat.

Rafael tracked her speedy climb to the top, where a little boy huddled.

Mother Moon! There were two of them. The boy was even younger. Maybe four.

Rafael started toward them, still unsure what the hell he could, or was willing to, do about the two young survivors. The girl was dressed in a plain cream-colored dress that covered her knees but not the lower half of her bruised legs. The boy wore a long, baggy gray shirt with a short length of rope tied around his middle like a belt.

When the boy saw him, his eyes widened. He wrapped his hands around the girl's waist and clung to her like she was his last hope. Rafael nearly stumbled as feelings flooded in of what he and Diego had gone through in the days following their mother's death.

These kids didn't stand a chance on their own. They were human. Rafael couldn't help them even if he wanted to. There was nothing he could do for them, and yet leaving left an acidic burn inside his gut. Maybe whatever was in the packs would help them for a little while.

When he reached the bottom of the boulder, he set the bags on the ground and looked up. The girl shoved her brother behind her and glared down at him.

"Stay away from us, werewolf!"

Her ferocity brought a chuckle to his lips. "I'm not a werewolf."

"Then what are you?" she demanded.

Damn, she had lip for a tiny human who knew her parents weren't coming to rescue her.

He took a step back and folded his arms. "Shapeshifter. Wolf."

The girl scowled. "How's that different from a werewolf?"

"Werewolves are slightly bigger, more humanoid in their animal form with the ability to walk on two legs. They become what they are from being bitten. Wolf shifters are born into their heritage. When we bite, it is with the intention of killing or claiming a mate."

It wasn't something either species went around broadcasting. Werewolves were made. Wolves were born. In Rafael's mind, it was obvious who the superior of the two groups were even if werewolves tended to be bigger and tougher than most urban wolf shifters. Rumor had it that there were no guarantees when it came to surviving the transition.

He kept this opinion to himself. Why was he getting chatty with a nosy human, no matter what her age, anyway? She stared at him, her jaw loosening. The little boy peered around her, his mouth slightly open as he took in Rafael's words.

"You don't walk on two legs when you're a wolf?" the girl asked.

Rafael shook his head and wrinkled his nose. "I wouldn't want to. That's what my human half is for."

He thought he caught a smile on the boy's lips before he ducked his face behind the girl as she put her hands on her hips.

"Are you a good wolf, or a bad wolf?"

"Depends on who you ask. The deer and rabbits don't think too highly of me."

There was a muffled giggle behind the girl. She rolled her eyes and huffed out a breath. "Do you harm children?"

Her question stole the mirth from his lips.

"Of course not!" He hadn't meant to snap. It was a fair question and showed a keen sense of self-preservation on the girl's part, but just the idea of treating young innocents poorly sickened him. He remembered the first time he shifted, around his twelfth year, confused and as unsteady as a toddler taking his first steps. There had been no one to guide Rafael or Diego through that first stage between wolf and human and back again. Like everything else, they had to figure it out for themselves. They only had each other—the way these two kids did now that their parents were dead. At least he assumed that was who that man and woman had been.

The girl went rigid at his tone and the little hands around her middle now clutched at her like she was the only thing preventing the boy from tumbling off the boulder.

With a heavy sigh, Rafael lowered one arm and lifted the other, running a hand through his hair.

"What are your names?

"What's yours?" the girl fired back.

"Rafael."

She pursed her lips and studied him for several beats before saying, "I'm Coral and this is my little brother Eco."

"What are you doing out here anyway? Don't you humans usually stick to your settlements?" Rafael scanned the woods as though someone might emerge and explain the queer circumstances that had left two children orphaned in the wild.

The girl cast a cool look over him. "We had to leave our home."

"Why?"

"We had to leave because of the werewolves."

"What do you mean? Was your settlement attacked?"

The girl shook her head of tangled auburn hair. "They said they were our protectors, but only if we did what they said. My father said they were the village overlords, and he wouldn't spend his life serving them."

Werewolf overlords? Rafael swallowed down his shock. He had always assumed that werewolves were as motivated as any other animal shifter to keep as far away from humans as possible.

"How many of these *overlords* are in your village?"

"There were six at first. When we left there were five."

Five werewolves. *¡Mierda!*

"How many people in your village?"

Coral screwed up her face and looked skywards in thought. "A lot."

Rafael nearly laughed at her childlike answer, but there was nothing funny about her situation or—more to the point—the one he had become a part of when he followed her to the boulder.

"More than thirty? Less?" he asked.

"More."

"More than fifty?"

Coral pursed her lips and shrugged.

With five werewolves lording over the place, it wouldn't matter if there were a hundred of them. Usually it was shifters avoiding humans, not the other way. Apparently, werewolves were an entirely different breed of crazy. Come to think of it, Rafael and Diego had rarely come across them in their travels. They had never seen one living among wolf shifters until meeting Aden in Wolf Hollow. He hadn't seemed like the type to want anything to do with lording over humans.

Rafael scrubbed the wiry hair covering his chin. "Do you have any family who stayed behind in the village?"

Coral inclined her head. "My aunt Autumn stayed behind."

Rafael nodded. It was unfortunate the place was run by werewolves, but it was a hell of a lot safer than the woods, and at least the kids still had family.

There was no doubt in his mind that he would help the girl and boy. When he looked at their tiny faces, he saw children, not humans. They were in a category of their own. And he couldn't help feeling that this was fate's way of intervening. He had been close to catching up to Hailey. Too close.

The horror he had stumbled upon along the hillside was a bleak reminder of why he did not want a mate and children. A warning.

Looking up at the sister and brother huddled together on the boulder, he felt a certain relief in knowing that it would never be his kids who had lost everything and been left to fend for themselves.

He would never have to worry about what he didn't have.

The thought brought him more emptiness than relief.

chapter twenty-three

HAILEY RETURNED TO her dream, standing naked on a sandy shore. She had never seen the ocean before, only heard descriptions from elders in her pack. But there it was at her feet, the tide rushing across her ankles as she searched the endless blue waves for other survivors.

What she saw was vivid, yet far away as past and present intertwined. She could not feel the wet sand beneath her toes, nor the chill of the wind on her exposed skin. She floated somewhere between the dream world and the prairie in which she slept hidden in the grass.

Her thoughts were for her luggage and the miniature portrait of her mother, which she valued above all else. Lost to the sea. She had more urgent matters to worry about, but thinking of the frivolous items that had sunk beyond reach delayed an all-out panic.

How far was she from New York?

She walked up the beach and made her way over a windswept dune to a grassy ledge, stepped on top, looked from side to side, then stared at the wall of green. There was no sign of civilization in sight.

A sequence of events unfolded, blurring and skipping as dreams do.

She was running through dense woods on four legs. The forest was endless, and she wondered if any other creatures existed here. Lonely howls rose from the depths of her soul every night. She felt so very alone. And then, one night, her call was answered.

The male appeared from the trees, a striking gray wolf who radiated primal dominion over those eternal woods. Over her.

They became mates, loyal and loving. No human had ever treated her as well as that wild wolf.

She birthed her first litter in the early summer—six healthy pups. Of those, two survived. A couple years later, she gave birth to a litter of four. The older two helped look after them. Her mate found it odd that their offspring stayed with them instead of forming their own packs with the wild wolves that sometimes called in the distance, but he allowed them all to remain. Like the wolf she had claimed, Hailey was a force to be reckoned with. Not once during their time together did she take on her human form. That part of her became a ghost.

She got six more years with her mate before he succumbed to old age, having lived the full, satisfying life of a natural wolf.

Although her pups were now older than her mate had been when she met him, they were curiously playful and dependent upon her, like adolescent children she recalled from her human life.

There were six of them, plus her, leading the family pack. Years passed. Seasons changed. The moon waxed and waned and still her pups did not succumb to their father's lifespan. It was around the time they should have been approaching their entry into the spirit world that Hailey came across the oldest two, now in their twelfth year, sitting beside the creek making sounds of dismay as they stared, and poked, and slapped at their arms and legs. Groans and bellows heaved from their lips. They looked at one another and cried out in terror.

Without a second thought, Hailey shed her fur for the first time in over a decade and stumbled toward her children. Her upper body hunched, as though she had forgotten how to walk upright.

"It's all right," she gasped.

Their eyes widened as she closed in. When she stretched her arms toward them, they scrambled away and tried to bark.

"Luna! Lupus!" she said sternly, pointing at her daughter, then son. "Hush!"

They went still.

She looked them over and nodded. "Good girl. Good boy." Then the words poured out of her, coming easier than her body movements. Her thoughts had been with her all along, though she'd had no one to share them with for many moons.

She explained to her children what they were. They didn't understand her words, or what was happening to them. Not at first. But they learned her language fast. Their younger siblings were afraid at first. Curiosity won out in the end. The four younger pups followed their siblings around and occasionally allowed themselves to be picked up, though they squirmed almost immediately after. When their first shift came, the transition was a great deal smoother having watched Luna and Lupus go through the transformation.

Hailey was happy in the dream. She had six beautiful, healthy children who were able to shift from wolf to human and back like her. They could carry on conversations. And they were strong.

Wildlife abounded and they were always well-fed. The forest provided. The native people left them alone, and they extended the same courtesy to those humans who respected the land and animals.

Although Hailey's wolf mate had died of old age, she was still a beauty in her prime. Her animal form aged at the same pace as her human side. Although her children kept her happy, there was a loneliness they could not completely fill inside her soul. She missed having a mate.

Her memories of the young bucks in London were like faded photographs. She had never been with a man and concluded she never would in this savage new life she had carved out for herself. That ship had sailed . . . and sunk.

Then one afternoon, as though sent by the moon goddess, a male wolf appeared at the edge of a pond as she was rinsing off alone in her human form while her children hunted. The wolf had a gorgeous coat of black fur edging his ears, upper head, and back. The coloring lightened to gray, brown, and tan over his muzzle and legs. Seeing her, he growled. When she looked into his eyes with no trace of fear, his snarling stopped.

"Hello there," she said.

He cocked his head to the side.

Emerging from the water, she chuckled. "Don't you know it's highly inappropriate to watch a woman bathe? Scandalous."

The wolf wagged his tail and she laughed, until his fur faded into tan skin and raven black hair that fell practically to his waist. He raised himself off the ground, standing proud and as naked as she. With a strangled gasp, she threw one arm over her breasts and the other in front of her sex.

She did not realize the indigenous people had beast forms, or perhaps he was a rarity like her. He grinned and fired off a string of words that had her shaking her head.

"Sorry. I don't understand."

Whatever he was saying, he looked quite happy. Walking backward, he stopped, crouched, and pointed to where her paw prints had turned to footprints.

She nodded and smiled. "Yes, that's right. I'm a shapeshifter like you, apparently. Are there more of you? More like *us*, that is?"

"Us?" His deep voice was as beautiful as the rest of him. There was an intensity about him when he listened. Wide, sensual lips parted slightly from beneath a long, elegant nose and soulful eyes. He had no facial hair and his body was all smooth, defined muscle.

"Yes, us," Hailey said enthusiastically. She had aided her children through the beginning and advanced stages of verbal communication. She could do so again with this male. "You and me. Us." She pointed at him then at herself.

In her eagerness to commune, she momentarily forgot about her bosom. That is, until she saw the man's lips stretch into a wide smile and his keen dark brown eyes look where they should not have been looking.

Over a decade spent living in the wild should have eroded the last of her inhibitions, but modesty clung to her like the moss to the trees. There was no shedding a proper British upbringing. Not entirely.

Hailey felt her cheeks turn hot. It crept across her fair skin down her neck to the valley between her breasts. She quickly used her arm to cover what she could.

The shifter spoke, then wiggled his eyebrows.

"I hope you did not say something inappropriate," Hailey admonished.

The man's smile was friendly and warm. He made no move toward her, instead pointing to the animal tracks. "*Maheegan*," he said.

"Wolf," she countered.

"Wolf," he repeated, then pointing at her, "wolf."

"Wolf." Hailey pointed at the tracks. "Woman." She exposed her bosom again briefly to point at herself.

"Woman." The reverent way he said it made her thighs heat and legs quiver.

She stole a look below his neck, running her eyes down his chiseled chest. Unlike her, he did not attempt to cover himself. He was tall, lean, tan-skinned, muscular, and . . .

Oh, my.

Her gaze snapped right back up in time to catch his knowing smirk.

Hailey's face burned. She backed up a couple steps, as though that might make up for their nudity and lack of a chaperone.

She was a widow, she reminded herself. A mother. And part beast. Perfectly capable of handling herself with a stranger.

The man remained in place, as though he did not want to scare her off, though she couldn't help noticing the way he posed, standing with his back straight, torso and chin lifted. When he fluffed his long, black hair over his shoulders as though to show it off, she couldn't help chuckling. "Indeed, you have the most gorgeous locks. Men and women alike would be envious."

He grinned and flattened his palm over his chest. "*Ininì*."

She repeated the word in her head. Was that his name?

"*Ikwe*." He pointed at her. "Woman."

Understanding brought the smile rushing back to her mouth.

"Woman." She pointed at herself. "Man." She pointed at him.

"Us," he said in a tone that brightened her entire world.

Over time, the native wolf shifter learned her language. Neither of them were in any hurry. There were other, more pleasurable, ways to get to know one another. He was her forever mate. Eventually they could speak. He learned English so that he could talk to her children, as well as her.

With Matwau, her shifter mate, she gave birth to her first child in human form. She joined Matwau's tribe, having discovered several months into her pregnancy she

238

could no longer shift. With that joining, her family grew into a community of people who accepted her with open arms and hearts. She found not only love with Matwau, but happiness in the tribe. Her children suddenly had playmates and role models. Together, they made new discoveries of who they were as man and beast.

Although she had more time with Matwau then she had with her wild wolf mate, it still slipped away too fast.

Blissful years passed until the inevitable ravages of age found the couple. As they lay side by side, wrinkled and gray, in their tepee, Matwau spoke his farewell for the parting that must temporarily take place.

"I will find you in the next life, my woman, my wolf, my heart. Until then—"

"Run forever free," she finished, cupping her mate's cheek.

 chapter twenty-four

WE NEED TO *go back.*

Hailey's friends obeyed her wolf's command without hesitation. She made no secret of her intentions to claim Rafael. It was only her human's folly that had sent her running away from her destiny. *Their* destiny.

She should have never left him, even if he was being a stubborn wretch. It was lucky they had found each other at all. To leave his side was lunacy.

Something had happened to Rafael in his early life. Something that had built a barrier between him and his deeper senses. It was up to Hailey to remain steadfast. To not give up on their love. He needed her as much as she needed him.

She set an arduous pace over the ever-changing terrain. No one complained. They were a good pack, one she hoped decided to stay with her for more than a temporary adventure.

After running all morning, Hailey allowed for a drink at a creek they had passed several moons prior. It stirred the wild heart inside her to see the land they had traveled from a new angle.

They reached a ledge where the plateau dropped into a wooded bowl before rising into a rim of jagged peaks. Beetles had gone to work on the surrounding trees, carving out tunnels that looked like claw marks through the timber.

Hailey trotted ahead of her pack along the bowl until reaching a rock outcrop that tumbled its way down a small cliff. Dead pines dove over the edge, hanging on by their roots at a horizontal tilt, their bark stripped by wind and sun.

Afternoon brought a hot sun tempered by a westerly wind.

Depending on which direction Rafael had taken, it could be weeks—months possibly—before they caught up to him. At least she had turned around before it was too late. Once Hailey picked up his scent, nothing in this world would stop her from hunting down her mate. If his human half still balked at the commitment, maybe they would have to remain wolves. She would be content in either form, so long as they were together.

In the evenings, Hailey called out just in case. If Rafael's wolf was close enough to hear her, she knew he would answer. Silence as infinite as the stars blinked back down every night, hollowing out her heart a little more, like the tiny holes made by the wood beetles in distressed trees.

How much distance separated them? Did she have any hope of catching up? If they had been running in opposite directions, maybe he had gotten too far. Forever out of reach.

A forlorn howl ripped through her. Her sad song was

joined by her friends, their sympathy a haunting echo in her soul.

She didn't shift on the trek back, and neither did her pack. They took all their cues from her, loyally following her lead. Obedient, like children. It made the maternal instinct within her all the more demanding. Future generations were depending on her and Rafael. The bloodline must continue. Purebloods had to go on.

For all of her friends' teasing about apprenticing to become a seer, Hailey felt she could read her own dreams without any need to consult Flora or any other soothsayer. What her dream had revealed was that in a world rife with perils, this was something Hailey had mastered. Survival. Reproduction. The cycle of life.

She could not risk disrupting the natural order.

Fear drove her as much as determination. Just when she thought her search would extend into winter, she caught her first scent of Rafael.

Hailey stopped on her front paws so abruptly, the rest of her body swung around as though it had been spun. Sniffing loudly, she stuck her nose directly against the earth. Her friends inspected the surrounding brush as she inhaled tiny particles of dirt. Tail wagging, she raced from one spot to the next, smelling and confirming Rafael had reached this spot not long ago.

He had been heading in their direction, following them. Her male had come for her.

Why, then, had he veered off? And why was it his human scent left behind?

He could not have gotten this far by walking. Hailey

sniffed harder and picked up other scents that made her growl.

Rafael was not alone.

The human scent had Hailey snarling at once. Had they captured Rafael? She clawed the earth as she isolated the individual smells until they were deep in her lungs and committed to memory. Next, Hailey shifted to get a look at the tracks with her human eyes. Her packmates did the same, stretching their arms then studying the set of footprints.

Walking along the trail several feet, Hailey was shocked to see the footprints that accompanied Rafael's were child-sized. Confusion swept through her mind like clouds, thickening and blocking out any trace of blue in the sky.

What was Rafael doing with children? What were kids doing out alone in the middle of nowhere?

There was only one way to find out.

Rafael was now on foot, which meant they could catch up on four legs. Hailey was about to convey this to her group when a monstrous shriek froze both her heart and speech.

A vulhena slunk forward in its ghoulish way, talons clicking against large slabs of rock embedded in the earth, moving like a dark shadow through the trees. The unnatural creature reminded Hailey of a spider the size of a mountain lion. Luckily, it only had two eyes and four legs. It was downwind, but as it drew near, it brought its rotten stink with it.

Hailey held stone still, watching its every movement. Since her group wasn't running in terror, the vulhena continued creeping forward.

The beast probably thought it had stumbled upon easy prey–defenseless humans. This wasn't the vulhena's lucky day. Hailey just needed time to shift without being attacked in the process.

Eyes never leaving the ominous mutant, Hailey spoke in a low voice to her group. "Skeet, there's a rock by your left foot. Violet, the branch behind you is broken and should come free if you tug hard. Byron, Layla, Hudson, and I will shift. If the vulhena comes at us, attack, but be careful."

"Ready," Violet whispered shakily.

"Ready," Skeet affirmed in a voice that was barely audible.

Inch by inch, Hailey lowered herself to the ground, glaring at the vulhena with promises of ripping it apart once she had her fangs and claws. The vulhena must have seen her actions as a challenge, because it sprang forward, screeching before Hailey was able to sprout one furry hair over her body.

Violet screamed bloody murder as Skeet pelted the vulhena in the head with a rock. Hailey would have to congratulate him on his aim later. The shriek that followed had them all wincing and pressing their fingers over their ears–all except for Violet. The mighty snap of wood breaking followed her arms as she wrenched a thick branch free.

The vulhena stood on two legs, talons clawing at the air as it swiped and shrieked, turning one way and the other, looking them all over as though unable to decide whom to attack first.

While it was standing, Violet ran up and swung her branch at its middle, knocking it back onto four legs.

Byron, Layla, and Hudson managed to shift during the

commotion. Their growls were the most beautiful sounds Hailey had heard all day.

The vulhena reared back and shrieked.

It should scream; it was about to become very dead and quiet.

The shrieking grew louder. Hailey, Skeet, and Violet crouched, their bodies folding in as though the ghastly sound carried weight. She thought it must be extreme fear or anger, but it was much worse.

A chorus of shrieks rose up, like vicious spirits swarming the woods.

The cold sweat of terror ran down Hailey's sides like an open, bleeding wound. She felt lost in a nightmare as the screeching continued, unable to count the number of foes headed for them. Usually she had a keen sense of what was coming, but this was like standing in the middle of a wailing windstorm. It sounded like hundreds of vulhena were descending from the woods.

They didn't stand a chance. There were no protected walls to run to. Not nearly enough of them to fight off a horde and live to see another moonrise.

She was left with one real question.

Die as a human, or die a wolf?

Hailey dropped to the ground. Skeet and Violet did the same. By the time her shift was complete, Byron, Layla, and Hudson had already killed the vulhena. Its screeching stopped, but the damage was done. They could hear the blasted shrieks of the quickly approaching swarm.

Her packmates growled, facing the direction of the threat.

Hailey barked at them to run.

They might have a chance if they ran. Could wolves outrun vulhena? She liked to think so, but she knew so little of this horrific species.

Their group flashed through the forest. She led them away from Rafael's trail, sending a plea up to the moon goddess that the foul creatures had not fallen upon him earlier. The sun flashed back at her in a reminder that the moon wasn't around to save her nor guide her flight.

It felt unnatural to run. Her wolf wanted to face the threat and fight. She knew her friends felt the same pull to attack these lesser creatures. They growled at the shrieking closing in on them.

Hailey took one look back and saw the horde spreading toward them like a shadow across the land or a swarm of beetles covering every last speck of surface.

She barked at her friends to run for their lives. The growls stopped as they broke into a breakneck speed, paws barely touching the earth as their legs sped in a blur of unflagging motion.

The vulhena fell behind, but not out of sight. It was enough to give Hailey hope. She careered through the forest with her packmates keeping pace. Adrenaline fueled her, powering her legs.

They ran and ran and ran, but still the vulhena shrieked at their backs.

Hailey's mind raced alongside her, a topographical map of the land they had traversed taking shape. She scanned over her memories of peaks, cliffsides, rivers, boulder fields, prairies, plateaus, caves, and lakes.

Could vulhena swim? Maybe they stood a chance of losing them at the lake. There was only one problem. The nearest lake they had passed was still too far to reach even at this relentless pace. There were probably closer ones, but running aimless over foreign territory was an extreme risk.

The network of caves, however, was coming up at the next ridge. They couldn't hide, but they could bottleneck the vulhena, who would have to come in a couple at a time. Hailey and her pack would be waiting to kill them one by one, however long it took.

With renewed purpose, she sprinted down their earlier trail, fated, for the moment, not to catch up to Rafael.

The caves loomed ahead—a whole network of dark holes in the cliff side. They had hurried by before after picking up the scent of bears.

She selected a hopefully unoccupied cave, but at this point, Hailey would take her chances with a grizzly or black bear over a swarm of vulhena. When she veered off the path and charged for the cliff, Layla yipped at her back, suggesting she'd gone crazy.

Hailey had one focus. Survival. She was responsible for her pack, and she would ensure they lived to howl at another moon.

Racing up a narrow, rocky path, she dashed past boulders, selecting a small opening to dive into. Is this how voles felt when being chased down? She didn't like being hunted. It had the fur rising along the ridge of her back and her canines grinding together.

As soon as her friends were all inside, she barked

out the plan right before the screeching bounced off the rock walls. Hailey and her friends growled in answer. They weren't here to hide. These were their killing grounds.

They braced themselves, all facing the opening with snarls on their lips.

The stench of countless vulhena rose up the cliff along with their deplorable shrieks. Without hesitating, the first vulhena entered the cave and was killed by Byron before it had a chance to fight. The next one crawled in, and the next. Dead in an instant. Talons reached in and tried to swipe at them from the next creature who was more cautious. Layla bit its leg, crunching down with a snap of bone.

The vulhena's scream blasted into the cave before it drew its forelegs out.

Hailey and her friends snarled. More shrieks went up and they growled viciously back, their snarls magnified by the cave walls.

The entire cliffside felt like it shook with the battling reverberations. Then the walls really did tremble as a roaring joined the bedlam. Pebbles rained down from the ceiling. The screeching outside the cave took on a fearful pitch.

Adrenaline shot through Hailey's blood like snake venom.

The roar magnified and was joined by more just like it.

The bears had awakened and, from the sound of it, the caves were full of them.

 chapter twenty-five

THE BELLOWING SHOOK the rock walls, sounding as though it came from the mountain itself. It was as though the tunnels made up multiple throats within one giant behemoth.

The screeching continued, but no more vulhena tried to get inside the space where Hailey and her pack stood at the ready. Cautiously, she approached the opening and stopped near the entrance, listening and sniffing the air, which was thick with stink and blood. She poked her head out, eyes widening at the sight of great big brown bears standing to swat vulhena dead like they were no more threatening than flies. Shrieks turned to yelps that were silenced as the bears crushed the vulhena.

Looking down, Hailey saw that there weren't hundreds of the foul creatures—not even a hundred—but still a lot. Maybe forty versus around a dozen brown bears.

Four vulhena surrounded a bear and attacked all at once. They slashed at the bear's legs as he turned in a circle roaring. He lunged forward and bit the closest vulhena's head off. Hailey was too far and there was too much noise to hear the crunch of bones, but she saw the bear spit the head out as though it had been a piece of gristle caught between his thick, pointed teeth. Another bear joined the head chomper, grabbed a vulhena, and threw it on the ground with bone-breaking force. The limp black body didn't even twitch after appearing to die on impact.

When a cub wandered out, three vulhena seized upon the poor bellowing young bear. Hailey was closer to it than the adult bears. She barked, then led her pack to charge at the vulhena terrorizing the cub.

As soon as they heard the snarls, the vulhena shrieked and jumped at her pack. A talon ripped through Hailey's fur, just missing the skin it covered. The cub cried in panic. At first, Hailey feared he had been hurt. The next roar was more deafening than any sound she had heard that day as a mountain of brown fur broke away from the fight and charged them.

Hailey barked at her friends to scatter. Her pack's safety came above all else. They were to her what this cub was to the ferocious mass barreling toward them.

Diving out of the way, she and her friends were able to dash to safety in time. The vulhena weren't as perceptive, or as lucky. Black wiry-haired limbs were torn off and tossed, bleeding, through the air. Hailey yipped, making sure she and her friends were far away when the bear finished with the vulhena that had gone after the cub.

Now that they had a chance at a fair fight, Hailey led her group into the fray, helping the bears pick off the vulhena one by one until the screeching stopped.

Detached limbs, broken and bloody, littered the rocks

and patches of thick mossy ground making up the mounds that sloped over the ground outside the caves.

The roars turned to low rumbling as the bears paced in agitation around their previously serene turf.

Hailey guessed that they must be shapeshifters. Wild bears didn't gather in groups. It was rare even for shifters of their kind, or so she had believed.

When her packmates began growling and the rumbling grew louder, one of the brown bears shifted into a tall, lean young man with black skin.

Hailey's friends snarled. She barked at them to stop and to keep to their wolf forms while she shifted.

Once she was on her feet, warm brown eyes looked her over while thick, sensual lips smiled. Before they had a chance to exchange words, another bear shifted. This one was tan-skinned, but not nearly as dark as the other. Not only towering, his shoulders were as thick as ancient tree trunks, and he had long black hair that reminded Hailey of the shifter in her dream. But this was no wolf, nor was he flashing her a dazzling smile. He glared at her and fired off a string of incomprehensible words. Hailey shivered as though seeing a ghost from long ago.

The male finished speaking and narrowed his eyes at her while the black-skinned male grinned, showing teeth that appeared to glow like a crescent moon in his dark face.

"Hello, my name is Chester." His friendly tone was at complete odds with the ferocity radiating from his friend.

Hailey lifted her head and chest. "My name is Hailey from Glenn Meadows."

Chester said something to his friend in a language

she could not follow. She assumed he was translating. The friend said nothing. His stone-cold expression didn't change as he continued to glower at her.

"We were just passing through on our way to locate a missing packmate," Hailey offered.

Before Chester could translate, his friend spoke to him in his grumpy tone.

Chester's smile didn't falter, as though his mouth had been permanently fixed in an upturned position. As he addressed Hailey, he chuckled. "Kohana is displeased that you led the shrieking devils to our dwelling."

Hailey addressed Kohana when she answered. "I'm sorry. They came out of nowhere."

"So you led them here." Chester folded his arms, still smiling in amusement, it seemed.

Hailey turned her attention back to him. "We were outnumbered. Thank you for evening the odds."

He laughed and nodded at her packmates. "Are you their leader?"

"Yes. And you?"

With a deep chuckle, Chester shook his head. "Kohana is the leader of our tribe. I am the translator."

Hailey squinted at him. She had never heard of anything like it—an indigenous bear shifter tribe with a translator. They certainly lived in strange times.

"You look confused," Chester said with another chuckle.

"I didn't realize bear shifters formed tribes."

"Depends on the bear shifters. There's a community spirit among Kohana's people."

Hailey studied the stoic young man, who could not

be much older than her.

"Does your tribe have any elders?"

"Yes, but not among us. When they reach a certain age, most choose to retire in their animal skin on their own or with their mate if they have one and they're still alive."

Hailey nodded. Bears clearly did not possess the same type of pack mentality as wolves—even these ones who had formed a tribe.

Chester lifted his hand to stroke his chin, his eyes sliding over the attentive wolves at her sides.

"I see two more females in your group. Are they as pretty as you?"

When Hailey narrowed her eyes, Chester laughed heartily. "Do not worry, Hailey from Glenn Meadows. I am not looking to breed with wolves. Kohana's ancestors have successfully produced bear shifters with humans, but they say mating with another species of shapeshifter doesn't guarantee which animal gene will take hold—the same way gender cannot be predetermined. I am simply a man who admires the female form. You are welcome to admire back." He stretched his arms to either side and performed a slow turn, smiling all the while.

Kohana snorted in what sounded like amused annoyance.

Feeling flustered, Hailey rolled her wrist in front of her. "Yes, well, as I said before, we were on the scent of a friend, so we'll be heading out. Thank you again for your assistance."

Chester translated. Kohana yelled out a response. Hailey's friends growled at his tone, their fangs bared. A rumbling picked up among the bears at the two males' backs.

Chester clucked his tongue. "What about all these stinking, rotting bodies? Do you plan to leave them for us to clean up?"

Hailey's mouth fell open. "Oh, um, I hadn't considered that." Her cheeks heated. It did seem rather uncouth after the bears had helped save their lives, even as her soul howled at her to go after Rafael.

At least she didn't have to worry about the vulhena backtracking and finding him. But what if they had gotten to him before they were killed?

It was a thought she refused to feed.

"We'll help," Hailey announced. She looked from side to side, giving her packmates a nod.

They shifted and lifted themselves gracefully off the ground. Skeet and Hudson glanced around at the carnage, wearing twin smirks of satisfaction. Byron and Layla eyed the bears warily. Violet fluffed out her hair and flashed Chester a dazzling smile. "Well, hello, tall, dark and handsome."

His return grin was blinding. "My name is Chester. May I have the pleasure of knowing yours?"

Violet looked at Hailey quickly with an impressed lift of her eyebrows before returning her attention to Chester. "My name is Violet."

"Such a beautiful name for an exquisite flower such as yourself."

Violet giggled and twirled a curl around her finger.

Kohana grumbled some words.

"I'm guessing he said we should stop standing around and get to work," Hailey said.

Chester laughed. "Impressive."

Hailey addressed her packmates. "We need to clear these bodies."

Byron nodded. "Understood."

"After we killed a horde by our southern border, we burned the bodies," Hudson offered.

Hailey's jaw dropped. "The Wolf Hollow pack killed a swarm like this?" She jerked her chin at the dead vulhena. Running from the horrid black mass had been the most frightening encounter she had experienced.

Hudson chewed the inside of his cheek momentarily. "Yeah, actually it was Tabor's magic that knocked them unconscious before our pack finished them off. Not that hard to decimate a swarm of vulhena when they aren't putting up any fight." He shrugged.

If anything, Hailey's eyes went wider. It had never made sense to her why Sasha had turned down two pureblooded males in favor of a half-breed, but it seemed she had chosen a powerful mate capable of protecting their pack better than any other shifter.

"Might I suggest throwing them over the cliff?" Chester said, in a tone that was more directional than suggestive.

The bears lumbered back to their caves, making it clear they did not intend to shift and help. Hailey supposed she and her friends were in their debt as it was.

Layla wrinkled her nose as she looked at all the bodies, while Violet continued smiling and playing with her hair. "Are you going to help us?" she asked Chester sweetly.

He beamed at her. "I am at your service."

Apparently, Kohana was as well, though Hailey suspected it was to keep an eye on their activity. While they filled their arms with stinking vulhena, Chester asked a myriad of questions. Although he didn't speak their language, Kohana listened intently. He seemed to be the only one among them not gagging from the reek. Even Chester's bright smile faltered when he lifted one of the few vulhena still fully intact.

Hailey grabbed as much as she could carry, feeling her skin crawl when she touched the wiry hairs covering the dismembered vulhena. The fewer trips she had to make, the better. Chester fell into step beside her, smiling even as one of the legs he carried dangled and knocked against his thigh.

"How far are you from home, Hailey of Glenn Meadows?"

"Several weeks, give or take."

Her packmates offered nothing extra, which pleased her. It was none of Chester's business, nor Kohana's, knowing they were on a scouting adventure.

But, of course, Chester asked, "Why are you so far from home?"

Hailey held tight to her revolting load as she navigated a series of jagged-edged rocks embedded in the rough terrain. The last thing she wanted was to drop any bits and have to gather them up again. It was a struggle not to grimace with every step and brush of vulhena pressed against her. She needed a thorough rinsing off once this repulsive task was complete.

Chester's question went unanswered until Hailey

stepped onto even ground.

"I am a wild animal. All the woods are my home. Do you not roam from your caves?"

Chester laughed in delight and translated to his young chief. Kohana chuckled and said something back.

Nodding his head, Chester said, "Indeed, Hailey of the woods. We are all wild beasts."

She wasn't sure if the response was from Chester or Kohana.

The black-skinned bear shifter looked at Violet and winked. Skeet rolled his eyes but said nothing.

"Who is your missing friend?" Chester asked.

"My mate." The words came out strong and sure. She didn't remember thinking or even saying them, but there they were.

As silence settled over the group, Hailey tried not to think about how much ground they had to cover to reach the cliff on foot, and how many trips it would take to dispose of the bodies. Nightfall would come before the last limb could be chucked over the edge.

"Do you have a mate?" Violet asked Chester.

"Unfortunately, female bear shifters are a rarity–highly prized among our kind–which is why our males will sometimes breed with strong human women."

Yet again, Hailey felt her world knowledge opening up with new discoveries. Curiosity helped subdue the stink of the carcass she carried. "These human women your kind breed with have successfully birthed shifters?"

"Every time. My own dear mother was full human, as were the mothers of three other males in our tribe. The bear gene is strong." Chester's chest puffed up higher, if that was possible.

"But female bear shifters are uncommon," Hailey mused in wonder.

Chester inclined his head. "We only have one female bear shifter among us."

Skeet moved closer to Chester. "Let me guess," he said, "the one female in your tribe is mated to the chief." He inclined his head toward Kohana.

Chester burst into laughter, his shoulders shaking with mirth. At least he managed to hold on to his load.

Skeet narrowed his eyes and pursed his lips.

Still chuckling, Chester said, "Nita is Kohana's sister."

Kohana huffed, leading Hailey to believe he understood the gist of this exchange.

"Mahkah is her mate, and their son, Nikiti, was the cub you aided."

"I'm glad we could be of some help," Hailey muttered.

Chester just laughed.

After that, they fell into easy conversation. Hailey's friends joined in, recounting the beautiful sights they had seen. Chester spoke of lands to the east. It turned out his tribe was on the move in search of an ideal spot to settle in. They were hoping to come across females along the way.

"Human women aren't fearful of your kind?" Violet asked dubiously.

Her friend had every reason to question the bear shifters' intentions. Hailey's focus shot to Chester and caught the flashing of his teeth, which looked whiter as daylight dimmed.

"Rest assured that every female who accepts a bear shifter as her mate is willing and eager. Our brides are treated like goddesses beyond courtship, and we are exceptionally skilled lovers." Predictably, Chester laughed.

Hudson glared at him. "Your tribe might not be interested in wolves, but a bear shifter back home tried to force a female from my pack to be his mate."

Chester looked from Hudson to Hailey in confusion.

"His old pack," she clarified, though she knew nothing about his claim. Just more Wolf Hollow drama.

"I do not know about this bear, but we would never do anything so offensive."

Kohana cleared his throat, his dark eyebrows rising in question. When Chester translated, Kohana scoffed and answered gruffly. Chester laughed.

"Yes, this is true."

"What?" Violet asked.

"A bear has no need to coerce a female of any breed. We are—what is the word—most desirable among species."

It was Hailey's turn to snort. Chester merely puffed up, looking proud. Kohana shared his grin.

"Sounds more like a group of cavemen," Layla muttered, setting off Chester's laughter once more.

"They're becoming too meddlesome for my liking," Skeet grumbled.

"Your pride's just hurt that the vulhena are more afraid of bears than wolves," Violet said.

"Shapeshifters should only mate with their own kind," Skeet fired back.

"Moon above, cuz, chill," Layla said. "You do realize

we'd be dead if the bears hadn't helped us."

Skeet dropped a vulhena leg and swore. He scowled at Chester as though the bear shifter had been the one to knock it out of his grip. It didn't help matters that Chester smiled back.

"All of you simmer down," Hailey said. "What happened with the vulhena was terrifying. Thank the moon we're all alive and unharmed. Now, let's finish disposing of these bodies so we can be on our way." Her heart raged inside her chest. Rafael was still missing. He had to be alive. She believed she would have felt something if he had crossed over to the spirit realm. But he might very well be in trouble while they wasted their breath on customs that did not concern her. While there were plenty of wolves in the woods, it sounded like options were limited for the bear shifters. If they could pass on their shapeshifting gene to a favorable human, she saw nothing objectionable about bear shifters wanting to ensure the continuation of their species.

Skeet bent down and picked up the leg.

"No more grumbling or posturing," Hailey said. "This is merely a pleasant conversation with our new friends."

"Friends?" Byron asked in a doubtful voice, casting a sidelong glance at Kohana.

"Yes, friends," Hailey stated. "What better alliance than with bears?" When Chester's eyebrows jumped, she added, "And what better ally could a bear hope for than the loyalty of a wolf?"

Chester paused to translate while Hailey pushed forward. All this chitchat was stalling their progress. Still, in the spirit of making allies, she felt inclined to share the scent of humans they had picked up right before the vulhena chased them down. Mankind was an enemy of both wolves and bears. It sickened her to think of anything happening to the tribe's one cub. A lack of females meant even rarer cubs.

Darkness blanketed the land before their task was finished, just as Hailey had calculated. When it was done, Chester led them to a small, pristine lake where they all submerged themselves in chilly waters and swiped their hands over their skin.

Once refreshed, Chester announced, "You must stay the night. Our caves, as you have seen, are a safe haven for sleep. In the morning, Kohana and I will accompany you in locating your mate." Hailey folded her arms. Before she could protest, Chester continued. "All those vulhena indicate humans are somewhere in the area. We will look into the matter before our tribe moves out of the caves."

Perhaps Hailey's reunion with Rafael would lead the bear shifters to potential mates. She hoped that a human settlement this deep in the wilderness was made up of good people, respectful of Mother Earth and all her creatures. Why else would Rafael risk revealing himself to their children?

chapter twenty-six

ECO HAD A tight grip for such a young boy. Small fingers curled over Rafael's as bright blue eyes stared up at him with a look of wonder and trust.

Rafael needed to get these kids to their village before they became too attached. But it was a little hard picking up the pace with two tiny humans in tow.

Coral's longer legs had her skipping ahead, leading the way with a kind of shrill enthusiasm that suggested she believed her parents would be magically waiting for them back home. Or maybe she just needed the distraction. Every leap and bound forward was another step away from the horror of what had occurred.

"Are there any weapons in your village?" Rafael asked. He needed as much intel as he could gather before stepping a toe near a human settlement. His skin itched as fur rose to the surface just thinking about it.

"We have knives for preparing meals," Coral said.

One of the many commendable qualities about the girl was the way she answered his questions willingly.

"Any guns?"

"What's a gun?" she turned to look over her shoulder at Rafael, hopping over a root, as sure-footed as any shifter child. More sure-footed than Hailey, he thought wryly. But Coral wasn't trying to run away from him.

Because she answered his questions honestly, he returned the favor, explaining guns as best he could.

Coral's forehead wrinkled. "That sounds dangerous."

"It is, especially in the wrong hands."

"I've never seen or heard of anything like that." Coral skipped forward. Her hair was a long, tangled mess. Rafael had found a comb in one of the packs, but he wasn't about to stop and groom the child. He had extracted an extra set of clothing from what he gathered were the father's things. The shirt was hand-stitched and ragged. As for the pants, Rafael had to leave them unfastened to fit his wide hips. Waltzing into a human settlement naked was akin to announcing himself as a shapeshifter. That wasn't something he wanted to give away too soon.

"Tell me everything about your settlement," Rafael said.

"What do you mean?"

Apparently that was too broad a question.

"Where do you eat, sleep, poop—" Eco's giggle tugged a smile over Rafael's lips.

"We eat at our tables and sleep in our beds and do potty in the outhouse." Coral said all this as though it should be obvious.

"How is it that you have tables and beds in the wilderness?"

"Papa told me that when the sickness first started to spread, his grandfather and his friends brought supplies out here and built our settlement before the big die-off. He said his grandfather flew an airplane in the sky." She pointed up. Rafael followed her finger even though the only thing above their heads were a few puffy clouds.

Coral scampered up the next incline, going out of her way to jump over a rock.

"How do you feed yourselves? What do you eat?" More importantly, how did this group of humans hunt without guns? Rafael didn't believe they were unarmed for one second.

"We eat vegetables, grains, and meat," Coral said.

"And fish," Eco added. It was the first time the boy had spoken in hours. "Papa used to take us fishing." Tears glossed his blue eyes. Rafael gave him privacy by refocusing on Coral.

"Where was your family planning to go?" Their parents must have been idiots, or extremely desperate, to leave the safety of their settlement, along with the other unfortunate souls scattered over the hillside.

"Mama and Papa said there are other villages. Papa's grandfather said that if they established more than one, our chances of survival would be better. We were on our way to one of them."

Wonderful. More humans.

"Aunt Autumn didn't want us to go," Eco said softly. "She said it was too dangerous."

"Your aunt was right to worry. The wilderness is no place for humans to wander," Rafael said.

Coral's footsteps slowed and her small hands balled into fists. She swung around and aimed a fierce gaze at him. "Will you help us get our village back, Rafael?"

"I can't fight off five werewolves."

"We'll help you," Coral insisted.

Rafael shook his head. "If your village could have fought them all off, they would have done so rather than fleeing. The best I can do is deliver you back safely to your aunt."

Eco's lower lip trembled. Rafael felt as though the ground was quaking, shaking his soul. He crouched down. "Hey, how about a piggyback ride? Ever had one of those?"

Eco nodded solemnly while picking at the rope around his waist, avoiding eye contact. The boy was likely trying his hardest not to cry in front of Rafael and his sister. He was a brave little guy. Rafael still remembered Diego's howls after learning their mother was dead. The nonstop whimpering had been enough for Rafael to bite him for making everything feel worse.

Still staring downward, Eco moved around Rafael to his back. Once he was in position, Rafael reached back for his legs. "Hold on." Tiny arms circled his neck. They felt feather light wrapped around Rafael.

A feeling of love and lightness filled his heart, and it scared Rafael the same way his feelings for Hailey peeled away at his self-preservation.

Coral picked up a stick and threw it roughly at a tree, yelling, "It's not fair!"

Such was life. It was an infuriating slap to the face, but the sooner she accepted it, the better.

Rafael frowned, unconvinced of his own thoughts.

Coral grabbed pebbles as she walked, chucking them at tree trunks. She had remarkable aim. Her brother didn't make a peep, keeping a hold of Rafael with the softest press of his fingers.

After Coral had cooled off, Rafael found himself saying, "Tell me about these werewolves. Are they all males? Do they stay in the settlement all the time or do they leave? If so, how often? What is it they want from your village? Have they harmed anyone? Killed?"

This time he made sure to ask specific questions from the get-go.

Coral fell back into step beside him. "There are three males and two females. At first there were four males, but one of them was killed. That made them really angry." There was no triumph in Coral's voice, only numb detachment. Rafael could only guess what kind of punishment the remaining werewolves would have taken out on those responsible, and possibly the entire village. Coral pulled in a deep breath and continued. "The females always stay in the settlement in their human shape unless they want to threaten someone. The males mostly stay around too, unless they're out hunting together. Usually, one male stays to keep an eye on us."

Hmm. Rafael rubbed his lips together. He might have a chance against two werewolves if he could pick them off while they were out hunting. Laughter burbled up his throat. Was he seriously considering attacking werewolves to protect humans?

Diego had been right. It wasn't healthy to venture into the wilderness alone. He was clearly out of his mind.

Then he felt Eco's tiny arms hugging him.

Ay caray! Why did these kids have to be so cute? With

their parents dead, they had no one to protect them.

"They killed the men who tried to fight them," Coral said. "They murdered my uncle."

"*Hijo de puta!*" These kids were losing family members left and right.

Rafael hadn't realized that he'd cursed out loud until Coral repeated his words in confusion.

"What does '*Hijo de puta*' mean?"

Rafael's lips twitched. Her pronunciation was near perfect.

"It means son of a bitch, which is quite fitting when it comes to my species." Eco giggled against his back. "Oh, you find that funny, do you?" This set Eco off again, bringing a grin to Rafael's lips. It wasn't like the parents were around to lecture him on language.

"They're all a bunch of *hijo de putas*," Coral said. "Not you. The werewolves."

Sobering up, Rafael asked, "What do they want from your village?"

"They want us to be their servants." Coral glared down at a rock before kicking it out of the path, not even wincing as she did so with her bare toes.

"How so?"

"The adults have to cook, serve, and clean up after them. And they have to provide entertainment whenever the werewolves demand it."

Rafael's jaw tightened. He'd heard enough to understand the torment taking place under the werewolves' dictatorship. No one deserved that kind of misery, not even humans. He stopped asking questions, mindful of the things Coral might not be fully aware of.

From this point on, she and Eco would grow up faster than their parents would have wanted. But the world they lived in was savage, and Rafael believed they would adapt and become stronger for it.

These were the kind of people the world needed—the sort who wanted only to live peacefully in the woods, if Rafael was reading the situation correctly.

Why couldn't these werewolves go after the derelicts polluting the cities and suburbs?

He knew why. Because the strong always preyed on the weak.

Well, he was a pureblood. In his species, it didn't get any stronger than that.

To pull off what he had planned, Coral and Eco would need to be strong too.

chapter twenty-seven

DAWN TOUCHED THE corners of the curtain, and the warm bodies pressed against Autumn on the shared bed felt like a safe cocoon she did not wish to disturb.

It was the same thing every night when the three widows settled beneath the covers. The sniffling started. Muffled sobs from her companions kept Autumn awake when she desperately needed to rest.

She lived for daybreak and the brief respite upon first waking, that time of total peace, of lying on her back in stillness and blessed silence.

She opened her eyes, exhaled, and watched her breath fog past her nose. Soon they would need to light the stoves before bed and take turns waking to add wood throughout the night. Once her widowed companions cried themselves to sleep, they dozed through the night like bears hibernating. Autumn had no wish to rouse them for fire duty, and already planned to take that responsibility on as her own. She had for her late husband.

The edges of the blue, purple, and pink patchwork curtains turned luminous inside the log cabin's small bedroom. Dried flowers clung to pieces of branches arranged cheerfully around the space Blossom had put so much love into. It had not been to the werewolves' liking. Autumn and Willow had not been so fortunate. The worst of the werewolves had killed Autumn's husband and taken their cabin. Willow's husband had died refusing to let one of the beastly females have his home. Afterward, Blossom had offered both Willow and Autumn a place to stay.

Looking over at her slumbering friends, Autumn's heart squeezed. They had loving, kind husbands slaughtered right in front of them. Every night and every morning, Autumn vowed she'd make the werewolves pay for what they had done.

She inched away from Willow's soothing body heat to the edge of the bed, which wasn't far. Sliding one leg after the other out from under the covers, Autumn moved like a ghost out of the bedroom, closing the door gently behind her. She went to the pile of clothing she left folded on the rocking chair every night and pulled her nightgown over her head, then put on the frumpy, long, drab gray dress. Next, she grabbed a brush off the side table and yanked it through her thick red mane before pulling it back into a severe bun.

Fortunately, two of the three male werewolves had mates who didn't allow them to stray. But Gavner had already had his way with at least three of the women. Autumn had a sick feeling those were only the ones they knew of, who had spoken up or been overheard with Gavner. Those three women had left with her brother and his family, along with twenty-four other villagers who fled.

The next nearest settlement was a week's journey through the wilderness. It would have been fine, if not for the horrific shrieking creatures that seemed to appear from the pits of hell several years ago. They lurked outside the fortified walls, circling them for weeks, then disappearing for months. No matter how many times they left, they always came back.

Autumn had begged Fern not to go, or to at least leave Coral and Eco behind. The werewolves didn't bother the children so long as they kept out of the way. At least it was safe. There was no way of knowing that the other settlement hadn't fallen under the thumb of other werewolves. It might be the same, or worse. They might have all perished years ago. There had been no communication since the appearance of the four-legged creatures they had taken to calling werecats.

Autumn prayed that her brother and his family and the villagers he had taken with him made it. Every night before bed, Willow and Blossom got down on their knees and prayed they would bring help.

But Autumn knew better and saved her breath. Even if the other settlement remained untouched, they could no more save them than they had been able to save themselves. It had been the final argument between her and her brother. Autumn believed they should come up with a plan to rid themselves of the werewolves. To fight. Fern wanted to flee and start over. She already knew he would not be sending help.

Draping a black scarf over her head, Autumn eased open the front door and stepped into her rubber boots by the entrance. Her breaths came out in white puffs as she hurried to the children's cabin in the center of the settlement. The large structure was surrounded by wide areas of outdoor space, including trees left in place for rope swings and wooden steps leading up to forts.

The dewy grass slid across Autumn's boots as she crossed through the play area to the cabin. After removing her boots, she cracked open the door and slid in like the first ray of light bringing in a new day. Sixteen cots lined the wooden floor in neat rows. Half of those were now empty. Not all kids stayed in the children's cabin. Coral and Eco had lived with their parents. Autumn's two sons, ever at odds, slept on opposite sides of the main room. Spruce had insisted on weaning them young. Flint had been three and Lynx four when they were both sent to the children's cabin. Spruce said it was to toughen them up. He was the man in the home and his word was final. The fury still burned deep within her at the way Spruce had changed into an entirely different person after they wed. All the wooing and sweet talk turned from bright flames to charred ashes once she became "his."

The betrayal still stung. She did not cry for her deceased husband at night; she had not shed one tear over watching him get torn apart. He'd gone out of his way to insult the werewolves with no care over jeopardizing her safety along with his. Spruce had been the first to die. If not for the werewolves, Autumn would have been condemned to spend the remainder of her life with the bastard. But she wasn't about to thank the werewolves. They had killed beloved members of her village and enslaved those left behind. For Autumn, one aggressor had been replaced by five.

She blinked the fog from her eyes and gave a nod to Misty, who sat in the corner rocking chair nursing her five-month-old infant girl. Misty's husband, Ash, stood on his knees in front of the stove, poking logs into place above the crackle of flames. Misty and Ash were a young couple playing it safe. They stayed with the children, heads down, mouths shut, avoiding the werewolves as much as possible.

The once-joyful smile of a new mother was now small and sad, but every morning, Misty offered it to Autumn all the same.

"Good morning," Autumn mouthed. She removed the scarf from her head and set it on the nearest empty cot.

Ash looked over his shoulder and nodded his head in greeting. Setting the poker aside, he closed the door of the stove and joined Autumn at the worktable. He pulled a stool out from under it and stepped on it to reach one of the large sealed jars on the shelf above. Autumn reached up to take it from him and set the jar on the table. It was half full of ground maize and oats. Ash next handed down a large pot.

While Autumn poured out a generous amount of the mixture into the pot, Ash stepped out the back door, soon returning with a jug of water from the rain barrel kept beneath the roof. He poured the water in with the grits, then went out for more.

Autumn used a hand-carved wooden spoon to stir the grits and water. Setting the spoon down, she resealed the jar. Ash returned and set the water jug beside the pan.

He took the jar from Autumn, returned the grains to the shelf, then pushed the stool back under the table when he was finished.

Autumn looked at the back door and arched one brow in question. Ash shook his head. He aimed a gaze at the front door, then at her. Lips pursed, she gave a shake of her head.

No sign of werewolves yet.

The bastards liked to sleep in, but they could never be too cautious.

Ash pressed his palms together as though in prayer, opened them, then closed them again quickly. Autumn did the same, then lifted her hand, two fingers splayed. Their secret plans had become a daily obsession. She feared the fire in her eyes might give it away at any moment. For now, Gavner left the widows alone.

"What a sad lot you are," he had jeered cruelly on more than one occasion.

It was why Autumn never tried to comfort her friends. The longer their faces remained blotched and puffy, the better. Blossom was a beauty with light brown hair that flowed to her rear. After losing her husband, she looked like a mess. Autumn encouraged her and Willow to wear their worst clothing and hair secured tight the way she did.

There were other young women in need of protecting, but Autumn was powerless to help them all. That would change. She planned to free their entire village.

Ash made a walking motion with two of his fingers, followed by the opening and closing of his palms. They shared a rare and true smile.

The founders of their settlement had left many gifts to keep the village thriving: seeds, livestock, hens and roosters, the cabins, containers for food storage, root cellars, tools, and books on homesteading, though they had taught them everything they knew hands-on.

Early on, they had decided against guns and ammo. They made the decision to become pacifists. Ammo would run out, anyway. It was better to learn the old ways rather than force future generations to struggle through a rough transition as had befallen their parents when civilization failed them.

But they had stocked the settlement with fishing poles, gear, and nets. They had also flown in snares and traps.

Autumn's brother was their most skilled fisherman, while Autumn had a knack for placing traps in the paths of wandering critters. Envious of her trapping prowess, Spruce had forbidden her from stepping outside the village walls the moment she showed signs of pregnancy. The villagers saw it as a husband's concern for his pregnant wife, but Autumn had known Spruce better than anyone else and seen straight through to his jealousy. She had tried to talk to her brother about it, but Fern always waved it off and quickly changed the subject.

Rage engulfed her heart anew. She had to let it go and concentrate on the task at hand. Once that was complete, she would do her best to move on from the past seven years she'd spent beneath Spruce's thumb.

She placed the gruel on top of the stove to heat. Ash stood beside her, whispering while she stirred. "Clay told them the village needs firewood."

Autumn stared bleary-eyed at the gruel swirling with the spoon. The first time the werewolves had escorted two of their men out to fell trees, an ax had been thrown at one of their oppressors. There had been six werewolves in the beginning; now there were five. Both men had been killed immediately after. The rest of the villagers only knew what had happened from the raging werewolves, but not which of the men threw the fatal ax. It had to have been Fox, which had brought tears to Autumn's eyes that hadn't come for her husband.

Sly, stealthy Fox who always had a smile on his lips, a joke for every occasion, and a steady, true aim with an ax. Fox, with his red hair, had called Autumn his "ginger sister." In so many ways, he had been more of a brother to her than Fern. With cunning and patience, Fox had bided his time, waiting for the right opportunity, and taken it, the only villager who had managed to kill a werewolf.

One down. Five left to go.

Autumn knew the risk they were taking. They couldn't be killed one at a time, not without more death and punishment. Which was why they had to plan a coordinated   attack.

Since the incident with Fox and Briar, the werewolves were more watchful and cruel. Two of them would escort one man to do the chopping and bring along his wife or child to make sure that wood was the only element to feel the bite of his ax.

The shapeshifting monsters considered themselves above any sort of labor. They had killed all those they deemed too old or too weak to work.

Autumn's fist threatened to splinter the wooden spoon as she created a whirlpool in the gruel. A gentle hand pressed over her shoulder.

"This nightmare will end soon," Ash said in a low, solemn voice.

"The traps are set." Autumn's words were barely a whisper. They didn't dare risk anyone else hearing their plans, not even the sleeping children. "Clay knows where."

She, Blossom, and Willow had been allowed outside the walls to gather fall blueberries unchaperoned. So long as their tasks didn't involve sharp objects, the werewolves generally left them alone. The only good that had come of their presence was the absence of the werecats. The only screech to be heard for months had been from the nightly owls.

While in the nearby woods, Autumn had located the nearest traps and reset them by the stump they used as a chopping block. Clay's unflagging strength when chopping had made him the werewolves' prime pick to prepare firewood. They also liked to force his wife, Juniper, to waddle out and then rest the flat side of a knife against her bulging belly in warning before handing Clay the ax.

Clay had described to Autumn in minute detail the stumps the werewolves sat on to watch him work and the path they took to reach them. Even if he hadn't, she had a sixth sense when it came to identifying and predicting where an animal would walk. Autumn had studied the wood-chopping area from multiple angles, crouching low, standing on a log looking down, and even lying in the leaves on her side while Willow and Blossom filled baskets with berries that would be later devoured by the werewolves.

They could have fled if they wanted. Most of the villagers were allowed to leave at any time and need not return. It was a taunt. A dare. The werewolves did not know of the other settlements or, if they did, it did not concern them, which would have worried Autumn more if she didn't already have her hands full plotting her settlement's freedom. For whatever reason, the werewolves seemed to know that enough villagers would remain to do their bidding. There were mothers with infants like Misty, or those expecting like Juniper, who was seven months pregnant. Couples with young children they wanted to keep safe even if safety meant self-imprisonment. Then there was a group among them out for justice and liberation.

Ash left her side to bring down the bowls and spoons while Autumn stirred. The gruel didn't need that much attention, but it calmed the drum of her heart. She visualized their plan unfolding.

Two werewolves would accompany Clay and Juniper into the woods. Before they ever had a knife on Juniper, they would walk into the traps. Sky, Storm, and Rain would await them in hiding, and jump out at the first snap. The three sisters were tasked with protecting Juniper and her unborn child, and ensuring both werewolves ended up in traps—even if that meant pushing them in.

Their brother Sterling would be playing guitar for the two female werewolves while they lazed on the couch and chair smoking pipes in Willow's old home. While Sterling lulled them into a sense of tranquility, the women the females kept around to clean and cook would start a fire in the bedroom, then dash off before the werewolves knew what was happening. Their smell wasn't as keen in human form; plus they had developed a fondness for smoking the village's tobacco, which would help mask the fire at first. Sterling would next be fetched with a story of one of his sisters needing his help. Autumn, Willow, and Blossom would be waiting outside to block the entrances and barricade the windows.

Then those bitches would burn.

That left Gavner. Clay's sister, Hazel, had the worst task of all. She would lure the brute down to the root cellar. The bastard had been watching her the past couple days. It was one of a thousand reasons why they had to act soon. They had friends who would be looking out for Hazel as well. Autumn refused to accept any more casualties.

Gavner would be trapped in the root cellar. Once his friends were dealt with, they would all converge at the door of the cellar, armed to the teeth with every ax and kitchen knife the werewolves guarded when they weren't supervising chores. When they opened that door, they would attack the monster that emerged. Man or beast, they would be ready.

The werewolves would all die that afternoon.

chapter twenty-eight

"**C**HILDREN, BREAKFAST IS ready," Autumn called into the cabin, as she did every morning.

Several groans were muffled beneath blankets. Her eldest son, Lynx, was the first to toss his cover aside. His feet thumped to the wood floor. He stood and stretched, walked up to the stove, stood on his tiptoes in front of the pot, sniffed, and scowled.

"Gruel again?"

"Yes," Autumn answered tersely.

"How come the werewolves get all the eggs? It's not fair. Father would have never put up with that."

"Your father would want you and your little brother and mother to be safe," Ash cut in.

Autumn gave Ash a grateful smile. Lynx only huffed. Long dirty-blond bangs hung in his eyes and curled at the ends past his ears. He'd slept fully clothed in a pair of patched-up, faded jeans and a T-shirt with more holes than fabric.

Narrowing his eyes at Ash, Lynx said, "You don't know what my father wanted."

"Don't talk to your elders that way," Autumn snapped.

Lynx rolled his eyes at her. "I'm the man in our family now. You don't get to tell me what to do."

Anger roiled through her, hotter than the bubbling gruel. Autumn yanked the spoon from the pot so hard, blobs of steaming grains flew around her.

"I am your mother, and I am in charge, and you are not too old to receive a spanking." She shook the spoon at him as the words seethed out of her.

Lynx's face colored. "You're just a coward too afraid to speak out against the werewolves. Dad was the brave one. You're a disgrace!" he yelled, before turning and sprinting out of the cabin.

Autumn had half a mind to chase him down, spoon in hand, and paddle his bare ass, never mind the bits of gruel to go with his punishment.

But today wasn't the day to draw unnecessary attention. Breathing in and out deeply, Autumn dropped the spoon back into the pot.

"Children deal with grief in different ways," Misty offered from the rocking chair.

Autumn forced a smile rather than voice the truth, which was that Lynx was a little asshole just like his father.

The kids were all now wide awake and out of their cots. They shuffled over to Ash, grabbing bowls before lining up at the stove for Autumn to dish up their morning gruel. Halfway through the line, her youngest stepped up and lifted his bowl, avoiding eye contact. While Lynx was always looking to argue and insult, Flint pretended Autumn didn't exist. She hadn't decided which was worse.

Flint had not wanted to be moved to the children's cabin—had screamed and begged to stay with his mama. She wasn't sure he would ever forgive her for allowing Spruce to force him, along with Lynx, out of their cabin. Flint knew nothing of the fist his father had taken to her when she had tried to defy his orders. Again, her brother would not step in, would not help her. She had been a prisoner in this settlement long before the werewolves showed up.

Blinking away the dismal fog, Autumn finished serving the children and prepared bowls for Misty and Ash. She took their infant into her arms so that the young parents could eat their morning meal. Autumn cradled baby Meadow in her arms, a hollow ache tunneling down her chest as she looked down at the precious infant girl whose parents would give her all of the love and protection she deserved.

The older kids ate seated on their cots, then walked their empty bowls over to the table and set them down before exiting out the back door to make use of the outhouses.

Ash ate quickly, then took Meadow from Autumn. She slopped gruel into a bowl for herself as Misty went out back, returning with a second pot, this one filled with water, which she set on the stove to heat for cleaning dishes.

Autumn's spoon scraped against the side of the bowl. She forced the gruel past the knot in her throat and into the pit of her stomach. Halfway through, she felt as though she had gorged herself and could eat no more.

"Can you finish this for me?" she asked Ash. Misty took Meadow from him, and Ash accepted Autumn's leftovers. "I'll start on the dishes."

She carried the bowls, spoons, and heated pot of water outside to the washing bucket, taking her time scrubbing each one. Ash joined her and took the dishes back in as she cleaned them. When she was finished, he hauled the gray water off to the village garden. Autumn returned inside to dry off every bowl and spoon and return them to the shelf. She was grateful to be doing this for the children and not the werewolves, as other villagers had been ordered to do.

Autumn had one bowl left to dry when Sky, Storm, and Rain entered in their peasant skirts, blouses, and kerchiefs tied around the top of their heads. Long straight hair flowed down each of their backs. Storm and Rain were identical twins, and they preferred their names spoken in that order, rolling their eyes at anyone who tried to call them "Rainstorm."

"Got any extra firewood stashed in here?" Sky asked.

"It's getting chilly at night," Rain tossed in.

Autumn dried the last bowl slowly as she answered, "There's not much left in here, but I heard Clay volunteered to chop wood this afternoon."

Storm jerked her chin. "Good, we might as well do our part and collect kindling while he chops."

"Be safe," Autumn said.

"You too," the sisters answered in unison. They spun around and walked out the front door single file.

They would be on their way to tell Sterling.

Autumn's hand shook slightly as she set the last bowl with a clatter on the shelf. She concentrated on her breathing. Anyone who had gone against the werewolves had died, but they had all been single attempts. Today would be different. They were in this together. Everything had been carefully planned. The werewolves had let their guard down, believing there was no more fight in the villagers. How wrong they were.

Autumn headed for the front door, stopping to look back at Misty, whose baby was feeding again. The young mother met Autumn's eye.

"See you at dinner," Misty said.

Autumn tried for a reassuring smile. If everything went according to plan, the entire village should eat together in celebration.

"See you then," she said softly before stepping out.

The children were kicking around a ball patched together with deer hide. Lynx had not returned. He had probably run off to his friend Lake's cabin. Flint sat on a rope swing, pushing at the ground with his toe. When he caught Autumn looking his way, he frowned and twisted the rope around, giving her his back.

It felt like sand being kicked into a gaping wound over her chest, burying her barely beating heart.

Shoulders stooped, Autumn headed back to Blossom's cottage, noting the activity already starting as villagers emerged from cottages to use the outhouses and fetch water from rain barrels.

Back at Blossom's cottage, her friends were just finishing their morning porridge. They looked up from the oak table as Autumn entered.

"Good morning," she said.

Her friends returned her greeting somberly.

"Tonight we will have firewood," Autumn said.

"The nights will still be cold, but at least it will be done," Willow answered.

"This afternoon will be hot," Blossom reminded her. "Tea?" she asked Autumn, lifting the kettle.

"No, thank you. Are you both ready?"

"More than ready," Willow answered.

"I think I need to do some mending to calm my nerves." Blossom set the tea kettle back on the stove with a clunk and practically ran to her sewing basket.

Autumn didn't blame her; sitting still was the last thing she felt capable of. So she paced until the usual time she left to help in the village garden. It was fall harvest time with lots to do, and Autumn had found herself in charge after old Margret had passed on of pneumonia over the winter. Without the medical facilities of old, they didn't live as long as their ancestors had, though their elders said their quality of life and health were far superior and their years plentiful enough.

Autumn was the first to arrive at the village's sprawling garden. It took up nearly half the settlement. There were smaller gardens on the south-facing sides of every cabin, where couples and families tended to their personal vegetable and herb gardens.

Rows of cornstalks reached for the morning sun, taller than Autumn. It was a beautiful crop intended to feed far more mouths than were now necessary, as it was planted before the werewolves had descended on the village.

They could grieve later.

Autumn grabbed a basket from a large shed along

the garden and got to work. Checking the first stalk with brown tassels, she pulled back the silk and squeezed a kernel between her fingers. The milky fluid wetting her thumb showed her it was ready to harvest. She took hold of the stalk in one hand while twisting an ear of corn off with the other, then set it in the basket.

Her helpers, Clover and Ivy, arrived in the baggy dresses Autumn had instructed them to wear. Both young women wore their hair back in long braids. They were unmarried sisters without parents, having lost their father several years ago to one of the werecats while he had been out hunting, and more recently their mother, who was deemed too sick to serve a purpose by the werewolves. The bastards had said that the girls were wasting too much time taking care of their mom. So they killed the poor woman.

While other villagers wept into their pillows every night, Autumn wanted to press her face into hers and scream. More than anything, she wanted revenge.

After exchanging morning greetings, they got to work filling baskets with fresh corn. The garden had always been a place of peace. Even with all the bad that had happened, and all the fear that still remained, nothing could diminish the tranquility that came over Autumn when she worked with the soil and witnessed the magic of sun and water turning seeds into the thriving crops that fed their village. This simple, yet miraculous and vital task, was about the only activity that calmed her.

As the morning wore on, sweat dampened her hairline. They made trips to the root cellar, always together in their small group. If one woman filled her basket first, she helped the others fill theirs before transporting the harvest below the surface in the dark, cool cave of the cellar. The underground storage space felt good against Autumn's balmy skin as the midday sun beat down. Setting three more full baskets in the shade of the cellar, she, Clover, and Ivy wet rags in the shed's rain barrel and wrapped the corn in the damp rags before placing them in wooden crates on shelves in the cellar.

Slowing her pace, Autumn let Clover and Ivy finish first.

"I'm almost finished. Wait for me just outside the cellar," she instructed.

As soon as the girls' backs were turned, Autumn quickly finished covering her corn. When they left the cellar, she double-checked the sticks that had been whittled to sharp points with pieces of flint. Autumn had hidden eight of them in the cellar and showed their location only to Hazel.

The moment Clay and Juniper left to chop wood, it was up to Hazel to lure Gavner down there right away. Gavner needed to be taken care of first, in case one of his friends managed to shift in the trap and howl for help before Clay finished him off. The first had to happen around the same time Gavner went underground for the same reason, but not so soon that the smoke billowed into the sky and caught the others' attention before they walked into the traps. The timing of everything was critical.

It helped ease Autumn's nerves to double-check the wooden stakes hidden beneath potatoes, apples, carrots, beets, Jerusalem artichokes, and corn in easy to reach places. She had also placed fist-sized rocks in several crates, rocks Hazel had practiced bashing into spoiled squash, chewed on by vermin.

Hopefully Hazel would not have to use any of the rocks or wooden stakes. Two males were tasked with hiding in the cornstalks and waiting until they heard Hazel lead Gavner into the cellar. She would fabricate some story about wanting to close the door for privacy, then slam and secure it with the guys ready to reinforce the barrier. Or she would push Gavner or bring a crate of heavy squash down over his head. She would do whatever was necessary to get away, then close him in like a rat in a trap.

That time was fast approaching.

When she stepped out of the cellar, the sun pierced Autumn's eyes. Ivy and Clover stood with their slender arms wrapped around their middles, even though they had to be hot beneath their long gowns.

"That's all for today," Autumn spoke in a faraway voice. "Go home and stay inside for the rest of the afternoon until it is safe to leave. You'll know when."

For their safety, Autumn had told the girls there would be a coordinated attack, but only those in on the plan knew exactly what was happening.

"Please be careful," Clover said.

Ivy gave Autumn a quick, tight hug. Her throat tightened. There were words in her head, instructions to keep the garden going if something happened to her. But she didn't want to worry the sisters any more than they already looked, and such things did not need saying. Ivy and Clover knew what to do and would continue the harvest and seed saving with or without Autumn.

Once the girls were on their way, Autumn hurried back to Blossom's cottage to ready herself for her part in today's plan. She walked inside to find Hazel on the couch hyperventilating while Blossom tried to soothe the wild-eyed girl. Willow's words were harsher.

"There's no turning back, so get a hold of yourself before you ruin everything."

Autumn rushed over, her heart a drum against her chest. "What's going on?"

Hazel jerked her head up, her face ashen, breaths coming out in pants. "I can't do it, Autumn. Just thinking about it makes me feel like passing out. I'm sorry. You know I want to. I just can't. I can't. I can't."

Willow grabbed the girl's slender shoulders and shook her. "You have to!"

Hazel burst into tears. "I'm telling you I can't. Now please hurry and tell my brother, and the others."

"Goddammit!" Willow bellowed. Blossom sucked in a breath and looked upwards. Willow only scowled. "God wants us to put an end to these vile devils. He demands vengeance. We must do as He wills."

Two loud knocks at the door nearly had Autumn jumping out of her skin even though it had been planned. It meant Clay had been sighted leaving the settlement with the two werewolves. Their plan was in motion.

Hazel doubled over wheezing. "Clay. No," she moaned.

"It's too late!" Willow shrieked, waving her hands. "Get up, girl. You have to go now!"

Blossom bit down on her lower lip, her gaze downcast.

"I don't think she'll be able to manage."

A string of curses burst through Willow's lips. Autumn had never seen her so enraged, while Hazel, who had always seemed steadfast and brave, looked ready to expire on the ground from fear.

"I'll do it," Autumn said. "This has to happen. I'll take Hazel's place."

She didn't give herself time to think or feel; if she did, she might end up gasping for breath like Hazel. Instead, she rushed into the bedroom and yanked open the chest drawer where Blossom kept her summer clothes. Autumn had already pulled her gray dress over her head and was tossing it on the bed when Willow and Blossom entered.

Willow folded her arms tight over her bosom and frowned. "It shouldn't be you."

"I know where the rocks and stakes are. It has to be me." Autumn grabbed a short white sundress and put it on. It was neither tight nor too loose. It showed off her hips, curves, and large breasts.

Blossom retrieved the brush and came behind her, loosening the red knot before working the bristles through her thick locks, brushing her hair into a long, silky mane.

Autumn ignored the churning in her gut. The fear she felt was for her friends and for her children and the future of their village. For them, she would jump into the pits of hell, into the arms of the devil himself.

What she was about to do came pretty damn close.

On the plus side, she didn't have time to panic.

"How do I look?" she asked.

"Beautiful," Blossom whispered sadly.

Willow nodded grimly.

Lifting her head and shoulders, Autumn said, "This ends today."

"Pray with me?" Blossom asked.

Autumn looked into her friend's kind blue eyes. They had known each other their whole lives, but in the last few months, Blossom and Willow had become more than friends. They were family.

With a nod, Autumn and Willow joined Blossom, kneeling on her thick, round woven rug. They held hands, bowed their heads, closed their eyes, and prayed that God would give them strength and forgiveness for what they were about to do.

A wave of calm came over Autumn before turning into a tornado inside her chest as she found herself rushing out of the cabin, her bare feet imprinting the track leading to her old cottage.

Gavner was lazing in the hammock out front, wearing a pair of Spruce's shorts and no shirt.

Autumn stopped short when he sat up and ran his heinous dark brown eyes over her. Her entire body froze. She hadn't planned for this part. All she knew for certain was what came after. The root cellar. Securing the door. Her throat went dry. She tried to swallow past the lump threatening to choke away her ability to speak.

Gavner stood and smirked at her. Angry red scratch marks ran down his cheek, left over from one of his victims who had fought back. "What do we have here? You're one of the widows, aren't you?" He stared at her breasts. "Looks like you're no longer grieving. You came to the right place, Scarlet. I'll show you how a real man fucks."

Bile rose up her throat. No wonder Hazel had chickened out. They should have known it was too much to ask of the girl.

"I'm not here for that," Autumn spat.

Gavner laughed. "Oh, yeah? Then what are you here for?"

"You're in my house. I want it back." What was she saying? It was as though her mouth moved on its own.

"And you think granting me favors will get you back under this roof." Gavner looked her over again.

It had to appear odd, her coming around all gussied up. A hailstorm of cold panic pelted her mind and made her arms shake.

"Never mind. This was a mistake." She turned on her heel and hurried away, praying that he would follow. Isn't that what werewolves loved most—chasing down prey?

She could not pretend she wanted him, but in that regard, Gavner wouldn't care. Perhaps God had intended for her to take Hazel's place all along. Maybe she was the perfect bait. Lord knew she had enough determination to see it through.

Cruel and delighted laughter followed behind her. She had hooked him! Hurrying her pace, Autumn scurried toward the garden. She just needed to get him to the root cellar. She just needed—

"Aunt Autumn!"

She tripped and caught herself, whirling around in horror and relief at the sound of little Coral's voice. Her brother and his group must have turned around. But no, not now. Not now.

Coral and her little brother Eco ran toward her, holding hands. Autumn looked above their tiny heads, expecting to see her brother and sister-in-law, but there was no one else from the group who had left. She did, however, see the male werewolves returning, one holding the ax, and Clay with them, helping Juniper along. Sky, Storm, and Rain were right behind them. Their faces were all tight. If Clay was startled to see Autumn in a short dress with her hair unbound, he didn't show it. Nothing seemed to register beyond his panicked eyes. His gaze cut across to hers and he gave a shake of his head.

Coral and Eco reached Autumn and threw their arms around her legs.

"Aunt Autumn, mama and papa are dead," Coral cried. "Everyone who left is dead, besides me and Eco. We were able to find our way back."

Fern was dead? The whole group had perished?

Before Autumn could formulate a response, smoke and screams filled the air. Growls joined the clamor after the three male werewolves morphed into their beastly forms. The screams and snarls rang through her head and scorched the blood running through her veins.

No. They had a plan, a plan that had gone horribly wrong.

 chapter twenty-nine

HE HAD A plan. He just had to wait for the unsuspecting werewolves to leave the settlement on their next hunt.

Coral had said only two at a time ever left. Rafael could take on two. It wouldn't be pretty, but he had gone up against all manner of beasts during his life on the move, and always emerged the victor.

It would have been nice to have Diego to fight alongside him, but no matter. He would get the job done for two reasons alone: Coral and Eco. This was his chance to provide the help he and Diego had been denied.

Rafael waited in the woods in wolf form. First, he had made sure Coral and Eco made it to the tall wooden gate leading into the village. Crouched in the trees, he was surprised to see three females in long skirts emerge from the brush as the children approached. They appeared just as startled as they stared at Coral and Eco. Then the wooden gate opened and four figures emerged, shuffling at a slow pace.

Rafael felt relief settle over him as the group formed around the children. They stood for a while, no doubt asking the kids what had happened, before turning back to the settlement. Once the gate closed again, Rafael shifted. He didn't know how long he would have to wait. There would probably be a lot of questions and grief-stricken villagers making a scene inside about the fate of their fleeing people.

Well, it wasn't as if he had to be anywhere.

Rafael kept the walls in sight but didn't dare get too close. He had no intention of giving the werewolves a chance to detect him. Crouching over the ground on his belly, he kept his head lifted. The fresh forest air changed ever so slightly. The fur along the ridge of his back prickled. He inhaled, detecting smoke before it billowed above the village in a thick, gray stream.

Rafael jumped to all fours and ran to the gate. He had to shift in order to reach the latch. Luckily, the fortification had been built to keep out animals, not people. Cautiously, he cracked the gate a foot and peered in, afraid to find guns aimed at him. But there was no one guarding the entrance. When he stepped inside, the grounds were eerily deserted as a fire within raged.

Jogging naked, Rafael followed the smoke to a cabin engulfed in flames. The people standing outside the burning structure were too distracted to notice him slinking in the shadows of the other cabins as ash rained down.

The crackling fire seemed to encourage a growling werewolf that snapped its fangs at the crowd while a naked male tried to calm it down.

A young woman with hair like fire was on the ground sobbing, cradling another woman's head in her lap. From the neck down, her skin had been bitten and clawed open. Rafael was used to such grisly sights, but for some reason this one made him want to empty the contents of his stomach.

He scanned the area, looking for Coral and Eco. Unfortunately, they were in the crowd witnessing the horror unfolding, huddled together way too close to the red-haired female clutching the woman who had been brutally gouged by claws and teeth.

¡Mierda! He should have never sent them back in before the deed was done. But it wasn't as though they could have hidden in a tree for weeks either.

This had been the safest, surest plan . . . or so he had believed until the woman in the white dress was pulled up by her hair and the children began screaming. Blood stained her dress, which looked out of place with the drably clothed women around her.

"Let my aunt go!" Coral screamed at the naked male fisting the woman's hair as tears streamed down her cheeks.

"Hijo de puta!" This was the only family the kids had left.

"Were you in on it too?" The male snarled behind her. "Did you think you could lure me into that burning house? You're going to burn, bitch. You and everyone who conspired against us."

"No!" Coral yelled, as her brother burst into tears.

"Those two killed Stella," another naked man all but growled.

He pointed at a woman in a long pink-and-purple patchwork skirt and a skinny male with long dirty-blond hair tied in a low ponytail. The three women he had seen in the woods when he first arrived shrieked with sobs. One of them got on her knees in front of the male who had pointed.

"Please, there must be some misunderstanding. Sterling wouldn't hurt a fly."

With a raging snarl, the one werewolf in animal form lunged at the woman. She screamed. The young man named Sterling yelled, "No!" and sprinted to block the werewolf's path. The growling beast turned on him, tearing out a chunk of his arm. Blood sprayed. The screams were deafening.

Rafael might as well have been invisible as he got on the ground and shifted.

There were four werewolves, currently only one in animal form. He could sense her wild rage the moment his wolf took shape. Only her alpha's command kept her from ripping out the throats of every human gathered in front of the flaming cabin. Smoke and ash made Rafael's nose twitch in irritation. It nearly masked the scent of blood.

As the woman with the red hair was dragged toward the flames, Coral ran after her and pounded her small fists at the man who forced her toward the merciless heat. The male paused long enough to backhand Coral so hard her head twisted and she fell to the ground. Her aunt's scream was nothing to the earth-shaking snarl that thundered out of Rafael's throat.

He didn't remember running at the man. One second he was lurking behind the crowd, and the next he was airborne, jaw wide as his fangs sank into the male's arm and bit down, tearing through muscle, grabbing hold of the bone beneath.

The male howled in agony and released the woman, who rushed to Coral. With his jaw locked on the arm that had struck the girl, Rafael knocked the male on his back. As soon as his paws landed on solid ground, Rafael shook his head back and forth, tearing viciously through skin tissue. He wanted to tear the arm off completely, but the female werewolf snarled behind him as she charged to attack.

Rafael dropped the bleeding arm and spun around in time to leap and bite at the female. She stood upright on her two hind legs and swiped her claws at his belly, scratching exposed skin. Snarling, he grabbed hold of her neck and gave her a fierce shake.

"Rafael!" He heard Eco's panicked yelp.

The growls surrounding him confirmed that the males had shifted, including the one whose arm he had torn into. Unfortunately, the arm injury wouldn't slow down the male's beast.

The males attacked. They bit at his sides, forcing him to release the female. Rafael flipped around to face them, snarling as the fire roared behind the werewolves. With the black smoke at their backs, they looked like the hounds of hell.

Rafael's low growl vibrated in his throat.

The female let loose a manic snarl. Her rage reeked of fear, outrage, and vengeance. She was the first to lunge. Too bad the other three didn't hang back to watch. They were a snarling mass attacking Rafael from every angle. He jerked his head from side to side, snapping his teeth, biting as he was bit by the other werewolves. They clawed and bit him as he fought back, striking and chomping with canines that glistened with drool. The pain was piercing. He felt like he had landed on a porcupine who planned to shoot every last quill through his skin.

Four werewolves. He knew there was no winning, but that wouldn't stop him from fighting until the end. They were all over him in a snarling, salivating mass, which brought them close enough to bite. He made each slash of his nails and gnaw of his teeth count, tearing, ripping, and spilling blood.

Only, everything he did was done to him and magnified. A claw came at his face, missing his eye, but carving a trench across his muzzle. Blood gushed out.

"Rafael!" Coral yelled, fear swirling around the syllables.

The sound of her voice made him fight harder. She was alive. That was all that mattered.

He'd kill as many of the werewolves as he could before bleeding out. Give the humans a fighting chance. They had taken out two of the six. Rafael had a goal of two. He couldn't let the humans go showing him up.

If he had been in his upright form, he might have laughed at the surprise of it all. How he had chosen to go down defending a couple of human children as though they were his own. Most astounding of all, he couldn't think of a greater purpose than to protect those kids.

Another burning gash clawed over his hind leg. Hot blood flowed out. One of the werewolves stood up and threw himself over Rafael's back. The connecting force knocked him off his legs, flat on his belly. With snarls of bloodlust and excitement, the other three werewolves attacked.

"Rafael!" Eco yelled desperately.

Coral was sobbing hysterically. "Rafael. Rafael."

Nails clawed his back, skinning him alive. No. Not yet. He had to take at least one with him before his departure to the spirit realm. He snarled and snapped, refusing to whimper his way into the afterlife. Sharp teeth latched onto his ear and tore.

With a howl, Rafael jumped up and grabbed one of the werewolves by the throat, teeth locked. His captive cried out. One of its friends rammed into him over and over until his legs gave out. When his head hit the ground, his jaw sprang loose and the werewolf got away. There was a brief moment when he could have gotten up, but his legs were trembling with wounds, his fur matted with blood, and every muscle felt like pulp.

He lay bleeding on the ground while Coral and Eco sobbed his name.

"Rafael."

"Rafael."

"*Rafael*," his mother said in the far recesses of his mind. "*Levántate, mi pequeño lobo. Mi ángel. Levántate.*"

He tried to do as his mother commanded, tried to get up, but his legs gave out again.

"Rafael!"

"*Rafael.*"

"*Raphy.*"

A scream.

A whisper.

A memory.

A howl.

He supposed it was fitting that Hailey joined the hallucination. No matter how hard he had tried to fight it, they were bonded. He had known it from the moment he first laid eyes on her proud and elegant wolf. They were meant to be, if not in this life, perhaps in the next.

Her scent cut through the smoke and blood. It was that bewitching and familiar smell that convinced him she was really here.

With his last remaining energy, he lifted his head off the ground so that he could take one last look at the beautiful pureblood who had loved him even though he was a complete and utter wretch.

She looked from him to his assailants and bared her fangs.

The growl that tore through Hailey's fangs was a glorious and terrible sound that threatened to rip the world in half.

chapter thirty

BLOOD AND GORE.

Fire and smoke.

Screams and snarls.

So much death.

It was hell on earth.

Willow's blood soaked Autumn's dress straight through to her skin. She hadn't seen the female werewolf escape and rip her dear friend apart like a rag doll. But her mangled body was a sight that would haunt Autumn for the rest of her days. If she had days.

She didn't know where the new werewolf had come from. He was slightly smaller than the others, but that only appeared to make him more fierce. She was too shell-shocked to contemplate how her niece and nephew seemed to know him—know his name. The children were hysterical as the other werewolves tore into him . . . and had wrenched out of her hands when she tried to pull them away.

They didn't have much time before the werewolves finished him off. Once they did, Autumn, Blossom, and Sterling would be thrown into the flaming cabin, burned alive. The terror of it clawed down her spine like the nails digging into the lone werewolf who had tried to help.

Autumn and her friends had one chance to get away. She couldn't let it go. Looking over her shoulder, she saw that Sterling and his sisters had disappeared. That left Blossom, who stood rocking in place with a vacant stare.

"We have to go," Autumn hissed at the kids.

"But they're going to kill him," Coral sobbed.

"They're going to kill me too, if we don't go now."

Coral's nostrils flared. It brought a fresh surge of panic rushing over Autumn's heart. The girl looked like she wanted to join the fight. Autumn grabbed her hand and Eco's and yanked them toward Blossom.

"Let's go," she snapped at her friend. She had no more hands to spare so she had to use her voice to get through Blossom's inertia.

Blossom blinked once, then nodded.

"Rafael needs help," Eco said.

The kids were still dragging their heels until a new group of howling wolves ran toward them—six in total.

Oh, God, no. Please no. Terror paralyzed her. Blossom's face drained of all color, and she wobbled as though she might faint.

But then the new wolves began attacking the monstrous ones.

"See. Your werewolf friend has help. Come on now."

There were no assurances that this additional group would win or be any better than their oppressors. Maybe they were fighting for the chance to take control of the settlement. She had no way of knowing and every intention of getting the children out of harm's way.

They hurried toward the children's cabin. Misty and Ash would keep them safe. If something happened to Autumn, she knew the children would be protected. They had had no part in any of this, nor had Misty and Ash. They already had their instructions to deny all knowledge of the plot to kill off the werewolves should the mission fail.

Coral kept glancing over her shoulder. "Rafael's a wolf shifter, not a werewolf," she said.

"Is he going to be okay?" Eco asked in a watery voice.

Autumn had more pressing matters than the well-being of a werewolf or whatever he was.

"We'll drop the kids off at the children's cabin, then leave out the back gate and trek to the other settlement," she told Blossom.

Her friend stared back at her with a blank expression. At least her legs kept pace.

Coral's grip tightened around hers. "Nooo," her niece cried. "The werecats will get you. Please don't go, Aunt Autumn. Don't leave us."

Tears streamed down the children's cheeks. Pressure built in Autumn's chest, nearly pitching her forward onto her knees. It felt like a dam might burst open inside her heart.

"Shh. It will be okay. You're safe now," she said in a soothing voice. She ran a hand through Coral's tangled mess of hair, then bent over and kissed the top of Eco's head. "After the fighting's over, I'll come get you. Until then, you need to stay inside. Don't you want to see your cousins?"

Jaw clenched, Coral shook her head. At least she didn't pull out of her grasp. They hurried away from the smoke, skirting the garden and passing the root cellar.

The sky darkened beneath the ash cloud forming above the village. The air was still, not a wisp of wind, which was another reason they went ahead with their plans that day. If it had been blustery, they would have had to put their plans on hold. It had never been worth risking burning their settlement to the ground. That would have been a sure death sentence. One cottage was chancy enough. It had all been a grave and terrible risk. After holding her murdered friend in her lap, Autumn wasn't sure any of this had been worth it.

The children were safe. That was all that mattered right now. The wolves that had run in outnumbered their oppressors. She had to believe they would win and be on their way, and that Willow had not died in vain.

"Now where might you be off to in such a rush?"

The cold voice at their backs struck terror in Autumn's heart.

Gavner.

Did that mean his group had won the fight? Autumn wanted to sob in outrage. She dared a look over her shoulder. The monster was alone, lips clenched, injured arm bleeding, his gaze gleaming with savagery. Her stomach dropped like a stone.

"Blossom, take the kids," she rasped. "I'm the one he wants."

Autumn held Coral's and Eco's hands out to her friend.

"No," Coral whimpered, her lower lip trembling. Fresh tears spilled down her cheeks.

Blossom's eyes cleared. Steady, unadulterated

understanding and determination seemed to pull her out of her stupor as she took the kids' hands and squeezed them in her own.

"Godspeed, Autumn," Blossom said in a low, fierce voice. "Godspeed." She made it sound like an order rather than a farewell.

Coral tried to shake free of Blossom's grip, but the young widow held on tight.

With one last look at them, Autumn took off sprinting into the cornfield. The dry stalks whipped over her arms, legs, and face. The sound of Coral screaming her name made her run faster. She didn't want the kids to hear what happened to her if Gavner caught up.

Gritting her teeth, she threw her arms out to knock cornstalks aside. Defeat was not an option. She knew these gardens better than anyone, certainly better than Gavner. So, unless he—

Her thoughts were cut off by a low, bone-chilling growl. Terror wrapped itself around Autumn, choking her before the werewolf found her. Horrific images flashed through her head of the villagers she had seen torn apart— of Willow's mangled body. The cornstalks rustled in a slow, methodical crackle. He was stalking her. Gavner knew there was nowhere she could run, no place she could hide from his beast.

She wished and prayed that if she held still enough, she would blend into the cornstalks.

When Gavner emerged in his werewolf form through the stalks, it was upright on two legs in that monstrous form, smiling with canines that dripped saliva.

Autumn's bones turned to mush right before she fainted.

There was only one safe place for her, and that was oblivion—until a hard slap to her face smacked her back to reality.

Rough hands yanked her dress up to her waist. She jerked awake and grabbed Gavner's wrists, digging her nails into his skin. He had changed forms while she was unconscious, turning himself into his brute form. Naked. Erect.

Autumn screamed in fury when he pulled his wrists free and tore her dress and kneed her legs apart.

She dug her fingers into the soil, scooping up chunks of earth, which she lobbed into Gavner's eyes before pushing him off. The snarling sound he made reminded Autumn that if she ran, he would transform and hunt her down again—probably rip her apart after this stunt. So she launched herself at him, kicking and biting and screaming. The war cry gave her a boost of energy as she kicked at his genitals and rained her fists over his head.

"You bitch!" he seethed.

Another kick to his groin had him curling up to protect his sensitive organs. Maybe God had been looking out for women when he created that rare advantage a woman had against a man.

While Gavner was groaning, Autumn stumbled away, racing through the corn, heading back out. If she could reach the root cellar, she could barricade herself inside and gather up the wooden stakes. At least she would be armed to defend herself.

A menacing snarl made her jerk around so quickly, she tripped and fell on her back.

No! She thought he wouldn't be able to transform until the pain in his groin subsided.

But there Gavner was, stalking toward her on all fours through the cornstalks. His snarl was a continuous, angry vibration with no end.

As soon as their eyes met, he ran, whipping through the stalks, his deafening snarl threatening to loosen her bowels.

Autumn screamed and threw her arms up in front of her face as the werewolf hurtled through the air and stalks straight for her. Then a mass of brown fur erupted through the corn, knocking into Gavner. The werewolf gave a cry of dismay. Then he was on his feet growling at the mighty brown bear who roared in return.

Autumn winced and shrunk back, terror pressing down in new layers.

Gavner charged the bear in a snarling rage. The bear took one gigantic paw and smacked Gavner to the ground, then set upon him. The werewolf's growls turned to whimpers and then terrorized cries.

Autumn scrambled back. She turned over and crawled on her hands and knees as fast as she could through the corn field while the bear was busy tearing Gavner apart. The crunch of bones made her stomach roil. Gavner's piercing shrieks cut through the air. That could be her next if she didn't get away.

Heart drumming against her ribcage and corn rustling against her body, she made her way to the outer edge of the garden. Instinct told her to stop and listen, even as her mind screamed to get up and run. She stopped, crouched in the soil, and noticed the garden had gone eerily silent.

Was the bear already finished eating Gavner? So soon? Was he still hungry? Did he want seconds?

Her heart beat all the way into her ears, making it difficult to listen. Chest rising and falling rapidly, Autumn focused on her breathing, concentrated on pushing the panic off and making it to safety.

A rustling in the corn made her heart stop altogether. She held her breath.

Something was moving toward her. Its movements sounded more like a gentle murmur than a predatory hiss.

She turned to face whatever it was and gasped as she looked up at the most striking man she had ever seen. Hard brown muscles covered his chest, arms, and thighs. Raven-black hair streaked past wide shoulders, brushing over abs that looked as though they had been carved out of granite.

He walked up to her, smiled, and held out his hand to help her up.

Autumn's eyes widened. "Be careful. There's a bear," she whispered urgently, pointing in the direction she had crawled from.

The deep voice that answered had her body relaxing, as though on a sigh. She didn't recognize a word he said, but she understood that he meant her no harm. But there was still the matter of the bear. The man didn't even turn around when she pointed again. Instead, he took her hand, lifting her to her feet. Once steady, Autumn snatched her hand back and craned her head, searching the field for the brown bear. But there were no signs of the beast, as though she had conjured him up in her imagination or God had sent the bear in at the last second to protect her. Whichever the case, she had narrowly escaped a gruesome death, and now there was a gorgeous man looking her over.

Creases appeared over his forehead and his lips settled into a firm line. There was nothing vulgar in his gaze. He seemed to want to make sure she wasn't harmed.

Autumn felt her cheeks turn the color of her hair. Her short dress was bloody, dirty, and torn. Feeling self-conscious, she pulled together the loose pieces over her left thigh where Gavner had torn a slit up to her navel. Her fumbling fingers drew the man's attention to the exact spot she was attempting to hide.

His tone sounded harsh when his next words came out. Autumn's eyes widened. The man pointed in the direction she had last seen Gavner then pointed between her legs.

Understanding loosened her tongue from its cage behind her clenched teeth. "Oh, God. No. He didn't have his way with me. Thank God."

The man squinted. His frown didn't diminish his good looks, but it did tell Autumn he was having trouble deciphering the tone of her answer, which had come out a bit frantic.

She tried again in a calmer voice, "I'm okay. He didn't–"

The man crouched in front of her, parted the ripped section of the dress, and took a deep inhale in front of her privates.

With a shriek of dismay, Autumn turned away, recovering

herself with the torn sections of fabric. Holding the dress in place, she faced the man and glared at him.

He straightened and gave a satisfied nod like it was perfectly normal for a stranger to sniff a woman's sacred flower.

The man said something before walking at a brisk pace through the corn. Well, she had tried to warn him. He looked like he could handle himself, and Autumn desperately needed to get her village under control.

There were still three werewolves unaccounted for, a new group of wolves, and a bear loose in their settlement—not to mention the attractive mystery man who disappeared into the cornstalks.

chapter thirty-one

Hailey's Growl Would have frightened thunder from the sky. She felt lightning in her veins the moment she saw Rafael injured on the ground.

Four werewolves surrounded him, blood glistening on their canines.

Rafael's blood.

Hailey's human half was screaming inside her subconscious. The forlorn echo faded as she let go and gave herself over entirely to her wolf. Everything blurred around her in her vicious attack on the werewolves. Between snarls, snaps, and growls, they cried out every time Hailey got her fangs on them.

Her friends joined the fight and Hailey had to watch that she didn't hurt them as she went rabid with rage. Werewolf blood coated her tongue and stained her white fur. Her nails clawed through flesh and bloodied her paws. One of the werewolves began wailing in panic, and it only encouraged Hailey to finish the job. While biting the flailing creature over and over, another one managed to attack Layla and get hold of her neck. She snarled frantically. Byron, Skeet, and Hudson pounced on the werewolf who had her in its grip. Another werewolf took off running, fleeing from the brawl. Hailey hungered to chase him down and rip him apart, but she would not leave Rafael's side.

The werewolf she currently fought managed to bite her leg. She didn't even feel it. With a savage snarl, she sank her fangs into its throat and jerked, tearing flesh, ripping it wide open. Hot blood gushed out as it fell dead on the ground. Hailey lunged at the werewolf fighting Violet. The beast was already wounded, and Violet appeared to have it under control, but Hailey was blind with bloodlust. While the werewolf swiped frantically at Violet, Hailey lunged and ripped into its side with tooth and claw. The animal's cries didn't stop until it was dead, and still Hailey dug into its chest cavity, pulling out its entrails and tearing open organs.

Another cry had her whipping around. The third werewolf issued its last whimpers before her friends finished it off.

The world went silent. Quiet. Too quiet. Deathly quiet.

Rafael's eyes were closed, his body still.

With a strangled cry, Hailey transformed abruptly from beast to human. She rolled head over ass across the bloodied earth, then scrambled over to the injured wolf.

"Rafael!" Hailey took care not to shake him as her fingers brushed over his fur. "Shift, my love. Shift." She put her hand in front of his muzzle, feeling for breath. None came. "Shift," she begged. Tears tracked her cheeks, spilling faster than blood.

Then she saw it, the faintest rise and fall of his fur. Gulping down her tears, she squared her shoulders and issued an alpha's command.

"Shift."

 # chapter thirty-two

THE SECOND RAFAEL completed his shift, Hailey was on top of him, grasping his face and kissing him between sobs. He barely recognized the usually composed pureblood who currently straddled him wild-eyed and frenzied. It was a bit scary and oddly enticing.

When he smiled, Hailey broke off her next kiss and dug her fingers into his shoulders. "You're not allowed to die on me. Do you hear me, Rafael?"

"Everyone dies." His smile faded and voice turned solemn.

The blonde beauty on top of him growled. "Before that final hour comes, I want to truly live. Don't you?"

Their eyes locked. Hailey's gaze was fierce, frightening . . . full of strength.

Rafael reached a hand up and brushed her hair behind one ear. "You came back for me," he said in wonder.

Hailey's nostrils flared. "And this time, I'm not letting you get away."

"So stubborn." Rafael chuckled.

"Have I told you lately what a wretch you are?"

"Only a thousand times, but why don't you tell me once more."

He sat up, arms circling her back, pulling her against him. Their mouths crushed together, tongues invading between lips that devoured. Hailey gripped his hair tightly and kissed him roughly.

"Um, guys?" Layla said.

Skeet made a coughing sound.

Hailey groaned as though it physically pained her to pull away from Rafael. She looked warily around as though seeing their surroundings for the first time. Hailey's packmates were all standing grim-faced. Alarm had Rafael on his feet, pulling Hailey up with him.

They were surrounded by villagers holding flaming torches. The humans had formed a circle around them. Fools. All Rafael, Hailey, and the rest of her pack had to do was get down and shift . . . except Rafael couldn't shift, not until his wolf had a chance to heal. He clenched his jaw. People never changed.

Hailey glared around the circle. "Don't worry," she said to Rafael. "We'll take care of them."

Rafael's heart gave a lurch. He should be the one protecting her, and yet here she was about to save him a second time in a row. It struck him as comical that he had spent so much time worrying about losing her. Hailey had proven over and over that she was more than capable of surviving in the wild.

As Hailey lowered herself to the ground, a scrawny young man thrust his torch in her direction.

"Stay where you are," he yelled. "If you try to transform,

we will burn you."

Rafael growled.

The humans moved in closer, their torches sending waves of heat over the pack's naked flesh.

"Wait!" came a familiar cry as Coral raced over with her brother, the woman she had called her aunt running close behind. "Stop it," Coral shouted. "The wolves are our friends! Rafael saved me and Eco after mama and papa were killed by werecats."

The scrawny guy gaped at Coral. "But they're were-wolves."

"No, they're not. They're wolf shifters—big difference." Coral's haughty tone made Rafael's lips twitch. Tiny humans were so much wiser and likable than adults.

Rafael didn't need to be in wolf form to detect the fear in the pinched faces surrounding them. The villagers kept the circle tight and their torches grasped in their fists.

"Back off," Coral's aunt commanded. She pointed at Rafael. "This one saved the children and he came here, risked his life, to save us. Any friends of his are friends of ours. We owe them a debt of gratitude. It's over. We're free."

"Is it? Or are these wolves planning to take over where the werewolves left off?" demanded a young woman in a long frumpy brown dress, her hair tied in a scarf.

Hailey, being Hailey, took a step forward and announced, "I am Hailey from Glenn Meadows, which is a long way from here. Allow me to assure you that we have no intention, nor desire, of living within your walls. Our home is the open fields, mountains, streams, and woods. But we do need to stay here for a few days while

Rafael's wolf heals. He was badly injured while fighting to liberate this village."

It was that voice, those self-assured words, that finally got through to Rafael and made him realize there was no fighting this attraction, this bond, this love for Hailey that burned eternal inside his soul. He had been a brute to deny their connection, and an even bigger fool to try and run away from his destiny.

"You are welcome to stay as long as Rafael needs to recover," the redhead said. The villagers parted for her.

Coral ran past her aunt and threw her arms around Rafael's legs, squeezing tight. Eco hurried over and hugged him from behind.

"Told you wolf shifters kicked werewolf ass," Rafael boasted.

Behind him, Eco giggled.

Hailey stared at him like he was a stranger for several heartbeats before quirking a brow. Rafael grinned.

"Crazy story."

"So it would seem," she answered.

The redhead searched the gathering and frowned. "Your other wolf friend must still be in the garden."

Wolf friend? Rafael's forehead wrinkled in confusion.

"Chester or Kohana?" Hailey asked. Rafael whipped his head around to gape at her. "They're bear shifters."

Sounded like Hailey had her own crazy story to share.

It was the redhead's turn to gape. Her face turned ashen and her throat bobbed as she swallowed. "Shapeshifting bears?" Her voice was barely audible.

Hailey batted her hand through the air. "Don't worry.

They're friendly. The helped us kill a horde of vulhena."

"Vulhena?" the redhead asked.

"I think she means werecats, Aunt Autumn," Coral supplied. The little girl eased her fingers off Rafael to put her hands on her hips and glare at the villagers.

They looked at one another, still clutching their torches. When a naked man appeared behind them with skin as black as night, the villagers gasped in dismay and swung their torches in his direction.

With a wide, bright smile, the man stopped and lifted a hand in greeting. "Hello. My name is Chester."

"Are you a bear shifter?" Coral asked at the top of her lungs.

Eco peered around Rafael's legs.

Chester lowered his hand and laughed in delight. "Yes, I am. And, as you can see, I am also a man." He turned in a circle, showing himself off with a wink at the end.

"And what of your friend?" Autumn asked. "We heard there are two of you."

Chester nodded enthusiastically. "Yes. Kohana is doing a search of the settlement to ensure there are no more threats. He is the chief of our tribe and, like me, he is unmated."

For some reason, a blush appeared in Autumn's cheeks. Her bloody dress was now torn and covered in dirt, but not burnt. Rafael was just glad to see Coral and Eco still had their aunt.

"We must prepare a celebration feast," she said to the other villagers. "I lost a dear friend today"—she choked up a bit, then cleared her throat—"but I know Willow is

319

looking down and cheering our victory. Today, justice was served. Our loved ones' murderers have been killed. Good triumphed over evil. The monstrous beasts are dead. We are free and able to honor our loved ones at long last."

One by one, the torches were secured to posts spaced around the settlement. Everyone began hugging and crying. A woman appeared with a group of children who saw the dead werewolves and began skipping, jumping, and clapping.

Autumn raised both hands in the air. "Before you get too carried away, we have a fire to put out. We need all available hands."

The shifters stayed behind as Autumn led the villagers toward the smoke. Coral and Eco ran over to the group of children, following slowly behind the adults.

With a sparkle in her eyes, Hailey grabbed Rafael's hand and tugged him over to the bear shifter Chester.

"A whole horde of vulhena?" Rafael asked as they made their way over.

"I thought we were done for when they came upon us," Hailey said.

"Yeah, I know the feeling."

"Chester!" she exclaimed happily, her entire face lighting up. "This is Rafael."

The black-skinned male was tall, lean, and muscular with friendly eyes and the brightest smile. He threw out his arms and embraced Rafael in . . . well, a bear hug. "So, good to meet you, Hailey's mate."

Rafael didn't correct him. Instead, he smiled at how right it sounded that he and Hailey were mates. His chest puffed a little higher knowing Hailey had informed the self-proclaimed unmated, available bear shifters that she was already taken.

"Thank you for helping our pack. Great to meet you, *amigo*."

Eventually the smoke cleared, uncovering the stars and a waxing moon full of promise. The villagers had roasted an animal called a "pig" over an open fire. It was one of the most mouthwatering meats Hailey had ever tasted, or perhaps she was so ravenous that anything would have tasted delicious.

Along with the feasting, the humans danced and sang and played foreign instruments late into the night.

Several of the young women who had been wielding torches earlier still eyed their group warily.

They had lent the shifters clothing. Sadly, they had a surplus after so much death. Some of the villagers weren't ready to jubilate, choosing to pay their respects to the dead in the privacy of their cabins. Others appeared resolute on burying the past and savoring this victory.

Hailey and her pack sat on a blanket near the roasted pig, content to smell its lingering aroma long after they devoured their portions of the meat. She, Violet, and Layla had chosen short, airy dresses from among the clothing offered. Rafael, Byron, Skeet, and Hudson wore long khaki pants and off-white button up shirts. Chester and Kohana had torn and tied a couple articles of clothing, fashioning them into loincloths that made the villagers' eyes bulge.

They were speaking to the woman named Autumn, who seemed to be in charge of the settlement. The redhead had washed up and changed into one of the drab dresses that seemed to be a favorite among the women. Her hair was now secured into one long braid.

Layla lay on her back, arms behind her head, and sighed wistfully. "What now?"

Violet reached over and tickled her under her arms. Erupting into giggles, Layla sat up and smacked her playfully. "You're evil."

"Just lightening the mood," Violet said.

Skeet belched.

"Ew!" Layla glared at him.

He grinned. "Me too. Just lightening the mood."

Their group laughed, then went quiet again. Hailey glanced at the pig, wondering if it would be greedy of her to dish up thirds.

"I don't want to go back to Glenn Meadows," Layla said. "Ever since we left, I feel fully alive. You know? Like really, really awake."

They all nodded.

"Me too," Hudson said. "Makes me think I should have left home sooner. I mean, it's not as though I passed up opportunities to explore. I'm grateful you all gave me a chance to see more of the world."

Layla pressed her lips together and smiled at him.

Byron cleared his throat. "I'm glad Hailey chose the wild unknown over the sheltered familiar."

Taking up the thread, Hailey said, "And I'm happy Rafael agreed to join us on our grand adventure. We don't have to return right away. We don't have to go back ever—except to visit. I like our pack. I think we should stay together and keep going."

Layla clapped her hands in excitement. "Yay! We were hoping you would say that."

"What about Rafael?" Byron asked, shooting the pureblooded male a pointed look.

They all turned their heads to stare at Rafael, who smirked back at them. "Well, Hailey's probably told you what a wretch I am."

"She didn't have to tell us," Violet interjected. "It was sorta obvious from the moment we met you."

Hailey's eyes widened. Violet smiled cheekily. Hailey held back her scoff. She wanted to hear what Rafael had to say, not joke around.

Rafael ran a hand through his hair, seeming almost nervous. "Yes, well, it seems your alpha is willing to give me a second chance. At least, I think that's why she showed up to save my sorry hide." He flashed her a smile, but Hailey went still, her heart a star, suspended in the sky, waiting to either shine or implode. Rafael swallowed. "Can we take a walk, Hailey? There's something I want to ask you."

"Hell, no!" Violet said. "We want to hear it too."

She looked at Layla, who smiled mischievously before joining Violet in her chant of "Claim her! Claim her! Claim her!"

Hailey felt her cheeks heat. She scrambled to her feet and cast a silent command at her friends to simmer down, but they simply changed their words to, "Mate her! Mate her! Mate her!"

Rafael stood and winked at Violet and Layla.

"Come on," Hailey said, grabbing his arm and pulling him away.

Threading her fingers through Rafael's, they walked hand in hand through the celebratory crowd. A young man with long dark-blond hair and a freshly bandaged arm plucked at strings on his instrument, producing a merry tune. A few of the children held reed-like musical devices to their lips and blew while their fingers moved over tiny holes. Women spun in circles, their long skirts twirling with them. It gave Hailey a warm feeling of hope that humanity wasn't entirely doomed.

She gave Rafael's hand a squeeze. "You said I saved you, but you rescued this entire village. I never would have led the pack here if your scent had not brought us to this human settlement, of all places."

Rafael used his free hand to rub his hand through his stubble.

"I came across two little kids who needed help."

"I'd say you're their hero for life."

Rafael did not return her smile, shaking his head with a heavy exhale. "I always thought that people were the bad guys, but it turns out our shifter cousins were the villains—heinous ones at that."

"We all have the choice between good and bad, regardless of gender or breed," Hailey said.

He sniffed. "Which one am I?"

"Oh, you're a wretch, but at least you're the good variety."

Rafael laughed at that.

They meandered around dark cottages and entered an open space in front of a large cabin. Stars dotted the sky overhead, now clear of smoke. It felt like a fresh start.

"Hi!"

Craning their necks, they spotted a young boy in a cute little house in a tree.

"Hi," Hailey said, offering the child a smile.

His cheeks dimpled and he ducked down, then popped back up, giggled, and waved. Hailey and Rafael waved back.

"Is it just me, or does this feel like a totally bizarre dream?" Rafael asked as they strolled across the small clearing.

A secretive smile lifted Hailey's lips. "Definitely strange. Maybe one day we really will revisit this place in a dream, but for now, I've had enough of past reveries." Releasing his hand, she stepped in front of him and put her hands on her hips. "Are you going to claim me or what?"

Rafael's face lit up when he chuckled. "Stubborn, bossy, and all alpha . . . how can I refuse?" He stepped closer until only cloth and skin separated their beating hearts. Hand cupping one side of her face, Rafael stared into her eyes. "How do you want to do this, Hailey of Glenn Meadows?"

Her lips twitched, even as her heart sped up. "It's Hailey of the woods."

Rafael just chuckled and kissed her on the mouth, dragging the moment out in languid strokes of lips moving together and pressing hard.

He broke contact to say, "Hailey of the woods, I claim you as my one and only mate now and forever." Rafael moved back in, only to end up kissing air when Hailey drew back.

"I want pups—lots of them."

Rafael ran his hand through his hair. "*Dios mío*. What have I gotten myself into?"

Shoulders shaking with mirth, Hailey threw her arms around his neck and gave herself over to Rafael's kisses and the knowledge that theirs would be a happy bond filled with passion, respect, friendship, and cute little purebloods to continue the line until it was time to do it all over again.

"Bite me," she demanded.

Canines elongating, Rafael did as she commanded, sinking his fangs into her neck.

It was about time the male obeyed his alpha female.

epilogue

GOLDEN SUNLIGHT EDGED the green leaves beneath which the small group of adult wolves dozed. Birds chittered and cooed from the branches while another pair were intent on a whistling contest.

Rafael and Hailey lay side by side in Wolf Hollow's open glade, watching their six pups chase butterflies.

When his mate had demanded pups, she hadn't been kidding around. All six were from one litter.

A bear cub ambled through the grass to see what the pups found so entertaining and didn't seem too impressed with the winged insects flitting about. He made a soft bellowing sound, wanting to play.

Three of the pups were more than eager for a romp, especially with the adults more inclined to rest than roughhouse. Soon, the yipping started and Taryn's poor cub was up against six wolves. She stood on four legs and watched, as protective as any mama bear, despite being a wolf shifter. The pups would never hurt the cub, nor would the cub ever harm the pups. They were friends, though they made a ruckus and butted against one another.

Hailey didn't so much as growl when the cub batted one of their pups with enough force to knock him on his back. He rolled around and right onto four legs, wagging his tail as though he had performed a neat trick he could not wait to try again.

It was a strange and beautiful world they lived in.

To think Rafael might have missed out on so much happiness. He couldn't imagine.

Thank the moon above—no, thank Hailey, his sensible pureblooded mate, for not giving up on him.

He looked over at her, and she gave him a knowing flick of her tail.

They had not spoken in almost five years. Their wolves had communicated and mated plenty, but Hailey had chosen to remain in her wolf form so as not to confuse their pups. They had another five years, give or take, until they would be ready to shift.

Their pack had grown a little, and they continued to roam the wilds. They also returned to Wolf Hollow and Glenn Meadows at least once a year to visit family and friends, as they were doing now.

Diego and Lacy had two sons, but they would not be able to play with Rafael and Hailey's pups in one of their shared forms until their nephews could shift to wolf form or their pups into children. Rafael was betting on his offspring to be the first to pull it off.

He lifted his head high with pride, barely noticing the one ear that remained half-torn and hanging beside his eye.

That night, while their pups slept, Hailey shifted to

her human form and crept away from the spot they had taken outside the cave of Hudson's sister and her mate.

Rafael followed Hailey to the hollow's pond. While she waded up to her knees in the moonlit waters, he shifted.

"*¡Mierda!* I nearly forgot how sexy you are on two legs."

Splashing water as she spun around, Hailey looked him over with a wicked grin.

"You wretch."

His shoulders shook with laughter. "We haven't spoken in nearly five years and the first thing you have to say to me is 'you wretch'?"

Hailey shrugged. "It was the first thing that came to mind."

Wading into the water to join his mate, Rafael said, "*Mi amor*, I am going to give you better things to think about."

TARYN AND BRUTUS are up next! Return to Wolf Hollow in book 6, Bear Claimed. But first, turn the page to read Primal Bonds (Wolf Hollow Shifters book 5.5). After everything Autumn's been through, she deserves her happily ever after!

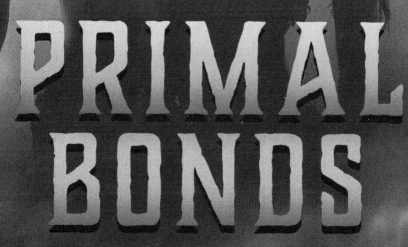

PRIMAL BONDS

A WOLF HOLLOW SHIFTERS NOVELLA

NIKKI JEFFORD

PRIMAL BONDS

LANGUAGE, CUSTOM, AND ANCESTRY FORGE SEEMINGLY IMPASSABLE BARRIERS BETWEEN A WOMAN AND A BEAR SHIFTER, but words cannot stand in the way when it comes to the language of the heart.

Autumn's settlement is still reeling in the wake of the werewolves' reign. If they are to protect themselves from future attacks, they will need help from their new bear guardians. The villagers are eager to give the bear shifters a reason to stay, especially after learning there are single males in the tribe interested in human wives. But before any of the bear shifters can court the village women, they must first wait for their chief to claim a mate.

Kohana saved Autumn from a vicious werewolf attack. When he offers to claim her as his mate, she is baffled. She's a human widow with two unruly boys. The mysterious and majestic indigenous bear shifter is chief of his tribe and the most gorgeous man she's ever seen. Surely he wants a young bride with her maidenhood intact.

The tribe's translator assures Autumn that she is the only female Kohana wants. He has witnessed her strength and position as a leader within her village. She has birthed two strong sons and looks out for her people.

AFTER A PASSIONLESS MARRIAGE, WILL AUTUMN MAKE PEACE WITH THE PAST AND GIVE IN TO HER DESIRES?

 chapter one

SOFT SOBBING WOKE Autumn from a slumber she did not remember falling into.

Her eyes opened to darkness and slowly adjusted, taking in the wooden chest of drawers against the log wall and, on the next wall, the blue, purple, and pink patchwork curtains. The groggy haze was replaced by panic. For several thundering heartbeats, she thought her village was still under siege. Her breaths sped out of her mouth. Blinking rapidly, she turned her head and saw Blossom curled up in the fetal position, her back to Autumn.

There was an empty space on the bed between them. It meant she hadn't dreamt the nightmare away. They were safe, but they had lost good people, most recently Willow. Silent tears spilled from Autumn's eyes and cooled over her cheeks. She could only pray that her friend was happier joining her beloved husband in heaven. Autumn wished she could burn the image of Willow's mangled body from her mind. After changing clothes, she had thrown the torn dress with her friend's blood into the flames of the cabin fire. They'd been lucky to lose only the one structure, not as lucky with the price of her friend's life. If they had waited another day or even another hour, Willow might still be with them.

She couldn't allow her mind to go down that dark path. The werewolves had done this to them. Everything that came after their arrival was entirely the fault of those ungodly creatures.

The cabin that had belonged to Autumn and her late husband was being temporarily used to shelter her niece and nephew's wolf friend, Rafael, and his mate Hailey while the shapeshifter waited for his animal to recover from the wounds he'd suffered.

They were more than welcome to her old home. Autumn had no intention of ever moving back in. There were no happy memories tied to Spruce lingering within those closed walls, even before Gavner took it as his personal lodgings. She could not think of a more fitting death than the one doled out by the bear shifter–Gavner in his beast form being mauled by a much larger creature. It was sinful to take pleasure in the suffering and death of another being, but if ever an exception was to be made, this was it. Gavner was a monster who deserved far worse.

A howl made Blossom shriek and fling herself into Autumn's arms. They were both sitting bolt upright on the bed, clutching each other.

After her heart dislodged from her throat, Autumn tried soothing her friend, which was challenging when she herself had broken out into a cold sweat.

"Hailey said that her friends would be checking the perimeter outside our village." Saying it aloud helped calm her nerves.

"Do they have to make that horrid sound?" Blossom asked in an angry, watery voice.

Autumn stroked the back of Blossom's head. "Once Rafael is recovered, they will leave."

Blossom's arms tightened around her middle. "And leave us vulnerable to the next werewolves who come along?"

"We don't know that more will come."

Blossom let go of Autumn and clutched the edge of the blanket in her lap. "Exactly, we don't know. Things were different for our parents. They never had to worry about monsters like werecats or werewolves or shapeshifters when they were our age. We're no match for them, Autumn. That's why God sent us the bears."

"What?" Startled, she turned to face her friend. The tears were gone from Blossom's face, replaced by gutsy determination.

The young woman had always been a sweet, sensitive soul, but that didn't make her weak. In spite of all of the hardships, loss, and suffering, their whole village remained strong. They had been taught as children that the world they inherited was not for the meek.

"Tell me again what Chester said to you last night," Blossom said, sounding resolute.

It took Autumn six long breaths to go back to that conversation. There had been so many, it felt like trying to separate one chirping cricket from all the rest . . . only that was a lie. She remembered that talk with Chester well.

The music and merriment of the night returned to her head. For the first time in three months, they had been able to harvest a pig to feed the village rather than the werewolves. Autumn had allowed herself to savor their newly won freedom.

Torches blazed from posts, lighting the settlement in the night. Chester, with his coal-black skin, saw her, smiled, and walked over with his muscular Native friend Kohana—his chief, she discovered later from Hailey. They had fashioned loincloths out of clothing the village offered, seeming to miss the intended point of the garments. Autumn kept her gaze level with theirs, or rather, tried to. The bear shifters towered about a foot above her.

"Thank you both again," she said, though it was Kohana who had saved her.

"It is our pleasure," Chester said. He stood with his legs a couple feet apart, tall and relaxed, the embodiment of ease.

What must it be like at the top of the food chain—to roam the world fearlessly?

"I will never forget what you did here tonight," she said to Chester, though her words were for Kohana. She found it difficult to look at him without her body reacting in ways unbecoming of a recently widowed woman. "You are always welcome in our village."

Chester beamed. "Your hospitality is greatly appreciated." He spoke in tongues to Kohana.

Autumn braced herself for the deep timbre of his response that had turned her heart into a drum the first time she heard him speak, but he merely nodded.

"We must rejoin our tribe," Chester announced. "Our group of ten was looking for a good place to spend the winter. We passed some caves near your settlement on our journey here. If you and your people are not opposed to shapeshifter neighbors, it would be our pleasure to winter in the caves."

"You mean hibernate?" Autumn asked, curious.

Chester repeated her question to Kohana and the two males broke out into laughter. The rumbling of Kohana's mirth vibrated through Autumn. She threaded her fingers over her abdomen, glad for the long wool gown covering her, which was far more appropriate than the short, torn dress Kohana had first seen her wearing when he—

Her cheeks blazed as she recalled his face in front of her nether regions, sniffing to determine whether Gavner had raped her. Thank God the monster had been unsuccessful and Kohana's bear appeared before the werewolf had a chance to rip her to pieces.

"We do not hibernate," Chester told her in that amused voice of his. Autumn watched him, waiting for more, and was glad to have somewhere to focus other than on the nearly naked man who had inhaled her as though she had a flower blooming between her legs. "But we do enjoy our rest," Chester continued.

"You said there are ten of you?" She had to fight down a flare of panic and remind herself the bear shifters had shown themselves to be friends, not conquerors. They were not ordering the village to provide cabins and meals. They weren't asking to stay in the settlement at all. Chester was asking permission to occupy the caves outside their perimeters through the cold season.

Chester bobbed his head. "Kohana's sister, Nita; her

mate Mahkah; and their son, Nikiti, will join us. The rest of our tribe is made up of unmated males." Again, there had been no comment from Kohana, who appeared content to let Chester do all the talking.

"No other females?" Autumn asked.

"Females are very rare and highly prized among our kind." It was the first time she'd seen Chester's smile sag. In a blink, his teeth were once more flashing in high spirits. "Luckily, we have an advantage over our wolf friends. Our species is able to impregnate human females with our shifter gene to birth offspring capable of transforming into bears."

Repeating that revelation to Blossom in the morning brought a fresh wave of heat to Autumn's face. "It would be an abomination," she whispered.

"Why?" Blossom demanded, surprising her with her conviction so at odds with what Autumn would expect. Her friend swung her legs off the bed, stood in her long light-blue cotton nightgown, and began to pace. "The bears have proven themselves to be protectors. If there are women in the village interested in taking them as husbands, why not? That gives the bears a reason to stay." She whirled around, placing her palms on the edge of the bed to lean forward and look into Autumn's eyes. "Think of their children. They could protect themselves, protect the village." Her eyes took on a gleam as she straightened and swooshed a hand through the air. "They could be the guardians of our village for generations to come."

It gave Autumn pause to see the murky light against the curtain at nearly the same moment, as though Blossom had summoned the dawn of a new day. Her mouth fell open. She felt like she was seeing Blossom for the very first time. "You think to domesticate the bears?"

"Not me personally, but do not forget that they are also men—human and bear—both God's creations. Men have need of brides—even men who transform into bears. They wish to procreate. If they don't find wives with the women in our village, they will move on and perhaps find their way to the other settlements. These are *our* bears, *our* men."

For a fleeting moment, Autumn wondered what it would be like to marry a strong, caring man like Kohana.

Spruce had been a weakling with no one to bully until taking Autumn as his wife, and she realized too late that she'd been baited by false kindness. He'd taken control of her life and treated her like she was a disobedient pet who needed breaking, rather than a treasure to be valued.

What would it be like to know tenderness?

Love?

Passion?

Heat radiated from her face and spread in a flush down her body. Feeling feverish, she flung the blanket aside and got out of bed. "It will be time to feed the children soon," she muttered.

"And what of my proposal?" Blossom asked. "What about the bears?"

"We will speak with our womenfolk first. They must be comfortable with the idea if we are to even consider it."

Blossom opened her dresser drawer and fished out a long skirt and blouse. "While you're feeding the children,

I will round up the women."

Autumn might have teased her about being on a mission if not for the melancholy that stole over her as she wondered which young women in their village might interest the bear chief.

Kohana had saved her. Smelled her. Seen her first.

But she was widowed with children. She'd had her turn as a wife. There were younger women in the village. Beauties just entering their prime, lovely and pure.

Still, she could not help thinking *my bear* with sad, wistful delusion.

chapter two

ONCE DRESSED IN a long, gray gown, her red hair woven into a long braid, Autumn made her way across the settlement, taking in the peaceful quiet. Birds tittered and a pair of squirrels circled around a thick tree trunk in playful chase. Even the forest animals appeared happy the werewolves were no more.

It was early yet, so she visited the graveyard outside the village church and paid her respects, head bowed over the fresh mound. Willow was the first to be buried since the reign of the werewolves. They'd forced the villagers to drag the bodies of their victims out of the settlement and into the woods for wild animals to feed on.

Such horrors could never be allowed to take place again. Maybe Blossom was right. Maybe the bears had been sent to them for a higher purpose.

Autumn's gaze went out of focus as she whispered prayers over Willow's grave, letting tears drip freely. When she was finished, she added, "We took care of every last one of those bastards, my friend. We did it. I just wish you were here to see the return of our village. Be at peace, dear one."

She rubbed the tears off her cheeks before heading to the children's cabin. Though it was getting much lighter, Autumn did not expect to see the kids up after the late-night celebrations and was surprised to find them in the yard outside their shared cabin. Her niece and nephew stood with Rafael and Hailey. The male had darker skin like Kohana, but his hair was short, if a bit shaggy, and he had stubble over his chin. His mate wore her white-blonde hair to her shoulders, shorter than any hair Autumn had ever seen on a female. Every movement and stance she took conveyed confidence, leaving Autumn to wonder once more what it must be like to have the ability to call upon a wild animal within to protect loved ones against the predators of the world.

"Aunt Autumn!" Coral yelled as soon as she saw her. The little girl raced straight for her with a huge grin.

It softened the sharp edges piercing Autumn's heart to see Coral smile after losing her parents at such a young age. Life had always been hard, but never as cruel as it had over the past few months.

Autumn stretched her arms wide, crouched, and wrapped Coral into a hug, squeezing and rocking her from side to side. After embracing her niece, she stood and held her out by her shoulders. "You must be hungry."

"We've already eaten."

"You have?"

Coral nodded enthusiastically as her little brother hurried over for a hug. Autumn picked him up and rubbed her nose against his, getting a dimpled smile and cute laugh out of him.

Rafael and Hailey joined them.

"Good morning," Hailey said in her friendly tone. Her olive-brown eyes were bright, and her smile filled with warmth any time she looked at Rafael.

"I hope you slept well in the cabin," Autumn said. The secretive grins the pair shared made her suspect that the bed had been used for more than slumber.

"We were very comfortable," Hailey said. "Thank you."

Coral pulled on Autumn's gown to get her attention. "Eco and I are going to give Rafael and Hailey the full tour of our village."

"That's a wonderful idea, but first we should offer them breakfast."

"They already ate porridge with us," Eco said. "Rafael, come see my cottage." The little boy took skipping steps in the direction of his family's cabin.

Autumn flashed the wolf shifters a grateful smile for distracting Coral and Eco. The Lord certainly worked in mysterious ways to send her niece and nephew a guardian angel in the form of a wolf man. She had witnessed the worst kind of evil after the werewolves took over their village and was grateful that not all shapeshifters were monsters.

Her youngest son, Flint, sat on the ground with his small wood carved horse, making it jump over a rock. When Autumn started his way, he frowned, got up, and headed in the opposite direction with his toy. The familiar anguish tugged at her chest. She was so tired of the heartache. This had to stop.

Autumn picked up her pace, but Lynx, her eldest, ran out from behind a tree, grabbed the horse carving from

Flint, and shoved him to the ground.

"Give it back!" Flint yelled.

Her nostrils flared as she ran over. "Lynx! What have I told you about pushing? Give your brother back his toy, then apologize."

Lynx scowled at her, stuck his tongue out at Flint, and took off running for the tree fort. Lord give her strength. That boy needed paddling.

Autumn sprinted as best she could in the wool dress, determined to reach Lynx before he made it to the rope ladder. If she had to climb up after him, so be it. When Spruce was alive, they'd battled over discipline. While the werewolves were in charge, she'd done as little as possible to draw attention to herself or her children. Today was a new day, and it was time to remind the boys who was in charge.

Unfortunately, Lynx had the head start—not to mention pants—and reached the tree first. He dropped the wooden horse to free his hands and climbed the rope ladder, scrambling up like a deranged raccoon.

Autumn reached the bottom of the ladder as he began to tug it up. Not happening! She was behind, but she was tall, fast, and feeling half-feral after seven years of suppression. She grabbed the rope, nearly yanking Lynx over. Her heart gave a sickening lurch when his head and torso tipped over and alarm filled his wide eyes. As soon as he righted himself, a ferocious snarl curled his upper lip.

"You tried to kill me!" he screamed. Autumn began climbing as Lynx hollered, "Help! My mom's trying to murder me!"

She had to bite her tongue to keep herself from

yelling back, "Don't tempt me." His outburst wouldn't save him from a spanking this time. Once that joyful chore was complete, she'd trim the dark blond mop hanging over his eyes and shoulders, bathe him, and burn the piece of scrap shirt that looked as though swan-sized moths had eaten through it.

When Autumn was halfway up the ladder, Lynx threw a thin branch at her. She closed her eyes and ducked her head as it sailed by the side of her head. It wasn't large enough to have hurt her, but it turned her vision red and limbs quaking with uncontrollable anger. On the next step up, Autumn missed the rope rung and slipped. Her shaky hands lost their grip and suddenly she was falling backwards, lungs frozen in horror as leaves and sky filled her vision.

There was nothing to grab hold of as she dropped . . . and landed in a pair of strong arms.

Autumn gasped in surprise, dismay, and relief. She turned to thank her rescuer only to have the air knocked from her lungs yet again. Kohana stood mere inches away, his hands on her hips to steady her. Even through the thick wool gown, she felt the heat and strength of those fingers and was shamefully aware of his bare chest and muscles filling the thin space between their bodies.

With a squeak, Autumn jumped back. Her heartbeat thundered as though she were still falling. "Thank you."

Kohana stared into her eyes and nodded, then looked into the tree. Autumn followed his gaze, but Lynx was now hiding somewhere inside the fort.

Kohana returned his attention to her and spoke in his deeply captivating voice.

Autumn found herself leaning forward, listening, momentarily spellbound until he finished speaking and she remembered she couldn't understand a word of his language.

He walked to the rope ladder and spoke again.

Autumn shook her head. "I wish I knew what you were saying."

As though magically summoned, Chester ran across the field, one hand lifted in a friendly wave. Being the darkest-skinned man the village had ever seen, Chester was impossible to miss even if he'd been the timid, quiet type. Long legs and arms flying, he sprinted the entire way over yet wasn't out of breath in the least when he arrived.

"Hello and good morning," he greeted Autumn, the whites of his eyes and teeth standing out in stark contrast with his coal-black skin. "It is a beautiful new day, is it not? What are you doing?" Kohana spoke while Chester continued grinning. "Ah," he said. "Kohana asks if you would like him to retrieve the boy for you."

Autumn clutched her fingers in her hand. While she was grateful to Kohana for catching her, she didn't want a stranger interfering with her family.

"Tell him that won't be necessary," she answered curtly.

Kohana studied her face. Autumn imagined her tone conveyed part of the message before Chester translated.

"This is your son," Chester said more than asked.

"Lynx is six and Flint five." Autumn looked upwards then turned her head in the direction of her youngest.

The bear shifters followed her gaze to each boy. Chester bobbed his head, then spoke quickly to Kohana.

A conversation ensued, leaving Autumn rocking in place awkwardly. She thought it would have been enough to scare Kohana away and let her get back to strangling her eldest.

When Kohana did turn and leave, she couldn't blame him for taking off. Chester, on the other hand, remained behind, beaming at her with his pearly white teeth.

"I suppose you find this entertaining," she said wryly.

There was something about Chester's merriment that helped defuse her anger. The man's eyes shone with humor as he chuckled. "Shall I fetch an ax . . . for the tree, of course?" Seeing Autumn's horror, Chester burst into laughter and pointed at her. "Autumn, I wish you could see your face." Tears leaked from the corners of his eyes as he doubled over and clutched his stomach and chortled.

"You're awful, Chester." But she was holding back a laugh.

He swiped tears from the edges of his eyes and straightened, smiling as bright as ever. "When you are finished here, Kohana has something he wishes for me to discuss with you."

Her mirth faded as she stood rigid in alarm. "What is it?" she half whispered.

Chester's lips pressed together and his eyebrows shot up. "Do not worry, Autumn. I am the bearer of good news. Bear-er, get it?" His joke and chuckle did nothing to allay her concern. Chester cleared his throat dramatically, pounded his chest with one fist, and lifted his chin. "Kohana would like me to convey his interest in claiming you as his mate."

chapter three

AUTUMN'S THROAT WENT summer dry. She had to moisten the roof of her mouth with her tongue before finding her voice. "But I am widowed with two sons. He could choose a woman with her maidenhood intact."

Chester leveled an assessing gaze over her as he stated, "You are a strong, fertile woman—the leader of your tribe."

"I'm—" Her mind went blank for a moment. Kohana had chosen her because he saw her as a leader. As a woman of strength—probably after watching her issue commands and directions to the villagers as soon as the last werewolf was killed. Everyone had looked a bit lost and numb. Autumn was all about action and getting things done.

It was difficult to fathom that a man might covet a dominant wife. Spruce used to call her bossy. A nag. He'd told her to lay off the boys. Keeping her mouth shut had felt as unnatural as a bird without song.

Chester had also called her fertile, which made the flush in her cheeks feel molten. Autumn wasn't sure whether to be flattered or offended.

Did she even want another child? If she had been

married to someone other than Spruce, she would have. After Flint was born, Blossom had secretly helped her with an herbal mix to ward off future pregnancies.

When Autumn was still a maiden, she had dreamed of having a daughter one day. Chester had confided to her the night they met that females were prized.

"Your chief wants a daughter," she said. "What makes him think I can give him one?"

"You already have two boys." Chester looked up at the tree fort, where Lynx was still hiding, and smirked.

Autumn laughed. "That reasoning makes no sense."

Chester shrugged. "My wise and magnanimous chief has the second sight. You would do him the greatest honor in becoming his beloved and the mother of a treasured baby girl." Autumn blinked several times, feeling the sweet promise of those words create fissures in the walls she had erected around her heart years ago. Chester, naturally, had to throw in his own comic commentary. "And you would do me and the other unmated males of our tribe a favor by allowing us to court the females in your village. Only if the women are interested, of course." He lifted his palms in a placating gesture.

"You're not allowed to find a wife until Kohana is married?" Her mouth hung open.

Chester nodded and beamed. "Yes, as it should be—with the exception of Kohana's sister Nita. Females, as we've mentioned, are rare among our kind. Your daughter would be treated as a princess with honors surpassing even that of a chief." Chester's eyebrows jumped to the hairline of his nearly shaved head.

"And what of my boys?"

"Kohana would claim them as his own, giving them his protection, love, and gentle guidance."

Autumn's heart fluttered with hope. She had to turn away before her face gave away the longing with which she wanted these promises to be true. But Kohana was still half beast. A savage from the wild. They were from two different worlds and could not even communicate without Chester. He was a gorgeous man proposing all the right things, but the divide felt as wide as the valleys between mountain peaks.

She looked into the sky, hoping for a sign.

The wife of a respected bear chief who would treasure her and her children—such an offer was not to be dismissed without consideration.

"We have husbands and wives in our village, not mates," Autumn informed Kohana's playful ambassador.

"Whatever you want to call it." Chester shrugged like it made no difference, but it certainly did. The sanctity of marriage was one of the last remaining vestiges of civilization they clung to.

"We would have to be married in church. I will not become a heathen."

Without her father or brother alive to discuss such delicate matters, it was up to Autumn to negotiate a potential union for herself.

Chester laughed again. "We are highly spiritual beings, Autumn, but Kohana understands and agrees to your terms."

Exasperated, Autumn flung out her arms. "How can he possibly agree when he's not yet heard my conditions?

Don't you need to run off and tell him first?"

Chester's chuckle was a language of its own. It had a chiding melody that seemed to convey there was no reason to complicate matters.

"As long as you do not ask Kohana to cut off his hair, all else is acceptable to him."

Her mouth opened, then quickly closed. She loved his hair, and it occurred to her that as Kohana's wife, she would be able to run her fingers through his midnight locks.

Autumn blushed.

"Is that a yes?" Chester asked, lifting onto his toes.

The man was already tall enough without adding extra inches on her.

Schooling her expression, she told him, "I will think on it."

As IT TURNED out, Autumn had nearly a week to ponder Kohana's proposal. The chief and his emissary left the village following her promise to consider accepting him as her husband. It was the bear shifters' intention to collect the rest of their tribe and set themselves up inside the caves. Which reminded Autumn, she needed to make it clear that she would not be living in a cave like a savage. Such thoughts were enough to convince her that a union between herself and the bear chief was impossible.

"You deserve this," Blossom said, as Autumn plaited her hair on the fifth morning since the bear shifters' departure.

After Autumn had repeated the proposal Chester had delivered on Kohana's behalf, Blossom had sighed wistfully and treated it like some kind of fairy tale. Her sweet friend remained stubbornly blind to the bawdy nature of a woman taking up with a beast man. It was an aspect of the arrangement Autumn could not clear from her head, especially in the darkest hours of the night, when wicked desires emerged in her mind.

"It will never work." She sighed sadly.

Blossom huffed and stormed over to where Autumn loomed in front of the window and took over braiding her hair. Her friend's usually gentle fingers tugged at each strand as she finished the weave down Autumn's back.

"If you don't make it work, someone else will, and that would be an absolute shame, Autumn. Stop obsessing over Kohana's background. From everything you've told me, he is a kind and decent man who wants to do right by you. What could be superior to a man who is pure of heart? I thought you above such judgment. Don't be so intolerant."

Autumn's eyes widened. She could barely form words past her sputtering. "I am not intolerant!"

"It's unkind to give a man false hope."

"Blossom! I did no such thing. I am giving the proposal proper consideration."

"I certainly hope so," Blossom said with a sniff.

"You remember my first marriage was an unhappy one," Autumn reminded her. "I will not rush into another."

Blossom's fingers stilled a moment before continuing in a softer manner. She secured the braid with a thin ribbon. "It pains my heart that you were mistreated, my dear, but I'm afraid you must make a decision sooner rather than later."

AUTUMN HAD SEEN enough tears to flood a river over the course of summer. It was inevitable that the day Rafael and his pack left the village, more would flow from the young eyes of Coral and Eco.

The wolf shifters gathered in the field outside the children's cabin to say goodbye.

Her nephew had his arms wrapped around the shapeshifter, face buried in his borrowed pant leg. Coral's eyes were puffy and her chin wobbled as she asked, "Will you come back to visit?"

"If it's okay with your village." Rafael got on his knees and pulled Eco into his arms.

Autumn had to blink rapidly to stop herself from crying at the sight.

"Of course it's okay!" Coral exclaimed. "Aunt Autumn, tell Rafael he can visit whenever he wants."

It was nice to have a reason to chuckle. "Yes, of course. Rafael and his friends are welcome any time."

Hailey stared at her mate with a warmth and tenderness that made Autumn's chest ache. Their five other packmates stood clustered at a distance, casting furtive glances in the direction of the gate. Unlike the werewolves who had taken over the settlement, these wolf shifters were obviously anxious to return to the wilderness.

It was a relief despite the children's distress. Better the wolf shifters go. The longer Rafael stayed, the harder it would be on the kids when he did leave.

"Okay, little man, it's time for this wolf to run free." Rafael stood and set Eco in front of him. The little boy bowed his head. "Do you want me to howl out a hello tonight from across the mountains?"

Autumn clenched her teeth but didn't have the heart to ask Rafael not to howl, especially when Eco was nodding eagerly.

"You and your sister look out for each other."

"We will," Coral informed him.

Rafael chuckled. "I have no doubt."

"Thank you again for bringing my niece and nephew back home safely." Tears filled Autumn's eyes. She picked Eco up and hugged him against her, hoping to bring him some measure of comfort.

"Be safe," Rafael said.

"Where would you like us to leave the clothing we borrowed?" Hailey asked.

"Outside the gate is fine," Autumn said quickly when one of the males in the pack started pulling down his pants. The dark, curly-haired female beside him giggled and said, "Someone's eager to let it all hang loose."

He scoffed. "These pants chafe."

"All right guys, let's head out," Hailey said. She and Rafael turned to lead the group at the same time and bumped into each other. They shared an intimate laugh, after which Hailey said, "Lead the way."

"After you," Rafael returned.

"Together," Hailey said, reaching for his hand.

As they walked away hand in hand, Autumn spared them one last wistful glance before turning her attention to the children. She clapped her hands. "Hey, everyone, how about a game of tug-of-war?"

The other kids, who couldn't care less about the wolf shifters' departure, hollered in earnest. Eco was still rubbing his eyes and watching woefully as Rafael left, But Coral's head lifted in interest.

"Flint, can you get the rope?" Autumn asked, pleased a second later when he nodded and ran to the children's cabin to fetch it.

He still wasn't speaking to her, but at least he did not ignore her entirely.

Ash stepped outside behind Flint as he ran back over with the rope. "I hear there's going to be a game of tug-of-war," Ash said.

Autumn smiled and nodded. "That's right. Want to pick out teams?"

"Happy to."

She watched while Ash paired up two teams that were evenly divided by age and size. His wife and infant girl were probably napping inside while they had a bit of peace and quiet. The young couple had not moved back into their own cabin yet, helping out until someone else volunteered to live in the children's cabin.

It made the most sense for Autumn to move in with the kids, since she was now directly responsible for four of them. With their kind hearts, Ash and Misty knew that Blossom needed Autumn in the wake of their friend's death. She had planned to stay with her friend for a week or two, then move into the children's cabin. That was before Kohana's proposal. Now Autumn didn't know where she'd end up. If she married Kohana, they would need their own cabin. Her boys were used to sleeping on their own, but Coral and Eco had lived with their parents.

She shoved her worries aside to cheer the teams on. Ash had put Flint and Coral together with Robin, which made it easy to root for one team. When she made a place in the grass to watch, Eco came over and sat in her lap, temporarily distracted by the activity.

"Go, Flint! Go, Coral!" Autumn yelled.

When her son's team pulled the other kids over a line dug in the ground, she and Eco clapped their hands. A grin spread across Flint's cheeks, and it was the most joyful sight she had seen in a long time.

When her son's team won again, Autumn lifted her hands high in the air and cheered.

"How about three out of five wins?" Ash said.

Coral squealed gleefully as she threw her weight back. The three kids on the other team gritted their teeth and shoved their toes into the ground, intent on winning the next round. As they were pulled closer to the line, Flint yelled in excitement, "We're going to win! Look, Mom!"

Her name on his lips was the sweetest sound she had heard in years. Autumn leaned forward, grinning . . . until Lynx ran over, grabbed hold of the opposing team's rope, and yanked.

Taken off guard, Flint, Coral, and Robin were pulled with enough force to bring them to their knees.

Leave it to Lynx to ruin her rare moment of parental bliss.

"No fair!" Coral yelled from the ground, glaring at her cousin.

Lynx's smug smile only lasted long enough for Autumn to set Eco aside and spring to her feet. She had him by his shirt before he could run away. The little terror tried to twist out of her grip. When that didn't work, he attempted to shove her away. Autumn grabbed his wrist so tightly, he cried out.

"That hurts!"

"Too bad," Autumn snapped. "I'm taking you around back for a spanking–unless you want to apologize. No? I didn't think so."

Lynx yelled and fought the whole time she dragged him around the children's cabin.

"She's breaking my arm," he screamed to Ash.

The young father rubbed the back of his neck and avoided eye contact. He was probably thanking his lucky stars for the sweet baby girl Misty had given birth to. Well, not all children were little angels–and not all mothers were saints. The eagerness to punish her son brought a sick wave of elation, followed by guilt. Autumn's stomach turned to acid.

On the other side of the cabin, she flipped Lynx around and paddled his bottom while he wailed. He should be grateful she had spared him the humiliation of a public spanking. Lynx didn't see it that way.

"I hate you!" he screamed when she was finished.

Her heart sank as she watched him flee. The boy needed a father to nurture him, not a weasel like Spruce, who had egged him on.

It was in that moment that she made up her mind to accept Kohana's proposal.

"I'm doing this for my boys," she whispered to herself. She said it again to quiet the voice telling her she wanted to marry Kohana for selfish, wanton reasons.

The moment the man had kneeled naked in front of her, something powerful had awoken inside her neglected body and spirit. She wanted him as she had never dared want something for herself before. Autumn longed for a good husband to help her raise her boys. She wanted to expand her family. Lord help her, she wanted love and passion too.

 chapter four

"WHAT IF THE bears don't return?"

The small group of young women and one man Blossom had invited to her cabin filled every available seating space. Sky, Storm, and Rain were all present, along with their brother Sterling. Autumn wasn't sure how she felt about Ivy and Clover's attendance. The two sisters had become Autumn's responsibility after the werewolves killed their mother—no thanks to her brother, their uncle Harvey. The man had closed himself and his friends inside the village bunker soon after the werewolves made their first kill. The traitorous man would not even wait for his own sister to be transported to safety.

Clay and Hazel's father, Pete, was inside as well. Clay had tried knocking to give the cowards the all-clear, but they had not opened the door. They probably thought it was villagers desperate to get away from the werewolves, which made it all the more sinful. The men in the bunker were not Autumn's priority, and Harvey had lost any future guardianship over his nieces as far as she was concerned.

At ages eighteen and nineteen, Ivy and Clover were

old enough to take care of themselves, but that had not stopped Autumn from doing everything in her power to shield them from Gavner's perverse appetite.

Autumn helped Blossom hand out steaming cups of tea.

Sky stood in the middle of the room with her hands on her hips as though she were the one in charge. "Our wolf allies have left us. If the bears don't come back, we'll be sitting ducks the next time werewolves or werecats stumble upon our settlement."

"A man doesn't propose to a woman without returning for an answer," Blossom said in a sweet, yet firm, voice. When she offered a cup of tea to the outspoken young woman, Sky shook her head. Blossom next tried handing it to Autumn.

"You have it, my dear. I'm not thirsty."

"I had some earlier. Take it. It's my calming blend."

Smiling her thanks, Autumn took the tea and sipped it while standing. She and Blossom remained on their feet to give their guests the sitting spots.

Sky looked at Autumn and lifted a brow. "You plan to accept?"

"Yes."

"Then you must be married as soon as can be to secure the tribe's loyalty."

Rain snorted. "Sky's just impatient to be courted by a bear man."

"And you're not?" Sky challenged with an arch of her brow.

Rain smiled sheepishly.

Cupping her tea in both hands, Autumn peered

through the steam to where Sterling sat at the edge of the rocker, feet planted flat on the ground. There were stitches in his off-white socks where the material had been mended. He and his three sisters, like Ivy and Clover, had lost both parents. With modern medicine a luxury of the past, their life expectancies weren't incredibly long. It sickened Autumn that many of the elders who had held out were the first to be culled by the werewolves.

What would Autumn's parents have thought of her marrying a shapeshifter? Perhaps it was better that they were not around to see such things.

With the exception of Blossom and Autumn, no one else gathered had been married. Sky was the oldest of the younger women. It made sense that she would consider a union with a strong man who could protect her and her siblings.

"Sterling, what are your thoughts on the matter?" Blossom asked, voicing the question Autumn shared.

Sterling's hand went to the bandage on his arm, a stark reminder that he had not been able to defend himself against the werewolves. If not for Rafael's interference, he would have been killed as mercilessly as Willow.

"My sisters are in need of husbands. If there is a worthy man among the bear shifters, he will have my blessings."

"Hopefully there is more than one worthy man," Rain said.

Her twin sister, Storm, nodded.

"You all wish to become brides of bears?" Autumn asked.

The three sisters exchanged glances.

"If they are anything like Kohana, then yes," Storm said.

"I like Chester," Sky announced. When her siblings looked at her wide-eyed, she threw her arms out to her sides. "What? He makes me laugh, and he speaks English."

There was a lull in the conversation as they reflected on that truth. While the room was quiet, Clover cleared her throat gently and spoke with her head and eyes downcast. "Will the other men learn our language or must we learn theirs?"

"I expect Kohana to learn English." Autumn didn't mean for her answer to come out sounding harsh, but she had no intention of speaking in tongues.

The maternal instinct she felt toward Clover and Ivy also left her conflicted as to her feelings about one, or both, of the girls marrying a bear shifter. Sky, she knew, could handle a bit of wildness, as could Storm and Rain.

As could Autumn.

But Clover and Ivy were sweet girls. Until Autumn met the rest of the tribe, she would voice caution.

TWO DAYS AFTER the meeting in Blossom's cabin, the bears returned. Chester arrived alone to deliver the news that they had reached the caves and that he would visit again once they were settled.

What exactly was required for a bear shifter to settle in a cave? Autumn wondered. And more importantly, why hadn't Kohana accompanied Chester? Was he still interested in marrying her? Chester had not inquired, and Autumn wasn't about to volunteer her answer freely.

Several more days passed before Chester returned, this time with Kohana, in the early afternoon. Autumn stood under the shade of a tree, supervising the children with Ash. The instant her eyes landed on Kohana striding over, her heart shot off like a comet. His muscles gleamed in the sun, hard ridges rising from his chest like mountains over God's green earth. The sounds of the kids playing faded into the distance as Autumn basked in the glorious view of such a magnificent man. Was he truly to become hers? What if Chester was playing a trick on her?

Before another second of doubt could pass, Kohana met her gaze and flashed her a smile that turned her insides into breakfast mush.

"Hello," he said.

Autumn's mouth opened wide in surprised delight. Had Chester been teaching him English during their absence? "Hello," she responded eagerly.

Kohana's next words were indecipherable, but she loved hearing the sound of his deep, melodic voice.

Chester took a step forward to address Autumn. "Kohana would like me to introduce you to his sister and brother-in-law. May I bring them by tomorrow?"

"Yes, of course. The entire tribe is welcome to visit."

As soon as Chester translated, Kohana beamed. The pleased look he gave her made Autumn's tummy flutter like a young maiden in the throes of her first crush.

"What are they doing here?" Her son's indignant voice chased the butterflies right out of her belly.

She'd managed to get his ratty shirt off him, but that was about all. He was still unbathed, shaggy-haired, and now bare-chested—refusing to wear any kind of top if he couldn't have his favorite piece of scrap.

Lynx had his hands on his hips, glowering at Chester.

Kohana spoke and Chester's head bobbed as he listened. "Yes. Very true."

Lynx narrowed his eyes. "What did he say?"

Chester gave Lynx a considering look, taking his time answering. Autumn felt just as impatient to understand Kohana's words. Finally, Chester obliged. "My chief says that you are very strong and will become a skilled hunter admired by your village."

Lynx pursed his lips and gave Chester a hard stare as though determining whether these words had been spoken in earnest or jest.

Kohana spoke again and Chester translated, "Kohana would like to take you hunting tomorrow morning."

Autumn sucked air in through her nose. The extra oxygen seemed to fill her eyes. She grabbed hold of Lynx and pulled him to her. "It is too dangerous."

"There is no place safer than with Kohana, I assure you," Chester said.

"Mom," Lynx grumbled, pulling out of her grasp. At least he did not yank himself away. He straightened his back and held his chin high. "I am old enough to go outside the walls."

"What about me?" Flint asked.

Autumn craned her neck and saw her youngest son, along with Coral and Eco, peering down from the tree fort.

"You are too young," Lynx informed him. "Kohana chose me."

"What about the werecats?" Coral asked. When Lynx scoffed, her lips drew back, revealing all of her teeth. "They killed my parents and the rest of our group—everyone besides me and my brother," she yelled at her cousin.

"They should have never left the settlement," Lynx fired back.

"You're a bully and a jerk, Lynx!"

"No, I'm strong."

While the cousins argued, Chester and Kohana conferred in low voices until Chester lifted his voice. "Children, it is all right. The beasts who killed your fleeing villagers are all dead now. Our tribe took care of them with the help of our wolf friends—though mostly us, as the wolves were fleeing and unable to handle such a large horde. These unnatural creatures are no match for bears. If any more come around, they will be most unfortunate."

Lynx smirked as though he were one of the bears, ready to take down a shrieking monster with his bare fists.

The bear shifters shared a look before Chester continued. "Kohana and his best tracker Maska will take both boys out tomorrow morning, if Autumn agrees."

Lynx whipped around with a pleading look that made her question whether her sight had gone fuzzy. "Please, Mom, you have to let me go. I'll be fine. No one messes with a bear."

Flint scrambled down the rope ladder and hurried over, standing beside his brother. "I want to go too, Mom. Kohana said I could come."

Lynx's jaw tightened, but he seemed to think better of picking a fight with Flint. Autumn couldn't get the grimace off her face. She had no doubt Kohana could protect her boys—she had seen what his bear had done to Gavner—but there were far too many ways to get hurt in the wilderness. A wrong step along a bluff could lead to a fatal tumble. A hidden snake could strike with its poisonous venom. A tree could fall on them.

Capturing her bottom lip with her front teeth, Autumn hedged. "I don't know."

Lynx stepped in front of her, palms open to the sky. "We've lost a lot of men. The village needs me to step up and hunt wild game," he reasoned.

"Feeding the settlement is not your responsibility," Autumn said.

Chester cleared his throat. "Perhaps not, but now is the best time to build the boys' hunting skills. They will become the most able men in your village—highly coveted by the females."

Up in the tree fort, Coral snorted. Flint tugged gently on her skirt. "Please, Mom. Please. I'll be careful."

"You'll scare off all the animals with your whining," Lynx snapped.

Autumn folded her arms. "Either you both go or neither goes."

Lynx huffed and rolled his eyes. "Fine."

"I haven't agreed to anything yet."

"But—"

"Do you promise to look out for your little brother while you're in the woods?"

"Yes."

"And do you agree to do as Kohana tells you while

you're in his care?"

Lynx took a little longer to answer, but his yes was no less determined.

"What about you, Flint? Do you agree to behave yourself and listen to Kohana?"

"How are we supposed to listen to him when we don't understand what he's saying?" Flint peered up at Kohana.

Her boy had a good point. Autumn looked at Chester who grinned and winked. "Kohana and Maska are experts in hunting, tracking, *and* nonverbal communication."

"Okay," Flint said.

Chester clapped his hands together. "Excellent. It's all settled." Kohana nodded stoically. After the boys ran off to tell their friends, Chester took up the spot beside her and lowered his voice. "And what about you, Autumn? Are you agreeable to accepting my chief as your mate? In your case, there is no obligation to obey or behave yourself in Kohana's company."

Autumn's face flushed hot, setting Chester off laughing.

Kohana sighed heavily as though knowing exactly what type of fun Chester was having at Autumn's expense. Whatever the bear chief said next had his friend sobering up quickly.

Turning away from the black-skinned jester, Autumn faced Kohana.

"Yes," she said, nodding.

It was one of the few words that required no translating.

 chapter five

THE NEXT MORNING, Autumn threw herself into finishing the corn harvest with Clover and Ivy. The grueling pace she set kept her from pulling on her braid with worry for her boys and eased the anxiety about her upcoming betrothal to a man who was part bear.

"We must plan a big celebration feast," Clover said to Ivy, as the older of the two sisters filled her basket with ears of corn.

Autumn swiped her long sleeve over her sweaty forehead. "I don't want a fuss being made over me. I've already been married once before."

"But Kohana hasn't," Clover argued. "We want to show our respect to the tribe's chief."

"Plus, the village could really use more reasons to rejoice," Ivy said as she added an armload of corn to her basket.

"Don't worry. We'll take care of all the planning," Clover said. She grabbed her basket and headed for the root cellar.

Ivy quickly finished filling hers and took off after her sister.

Autumn watched them a moment, an ear of corn in one hand. Without the werewolves around to intimidate them, the two young women were spreading their wings. A sense of pride swelled inside her chest, along with a few tears. With the sun beaming down over the tall stalks, Autumn knew that the girls' parents were looking down on their daughters with love.

As for their craven uncle, well, Harvey could remain in the bunker for the next decade for all Autumn cared.

THAT AFTERNOON, CHESTER arrived with Kohana's sister and brother-in-law. Autumn half expected them to lumber into the settlement in bear form, but the couple arrived on foot and dressed in clothes made from animal hide. They were tan-skinned, dark-haired, and looked at least five years older than Autumn. The man's hair was short, making her wonder if Kohana was the only male in his tribe who wore it long.

Bright smile in place, Chester made introductions in front of Blossom's cottage. When Autumn invited the couple in, Chester translated that they wished to have a tour of the settlement first.

"This is Nita and Mahkah. Autumn." Chester pointed everyone out, however unnecessary.

"Hello," Nita said, holding her right palm open. Her husband did the same.

"Hello, and welcome to our village," Autumn said, showing teeth when she smiled.

Chester translated, which led her to conclude that Nita's

command of the English language was as limited as her brother's. The woman's tall, lean body was only half covered by the short skin dress that clung to her full breasts and hips. Her long hair cascading down both shoulders provided nearly as much coverage as the homemade garment.

"Where is your son?"

"Nikiti is at the caves with our tribe," Chester answered.

Hearing her son's name, Nita smiled and nodded. The bears appeared to put their full faith into Chester's communications. He could alter their words at will and they would be none the wiser, but the man had a good-natured and trustworthy air about him—even with his comic delivery.

"Well, I'll go ahead and show you around. These cabins, as you see, are all fairly similar. Larger cottages accommodate larger families. We also have communal structures for big gatherings such as worship in our church and the children's cabin, where the older kids move to make room for younger siblings in expanding families." That or be kicked out, as Spruce had done to their boys, but she kept that bit to herself.

Nita and Mahkah did not ask many questions, but they watched her with rapt attention and took everything in with bright eyes. Their heads moved with Autumn's finger every time she pointed something out. It felt soothing to speak, even though they could not understand her. More than the gardening, this helped ease Autumn's anxiety over her sons.

When they reached the garden, Nita made a joyful sound. She touched the crops they passed with reverence, rubbing plant leaves between her thumb and forefinger gently with a beaming smile. Her voice was low as she made quick comments to her husband, who answered in soft grunts. Not wanting to interrupt the woman as she explored the garden, Autumn slowed her steps as she led the small group to each flourishing area. She was proud of their produce, grains, herbs, and fruits. Seeing it through a newcomer's eyes deepened her satisfaction.

Chester strolled over to Autumn with his brilliant smile. "Nita is in love with your gardens. We're always on the move, which means whatever we eat fresh has to be foraged."

"Tell her she's welcome to plant and harvest in our garden anytime she wants."

When Chester translated, Nita looked at Autumn and flashed her a smile full of teeth. She said something to Chester, to which he responded, "Thank you."

Eyes back on Autumn's, Nita sounded the words out slowly. "Thank you."

"You are most welcome anytime." Autumn grinned. She had a good feeling that she and her sister-in-law-to-be were going to get along very well together.

They walked by Clover and Ivy, who were keeping their heads down as they dug potatoes out of the earth. After introductions were made, Nita said something to Chester.

"Ah, Lady Clover, Nita asks if she can look at one of the potatoes you have dug up?"

"Of course," Clover said, holding out a potato so big her fingers were unable to close around the middle.

Nita took it carefully, as though it were a sparrow

she did not wish to scare off. She studied it up close and showed it to her mate, who brushed her hair back and smiled at her kindly. If all of the men in Kohana's tribe were as gentle as the ones Autumn had met, they would make good husbands for the village women.

As Nita handed the potato back to Clover, she said, "Thank you."

"You're welcome. Do you want to take it with you back to the caves? It tastes wonderful cooked."

After Chester translated, Nita took the potato back with another "Thank you."

From the garden, Autumn led her guests to the church, a beautiful structure made from bricks their founders had flown in so that it might weather the turbulent decades ahead. The iron cross rising from the highest point of the structure was like a weather vane directing all of Autumn's hopes and prayers into the heavens—giving her courage and strength through all of life's trials.

Nita appeared more impressed by the rose bushes lovingly cultivated on the church grounds in red, pink, and yellow than by the brick construction. The female bear shifter leaned in to smell the yellow roses with a smile that widened in delight. Her attention was next drawn to the church's window boxes spilling over with purple petunias and delicate white sweet alyssum. Vibrant pink asters popped cheerfully along the walls.

"It is a beautiful place to be married," Chester offered.

"Yes," Autumn said. Now Kohana had only to bring her boys back unharmed, and they could set a date to exchange vows.

"Kohana has one request."

A tremor of unease descended rapidly across her sinking chest at the earnest look on Chester's face and the serious note his tone had taken.

While Nita and Mahkah circled the church, she stayed behind to talk to Chester.

"What is it?" she asked, unable to take the suspense any longer.

"After you are married, Kohana would like to bring you back to his cave—not to live—but to conceive." Her mouth hung open, which seemed to suit Chester just fine, as he continued before she could interrupt with protests. "You must understand that caves are a sacred place for us—like your church. It is a fathomless well of mythical power that gifts our offspring with shapeshifting abilities."

Her attempt to respond came out as a gurgle of dismay. Chester laughed, returning to his smiles and light tone.

"Do not worry, Autumn. Once you are pregnant, you need not bestow your affections on one another in the caves—unless you want to." Her glare set him off laughing again.

The stiff press of her arms made her shoulders ache. "I am not an animal," she informed him pertly.

"No, but you wish for your child to be born with abilities, yes?"

Folding her arms and pursing her lips, Autumn responded, "I want all of my children to be safe. If God sees fit to grant my next baby extra strength, I will be grateful, though I will love that child no more and no less whether that comes to pass."

Chester clucked his tongue and shook his head. "Conceive in a cave and you will have no need to leave things to chance."

She heaved out a huff. "I will think on it." And likely say yes because it was the only request Kohana had asked of her, and because it wasn't for himself but for their child.

"Do not worry," Chester repeated in his relaxed tone. "Kohana will impregnate you in no time."

Heat blasted in multiple directions—up Autumn's neck to her hairline and down her belly to her thighs. It spread across her arms, which loosened and fell to her sides. At least Chester wasn't laughing at her expense. He had turned to the red roses. "May I pick one?"

"Watch out for the thorns," Autumn mumbled.

Nita and Mahkah rounded the church.

"Are you ready to visit the children's cabin?" Autumn asked.

After Chester translated, Nita nodded eagerly.

They walked by the garden again, only to lose their translator when Chester dashed down the beaten dirt path to present Clover with the rose he had picked. Autumn stopped to gape as Clover brushed the dirt off her hands before accepting the rose with a bashful smile. While she stared at it in her hand, her grin widened. Chester ran back beaming with an extra sparkle in his eyes.

"Clover is like a daughter to me," Autumn warned him. She would prefer for the man to redirect his attention on someone else—someone a few years older and less delicate. Someone like Sky.

Chester placed his hand over his heart. "Let me assure

you, Autumn, that the happiness of my wife will become more dear to me than my own. Her joy is my joy. I believe we all want the same thing." The man certainly did not lack in confidence, but she liked what he was saying. Autumn did not doubt that Chester's use of the word *wife* rather than *mate* had been a calculated choice. The man was too clever by half.

But there was still the issue of the consummation caves, as she was beginning to think of them. Clover, and the rest of the village's young women, deserved a respectable deflowering on a proper bed surrounded by four walls, not rocks.

The more Autumn thought on it, the more she felt she must insist that the first night be within the new couple's cabin.

As for herself, she was no maiden, so perhaps she could grant Kohana the wedding night he desired from her. Once with child, she could put the cave sex behind her.

A fresh wave of heat licked up her thighs. She clamped her jaw shut and mentally boxed up the naughty images to examine later while the village slumbered.

The children were running around the lawn outside the cabin when Autumn brought their guests over. Waving at them, Coral raced over while Eco trailed after her. Sadness that life had forced Coral to become a sister and mother to the boy was buffered by her gratitude that the siblings had each other for company. It also reminded Autumn that she had lost her own brother. She would have appreciated support from him while married to Spruce, but Fern had his own family to take care of. Autumn loved and mourned him, along with the rest of the villagers they had lost. All except Spruce, but she would never admit something so unholy out loud.

"Hi," Coral said eagerly, coming to a jumping stop in front of Nita.

"Hi," Nita repeated.

Eco caught up in time as Coral made her own introduction. "I am Coral, and this is my little brother, Eco."

Blushing, Eco dashed behind his sister to hide.

Chester had barely finished translating before Coral said, "I heard you have a son. Where is he?"

"He is at the caves," Autumn said gently.

"How old is he? When can we meet him?"

Upon translating, Nita and Mahkah looked at one another and shared a smile. Nita sounded excited as she spoke to Chester. He grinned while she talked, waiting until she finished to relay her words.

"Nikiti has been with us these past seven years. He was born in his bear form and is a year past the age when a bear shifter is capable of his first transformation. Our tribe has been unable to coax him into his two-legged form." Nita spoke animatedly again. Chester nodded. "Nita believes that if he spends time with the children, he will transform."

"Cool!" Coral exclaimed at the same time as Autumn's heart dropped into her stomach like a ladle sinking to the bottom of a soup pot.

"Is it safe to have a bear cub around human children?" she asked, as claws slashed across her mind.

"Yes, yes," Chester said, bobbing his head. "Nikiti would not harm a butterfly. Behind all that fur, he understands how to behave himself. The cub is harmless, I promise you, Autumn."

She gripped her fingers, not feeling reassured at all.

"Aunt Autumn, I want to meet Nikiti," Coral said. "Can he come tomorrow? Please?"

"The adults need to speak on it first," Autumn said.

Coral's lower lip pouted. "I want to play with a bear cub."

"We'll see."

Betrothals with bears.

Sex caves.

Bear cubs playing with children.

Lord help them, village life was about to change forever.

chapter six

"MOM! MOM!"

Autumn was chopping potatoes with Blossom when she heard Flint's excited voice calling to her through the open door. She dropped what she was doing and ran outside where the men and boys stood grinning from ear to ear. Kohana and Maska each held one end of a deer. Like Kohana, Maska wore pants made of animal skin. His hair was short, leading her to believe that she might be correct in assuming only the chief grew his long. There was a quiver filled with arrows strapped to his back. Lynx held the bow.

"Look what we caught," Flint said, pointing at the deer.

"Now we're going to skin it," Lynx said with an eager gleam in his eyes. "Where are the knives?"

Her stomach lurched. "You need to learn to handle a blade safely first."

Lynx rolled his eyes, setting her teeth on edge.

Blossom walked out in a swirl of floral patchwork skirts and woven, beaded anklets above her bare feet. Her long light-brown hair was loose, with a thin braid that started near the middle of her head and ended at her rear.

"My gosh. Look what you boys caught. It's a beauty," she gushed.

The boys weren't the only ones beaming. Kohana's friend grinned and stared at Blossom like she was the first sunrise he had seen in months. He said something to Kohana, who raised his brows before addressing Autumn with his foreign words.

"Um, Chester went back to the caves with your sister and brother-in-law." After Kohana squinted, she tried again with hand gestures. "Chester, Nita, and Mahkah returned to the caves." Autumn pointed in the direction of the village gate.

Kohana answered and kept talking, saying more words at once then she had ever heard. Then he and his friend were speaking.

"That deer must be getting heavy," Autumn tried to reason. The men had yet to set it down.

Lynx huffed. "They don't want the meat to get any dirtier than it has to. Come on, Mom. Get us the knives already." When she shot him a warning glare, he changed his tone. "Kohana will show me how to skin the deer."

At the mention of his name, Kohana paused, looked at Lynx and nodded as though he understood English from a child's mouth perfectly. It was sweet, endearing, and beyond exasperating. When Autumn looked at Blossom, her friend shrugged and smiled sweetly.

"Fine," she said with a sigh. "Wait here." Autumn returned to the cabin and selected a sharpened skinning knife sheathed in leather from a drawer in Blossom's kitchen. When she stepped outside, it was to see Sky, Storm, and Rain swarming Kohana's friend, who suddenly looked extremely overwhelmed.

"Sky," Sky said pressing her palm to her chest. "Storm." She pushed her sister, who yelped, "Hey!" Smirking, Sky continued introductions. When she reached out for Rain, her sister wisely took a step back.

"Rain," she said for herself.

"And you are?" Sky asked, raising a brow.

The male just stared at her. She repeated her introductions then pointed at him and spread her arms open in question.

With a heavy huff, and eyes lifting skywards, Lynx stepped over and said, "This is Maska."

"Maska," Sky repeated, giving him a flirty once-over.

Maska clutched the deer and looked sideways at Kohana with an expression that looked to Autumn like "Help." Kohana gave the barest shrug.

"You are making him totally uncomfortable, Sky," Rain admonished.

"What? I'm just saying hello and yes, I'm available." Sky winked at Maska.

His tanned cheeks flushed. Taking pity on the shy man, Autumn strode over and held the knife out to Kohana. He flashed her a smile that traveled across her body like a rainbow and then spoke. The only thing Autumn understood was that he was not taking the knife from her.

"Mom, can't you see his hands are full?" Lynx asked impatiently. "Give the knife to me."

"Absolutely not." She laughed humorlessly.

"Mom," Lynx groaned.

Ever watchful, Kohana followed the exchange and spoke. He nodded at Lynx.

"He wants you to give me the knife," Lynx said.

"Do you suddenly speak his language?"

"I'm learning."

"Well, I doubt you learned that much in one day."

"I do think that's what he's communicating, though," Blossom said, as Kohana spoke and nodded at Lynx again.

"Mom," Lynx coaxed.

"Mom," Flint echoed. "The deer needs dressing."

Maybe she would hold onto the knife for a few more minutes, just to hear her sons call her Mom a dozen more times. But Kohana and Maska had been kept waiting long enough.

With a stern glare, Autumn crouched in front of Lynx, holding up the knife with a warning. "You are carrying it only. Do not take it out of its sheath. It's extremely sharp. Give it to Kohana as soon as his hands are free. Do you understand?" When he nodded, she said, "Tell me you understand."

"I understand. Now will you please give me the knife?"

Autumn narrowed her eyes before handing it to him.

Kohana said something and grinned at her.

"We can use a worktable at the butchering quarters," Lynx announced. "Follow me."

"See you later, Maska," Sky said in an overly sweet voice, throwing in a wave of her fingers as though strumming the air.

Maska's dark eyebrows drew together and his forehead wrinkled.

"I don't think you're his type," Storm said.

Sky placed one hand on her hip and smirked. "He's just trying to decipher what I'm saying. Maybe I need to find another way to express my interest."

"Sister," Rain said, "I'm fairly certain he knows."

Storm grunted her agreement. "We all know. Even Lynx and Flint picked up on your not-so-subtle hints."

"Who said I was trying to be subtle?" Sky's question was met with shared laughter between the women.

AFTER THE DEER was skinned, gutted, and bled, the men set aside choice pieces before putting the rest in the village's smoker. When Autumn tried to invite Kohana and Maska to stay for dinner, they smiled and shook their heads before departing, leaving behind all of the meat and skin.

"How about the four of us enjoy this fine meat you've caught with a side of boiled potatoes?" Blossom suggested.

Flint nodded. Autumn hoped he would not relapse into non-speaking terms around her.

The boys followed them inside Blossom's cabin.

"Sit and relax while we cook up the deer meat. You boys have had a long day," Blossom said.

Lynx held on to the deer's antlers. "I'm going to hang these up over my bed," he announced.

"Kohana said I get to keep the next pair," Flint said.

"How do you know what he's saying?" Autumn asked.

Flint walked over to the kitchen and leaned against Blossom's worktable. "Mom, it's easy. You just have to pay attention."

"Oh, it's that easy, is it?" She chuckled, feeling a lightheartedness as foreign to her as Kohana's language.

Flint pushed away and walked over to his brother. "Can I hold them?"

"No."

"I want to hold them for a moment."

"They're mine."

"Mom!"

"Leave your brother alone." She nearly laughed at the irony. Usually Lynx was the one bothering Flint. "You'll have your own pair the next time you get a deer with Kohana."

Flint dropped into Blossom's rocking chair and pushed it into motion with his toes, a pout on his lips. Autumn watched for several seconds to make sure he wasn't being too rough on her friend's furniture before turning away. Blossom already had the deer steaks sizzling in a pan of animal fat over her kitchen's wood stove.

"That was nice of the men to clean and cut these up all nice for us. You should bring them some of the smoked meat tomorrow," Blossom suggested. "See how they're getting on in the caves."

Autumn's heart did a little flip remembering her concession about the caves. She breathed in the smell of cooked meat and rubbed the back of her neck.

"You should come with me. I think Maska likes you."

Blossom tested the deer steaks with a knife and left them to cook longer before flipping them over. She looked over with a smile and a shake of her head. "I've already been a bride."

"But not a mother."

It seemed unfair given all of the cute infant hats and socks Blossom had knitted and gifted over the years—even before she was married. Autumn tried to read the seemingly blank stare in Blossom's eyes. She couldn't tell if her friend felt wistful or resigned to remaining single and childless.

Clearing her throat, Blossom announced, "I think the meat is about ready," in her usual cheerful voice.

chapter seven

THE FOLLOWING DAY, Autumn did as Blossom suggested, even though her friend declined joining her on an excursion to the caves.

She filled a basket with smoked deer strips, along with a jar of Blossom's blueberry preserves and a coarse rye bread loaf baked early that morning.

Autumn set out in the late afternoon, having waited to see if Kohana or Chester would come by first, but no bear shifters had entered their village that day. Clutching the delivery, she made her way to the caves, feeling freer with each step outside the settlement. Spruce had made the village feel more like a prison than a home after he forbade her from venturing out alone.

A gentle breeze rustled the leaves around her—the woods welcoming her back. There was a worn path to the caves, as the village teenagers used to spend time with friends in the cool shade away from prying eyes. Autumn had shared her first kiss with Spruce in the caves, back when she believed him to be honorable.

"Hello?" she called out when she reached the first

large opening set among moss-covered rocks and surrounding trees.

She was met with silence.

Hmm. Maybe the shifters were out hunting. Or were they perhaps sleeping?

"Hello?" Autumn called louder.

Balancing the basket between her hip and arm, she stepped into the largest and easiest to enter cave at ground level. Enough light entered to see that it was currently vacant, but there were spears, bows, and arrows stacked neatly inside. Maybe the shifters were out hunting in their animal forms.

A slight shiver trickled down her spine as she stepped in deeper, trying to decide whether to leave the basket, wait, or deliver it at another time.

Then she noticed the primitive cave drawings etched into the rock—crude scenes that made Autumn flush all the way to the roots of her hair. She should leave right away, but shock suspended her in place as her eyes moved from one drawing to the next. Naked men and women covered the walls. Penises protruded longer and thicker than the arms on the men. The women had been given mountainous breasts. Men were depicted sheathed behind women. Other drawings showed women with rounded bellies. Then she noticed the one of a bear making love to a human woman.

Autumn's eyes rounded like an owl's.

Amused laughter rolled through the cave. She knew the sound well enough not to break out into a cold sweat of panic. Her only hope was that Chester was alone.

Rather than run out, Autumn turned and kept to the shadows, hoping to hide her flaming cheeks. Luckily, there was no one with Chester. As he walked into the cave, his smiling teeth beamed brighter against his dark skin.

He looked at the rocky canvas and bobbed his head. "Our tribe enjoys having art on our walls."

"Art?" Autumn's eyebrows rose to her hairline.

"Do not worry, Autumn. The etchings are a harmless activity enjoyed by the men."

"Is any of this your work?"

Chester shrugged and smiled wider.

Somehow, she needed to get the wily man to redirect his attentions from Clover to Sky.

Autumn clutched her stomach. The back of her neck prickled with heat that even the shade could not cool. "Kohana didn't draw any of these, did he?"

"No, no. Kohana is much too serious for drawing on walls." Chester lifted his hands, the lighter skin on his palms facing her as he shook his head.

Autumn released a breath of relief, eyes momentarily closing out the erotic images.

"He would rather do these things *with* you."

When her eyes flew open and jaw dropped, Chester's laughter bounced off the walls and echoed deep within the cavern.

"Very funny," Autumn huffed. She hurried out and looked around the surrounding forest. "Where is Kohana, anyway?"

Chester strolled out behind her. "He and the others are out hunting."

"As bears?"

"Yes, Autumn, as bears."

She blew a loose tuft of red hair off of her forehead. "I brought him and Maska this basket of food—to share if they like."

Chester peered inside and grinned. "Did Clover not wish to bring me a basket?"

Autumn narrowed her eyes. "This is smoked meat from the kill Kohana and Maska prepared."

"Kohana and Maska did not make the bread and jam," he noted. When Autumn didn't respond, he raised two slender brows, grinning the entire time. Finally, he laughed and held out an arm. "I will see to it that Kohana receives the basket when he returns, and I promise the bread will still be there, and at least half of the jam."

"Chester!"

He burst into laughter, doubling over and clutching his stomach as he continued. After he got a hold of himself, he straightened and looked at Autumn with eyes that still laughed. "You are fun to tease, Autumn. I will not take a single crumb or taste of the jam or jerky. Hopefully one day soon I will have a sweet bride to make me a basket. Until then, I will guard this one for my chief."

In spite of his teasing, Autumn trusted him to deliver the basket in full to Kohana, so she handed it over.

After seeing the erotic cave drawings, she felt eager to get back to the village before the bears returned. A question that had been nagging at her made her hang back a moment.

"Chester, you said that Nita gave birth to a bear cub. There's no way that could happen to me or the other women, right? I won't have an actual bear in my belly?" She pressed her fingers over her stomach, her breaths becoming strained as her imagination ran wild.

Chester did not laugh at her question. He set the basket on the ground beside his left foot and addressed her concern in reassuring tones. "A human woman cannot birth a bear in its animal form. Your child will grow inside of you with tiny fingers and toes, not claws. I swear on the sun and the moon. Around the age of six, your child will have the ability to transform, but not a moment sooner."

She blinked back tears, not realizing until that moment how scared she had been. "Thank you, Chester."

He bobbed his head. "All will be well, Autumn."

With that reassurance, she returned to her village.

"**N**IKITI, OVER HERE!" Coral yelled, waving both arms in the air after popping out from behind a tree.

They were supposed to be playing hide-and-seek, but the bear cub had gotten distracted by the children beckoning him to climb up to the fort. He had done so the previous day and the kids could not stop talking about it.

"Nikiti!" Coral yelled louder.

The cub looked from the treetops to where Coral stood. Seeing her, he charged joyfully to reach her.

After several days of supervising the children playing with Nikiti in this manner, Autumn was finally starting to relax. Once the cub reached her, Coral threw her arms around Nikiti and hugged him.

"Coral has all but called dibs early. Smart girl," Sky

joked as she rocked on her heels.

Sky had never shown interest in the children's cabin and play area in the past. Now that Mahkah's brother Akando was spending time in the village with his nephew, Sky had taken to hanging around the kids.

"Don't you have berries or something to gather?" Autumn joked back, not taking her eyes off her niece with the cub.

Eco joined them tentatively and began petting Nikiti, which made Autumn chuckle. Beside her, Sky snorted. "I can't wait for you and Kohana to get married tomorrow so the rest of us can get on with the courting."

Autumn tugged her braid over her shoulder, an explosion of butterflies taking flight inside her belly.

"Are you . . . excited?" Sky asked.

Laughter burst from Autumn's tongue. She had been expecting Sky to ask if she was nervous, but of course she would wiggle her brows suggestively and say "excited" instead.

Smirking, Sky feigned ignorance. "What?" she asked. "He's one hot heathen."

"Sky!"

She rolled her eyes. "We all know Spruce wasn't making you happy. I bet Kohana won't have the same problem."

"My personal life is personal," Autumn informed her.

"Suit yourself." Sky gave her a lazy shrug and sauntered over to where Akando stood with his brother and Nita watching Nikiti with content smiles.

Autumn looked around the play area with a small

frown. Were her boys still inside the cabin? That wasn't like them, and yet they had been keeping oddly scarce all week. At first she had worried that they were upset about her upcoming betrothal, but that didn't fit with the excitement they expressed during their evening meals shared in Blossom's cottage. Misty had overheard Lynx boasting to the other kids that Kohana had chosen his mom as his bride because she was the most beautiful of all the women. Remembering what the young mother had shared made Autumn flush with pleasure every time she played her son's words in her mind.

She was still smiling when she reached the cabin door, which was closed despite the balmy afternoon. Opening it, she took a step inside, then heard Flint yell, "No!" Misty came running at her, infant jostling in her arms. Little Meadow started to wail as Misty yelped. "Don't come in!"

Autumn stood momentarily frozen. As Misty and her crying infant ran straight for her, she took a step back.

"Misty, what is going on?"

Misty hurried outside. "Close that for me, will you please?"

Autumn closed the door while Misty settled Meadow down. The infant girl's bellows turned to softer crying as Misty rocked her gently in her arms, talking soothingly the whole while. "It's okay, my little love. Had a bit of excitement back there, didn't we? You're a good girl. Mama's brave little sweetheart."

Meadow hiccupped and flashed her mother a toothless grin. It brought a smile to Autumn's lips remembering what cute babies her boys had been. The flutter returned to her stomach as she imagined holding a newborn in her arms again.

Meadow rested her head against Misty's chest, her eyelids quivering slightly before closing. Misty kissed the top of her little girl's head, then looked over her shoulder at the closed door before whispering to Autumn, "The boys are making you wedding gifts. They want it to be a surprise."

Autumn's hand went to her heart. "They're making me presents?"

With a big smile, Misty nodded. "They have been hard at work all week. It's so sweet."

Tears filled Autumn's eyes.

Maybe, just maybe, she would have the husband and family she always dreamed of.

Tomorrow she'd exchange vows with Kohana.

Tomorrow she would give the bear chief her love and loyalty. Hopefully, it would not take too long to give him a baby too.

chapter eight

DRESSED IN AN ivory gown with lace trim, Autumn
was walked down the village chapel's aisle by Sterling.
She wore a beautiful crown of wildflowers and ribbons
Blossom had made for her, and her red hair flowed in
silky waves down her back.

Her dear friend sat in the front pew with Lynx and
Flint—both of whom were bathed and dressed in clean
slacks and buttoned shirts. Behind their pew, Misty sat
with Coral and Eco, and behind them, Clover and Ivy,
followed by Sterling's sisters.

The gathering for the ceremony was a small and
intimate affair. On the groom's side, Nita and Mahkah took
the front pew. Akando was supervising their son outside,
who had not yet transformed into a boy, while the rest
of the tribe waited with the villagers for the festivities to
begin. Behind them, Maska sat on the edge of the bench,
bolt upright, observing the proceedings with keen interest.

Kohana had borrowed slacks and a buttoned shirt—at
Autumn's insistence. He stood near the pulpit with Chester
at his side. When Autumn had explained what a best man

was, Chester had jumped at the opportunity with gusto. The black-skinned man was beaming like the midday sun in a cloudless sky.

Kohana's eyes were on Autumn as Sterling delivered her to his side. A blush spread across her cheeks at his proximity and the raw strength emanating off every pore on his body. His inky hair was combed to a shine that made her mouth go dry as she imagined it brushing against her bare skin. The borrowed shirt stretched over muscles chiseled by toil and time.

Beautiful brown eyes drank her in. While the groom stood poised, Autumn felt like a riot of nerves as anticipation, excitement, jitters, and joy quaked through her. She could not pick out which emotion was the strongest.

Ash stepped up to the pulpit and began the proceedings. They had lost their old pastor to pneumonia two winters ago. The pastor's replacement had been among the villagers to flee and perish when they set off for the nearest neighboring settlement after the werewolves took over.

As of yet, it had not been decided who would lead sermons and ceremonies. Ash had kindly stepped in for the moment. Autumn hoped it became a permanent calling. The young man had patience, virtue, and kindness. She could not think of a villager more capable to guide their devotions. Perhaps her wedding would serve more than one purpose if it showed Ash the way.

In that moment she felt it. Joy. It overshadowed all the other emotions as she spoke her vows to Kohana. With help from Chester, Kohana repeated the vows, promising to love and honor her until death did them part.

Autumn heard someone sniffle, but her gaze remained on Kohana's as Ash pronounced them husband and wife.

"You may kiss the bride," Ash said.

Chester's translation brought the biggest grin to Kohana's lips. He reached for Autumn and drew her to him like a breath of fresh mountain air. Her bones turned doughy in his strong grasp and her lips pliant as he brought his mouth over hers. She melted against his kiss and savored his embrace. His hands, oh Lord, his hands felt so nice holding her waist.

Someone stood up and cheered—probably Sky.

Autumn blinked once, but there was no clearing her daze.

She was married to this gorgeous man. He was hers and she was his.

Hers.

His.

Her mind flicked back and forth on this glorious gift life had brought her.

"Let's celebrate!" Sky yelled.

Still flushed, and likely to remain that way for hours, Autumn laced her fingers through her husband's and gave him a gentle tug.

The children stood and tossed dried pink and yellow rose petals from small baskets into the aisle as they walked by hand in hand. Sterling and Sky hurried ahead of them to throw open the chapel doors and announce, "Husband and wife!"

Cheers went up, and when Autumn stepped outside

with Kohana, more rose petals were tossed at them amidst the whistles and congratulations. She was swept away with the crowd as they traveled in one boisterous and jolly mass to the celebration grounds. Mugs of Blossom's famous raspberry cordial were passed out to the adults, juice to the children, and her friend made a brief, though lovely, toast.

Autumn touched her mug to Kohana's. He watched her take a sip, then did the same. She watched his expression for a sign of pleasure, but his focus was fastened to her lips. Autumn tried to steady her hand as she lifted her mug and swallowed another sip of the cordial.

She had not expected to feel these kinds of nerves, being a woman of experience. But Kohana was unlike any male she had ever known. He took up so much physical space in the world and in her heart. Love was not something to trust, or so she had believed. Would Kohana change now that she was his?

He offered her a sweet smile, cupped her cheek, and murmured, "Autumn," reverently.

Her body melted and heart flipped at the soft sound of her name on his lips.

"Mom!" Flint yelled.

Autumn jerked, nearly spilling raspberry cordial on her gown. She never thought she would wear it again. Luckily, it still fit. Blossom had added extra lace and ribbon to make it different from the dress she had worn to exchange her vows with Spruce.

Flint hurried over, tugging Chester with him. When they reached Autumn and Kohana, the black-skinned man tipped his mug and gulped down the contents. "This is most delicious. Are you drinking yours?" he asked Kohana. Without bothering to translate, he plucked the mug from Kohana and downed it.

"Chester!" Autumn's forehead wrinkled.

Chester laughed. "I am merely serving my chief. Kohana prefers to keep a clear head at all times."

Autumn smiled with pleasure. "I am happy to hear it."

Chester translated. Kohana nodded at her and grinned.

"It is time for you to open your presents. Come on, Mom," Flint interjected with a tug at her skirt. "Lynx is waiting in the children's cabin. We need you, Kohana, and Chester."

"You made me gifts?" Chester exclaimed, batting his long eyelashes in a flurry.

Flint sighed with impatience. "No, we need you to translate to Kohana."

"Ah," Chester said, but his grin showed he had known this all along. He set the two mugs he had drained on the ground. Autumn placed hers beside them.

"Come on." Flint scooped his arm in the air for them to follow. Once the children's cabin was in sight, he ran for the door. Autumn was not about to jog in her wedding gown. Upon reaching the cabin, the first thing she noticed inside was a cot topped with gifts wrapped in cloth and tied with twine. Lynx and Flint stood on either side of the cot grinning from ear to ear.

Her vision went blurry with tears of happiness. This moment was more than she had ever dreamed of. She didn't need any presents. The best gifts were standing with her in this cabin right now.

Flint grabbed a bundle off the cot and ran up to her. "Mom! Mom! Open mine first."

"What can it be?" Autumn asked.

"Open it and find out."

She touched her boy's head gently before taking the bundle, loosening the twine, and unwrapping it slowly. Inside was a pair of fur-trimmed deerskin slippers.

"Flint! You made these?"

"Misty helped him," Lynx said.

"Only a little," Flint snapped at his big brother.

Autumn ran her fingers through the soft fur edging the rim. "These are beautiful." She couldn't stop a soft sniffle from escaping her nose.

"Open mine!" Lynx said. He hurried over and thrust a smaller item wrapped in cloth and tied much tighter than Flint's lopsided bow.

Not wanting to relinquish the slippers Flint had made her, Autumn pressed them between her arm and side while working the knot out of the twine. She unfolded the fabric, revealing a bone choker.

"Lynx, this is beautiful."

"Chester helped him," Flint said.

"I love my gifts." Autumn let a tear slip down her cheek as she hugged Lynx and then Flint.

"Put it on, Mom," Lynx said.

"Put them both on," Flint added.

Turning to Kohana, Autumn didn't have to say anything through Chester for him to understand as she handed her husband the bone choker. He ran his hand over the long, bone pipes, nodded, and spoke.

"Kohana says it's beautiful craftsmanship," Chester said to Lynx.

Autumn lifted her hair and held it over her head while her husband secured it around her neck.

"It looks cool," Lynx said.

"Put my gift on too, Mom," Flint said.

Autumn kicked off her ivory leather-soled slippers and put on the ones Flint had made her. "They fit perfectly," she said, as she looked down to admire them on her feet. "Thank you, boys. I will treasure these gifts forever."

Lynx and Flint beamed.

"Now Kohana!" Flint yelled as he ran to the cot.

It turned out the boys had both made arrowheads for Kohana. Translating through Chester, he praised the edgings, notches, and sharp tips, holding each one up to inspect and admire. The boys were utterly silent the entire time Kohana looked over their gifts to him. Watching the three of them—her husband with her two boys—Autumn felt like her heart might burst out of her chest with happiness.

Her earlier fear of birthing a cub faded like shadows in the sun.

She was ready for another baby to expand their happy family.

Kohana held the arrowheads in his palm and spoke.

"My chief requests that you keep these safe until he attaches them to arrow shafts. Perhaps you would like to help him in a few days' time."

"Here," Lynx said, cupping his hands to take the arrowheads. "I'll hide them where no one will find them."

"Come join the festivities afterwards," Autumn said. "There's juice and games. Blossom has a feast planned for tonight."

Lynx nodded, though his focus was intent on the arrowheads he carried toward the back door.

On the walk back to the glen, Kohana and Chester conversed in Kohana's native tongue while Autumn's mind drifted merrily along like a fluffy cloud in a warm and lazy sky.

The din from multiple conversations reached their ears as they returned to the celebration. Sky and Akando were making rapid hand gestures at one another. Noticing their approach, Akando called out, "Chester," in a commanding tone.

"Duty calls," Chester said, bobbing his head before setting off to join Sky and Akando.

The other bear shifters were clustered in a group together, conversing between sips of Blossom's raspberry cordial. Near their circle, Coral tried to share her juice with Nikiti. The cub's tongue dipped into the mug, setting Coral off into a fit of giggles. Nikiti tried to hold the mug between his paws only to drop it. When the contents spilled on the ground, he bellowed mournfully.

"It's okay, Nikiti," Coral said, petting his head. "I'll get you more juice."

She stood, but before she could step away, the cub's fur dissolved into skin and his claws retracted, replaced by fingers and toes. A brown-haired boy crouched in his place. Everyone went quiet. Then Nikiti got up on wobbly legs and said, "Juice!"

Laughter from the villagers and cries of joy from

the bear shifters were tossed into the air with the same merriment as the rose petals after the ceremony. Nita picked her son up and hugged him against her chest, words gushing out of her like water rushing from mountain falls. Mahkah joined her. After they had hugged, patted, and inspected their boy from head to toes, they brought him over to meet his uncle and new aunt.

Kohana said a few words, then grunted and smiled at the boy.

"It is very nice of you to join us in human form today," Autumn said.

Coral skipped over. "Hi, Nikiti."

"Coral, how about you find Nikiti some clothes to borrow?" Autumn suggested.

"Okay. Come on, Nikiti." Coral grabbed his hand and tugged him away.

The adults chuckled and Nita watched with happy tears filling her eyes.

When dusk came, the torches were lit and music started. Everyone wore smiles, and more of the bear shifters were venturing outside their group to mingle with the village women—with Chester's help. Autumn might have felt bad for him, but his language skills had the benefit of keeping him too occupied to flirt with Clover. Besides, Chester clearly enjoyed his duties.

Autumn was so caught up in her joy that she didn't immediately notice Kohana steering her away from the crowd until they were on the fringe of the gathering.

He spoke in a husky voice that filled her belly with molten heat.

"Yes," she whispered, even though he might not have asked a question. He could have just told her she looked beautiful. It didn't matter. She knew this moment was coming and she was ready.

Taking his hand, she walked with her husband out of the settlement to head to the caves.

 chapter nine

KOHANA HELPED AUTUMN up a rocky outcropping to a cave entrance about ten feet off the ground. It relieved her that he had not brought her to the lower cave with the erotic pictures. She had enough of those running through her mind without adding cheek-flaming visuals.

Deer skins had been piled on a smooth section of ground. Autumn willed her body not to turn sun-crisped red and tried not to visibly shake.

Was Kohana a virgin?

That was a mystery for another time. Right now, he did not hesitate when he stepped forward and stripped her of her floral headpiece, bone necklace, and slippers before lifting her gown.

Her chest rose and fell rapidly as he undressed her. Once she stood in front of him as naked as the day she had been born, she braced herself for his groping hands, but Kohana took a step back to look at her. His perusal was steady and sensual, beginning from her head and easing down like a feather floating softly to her toes.

Kohana said something and gave a nod.

"You find me acceptable, I take it," Autumn said. Her words dried up beneath his heated gaze.

She knew what came next. Their customs were different, but there was only one way to consummate a marriage. She had always found it best to count her blessings. Autumn had never been violated, never gone hungry or been without shelter. She could do her wifely duty. Had years of practice silencing her wanton desires. Being married to Spruce had made it easy to stifle all carnal pleasure. Perhaps, like Spruce, Kohana would leave her alone once she was pregnant. The sooner the better. She felt things for him that no pious woman should feel, especially not for a shapeshifting heathen. But he was good with her boys, and she trusted he would be good to their child and to her.

Already, he was showcasing the restraint he possessed over himself in all things, even this. He removed his borrowed clothing, tossed the garments aside, and pulled his shoulders back, his chest high, like he wanted Autumn to look him over as he had done with her.

The flush she felt heat her cheeks spread down her arms. It was as though her skin was leaching color from her hair.

This wasn't the first time she had seen him naked. That had been a panicked moment before she understood that he was the bear who had saved her from Gavner's murderous fangs. He had been beautiful then, her angelic savior with raven hair and the muscles of an avenging warrior. Language had not mattered, because in his eyes she had seen the goodness of his soul.

But now they stood alone together in a cave and he was erect, thick and long, his manhood already weeping at the tip. His gaze was savage, a man looking at his woman. It felt sinful how much that look excited her.

She felt a budding between her legs and dampness like dew glossing over flower petals. The tightening of her nipples made her blush deepen.

Kohana's deep voice startled her. She gave a slight jerk. He repeated his words, as though that would be of any help.

Well, she was certainly glad Chester wasn't around to translate or witness their union.

Was Kohana asking permission to consummate their marriage? She'd never heard of such a thing.

After Autumn nodded, a devilish smile appeared over Kohana's lips and he stepped forward to make her his. Her heart took off as the towering mass of muscle collided with her. Strong hands guided her over the deer skin.

Kohana's jet black hair fell over his shoulders, brushing over the hard planes of his pectorals as he leaned over her. Her heart pounded harder and her breaths came out in rapid bursts as he turned her around and positioned her on all fours. Autumn was no innocent, but she had only been with one man before, a weakling who had struggled to get it up half the time. She doubted Kohana would have that problem. His hands spreading her apart communicated his intent on breeding rather than foreplay, which filled her with as much relief as disappointment. Autumn did not know how she would handle those hands caressing her body or his tongue or teeth on her skin.

She was still imagining those sharp canines in his bear's jaw when he entered her. The sound that came out of her was a gasp of satisfaction. Mortification deluged her senses until fading altogether as Kohana took possession of her body. An approving grunt rumbled above her as his manhood burrowed inside her slick channel.

Oh, God. There was no hiding her wicked desires now.

I'm his wife, she admonished herself. There were women in her village who believed the act of lovemaking was beautiful and pure. To enjoy the activity was a show of gratitude both to the body God had granted her and to the husband who had pledged his love, loyalty, and protection. That was the idea, at least.

But years of suppression were hard to let go of. She had only to bite her tongue. He would probably finish soon. Spruce always got it over with fast.

But this man was also a beast, a chief, a hunter, and a predator. He moved with ardent thrusts that felt more like a merging of two souls than a bedding.

Kohana did not finish quickly. He did not stop. Did not slow.

Jaw clenched, sweat tracked between her heaving breasts that bounced with abandon while her husband fucked her like she was a four-legged beast. Instead of trying to tame her, she felt like he wanted her to turn feral and buck back, taking him in deeper and rougher.

She wouldn't. She couldn't. It wasn't decent.

Without words to communicate, she willed him to take his pleasure and end the torment. His relentless thrusts felt as though they might breach her womb. He rubbed at a hidden gate, loosening her hold over herself with each stroke.

The moan that inevitably tore through her lips sounded like a wild animal being released from her cage. Even more alarming, she couldn't stop. Her throat was a crashing waterfall of noise that pitched itself into the cave, flooding the walls with the echo of her pleasure.

The frenzy took hold. She bucked back, riding her husband's length, her hips jerking and sweat now dripping off her flushed skin. Her throat vibrated on a moan with no end—echoing across the universe.

Her husband rode her harder and faster, but still it wasn't enough. She made a growling sound and wondered if he wasn't somehow turning her into a beast. Without words to communicate, they were reduced to pants and grunts during their savage mating.

There was no going harder or faster or deeper than what Kohana did to her now. But he kept going until both their bodies were drenched in sweat. Bear-like grunts made Autumn's chest flare in panic, but the sight of Kohana's hands gripping her hips eased her fear that he had transformed behind her.

It was a powerful pelvis and a muscular lower abdomen thumping against her bottom—not fur. He was all man and all hers. This changed everything.

She shoved herself back, sheathing him fully, and moaned louder. Kohana drove forward, breaking through her gate, releasing a flood that swept through her passage and wrenched a scream of ecstasy right off her tongue.

Her belly sagged and her arms and legs spasmed as

though she had just run up and down the mountain peaks. Kohana's arms encircled her middle as he planted himself deep within her and flooded her womb with his seed.

His hands were the only things preventing her from collapsing face first onto the deerskin. She was glad she didn't have to face him immediately. Her hair stuck to her sweat-soaked skin, and the memory of her moans still echoed inside her head. Just as she was catching her breath, whoops and cheers arose outside the cave.

Oh, God. His tribe had heard everything. She had hoped they would remain at the celebration and give them a night of privacy.

While she tried not to die of mortification, words were shouted up. An amused chuckle had Kohana shaking against her backside. He spoke back to his tribe, not needing to yell as the rock walls amplified his words.

Which meant her moans had been broadcasting all over the forest. She winced in horror.

"Don't be mad at Kohana," Chester yelled. "We tried to stay behind as he instructed, but we are so happy for our chief and his new bride we returned to wish blessings on you both."

Autumn scowled, picturing Chester grinning up at the cave. There was no way she was going to have a conversation with him right now.

"Go away, Chester!" she yelled. "And take the rest of your tribe with you. Far away."

Laughter from outside followed her command. Chester translated to her husband, whose words didn't sound as amused as they had a moment before. The laughter ceased.

Was he angry at her for presuming to order his tribe? She braced herself for Chester's translation.

"Our chief tells us to obey the word of our chieftess." Autumn blinked several times in surprise. "We are leaving now," Chester assured her. "Many blessings on your union. May the seeds of your labor bear long-lasting fruit."

Kohana bellowed a single word that Autumn took to mean, "Go!"

Chester stopped talking, his laughter fading into the dusk.

Autumn's skin began to cool, but she still felt bashful about her actions during their coupling. Her husband stiffened and grew steadily inside her chamber still slick with his seed. She sucked in a breath, determined not to let go of all feminine decency the second time around.

Kohana seemed almost telepathic and most certainly unwilling to accept anything less than her complete and total abandon when it came to their joining. After several experimental thrusts that produced no sound from her lips, he reached around and stroked her nipples. A fresh wave of slick entered Autumn's passage as she moaned.

Kohana made a pleased grunt, then rocked his hips, riding her at a steady gallop that increased her body's temperature and made her pant. After bringing her to completion, he filled her again. There was no laughter or cheers this time. They were left to catch their breath and rest. She had never fallen asleep so quickly. When Autumn next woke, it was still night and there was a fire crackling gently between her and the cave's entrance.

Her husband sat on a boulder, leaning slightly

forward, watching her. Had he been like that all along, watching her sleep? She flushed in an instant. Her cheeks only grew hotter when she read the look of intention in Kohana's eyes.

"Again?" she rasped, sleep turning her voice husky.

She felt like a sweaty mess, but the look of worship in her husband's gaze made her feel like a goddess.

He dropped to his knees beside her and started to turn her around. Autumn grabbed his wrist and squeezed, stopping him. It occurred to her that perhaps Kohana was taking his instructions from the cave drawings and that it was time he received a little guidance from his new bride. She held her husband in her gaze as she tugged him on top of her and kissed him deeply. When they joined, Autumn didn't bite her tongue or hold back.

chapter ten

"**D**OES MY HUSBAND still believe I'm going to have a girl?" Autumn asked Chester.

Fall and winter had passed, giving way to an explosion of spring blossoms and warm days. The temperatures still dropped at night, but Autumn was currently soaking in the sunshine on a balmy afternoon watching the kids shout and play in the tree house and field below. She sat with her back propped against the children's cabin, a hand on her bulging belly. She was roughly seven months into her term, and even this far along, neither of her boys had grown so big at this stage.

Seated on her left side, Chester merely chuckled. The man had even more reason to be happy, with his upcoming marriage to Clover. They would be the fourth bear-and-woman couple to be married. As such, Autumn had insisted that Chester wear pants and a shirt. Some of the bear shifters still wore loincloths. Kohana had taken to wearing tight skin pants, but as the weather warmed, he didn't bother with a shirt. The sight of his tanned, muscular chest brought Autumn more pleasure than she would ever admit out loud.

Her husband did many things to please her, but he had his limits when it came to his appearance and independence. Chester, on the other hand, was ready to do backflips to keep in Autumn's good graces with his wedding to Clover fast approaching.

Ash, as Autumn had hoped, had taken on the role of village pastor.

Nita and Mahkah were now overseeing the children's cabin. Once Nikiti transformed, he had not wanted to return to his bear form. For now, the couple was content to see him making friends and learning both languages—unlike Kohana. Autumn's husband stubbornly refused more than rudimentary English. She supposed she was just as hardheaded, since she knew less of his language than he knew of hers.

He had moved with her into the cabin that had belonged to her brother and sister-in-law. When she invited the boys to join them, both had said a firm, "No." She supposed that independence, once achieved, was a hard thing to give up. It was better that way, especially since Kohana's nightly desires had not dwindled the slightest bit, no matter how large Autumn became with child.

Her husband and boys, along with Akando, were out hunting. Kohana had to replace his best tracker, since Maska would not leave Blossom's side once she started showing signs of the baby they had made together soon after their wedding.

Her friend sat to her right, about five months pregnant, knitting away at tiny socks and hats. Clay and Juniper's infant son had a matching set in blue and yellow, while Ash and Misty's little girl had a pink and white set. The two young mothers sat on a bench in the shade breastfeeding.

Sky ambled past them. Once she reached Autumn, she plopped down in the grass and leaned back on her wrists. "Look at the three of us all pregnant," she said by way of greeting.

Sky had yet to show signs of a baby, but her courses were over a month late and she said she felt changes in her body.

"Soon there will be a fourth," Chester boasted.

Sky snorted and rolled her eyes before refocusing them on the knitting needles in Blossom's ever busy hands. "Do you have a secret stash of yarn squirreled away? I swear you never run out of materials." Blossom flashed her a secretive smile. Her eyebrows jumped as she continued knitting. "Fine. Don't tell me. But can you add little bear ears to my baby's hat?"

Blossom paused her activity. "That could look really cute. Okay, I'll give it a try."

"I *know* it will look cute," Sky said. "I have complete confidence in you."

For the sake of her bladder, Autumn tried not to chuckle at Sky's antics. "Chester, help me up. I need to pee."

"It is my honor to serve you in my chief's absence." Chester leaped to his feet and held out his hand, tugging gently to pull Autumn off the ground.

Sky tilted her head back and grinned deviously. "Jeez, Autumn. You look ready to pop. Are you sure you and Kohana didn't sneak off to the caves before the wedding?"

"No, Sky, we did not," Autumn said with a huff.

When Chester offered to escort her, she waved him off and waddled to the nearest outhouse, which was behind the children's cabin. After doing her business, she stepped out of the wooden shack and found Hazel fidgeting in place.

Autumn moved out of the way, but Hazel did not step forward to use the outhouse. She pulled at her fingers and worried her lip. Hazel had been avoiding Autumn and her friends ever since she chickened out of luring Gavner away at the last minute. Autumn had tried to tell her it was okay—that she was in no way to blame for everything that had transpired with the werewolves. But Hazel had clearly struggled with guilt and mistrust of the bear shifters. She had been notably absent during the wedding celebrations and remained withdrawn despite the passing months of peace.

She avoided eye contact now, though it appeared she wanted to say something.

"Hazel, what is the matter?" Autumn asked gently.

Shoulders hunched, Hazel finally looked up. "It's my father. He and his friends have emerged from the bunker."

"Where are they?"

"My father is with Juniper meeting his new grandbaby." Hazel grimaced.

"And Harvey?"

Hazel's next words were cut off by a roar. The young woman's eyes expanded. Autumn hurried toward the glen, but Hazel stood in place—her face having gone pale.

"The bears are our friends," she reminded the terror-stricken woman. Poor Hazel had never been the same since the night Willow was murdered by the werewolves.

Autumn did not have time to comfort her, though. She hurried, as quickly as her body allowed, to the glen. The bellows intensified, making her heart jerk against her chest. After rounding the corner, she gasped when she saw four full-grown brown bears bellowing and pacing in agitation in the glen, children fleeing, Blossom hugging her knees crying, infants wailing, Coral clinging to her brother and to Nikiti, and Sky screaming at Harvey.

What in the world?

Autumn's attempt at running turned into more of a hop and jiggle. She went straight for Harvey, figuring he was the source of the upset.

"What did you do?" she demanded.

Sky jerked her thumb at the bearded man with the sunken cheeks, hard jaw, sandy hair, and protruding nose. "This idiot threatened Nikiti. Don't you know never to mess with a bear cub, especially around his parents?" Sky scoffed in disgust.

"You threatened the boy?" Autumn narrowed her eyes on Harvey, who glared back at her.

"I did not threaten the animal; I warned the children to stay away from him."

Autumn put her hands on her hips. "You've been hiding for over a year, so let me catch you up, Harvey. The bears are our allies and our friends. They're our husbands and—"

"I can see that." He sneered at her belly.

Gritting her teeth, Autumn finished, "They are full members of our village."

One of the bears got onto his hind legs and roared.

Autumn winced as her eardrums rang.

"Animals. Savages," Harvey spat.

"Oh, go back to your bunker, old man," Sky said.

"Is anyone hurt?" Autumn demanded.

Sky shook her head. "I think Chester and Maska are trying to calm Nita and Mahkah down. Dipshit here," she tilted her head at Harvey, "is lucky Kohana and Akando weren't present to overhear his insults."

Harvey's gaze hardened on Sky. "It's a good thing your parents are no longer around to see what's become of you. I'm going to see to it my nieces don't suffer the same shameful fate."

Autumn's nostrils flared. "Leave Clover and Ivy alone."

"I'm their family." Harvey jabbed his thumb into his chest. "The only family those poor girls got left. Clover won't be giving herself over to no heathen shapeshifter."

"You mean a black shapeshifter?" Sky challenged.

Harvey shot her a disturbing smile, then took off in the direction of the village garden. Heart lurching, Autumn felt like she was being tugged in opposite directions. The bears would never hurt the children, but the kids were clearly scared. Blossom was sobbing and now Eco was crying. The infants still wailed. Clay stood between Juniper and his father.

Autumn lifted her hands and pressed them to her forehead.

"What do you want me to do?" Sky asked.

Releasing a heavy breath, Autumn lowered her arms. "Find your brother and tell him to stay with Clover and Ivy until Harvey calms down. I'll sort all this out." She rolled her wrist at the activity in the glen.

"Why couldn't they have stayed in the bunker another fifty years?" Sky grumbled before taking off to do as Autumn had asked.

It wasn't like Blossom to openly cry, so Autumn went to her friend first. When she tried to squat beside her, Blossom yelped, "No! Don't strain yourself. I can stand." She scrambled to her feet and swiped the tears off her cheeks, sobs turning to sniffles.

"Did Harvey say something to you?" Autumn asked.

Blossom blinked several times, avoiding eye contact. "It doesn't matter," she said softly.

"It matters to me."

Blossom placed her hand on her belly. "I think the baby is just making me more sensitive. You should check on Coral and Eco."

Autumn frowned, watching Blossom gather up her yarn and knitting needles before heading for her cottage, her eyes downcast. A painful ache entered her heart before it was blasted away by anger that Harvey had clearly said something to upset such a sweet woman.

She wished the hateful man had fled with the group who left. She wished the werecats had— Autumn stopped herself before her next thought damned her soul. Jaw tight, she made her way to her niece and nephew in a wide arc around the bears who were still pacing, though no longer bellowing. Harvey's absence created its own kind of calm, though the infants still wailed while Misty and Juniper tried calming them. Ash ran over to Misty. Their foreheads practically touched and then he was escorting her toward their cabin.

When Autumn reached her niece and nephew, she wanted to drop to the ground and gather them in her arms, but her pregnancy made such basic actions a lot more difficult.

Coral held tight to Eco in one hand, and Nikiti in her other. The young bear shifter stared wide-eyed where his parents treaded over the grass in jerky strides. Eco gaped.

"Hey, you three. Don't worry about Harvey and his friends. They won't hurt Nikiti," Autumn said in her most reassuring voice.

"How do you know?" Coral demanded.

"Because Harvey is all bark and no bite, as the saying goes." Autumn offered her a smile, but Coral wasn't having it.

She lifted her chin high in the air and said, "Nikiti's parents *could* bite Harvey. He's lucky they didn't."

Autumn grimaced at the eager lilt in her voice.

If any of the bear shifters hurt a villager, no matter how much they might deserve it, the peace between the two species would crumble apart. One way or another, they all had to live together.

"Coral, I know you would never wish harm on a fellow villager." Autumn chose to ignore the roll of her niece's eyes. "Harvey was underground for over a year and is not thinking clearly."

Coral huffed. "He's a coward."

"All the more reason to pray for him to find his way and open his heart to our new friends."

"Whatever."

"Coral," Autumn warned.

"Nita and Mahkah are coming over," Coral said, jutting her chin out.

Heart pounding, Autumn turned. The sight of towering brown bears still set her on edge even knowing they meant no harm. But what she saw were naked humans running toward them. She avoided looking below the shifters' necks as they reached Nikiti. The boy's mother pulled him out of Coral's grasp and lifted him into her arms. She spoke rapidly. Nikiti tried pulling away, but her arms only tightened around her son.

Autumn saw that Chester and Maska had transformed, as well. Maska hurried off in the direction of Blossom's cottage, which was now his home as well. Chester reached to the ground for his discarded pants and shirt.

"Did you hear what Harvey said to Blossom?" Autumn asked.

Chester, for once, was not smiling. "I saw the man with the disagreeable face speak to her, but his words were too low for me to hear, and Maska does not know enough English to have understood. Where is this man now?" Chester twisted his neck from side to side.

If she told him he had gone for Clover and Ivy, it might anger Chester enough to transform, and then she would have no peacekeeper to calm him down.

She needed her husband's help setting things right.

"He's gone to visit family."

Chester's eyes narrowed. "Who is this man's family?" She sighed. "Autumn?" When she chewed on her bottom lip, Chester straightened and announced, "I am going to check on Clover and her sister."

421

Autumn's eyes expanded. "Chester, wait."

But the man was already striding away. Even if she had not been carrying a tiny human inside her, it would have been difficult to keep up when Chester took off at a jog with his long legs. He ran past cabins with Autumn lagging behind in pursuit. She lost sight of Chester when he darted behind the cottages on the path leading to Clover and Ivy's home.

Before she had a chance to reach the girls' cabin, a gunshot rang out, causing Autumn to stumble over her next step and clutch her racing heart.

The whole world went silent as her mind screamed, "No!"

 chapter eleven

"**Y**OU STAY AWAY from my niece, you hear me, beast?"

Autumn was out of breath when she reached the girls' cabin. Harvey stood in front of the door, shotgun pointed at Chester, whose teeth were bared and muscles corded, though he did not appear hurt.

"Don't you dare hurt him, Harvey!" Clover screamed.

She and Ivy glowered at their uncle from the side, hands fisted from roughly five feet away. Sterling stood with them, a hard gaze set on Harvey.

Nearby villagers had already gathered, watching the scene unfold from two sides of the cabin. No one congregated behind Chester. Heart still racing, Autumn gulped down several breaths, her voice shaking as she asked, "Where . . . did you . . . get . . . that gun?"

Harvey smirked with yellowing teeth. The bunker had not improved his questionable hygiene. "Not all of us were a hunch of hippy dippies like your granddaddy. My father made sure we had some guns and ammo in the bunker in case of an emergency."

A swarm of angry bees filled Autumn's head. "Where were you and your guns when the werewolves attacked?"

Harvey's smile dropped. "Don't you take that tone with me. Thanks to your granddaddy's misguided rules, my pa had to hide the guns. I went into the bunker to find them and liberate our village."

"It took you a year to locate your weapons?" She put her hands on her hips and arched a brow.

His jaw tightened. "Some of us got sick and needed tending to."

"For an entire year?" Autumn asked louder.

The shotgun in Harvey's hands made her nervous, but she had a temper to match her hair. When the older man glared at her, she glared back harder. His steely gaze drifted to her belly and his upper lip drew back. "What would Spruce say if he could see you now?"

"Oh, don't even start."

Harvey turned his head to look at Sterling while keeping the barrel of his shotgun on Chester. "What's your excuse for allowing your own sister to marry one of these beasts? Huh? You gonna let them have the other two as well, Sterling?"

"They're good men, Harvey."

The older man scoffed. "You all have gone weak. It's time a real man takes charge of the village. First order of business, the shapeshifting heathens have to go."

"The hell they do!" Sky yelled, running over with Storm and Rain to join their brother beside Clover and Ivy.

"You can leave the settlement with them, as can Autumn and Blossom."

Autumn's nostrils flared.

"You're delusional," Sky said. "Sterling, grab his gun before he hurts someone."

Before Sterling could take a step forward, Harvey fired a shot above their heads. Everyone gathered ducked. Someone yelped. Autumn's ears rang and her heart pounded in her throat, choking off a dismayed scream.

Clay came running, his face ashen. His father was right behind him.

"What is going on?" Clay yelled.

Harvey jutted his chin at Pete. "Good timing, Pete. Round up our men. We're bringing order back to the village."

Pete glanced from Harvey to his son and sighed. "I have a new grandbaby, Harvey. I don't want to make trouble."

"We already got ourselves trouble. Bear trouble."

Clay folded his arms over his chest. "If you help him, you can forget about seeing the baby."

Harvey scoffed. "You gonna let your boy talk to you that way, Pete?"

Pete rubbed the back of his neck, his eyes shifting from side to side, taking in all the eyes watching him. "From what I hear, the bears have kept my son, daughter-in-law, grandchild, and the rest of the village safe in our absence. I harbor no ill will toward them."

"Pathetic," Harvey sneered. "We'll see how the real men among us feel about that. In the meantime, you girls are coming with me."

"No, we're not," Clover said.

When Chester started for her, Harvey pumped his shotgun. Clover cried out and Chester froze in place. "The first two were warning shots," Harvey growled. "The next one goes through that black head of his unless he stays put and you girls come with me."

"Fine, I'll go with you," Clover said. "Just don't hurt him." She turned pleading eyes to Chester as his body twitched in their direction.

Fearing Harvey would take a shot at Chester, Autumn moved forward and spoke in a firm tone that did not match her rioting nerves. "It's all right. I'll go with them." Not waiting for an answer from either party, Autumn made her way to Clover and Ivy.

Sterling met her eyes and said, "I'm coming with you too."

Autumn gave a slight shake of her head. "Stay with your sisters and keep an eye out for my husband and boys. Let them know what's happening. Take Chester with you. Make sure Lynx and Flint stay out of harm's way."

"Enough of your plotting," Harvey snapped.

Sterling's lips drew back at the sound of the man's voice. He glared at Harvey but did as Autumn asked and strode away in a fury.

"We're not plotting, we're ensuring the safety of the village," Autumn informed him.

Harvey merely huffed. "You wanna spy on me, whore? Good luck keeping up."

Clover and Ivy gasped in outrage. Autumn was beyond anger. Her primary focus was on keeping everyone safe until they could get the gun away from Harvey. She also needed to know how many more weapons he had, where they were stashed, and if his friends were planning on joining his crusade.

In spite of his nasty comments, Harvey did not hurry, or maybe it simply placated him that Clover and Ivy were following even if they matched Autumn's sluggish pace. The girls linked arms with her, as though Autumn was the one who needed looking after.

"You shouldn't be putting undue stress on yourself and the baby," Ivy said softly.

That was an understatement.

Harvey strolled past cabins, leading them to the far edge of the settlement where an area of dense brush had been left to hide the bunker's entrance. Three men were standing outside holding shotguns, looking as unkempt as Harvey. They weren't men Autumn had socialized with in the past, though she recognized them behind their beards.

"Where's Thomas?" Harvey asked.

"He went to clean up," one of the men said.

Ironically, Autumn could not remember if his name was Scott or Steve. Jacob, who had been friends with Spruce's old man, looked at her belly and grimaced.

"So, it's true what we heard—you done taken up with a shapeshifter, Autumn?"

"My husband and I were married in the church," she informed him.

"That don't make it right," Harvey said. "Now, you two girls head inside the bunker and make yourselves comfortable."

"What? Why?" Clover asked shrilly. Ivy grabbed her hand, the skin stretching over knuckles as she squeezed tight.

Harvey looked at his friends. "Get the girls inside. Steve, you stay with them and make sure they don't leave until it's finished."

"Until what's finished?" Clover demanded.

Steve nodded. He, Jacob, and Harvey herded Clover and Ivy to the opening, and there was nothing Autumn could do to stop them without putting herself and her baby in jeopardy. The rage flamed up her throat. She had sworn to herself she would never again have to feel powerless, and here she was, unable to stop these men as the girls yelled.

"Until what's finished?" Clover screamed, as though hearing the answer might help her prevent it from happening. "Uncle Harvey, please don't hurt—"

The metal door clunked shut, drowning out the last of Clover's frantic plea.

"Now what?" Jacob asked.

Harvey's smile smelled of decay. "Now we grab Thomas and go bag ourselves some bears." Autumn's heart went cold as he trailed his eyes over her. "We've got the perfect bait right here."

chapter twelve

NO ONE COULD help Autumn as she was escorted across the village by Harvey, Jacob, and Thomas. The blackguards had shotguns, along with a backpack stuffed with extra guns and ammunition. Pleas and insults fell upon deaf ears.

There was no sign of Chester or any of the other bear shifters. She supposed they had gone to warn Kohana. Maska was probably comforting Blossom in their cabin. It was a relief that they were tucked away at the moment–an even bigger relief that Coral and Eco were absent.

"You should be ashamed of yourselves, threatening your own kin and a pregnant woman," a woman named Twilight spat out at the passing group.

Harvey ignored her the same as the rest of the villagers who jogged over, walking alongside at a distance. The man was delusional to think he would ever win the people over to his side. He had already lied about letting the bear shifters leave unharmed–that much had been made clear the moment his nieces were trapped inside the bunker. There was no hiding his intentions with so many witnesses gathered outside their cabins in an uproar.

Storm kept pace with them. Her sisters and brother were nowhere to be seen. Autumn had come to know the four siblings well during the werewolves' rule and, knowing them as she did, she guessed they were scrambling to organize some kind of ambush on the men. Storm had likely stayed behind to keep an eye on what was happening. But whenever Autumn tried to meet her gaze for a sign of a plan, Storm avoided looking directly at her. The young woman looked as enraged as the rest of the villagers. It wasn't exactly reassuring.

As they approached the village gate, Ash came running, waving frantic arms in the air. "Stop! You can't do this."

Harvey had not made his wicked intentions secret. He planned to use Autumn as bait against her own husband, lure him to the caves, and turn his gun on the bears—starting with their chief. The bastard was hoping for them to shift to get himself "trophies." It made her want to retch.

Harvey stopped and sneered. "I'm disappointed in you, Ash. I heard you're the one that's done and performed these unnatural ceremonies with the heathen beasts and our women. You and I are going to have a chat later."

Ash stepped in front of them and spread his arms wide, appearing before them like a human cross. "I won't allow you to take Autumn outside the settlement."

"My gun says otherwise."

Everyone around them gasped when Harvey aimed the barrel at Ash.

"You wouldn't murder me," Ash said

"I'll do what I must to save our people." The cold

conviction in Harvey's words trailed dreadful chills along Autumn's spine.

"It's okay, Ash," she said, even though they were a world away from okay. "The good Lord will watch over me. Let us pass." Jaw set, Ash stood his ground. "Think of your wife and daughter." Autumn didn't plead, merely stated a fact that made Ash hesitate. Ever so slowly, he lowered his arms and stepped aside.

Harvey kept a firm grip on his shotgun. "Everyone out of the way and don't try to follow us. When the bear chief returns, let him know we've got his woman at the caves."

"You're worse than the werewolves," Storm yelled at him.

"And you've lost your way, so get out of mine," Harvey returned.

Autumn was walked out the gate. She half expected to see Kohana or Sterling, Sky, and Rain waiting for them, but the woods were silent.

Thomas blew out a whistle. "The entire village is against us."

"It only seems that way," Harvey said. "For every loudmouth, there are at least a dozen more who are afraid to speak out against the bears."

Autumn didn't bother telling the man how wrong he was. These men had spent too long in the bunker and were beyond the point of reason.

"What did you say to upset Blossom?" she demanded instead.

"Keep moving," Harvey said, leading their slow procession to the caves. She kept her eyes on the ground, careful of every step, taking her time. At least the men did not rush her.

"I told Blossom the same thing I'll tell you," Harvey said. "You didn't wait long to spread your legs for another man. Poor Spruce would be rolling in his grave if he had one. From what I hear, his body was dragged into the wilderness for the wild animals to feed on. No one deserves that."

His hateful words rolled right off of Autumn, but Blossom would have taken them like blows. She had loved her husband dearly. To be called a faithless widow, as Harvey called Autumn now, would have been like a knife cutting into her heart.

How dare this cowardly maniac cause such a sweet woman to cry? Even worse, Blossom would likely carry his words around for days and weeks to come. She had a baby on the way, and such toxic emotions should not be allowed to burden her.

Knowing what Harvey had said would ease Autumn's conscience when her husband tore him apart.

Thomas, who walked ahead with Harvey, stopped and crouched over the ground. "Uh, these bear tracks look fresh."

Behind her, Autumn heard the rustle of Jacob's gun as he clutched it. Harvey merely bobbed his head. "Good. We want to take them in their beast forms. A bear makes a better blanket than a savage."

Autumn's stomach roiled. "You're sick."

Harvey shrugged. When they reached the caves, Harvey used the barrel of his gun to point. "Up there. Now."

Autumn took extra precaution scaling the rocky slope

to the cave where she and Kohana had created the child growing inside her belly. Entering the cave first, she looked around quickly for a weapon, but there were none to be seen. This was a place of love and conception. The lower caves held the spears, bows, and arrows.

"Take up positions, boys," Harvey said. There was no stress in his voice or the slouch of his shoulders. He was a coward with a gun. Even so, a bear was no match for bullets.

Autumn fought back tears. The mere thought of losing Kohana made her want to wail until the cave walls crumbled and caved in over the men. How was she supposed to protect her husband and unborn child?

Then she felt it . . . a tiny kick inside her womb. Her breathing calmed and her heart thudded steadily against her chest.

Have faith, she felt her baby telling her.

Autumn gave herself over to the unspoken reminder.

She had faith in her husband. Faith that their love story had only just begun.

Jacob stood in the opening of the cave looking out at the forest. "Now what?"

"Now we wait," Harvey said. "Stay alert. It's only a matter of time." It was a sentence Harvey would continue to repeat. The more he did, the more his gusto drained and the words soured in his mouth.

Autumn sat on the smoothest rock she could find inside the cave. Now that Harvey had her here, he left her alone with the exception of a pee break she demanded. The insensitive brute made her go inside the cave.

They waited and waited. The sky dimmed. Autumn's

eyes adjusted to the darkening cave. Dusk turned the men's backs into silhouettes at the opening of the cave. Their voices echoed back to her.

"Are you sure they're coming? Maybe they fled," Thomas said.

"Oh, they'll come," Harvey assured him. "The chief, at least. He won't leave the woman carrying his young."

"Maybe they are out on a long hunting trip and won't return for days," Jacob said.

"If that's the case, we should take turns on lookout," Thomas said.

"No," Harvey growled. "That's exactly what they want—to catch us with our guard down. What is your shapeshifter up to?"

Autumn didn't realize he was addressing her at first. By now it was so dark inside the cave that she couldn't make out Harvey's eyes.

Lifting her chin, she groused, "How should I know? I'm just a woman carrying his young."

"Maybe he's out there right now, but he's not properly motivated."

A figure, one she assumed was Harvey, started for her, setting her heart racing. He had barely made it two steps before crying out in surprise, then falling forward, arms flinging forward to catch himself on the ground. The other two men fired their guns over and over. Autumn shrank down and covered her ears, wincing with each explosion. The terrible sound rivaled her fear of the growling werewolves.

The man who had fallen got back up and tried to

reach around his back before giving up and coming at her. She could not hear him over the gunshots, but then Harvey was right in front of her, his teeth clenched and eyes blazing with fury.

Autumn jerked away, but Harvey's rough hands grabbed hold of her arm and hauled her up. She cradled her belly in one arm, wishing she could shield her baby from the horrifying cracks and bursts. It was her little one she thought of as she tried to calm her racing heart.

Harvey's fingers dug into Autumn's shoulder.

"You're hurting me," she screamed over the gunfire.

"Well, your heathen friends shot an arrow in my back!"

With stumbling steps, he pulled her toward the cave entrance. Her heart thundered inside her ears as they neared the blasts. Harvey nearly fell and pulled her with him. She threw her arms out, prepared to take the weight in her wrists and protect her belly, but Harvey righted them both before they could tumble.

When they reached the entrance, he screamed at his friends to cease fire. Autumn's ears still rang after the gunshots stopped.

"You okay?" Jacob whispered.

"I'll be fine," Harvey gritted out his words. "Did you hit any of them?"

"Can't see, but I reckon we must have."

Harvey gave a pained grunt. He released Autumn, but only to set his shotgun down and grab a smaller weapon, which he pressed against her temple. Her heart beat wildly, knocking against her ribs like a trapped bird.

"You want to save your woman?" Harvey yelled into

the dark woods below. "You come out now, you hear me?"

His foul breath hit Autumn's cheek. She sucked in a breath, wrinkled her nose, and clenched her teeth.

No answer came. Not a single sound from the forest reached them. The next noise was the click from the gun pressed to her head.

Horror cascaded over her. "He doesn't speak any English," Autumn cried.

"He'll understand my gun pointed at you," Harvey growled.

"How is he supposed to see in the dark?" she tried desperately to reason.

"He had no problem firing his arrow at me in the dark."

A deafening roar blasted from the woods. Harvey's gun left her head as he swung his arm forward, aiming out of the cave entrance.

"Hold your fire. Wait for the bears to get closer," he instructed his friends.

Jacob and Thomas crouched from opposite sides of the entrance. They pumped their shot guns and lay in wait.

There were more roars within the trees. They sounded near, but none ventured into the opening in front of the caves.

"How many do you think?" Jacob whispered.

No one answered. Harvey's fingers dug into Autumn again, and he held her in front of him, his breath moving to her shoulder.

When the roaring intensified, Jacob and Thomas crouched lower. They were pressed against the rocks when a large, shadow-like figure appeared to peel away from the wall. An ax lifted above his towering frame and came down over Jacob before he could scream.

Autumn slammed her full weight into Harvey as he fired off a round at her husband. Then she was being dragged backwards into the cave as Thomas shrieked in terror. A wet *thunk* ended his scream.

"Stop right there," Harvey said coolly when Kohana started toward them. The end of the horrid gun was pressed against Autumn's temple once more.

She could just make out her husband's features in the dark. He stood naked from the waist up, midnight hair flowing behind his back, his jaw set in rough edges. Facing them, Kohana threw his ax down. That was when Harvey fired and fired again.

Autumn screamed as Kohana ducked and rolled over the ground. But Harvey just shot again and again until her husband went still. The next scream to erupt from her lips was a volcanic, savage, inhuman detonation that should have leveled the cave.

 # chapter thirteen

AUTUMN FELL TO her knees beside her husband, tears gushing out of her eyes and falling over his motionless body like a rainstorm.

When Harvey tried to pull her away, she snarled and clawed at his arms with her nails drawing blood.

"You killed him!" she screamed. "Murderer! You will go straight to Hell for this, Harvey." She turned back to Kohana, wrapped her arms around his back and wailed against his still warm skin.

Don't leave me, she chanted inside her head. *Please God, don't take my husband from me. I can't live without him. Don't leave me.* "Don't leave me, my love."

Harvey moved around them, heading for the entrance of the cave. The bastard was getting away, but there was nothing Autumn could do. Even if she could, she would not leave her husband's side.

She buried her tear-drenched face into his firm back. Autumn breathed in his familiar scent and prayed for him to survive. The pain of losing him was too much—too high a price. There was no life without Kohana.

Her sobs were muffled against him—even more so when thick fur grew out of his back. She felt herself rising off the ground as his form expanded. Holding back her gasp, Autumn quickly moved away, giving Kohana space as he transformed.

She could still hear Harvey's footsteps leaving the cave, but the hateful man had yet to sense what was happening. Autumn moved back, keeping still and silent as she watched the bear take shape.

Without warning, he charged Harvey, holding back his roar until it was too late for the man to fire his weapon. Once Kohana had him pinned, he bellowed right before Harvey's screams were joined by the crunch of bones and tearing of flesh. Outside the cave, Kohana's tribe joined their chief's roars. It helped cover the gruesome, wet sounds of Harvey's body being torn apart as he continued to scream. Autumn supposed Kohana saved his throat for last.

She pressed her fingers against her ears and curled over her belly, her shoulders hunched.

When it was over, she started crying again. She sobbed with relief and sorrow and fear that her husband's injuries might be fatal—that this was his last act of bravery before death came for him.

The coppery scent of blood filled her nostrils as she made her way toward the bear. Low huffing sounds streamed from his massive jaw and she could not help noticing how large his claws were. They glistened with blood. But her fear was not *of* him, but *for* him.

"Kohana," She wept his name.

His large brown head faced her. Animal eyes stared

into hers, deep into her soul. A small kick inside her stomach had her pressing her palms against her belly.

"Autumn!" Chester yelled from below.

Her heart lurched. "Chester!"

"Are you all right?"

"I'm fine, but he shot Kohana. Will he be okay? Ask him if he is all right!" Her voice became shrill.

The sound of someone scrambling up the rocky trail was followed by a tall dark form taking shape in the entrance.

Autumn felt like weeping all over again to see her dear friend unharmed. It was hard to make out Chester's expression in the dark, but his words were comforting. "We are all fine, Autumn. The danger has passed."

"But what about Kohana? Why isn't he transforming?"

Chester clucked his tongue and turned his head to the bear. Despite the gore surrounding him, he now appeared calm. Jacob and Thomas lay motionless. Kohana had dealt them swift blows with the ax, not wasting time to reach her. She averted her eyes, grateful the darkness helped cover what had to be a gruesome sight.

"He must be badly wounded, otherwise he would shift into a man."

A wave of dizziness had Autumn spreading her arms to steady herself. Chester leaped to her side and took her arm gently. The fear welling inside her chest felt ready to burst. She remembered how Rafael's wolf had been hurt and unable to shift from his human to his animal form for a week. Would it be the same way for her husband? His human form injured so bad that he couldn't shift back?

What if transforming killed him? What if he was stuck as a bear for the remainder of his life?

Bitter laughter churned up her throat.

Together, yet apart. Would life be that cruel?

"Kohana is a strong man," Chester said. "He will heal, I promise you. His tribe will help him."

Autumn nodded numbly. Another little kick caught her attention—followed by a harder one. The baby seemed to be telling her to get a hold of herself and have faith.

"All right, little one," Autumn whispered, one hand on her belly. "Your daddy's going to be fine."

Chester nodded. "Kohana will be recovered in time to hold his newborn in his arms. This I promise you, Autumn."

If Chester had faith, then so could she.

Kohana would recover. He would transform again. Her husband would return to her.

He was her life, her love—her forever mate.

She walked over to Kohana and placed her fingers over his fur. "I love you." Fresh tears glossed over her eyes. "I can't even comfort him."

"Believe me, Autumn. Your safety and your baby's are all the comfort Kohana requires."

She sniffed, knowing it was true. He was a good man. The best husband. Her love for him knew no end. She pressed her forehead against his side and rubbed her face against his fur.

Chester coughed. "Autumn, what about Clover and Ivy?"

She lifted her head, glad for a distraction. "Right. We have unfinished business to attend to. Help me gather the guns. We're going to pay Pete a visit."

KOHANA'S TRIBE WAS waiting in the woods outside the caves in their fur forms. The bears joined their chief. Two of them lumbered over in the dark and transformed into men. Chester carried the bag of guns while Autumn held on to Harvey's shotgun. The tribe's translator said something to the two men, then told Autumn to wait for a torch to be lit.

The men made quick work of sparking a flame to life. When they came closer, Autumn saw that it was Sky's husband, Akando, and a male named Keyan, who had shown interest in Storm.

Chester spoke rapidly with the men, his tone devoid of its usually jovial notes. Once they finished their discussion, he told Autumn that Akando would hold the shotgun for her and Keyan would light the path back to the village.

She was only too happy to pass on the shotgun. She hated the thing–wanted all of the weapons destroyed once they got the girls out of the bunker.

Sterling, Sky, and Rain were waiting outside the gate, along with Lynx. Autumn's heart skipped a beat. "The children–"

"Are safe," Sterling said. "Flint, Coral, Eco, and Nikiti are with Ash and Misty."

As they drew near to the group, she saw that Lynx held a slingshot in one hand and a rock in the other. There were brown lines smeared across his cheeks. He looked like a little heathen going to war.

"Are they dead?" Sky demanded.

"Yes," Chester answered.

"Where's Kohana?" Sterling asked.

"He was shot." Chester's announcement was met with gasped dismay. "But he is with us," Chester continued, indicating the large bear at their backs. "He must stay in his animal form until we are able to gather what we need to help heal his human."

Lynx set his slingshot to the side of the path, then thrust his hand out to Chester. "Give me a gun," he said.

"Absolutely not," Autumn said as she sucked air in through her teeth.

"Don't worry, Lynx. We'll take care of Steve," Sterling said.

Sky nodded. "The bastard is up against all of us. We'll crush him like a spider."

"First we have to get him to open the bunker door," Autumn reminded them. "Where's Pete?"

Rain cleared her throat. "Last we heard from Storm, he's still with Clay, Juniper, and their baby inside their cabin."

"Let's go," Autumn said.

Pete was exactly where Storm had said he would be, and he didn't require much convincing to help them. The man claimed he wanted back in the village's good graces.

At the bunker door, Pete pounded out a coded knock while the rest of them stood back. Metal creaked as the door opened a crack.

"Pete," Steve's voice sounded surprised. "What–" Before he could say another word, Chester ran at the barrier and shoved, knocking Steve back as he slammed into the door.

"Clover!"

"Chester!" Clover flung herself into Chester's arms. He hugged her against him. Ivy hurried past them, fleeing the bunker and gulping down air as though deprived of oxygen.

The younger sister ran to Autumn, her eyes wide. "You're okay! What about Kohana and the rest of the bears?"

"We're all safe. What about you and your sister? Did Steve hurt either of you?" Autumn demanded.

Ivy shook her head. "We're fine—just sick with worry."

Sterling dragged Steve out while Sky kept a gun aimed at him. Autumn knew the woman had never held a gun before now, let alone fired one, but that didn't make her appear any less menacing as she pointed the weapon at the bearded man.

"Where's Harvey, Jacob, and Thomas?" Steve asked.

"Dead, dead, and dead," Sky replied.

"You killed them?" Steve's voice pierced the night's sky.

"Not me personally, but they're gone and you're next."

"Sis, maybe you want to tone it down?" Sterling suggested.

"Why?" Sky demanded. "This bastard would murder my husband given the chance."

Steve's face turned pale in the torchlight. "I was just following orders."

"Well, you picked the wrong side."

"Pete," Steve said desperately.

Pete scratched his jaw. "Sorry, Steve, but things have changed. You should have never gone along with Harvey's plans. This is supposed to be a peaceful settlement. Guns have no place here, nor does violence against our own people. Now, excuse me. I've got time to make up for with my son and new grandbaby." Pete took off, disappearing into the dark without a glance back.

"So, what are we going to do with him?" Rain asked.

"Our tribe can take him into the woods and make him disappear," Chester offered. He held Clover protectively against his side.

Steve's eyes went wide. "No, please. Have mercy." He dropped to his knees with a sob. "I'll do anything you ask of me. I love this village. I should have never gone in that bunker with the others. Please, allow me to make up for my mistakes."

Sky folded her arms over her chest and huffed. Autumn chewed on her lower lip and considered the man begging at their feet. "We give him a chance to redeem himself," she said.

"What?" Sky's nostrils flared. "How can you say that after your husband was shot by his friend?"

Autumn pursed her lips. "This isn't up for debate. Steve, you can start atoning by showing Sterling where the rest of the guns and ammo are hidden. I want it all destroyed at sunup." Steve lifted his head and nodded eagerly. "And I expect to see you in church every Sunday."

"Yes, Autumn. Bless your heart."

epilogue

BUTTERY SUNLIGHT POURED over the pews from the church windows as Ash concluded another beautiful sermon. As promised, Steve had not missed a single Sunday gathering. He sat up front as though making a point.

Autumn sat between her boys, cradling her sweet bundle of joy. Dyani was the cutest baby girl to ever grace the village—not to mention the best behaved. The girl was an absolute angel who never cried or even fussed. Barely three months old, and she was all smiles, curiosity, and delight in the world and people around her. Blossom, Maska, and their newborn boy Hopi shared the bench with them.

After repeating Ash's "Amen", they shuffled out of the church and into the sunshine to enjoy an afternoon picnic Misty had organized.

Kohana was waiting outside. His face lit up into a huge grin the moment he spotted Autumn, and he did not waste another moment before striding over in his deerskin pants and shirt. "Daughter," he said, then kissed Dyani's head. Flashing Autumn a cheeky smile, he next said, "Wife," before kissing her on the lips.

Autumn's lashes fluttered and her toes curled inside the slippers Flint had made her. She also wore Lynx's bone choker. The items weren't what she would have considered church attire in the past, but times were changing and cultures blending. Best of all, Kohana had been the first to break and begin learning English. She smiled to herself smugly.

"Hello, husband."

Kohana's grin turned wicked as he cocked one brow that promised wicked delights later that night. Cheeks heating, Autumn clutched Dyani to her chest, a motion that drew her husband's proud gaze down. He beamed happily. Every day she gave thanks that her wonderful man was alive and well. His tribe had borrowed a few medical supplies to dig out the bullets and patch him up inside the caves. When Autumn had tried to reason with them to use the village facilities and healers, Chester had patiently explained that they needed to do things their own way. Whatever they had done, it had worked. There were scars where the bullets had entered her husband's body, but the wounds had healed and he had returned to her with all his fingers and toes—all man and all hers.

Kohana gave her another kiss, then pressed his shoulder against hers to walk by her side.

"Mom, I'm going to eat with Coral and Eco, okay?" Flint asked.

Smiling at her youngest son, Autumn nodded.

Flint jogged to the blanket Coral was helping Ivy smooth out over the church lawn.

"I want to hold the baby," Lynx said. He was always asking—well, more like demanding—a chance to hold his baby sister.

"We'll sit down first," Autumn said.

They found a large blanket and were joined by Blossom, Maska, and their baby. Chester set a blanket out beside theirs and held Clover's hand as she sat down. The village's newest married couple glowed with happiness.

Once settled, Autumn gently handed Lynx her baby. He cradled Dyani and stared down with the same adoration she saw in Kohana's eyes whenever he looked at their daughter.

When Hopi began wailing, Blossom rocked him gently. From several blankets away, Clay and Juniper's little boy started crying. Dyani looked from side to side and puckered her lips as though thinking, *What's the deal with these whiny boys?* Lynx held his thumb out for her, and she wrapped her tiny fingers around it and giggled.

Sky, whose belly was now rounded, pulled her husband over by the hand. "Got room over here?" she asked, plopping down on Chester and Clover's blanket without waiting for an answer. "Dyani is such a darling. If Akando and I have a boy, we want to set him up with her when they're older." She inclined her head to her husband as he settled onto the blanket beside her.

"Yes," Akando agreed.

Kohana grunted and folded his arms over his chest.

Blossom succeeded in hushing her newborn by giving him her breast. "I must warn you, Hopi and Dyani are quite fond of one another," she said, as the babe latched on to her nipple.

Autumn grinned at Blossom's competitive spirit.

"Well, we were waiting to share this, but maybe now

is the time," Clover said. "My courses are seven weeks late. If Chester and I have a son, we're going to want you to consider our boy for Dyani."

Autumn barely registered the last part of Clover's words. Tears flowed down her cheeks as she got to her feet and rushed over, pulling Clover up and into a hug. "You're pregnant?"

"Pretty sure."

"Oh, Clover, that's wonderful news. Congratulations to you both." Autumn flashed Chester a watery smile. The man beamed proudly.

"You did not think we would let the rest of you have all the fun, did you?" Chester asked.

Autumn laughed in answer. She let go of Clover and returned to her blanket, where Kohana opened his legs and patted the spot in front of him. Feeling a blush coming on, she took a seat between his muscled legs, her heart beating faster when he wrapped his arms around her waist and pulled her against him.

"Lord almighty, so much competition already. What happens when the rest of the bears claim brides?" Sky groaned. "Autumn, you and Kohana had better get started on another daughter soon."

"Yes," Kohana said, causing their group to erupt into laughter.

Autumn's face filled with heat.

"Autumn, you should see your face. It's as red as your hair." Chester chuckled.

"Thanks, Chester," Autumn huffed, but it was impossible to contain her smile.

When the conversation shifted to baby names for Sky and Clover to consider, Autumn nestled back into her husband's arms and looked over her family and friends with a happiness as vast and glorious as the natural world surrounding them.

Life was good, and love lived on.

author's note

Animal Attraction was a tale that took shape at the end of Moon Cursed... then crawled off into a cave to hibernate while the real world got a little too dystopian. It was a drive through Canada and the hypnotic stare of a wild wolf that brought me back to this series.

Seb, Cosmo, and I lived in a truck camper during the second half of 2020. The most memorable experience was what I call a "wildlife safari" through British Columbia and the Yukon. We are forever grateful that Canada allowed us to drive through and help my family out in Alaska, (and then back down to the lower 48 at the end of the summer season).

With border restrictions keeping out the usual tourist traffic, we drove for hours without glimpsing a single car, truck, or living soul along the Alaska Highway. What we did see was a vast and magnificent kaleidoscope of wildlife, wilderness, starry skies, and beauty beyond expression. I lost track of the number of black bears and cubs we passed digging out tubers along the side of the road close enough to high five. There were herds of bison, rock sheep, and reindeer; foxes, moose, eagles, and—on the way back down—that rare and majestic wolf standing upland beside the road. At first we thought it was a mountain goat. As we drove closer, the pointed ears, proud muzzle, and long tail took shape. The wolf appeared to have taken an "I'm the king of the world" stance atop the rocky outcrop. Our heads turned as we drove by. Our eyes locked. A moment of wonder and kinship passed between us, stalling my breath. Then we passed and the world and the empty road opened back up. "Did that just happen?" I asked Seb. We were both left awestruck for the rest of the afternoon.

I wish we could have spent more time on the road and in nature before Seb's new job started. It would have been amazing to stop for a month and start writing Animal Attraction while the outdoor experience was fresh in my head. As it was, we passed most of that time inside the truck watching the landscape whiz by the windows on our way to North Carolina. We did get a chance to go wild camping during our stay in Alaska. I never enjoyed tent camping growing up but was happily surprised to discover how much I love the RV experience, which has only stoked my dream of getting back out on the open road.

We are housebound once more but writing this book and novella transported me to a place beyond cities, suburbs, and the walls that enclose us. Wolf Hollow is a series that first howled to my soul during a time when I felt trapped in an endless drudge. I hope the hollow's wild calling has fed your untamed spirit as it has mine, and brought a little love, beauty, and zest to your day.

Special thanks to my editors Roxanne Willis and Liz Ferry who had their hands full with this one. While working on Animal Attraction I was experiencing the worst brain fog of my life, which turned out to be advanced stages of thyroid disease. These ladies lent extra mind power where mine faded. I am so grateful for all their fixes, finds, and suggestions. *Muchas gracias* to my girl Deissy Hermunslie for cleaning up my Spanish!

I look forward to welcoming you back to Wolf Hollow in Bear Claimed!

As always, take good care, look for the beauty, and may you run forever free.

Nikki Jefford
April 2021

Nikki News!

Sign up for Nikki's spam-free newsletter. Receive cover reveals, excerpts, and new release news before the general public; enter to win prizes; and get the scoop on special offers, contests, and more.

Visit Nikki's website to put your name on the list. Make sure to confirm your email so you won't miss out: *nikkijefford.com*

See you on the other side!

MORE PLACES TO FIND NIKKI JEFFORD

Instagram:

www.instagram.com/nikkijefford

Facebook:

www.facebook.com/authornikkijefford

Twitter:

@NikkiJefford

BookBub:

www.bookbub.com/profile/nikki-jefford

GoodReads:

www.goodreads.com/author/show/5424286.Nikki_Jefford

SLAYING, MAGIC MAKING, RUNNING WILD, AND RULING THE WORLD!

Discover your next fantasy fix with these riveting paranormal romance and fantasy titles by Nikki Jefford:

AURORA SKY: VAMPIRE HUNTER

Night Stalker
Aurora Sky: Vampire Hunter
Northern Bites
Stakeout
Evil Red
Bad Blood
Hunting Season
Night of the Living Dante
Whiteout
True North

SPELLBOUND TRILOGY

Entangled
Duplicity
Enchantment
Holiday Magic

WOLF HOLLOW SHIFTERS

Wolf Hollow
Mating Games
Born Wild
Moon Cursed
Animal Attraction
Primal Bonds
Bear Claimed
Forever Free

ROYAL CONQUEST SAGA

Stolen Princess
False Queen
Three Kings
Holiday Crown
The Golden Prince
The Dark Pretender
The Ice Twins
The Forever Princess

about the author

NIKKI JEFFORD loves fictional bad boys and heroines who kick butt. Books, travel, TV series, hiking, writing, and motorcycle riding are her favorite escapes. She is a third-generation Alaskan, a free-spirit, nomad, Westie mama, and wouldn't trade her French husband in for anyone – not even for Rafael or Kohana!

Printed in Great Britain
by Amazon